SHAKEDOWN

The timing countdown was dropping drastically. "This is Commander Ariane Austin," she said, using for the first time the title she'd been accorded as the ultimate backup pilot for the mission. "We're almost to the activation point."

She reached out and grasped the manual controls. She'd decided it was best to cut out the direct connects. If she was really going to be needed, these were the controls she'd need.

Five seconds. Sandrisson coils charging.

The field strength built swiftly, symmetrically. If Sandrisson was correct, the Drive would cause them to be catapulted into the parallel related spacetime represented by the Kanzaki-Locke context parameter ma

Two second

One second

Activation.

In the sudden silent blackness, Ariane heard Dr. Sandrisson scream.

BAEN BOOKS
by RYK E. SPOOR

Grand Central Arena
Mountain Magic, with David Drake,
Eric Flint, & Henry Kuttner
Digital Knight

Boundary, with Eric Flint
Threshold, with Eric Flint (forthcoming)

GRAND CENTRAL ARENA

Ryk E. Spoor

GRAND CENTRAL ARENA

Copyright © 2010 by Ryk E. Spoor

A Baen Books Original

Baen Publishing Enterprises
P.O. Box 1403
Riverdale, NY 10471
www.baen.com

ISBN: 978-1-4391-3355-2

Cover art by Stephen Hickman

First printing, May 2010

Distributed by Simon & Schuster
1230 Avenue of the Americas
New York, NY 10020

Printed in the United States of America

10 9 8 7 6 5 4 3 2 1

Acknowledgements

Many people supported me in one way or another in this project, and deserve to be acknowledged. For sacrificing many weekend days so I could write, my wife Kathleen. Eric Flint, for giving me the general thought that became Grand Central Arena; my beta-reading group, especially my Loyal Lieutenant Shana; and Keith Morrison and Mary Dell, who helped bring the images in my head to life (as can be seen at www.grandcentralarena.com).

Dedication

This novel is dedicated to the memory of E. E. "Doc" Smith, the father of space opera and the author who showed me the most pure and undiluted sense of wonder I have ever known. In my "poor, limited, and thoroughly inadequate" way, I hope to give something of that same sweep of vision and thrill of adventure to a new generation of readers. There was, and will be, only one Doc Smith, but he lives through the memory of those he inspired.

GRAND CENTRAL ARENA

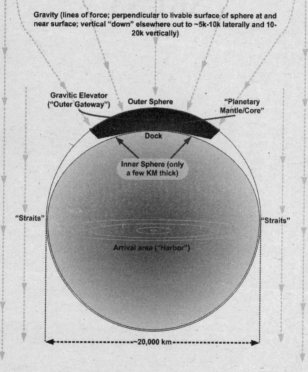

Gravity (lines of force; perpendicular to livable surface of sphere at and near surface; vertical "down" elsewhere out to ~5k-10k laterally and 10-20k vertically)

Gravitic Elevator ("Outer Gateway")

Outer Sphere

"Planetary Mantle/Core"

Dock

Inner Sphere (only a few KM thick)

"Straits"

"Straits"

Arrival area ("Harbor")

←------------------- ~20,000 km -------------------→

Arena Sphere (basic diagram)
Credit: Ryk E. Spoor

Spheres move in parallel to corresponding stars; slow change in relationships

Between-Sphere matter follows Spherepool gravity, air currents, Sphere gravity; general movement spiral towards center, but highly chaotic; many currents, upwellings, etc., to affect and be used by travelling Spherenauts

Center takes in matter and recycles Elsewhere

Gravity in towards core

No vertical component to gravity at galactic equator

~750,000,000 ~ 1,000,000,000 km

Spherepool Diagram
Credit: Ryk E. Spoor

Earth FTL Vessel *Holy Grail*
Credit: Keith Morrison

Chapter 1

"Watch the next keyhole, Ariane, that bastard's going to try to force a scrape—or worse!"

Ariane Austin heard the concerned voice in her helmet as she pulled round the third turn, spinning *Whip Hand* and then relaxing the gyros, lining up the nuclear rocket blast through instinct and experience, firing to skirt the marker asteroid and get on a vector to pass through the next course obstacle—the "keyhole" that Carl had mentioned. The power of the rocket pinned her to the acceleration chair with the thrilling force she sometimes felt was drawn from and through her, making her feel a part of the little racing ship.

Just ahead of her, no more than twenty kilometers—or about a second and a half at their current course-relative speed—was "that bastard," Hawke, the legend of the racing circuit. With enhanced vision, she could just make out the dagger-sharp shape of Hawke's ship *Lobo*, with its stubby wings for racing courses that had atmospheric sections. "Carl, he's not going to try that. He's got a one-point-five lead on me; why would he cut it down low enough to make the keyhole an issue?"

"Because," the voice of her control engineer and crew chief answered, "he knows you're better than he is at the driftmaze part of the course."

Ariane couldn't argue that he might have a point. She'd shaved almost three seconds off the last time through the driftmaze, and the rest of the pack was so far back that they weren't even contenders. If all Hawke had coming out was that one-point-five, there was a good chance she'd pass him in the driftmaze, and with only half the circuit left, Hawke would have damn few chances to make that up.

And Hawke is slowing, dammit. I'm catching him.

Unlimited Space Obstacle Racing rules were pretty relaxed. You couldn't deliberately *ram* your opponent . . . but forcing them off the course, bumping them pretty roughly by "accident" at critical moments, or even hitting something in order to leave debris behind you and in your opponent's way were not against the rules. It was that kind of no-holds-barred competition that made it a very, very popular viewing sport . . . and one with the highest mortality rate of any sport in the system.

She didn't mind matching scrapes with most people, but Hawke was a different matter. Scrape in a keyhole, that was even worse. The hundred kilometer-long hollow obstacles were basically tunnels a hundred meters across and two hundred high—something very, very narrow when you were in a craft with a twenty-meter wingspan moving at several kilometers per second, and even narrower if you had another twenty-meter craft with you. Even the fact that the keyholes were mostly made of aerogel and the racing craft of ring-carbon composite didn't make it comfortable; yes, many craft and their pilots had survived collision with the keyhole wall, but many hadn't, often by hitting one of the widely-spaced, but much more solid, supports for the keyhole. Even if you survived, of course, you would have lost so much time that you might not even finish the race.

"How're our numbers, Carl?"

"High," he answered instantly. "This being the first time this season you've faced off with Hawke, and being as you're currently the USORA league leader, that was a big draw. Now that it's down to just you and Hawke in a race this tight . . . flashpings are up three hundred percent over last, drawing in at least double the virtual audience. Plus we've got confirmed two hundred-seventeen physical presence attendees for the after-race party. If you don't screw anything up, we'll be ahead of Hawke on the Interest vector and pulling close on contributed E-dollars."

Ariane sucked in her breath. *Ahead of Hawke on interest?* The taciturn veteran had dominated the sport for almost ten years, and at first she'd thought he was untouchable. This year, finally, she thought she might even have a chance against him . . . but she'd never imagined other people cared that much. And the contributed E-dollars were critical for fast refuellings, transfers from one racecourse to another, and, of course, for paying her crew.

The question was . . . how to answer Hawke's obvious challenge?

Even before she consciously realized it, her body had answered. The drive roared again, sending her charging to meet Hawke. *People don't watch this sport to see someone who's playing it safe.*

The other pilot responded, accelerating, but not quite so fast. No calculations—no AISages or even less-intelligent advisors were allowed here. You had to guess the acceleration, judge the distance by eye and instrument, figure out the right moment to speed up or slow down. Hawke, of course, was trying to match up with her just as they entered the keyhole; she wanted to get ahead of him. If she *could* pass him, she might even have a chance of winning this race.

He's too good. He's judged it perfectly. I'm varying my acceleration, but he's matching me . . . here it comes!

Two ships flashed into the keyhole at a speed of five kilometers a second, nearly wing to wing. Hawke's *Lobo* spun, trying to slap her wing and send her spinning, but she matched rotation, then suddenly reversed. *If my wing's getting hit, I'm damn well going to be the one doing the hitting!*

But Hawke seemed to have read her mind. He reversed at the same moment, killing and reversing spin with the wingtip jets. Only a few more seconds in the keyhole—*he's swerving!* She kicked in the side and bottom jets, rose up and spun around again, barely evading the darting hummingbird of *Lobo*, jinking herself to force him to shift course . . .

Lobo and *Whip Hand* burst from the keyhole and separated, heading for the driftmaze.

Chapter 2

Simon Sandrisson watched from a nearby observation window as the woman shot from the cockpit of her racing ship like a rocket herself, the pilot's suit automatically retracting the helmet and then unfastening as she flew through the weightless docking bay towards her racing crew. Deep blue hair cascaded around her and the two men who arrested her headlong flight with enthusiastic hugs. He could hear Ariane Austin's elated contralto shout, "We *did it!*"

"*You* did it, you lunatic!" Carl Edlund, her crew chief and controls expert, answered, as he guided them toward the entrance to the station interior that was nearest to Simon. "Were you and Hawke *trying* to get killed in there?"

"Oh, stop it. It's not like you haven't seen worse."

"True," Edlund said as they emerged from the lock. "But usually 'worse' means 'someone got killed,' so I would rather compare it to 'sane,' which doesn't get seen very often either."

Simon was about to speak when another man whipped right past him and stopped directly between him and the racing crew. The sandy blond hair and emblem on his jacket—a wolf-head between hawk wings—was immediately recognizable. "Austin," Hawke said.

"Hawke."

The other pilot flipped forward and grabbed her up in a bearhug. *That was fantastic!*

Simon could see Ariane was startled but gratified. Now he became aware of more and more people making their way into the area. *A victory party*, Mio said. *It's going to be noisy here for a while. Why not come back later?*

I suppose I could, he said to his AISage companion. Mio's avatar, currently visible only to him, showed the synthetic intelligence—friend, confidant, research partner, advisor, a part of him since he had the headware installed nearly twenty years ago—as a pretty, diminutive, Asian woman with long, dark hair, wearing a white suit styled, as was his own, to echo the appearance of the ancient and venerable scientist's laboratory coat. *But what better time to catch Dr. Carl Edlund and his partner in a good mood?*

There is that, Mio said with a smile. *And while she seems oblivious to risk, Dr. Edlund may not be.*

Oh, hardly oblivious. Judging by her actions, I'd say she enjoys risk. He watched the dark blue-haired woman adjust without apparent conscious thought as the station "spun up" to provide about a third of a G for people to stand in. She was tall—just a few centimeters below his one hundred-ninety—and aside from her hair showed no obvious biomods; her eyes appeared to be almost the same shade as her hair, and her complexion was tanned but clear.

Hawke, as he turned, showed tiger-like facial striping; some of the others coming in sported mods ranging from full-size angel wings (*Kami, those have got to be a pain to live with!* he thought) to cat-like claws, fur, a couple of scaled individuals, and more. *In a way, being without mods makes one stand out these days,* he mused.

True enough, Mio agreed. *Of the over two hundred people physically here, there appear to be no more than ten with no visible modifications. And that ten does not include you.*

Well, yes, my hair is visible, but it could be natural. Just very unlikely to be so pure white at the age of thirty-two or to fall just so.

Are you not going to approach Ms. Austin or Dr. Edlund?

There is no great rush. I spent two weeks on a ship just to get here; no reason to get impatient now. I'm sure I can catch up with Dr. Edlund at some point, even if Ms. Austin is the constant focus of attention. You might ping her AISage and let her know I'm here physically to talk to her.

A pause. *She doesn't appear to have one.*

"What?" Simon was so startled that he realized he'd spoken aloud. It was rare enough to find someone who didn't keep their AISage head-resident (Simon, in fact, could only think of one person he'd ever met who didn't), but someone who didn't have one *at all?*

Wait. She does have one, according to records . . . but he's only rarely on the Nets, at least visibly. There, that ovoid box. Mio's directives highlighted in red a slightly larger than hand-sized object something like a high-tech turtle shell clipped to Ariane Austin's belt. *That's her AISage's resident housing.*

Simon shook his head. What was the point of having an AISage if you didn't even let it do its *job*? Perhaps he should be speaking with the other pilot, Hawke. But the reasons they'd focused on Austin remained valid; she had so many good connections that it would be a shame to waste them. *That's a clumsy housing, too.*

Mio was uncharacteristically silent for a moment. *Actually, it's about as small as it can be. Simon, her AISage is a T-5.*

That explained the casing. A Tayler-5 was the highest permitted AI rating outside of special research, and even with modern equipment, you weren't fitting a T-5 in ordinary headware. A T-1 was generally considered equal to an ordinary human, and Mio—just about top of the line for a headware AISage—had a Tayler rating of 2.5.

What a racing pilot needed, or wanted, with a T-5 AISage, now that was a mystery. Simon liked mysteries —it was part of what had drawn him into physics, unravelling the mysteries of how and why the universe worked the way it did—and now Ariane Austin wasn't just a daredevil in a totally anachronistic sport . . . she was a puzzle.

Simon smiled. He was looking forward to meeting her after all!

Chapter 3

Ariane was feeling her usual post-race high, nervousness and excitement combined with a need to get *out* and do something. The party wasn't bad, especially with Hawke showing that he was actually enjoying her competition rather than resenting it (the sudden grin on the usually deadpan face had taken her entirely by surprise), but she still was balanced on a hair-trigger and needed a distraction.

Through the crowd, she saw an arm gesturing in her direction. She bounced higher in the low gravity and was able to see Carl Edlund waving her over to a side alcove. With some guys, that might have been just an invitation to join them, now or later, for some more private recreation, but Carl knew she never played around with anyone on her team—conflict of interest. Besides, she was pretty sure he had someone.

There was someone else in the alcove next to the whip-cord-slender Edlund, but Ariane couldn't immediately make out who. She triggered her vision mods, and it seemed as though a spotlight was shining into the side room, showing a tall, elegant figure in white, light glinting opaquely from a pair of round-lensed glasses, equally white hair falling in a carefully-sculpted fashion around a narrow, intelligent face. *Who the heck is that, I wonder. He looks familiar.*

Ah, Ariane Austin of Tellus, now you embark upon your true destiny, thundered a deeply-resonant *basso profundo* voice within her mind. *You are about to meet Dr. Sandrisson, a Mind of considerable ability and, if my Visualization is correct, already known to you by reputation.*

"Sandrisson—Dr. *Simon* Sandrisson?" she echoed aloud in complete astonishment. To someone like Ariane, who—when not racing spaceships at unsafe speeds—preferred to spend her time virtually adventuring in other worlds (whether by reading books so old they were on paper, or by travelling directly to those worlds in a simgame as one of the heroes), Dr. Simon Sakuraba Sandrisson was someone almost mythical, a figure out of her favorite books come to life. Sandrisson had turned the world of physics upside-down almost a decade ago by declaring that the "context parameter matrix" in the Kanzaki-Locke Unified Field Theory was not, as many had thought, something like Einstein's Cosmological Constant—a "fudge factor" that made everything come out right—but was a factual and accurate physical description of the universe. As the "parameter matrix" in question involved methods of reconciling time and space differentials between widely separated points, the implication was that there was, in fact, a Universal Frame of Reference, a privileged perspective location from which the universe could be viewed.

Which, in turn, meant—if Sandrisson was right—that real, honest-to-God faster-than-light travel should be not only theoretically, but practically, possible.

Only a few weeks ago, Sandrisson had gone before the Space Security Council and the Combined Space Forces to seek permission to perform a manned test mission —one of the few types of experiments that he could not perform without the permission and oversight of the SSC and CSF.

And he'd been granted permission.

Ariane began bulling her way through the crowd, or jumping over particularly thick clumps of people, the low gravity allowing this maneuver. *You know perfectly well that I know ALL about him, Mentor. That I'd have given my last victory to meet him! If you knew he was here, why didn't you tell me?*

You speak loosely and muddily, child; it is not possible, either for an intellect at your level of development or any currently known to me, to know ALL about any being, the sonorously echoing pseudo-voice said chidingly. *As for notifying you of his presence, it was not necessary that I do so.* She saw Mentor's avatar—a glowing ball of energy with multiple complex winding patterns—give the rippling flicker that was his equivalent of an indulgent chuckle. *As Doctor Sandrisson is not, himself, a follower of the sport, and as his own AISage was studying us intently for some thirty-seven of your seconds, it was well within any competent mind to Visualize that his purpose here was to speak with you, and with Dr. Edlund as well.*

With ME? *Carl I can understand, but why me?*

Ariane Austin of Tellus, at times I despair of you. Think, child, THINK! *The limitations of your current Civilization constrain you too heavily!*

Sometimes I think I gave them TOO *good a template for your design, Mentor,* she said with a mental laugh. *There really are times I believe you're just* pretending *to be an AISage and really* ARE *a vast and unknowable intellect of starkly inconceivable age and power.* She waited as a logjam of people cleared before her, while exchanging a couple of toasts with those standing around.

The reply was more muted. *Alas, I am but what I was made to be. I hope you are not tired of this, my persona.*

Never. I just hope you're not tired of having to be constantly at my beck and call.

Mentor did not immediately reply. When he did, it was in a serious tone. *Ariane Austin, there are many of your people who show no concern for the thoughts or feelings of the created intellects that they call AISages; others who fear us. You do neither, and that gives me, and others, hope, that we can find a path beyond this—some way of proving, to both machine and biological intellects that both shall be needed, that both are worthy and equal.*

Ariane nodded inwardly. The name "Frankenstein," along with names of more recent vintage—"Skynet," "Monolith," and in a much more recent vein, "Hyperion" —kept all of their power to generate paranoia and fear, and even with the ubiquity of AISages and other artificial intelligences to perform endless tasks for people, the fear of their ultimate capabilities and what that might mean for humanity had meant that strict rules on the independence and capabilities of such artificial intellects were still maintained now, centuries after the first true successful AI was created.

Ariane knew she had her own brand of that fear—that was why she had no headware beyond the minimum necessary, no resident AI in her head; a fear of something else sitting in her head, thinking thoughts for her. At the same time, that was a purely personal fear, not one of the AIs in general; for them, she felt concern and pity that their lives were so heavily defined and constrained . . . and a worry that they would come, through all those constraints, to resent their creators, thus making all the precautions the cause of the very thing they were meant to prevent.

Enough of your introspection, Ariane Austin! You focus on the future when the present confronts you!

She saw with a start that she was nearly to the alcove. *Okay, thanks, Mentor. You can go now. I'll handle the discussion myself.*

It is well that you attempt all things in your own way. I shall be here, if you need me. The avatar-image faded, showing that Mentor was now no longer directly in contact with her and was presumably off amusing himself in whatever way suited his particular preferences.

"Ariane! Thanks for plowing your way over here!" Carl said, pulling her the rest of the way. "This is—"

"Dr. Simon Sandrisson, yes, I know. An honor, Doctor."

The long, elegant hand pressed her own with sufficient force to show that Dr. Sandrisson wasn't a completely cloistered academic. "Thank you, Ms. Austin. I'm surprised you recognized me."

"Ariane, please. It took a moment," she said, "but I have been following your work and recent announcement, so it's not surprising I'd know who you are." She rather liked the unexpected English accent, and the glint in his slightly oblique emerald eyes, slightly higher than her own, that showed the only really visible traces of his half-Japanese ancestry. "I'd guess you're here to try to steal away my crew chief, Doctor?"

Sandrisson smiled. "If I am to address you as Ariane, then please call me Simon. It is true that Dr. Edlund is on the very short list of candidates for control design and integration for the test vessel, but I also came here to speak with you."

"*Me?*" Ariane was startled. Despite Mentor's classically overdramatic statement about "destiny," she hadn't had any expectation of Sandrisson being actually interested in her.

"Indeed." Sandrisson's expression flickered as she felt an aborted ping at her headport—typical of an AISage trying to make a full manifestation connection and failing. "I . . . why don't you have your AISage connect and I can show you?"

"Because I prefer to see and understand things myself, not using someone else to do my thinking for me," she answered. She realized that this wasn't the most diplomatic thing she could have said, but she was still on the jittery edge from the race.

Sandrisson either couldn't or didn't bother to restrain a roll of his eyes skyward. "This will take five times as long to explain accurately, then."

Ariane ignored the all-too-familiar pang of annoyance combined with a vague overall guilt for being out of step with the world. "But I'll understand it better that way."

The elegant eyebrows rose, but Sandrisson flashed a smile and shrugged. "I will admit that I have little reluctance to talking about myself and my work. Very well."

He glanced at the wall of the niche, and touched the subtle marks that caused the hidden table and chairs to extrude, along with a privacy shield that dropped across the front of the niche (to some minor consternation of partygoers who had been closing in on Ariane).

"I'll assume," Sandrisson said, seating himself, "that, as you have been following my work, I don't have to detail the prelude. In short, we've certainly demonstrated that it is possible to cause an object to move from one point to another in time that, perceived from our locations in spacetime, appears to exceed the speed of light in a manner similar to that which was predicted.

"However, there are some . . . oddities. Some of the probes demonstrated effective velocities that were quite high, but well below c. A few—three, to be precise—never emerged at all after transition. Aside from the three lost probes, none of the probes were destroyed or damaged in any detectable way. However, even the ones which remained in, well, wherever they went, for a significant length of time—several seconds—returned no additional data. As you can see from the specifications—" He broke off, realizing that his instinctual triggering of some virtual presentation was not, of course, reaching Ariane, and winced. "Pardon me; I should have said, as you may know from examining our released data, all of the probes were well-supplied with multiple sensing modalities and controlled by AIs rated from 0.1 to 0.5 Taylers."

Ariane nodded her understanding, as did Carl (whose momentarily-unfocused gaze had shown that *he* had, indeed, seen the display Sandrisson had supplied). An AI of 0.1 Taylers was normal "smart sensor" automation; it could do a lot of the same sensing and perception and relationship evaluations of humans, but couldn't *think* about it much. Anything over 0.5 Taylers was closing in on human capabilities—and was never allowed to operate completely independently.

"Despite this," Sandrisson continued, "not a single byte of data was recorded from any sensors following transition."

"Well," Ariane said, thinking back to multiple fictional depictions of stardrives, "isn't it possible that from the point of view of the probe, no actual time elapsed? That is, that the transition from one point to another was accomplished instantaneously?"

"This was, in fact, my first working hypothesis once the pattern became obvious," Sandrisson said, with a shrug and another quick, bright smile. "However, several tests showed that this simply was not the case. Battery draw indicated that some period of time had elapsed during the transition; mechanical timers placed on board continued to run and showed the equivalance of the apparent lapse of time."

"Have you tried using direct recording methods?" Carl asked, leaning forward. By this, Ariane knew, he meant non-automated or minimally-automated sensor systems —dumb cameras, radar, and so on.

The white-haired head dipped in assent. "Certainly. But, unfortunately, such methods are little-used today, and while they have so far shown that they do record during the transition, none of the sensors we've used so far have shown anything outside the probe. It may be a completely featureless void, or it may simply be a lack of sensitivity or range, but it puzzles me as to why the main systems seem to notice nothing unusual at all.

"Now, on the most recent series of runs, we have tested probes carrying live test subjects, such as guinea pigs and rats. Biologically they appear, as near as we can tell, to continue functioning throughout the transition, and have suffered no detectable ill effects. The longest transition experiments have allowed me to test, using very simple automation, whether they can react during transition, and they do."

Carl, who was extremely familiar with automated controls and systems of the sort that Sandrisson's probes were using, looked up sharply at that. "But . . . something like a white rat is effectively running around 0.15 to 0.2 Taylers."

"Indeed," Sandrisson said, "but living creatures are essentially biological carbon-based nanotech, while most low-level automation—to the 0.5 Tayler limit—is monolithic carbosilicate optical junction circuitry. Very different physical operating principles."

The reason for Sandrisson's need for a manned flight suddenly burst in on Ariane, and she laughed. "Oh, my. The only solution you could use in the probes, you can't use, right?"

The physicist gave her an appreciative glance. "Very good, Ariane. I could equip the probes with nanotech-based AI, just like those used in our AISages and in the more advanced AIWish nanotech universal manufacturing units, but it is one of our few absolute laws that no AI of that level be placed in independent operation —which it would be, when placed on a potentially faster than light probe. So I have a technology which would probably solve my problem, but it's not legal for me to do so.

"Thus, no matter which way I look at it, I have to send a human being—or more than one—along with the next probe. And I might as well make it a full crew if I'm going to do this at all."

Her role in the mission seemed pretty clear now. Minimal, but clear. "So basically you want me there as an ultimate backup? Since you don't know what's going wrong with the normal controls, you figure that in the worst-case scenario, I can grab the joystick and fly us out of danger."

"Exactly!" Sandrisson said, enthusiasm having returned during their conversation. "I will confess that I had not thought of needing a pilot, but Dr. DuQuesne—our power engineer, whom you will meet on Kanzaki-Three—pointed out to me the possibility of unknown failures and the need for a human fail-safe. Sounds rather twentieth century, I know, but just for the sensing experiments I've had to revive a number of other astoundingly primitive approaches."

Somewhat to his credit, Sandrisson seemed to belatedly realize that this was rather unfortunate phrasing. "Ah, I did not exactly mean—"

"I suspect you did, Simon," she cut him off, "but you aren't the first and won't be the last. You need my primitive approach, and you want Carl as a control and integration specialist, so I'm not about to torpedo this chance just because you inserted your foot into your mouth."

The green eyes looked both relieved and apologetic behind the glasses, but she wasn't in the mood to let him off the hook right now. "From my point of view, you keep someone in your head all the time, I have to wonder how well you could do without them propping you up."

Sandrisson bit his lip, then gave a rueful smile. "Touché, Ms. Austin. Whether I find your choices . . . odd, even incomprehensible, I should be capable of rudimentary diplomacy. My apologies. And I will owe you a much more detailed and involved apology if it does turn out that you are required to act."

Carl held out a hand. "Okay, let's stop there before we turn this into a real argument." He was looking at Ariane when he said this, and much as she hated to admit it, he was probably right to be doing that; she *did* tend to look for trouble, sometimes when it wasn't a good idea. "Doc, you also said there was another reason you ended up here."

"Yes, as a matter of fact," Sandrisson said quickly. "It was actually rather surprising, although perhaps given Ms . . . er, Ariane's rather unusual and demanding career, not quite as surprising as it might have been. Our research showed that you have connections to several of our candidates of interest in other areas. Specifically," he turned back to Ariane, "in addition to Dr. Edlund, I understand that you know one of our top conceptual design engineer candidates as well as our first choice for medical officer."

Of course. "And if we're all satisfactory, it means it's a much easier crew to integrate and prep for the final test?"

Sandrisson nodded.

She tried to look as though she were thinking, then gave it up. "Much as I'd like to keep you hanging, Simon, I can't. The chance to be on the crew of the first FTL ship ever made? Even as a probably-useless supernumerary? You just try to keep me *out* of your ship!"

Simon's face relaxed slightly. "That's gratifying, I will admit. Now, I have to emphasize that there is a quite significant risk involved in this—"

She burst out laughing. "*Risk*? Dr. Sandrisson, I just ran a race where I tried—with my opponent—to get one of us run into a keyhole barrier at several kliks a second!" She laughed again. "One and a half percent chance of something going wrong? Without that, it wouldn't even be worth *flying* your little toy."

She found the expression of uncomprehending discomfort on Sandrisson's face quite satisfying.

Chapter 4

"You understand all of my instructions exactly?" DuQuesne asked.

"I believe so," replied Dr. Davison, looking up with slightly puzzled eyes at DuQuesne. "I am not entirely sure *why* you have to be so . . . emphatic, but they are your arrangements to make."

Yes, they are *my arrangements to make. Never thought I'd have to do this, but if what Sandrisson's got is for real . . . I have to be ready. It's potentially the kind of chance I've been waiting for all this time. But I still really, really* hate *having to take off like this. If I'm gone, even Saul and all my precautions might not be enough.*

Davison summoned up an image of the hospital agreement. "Support for all individuals named is to continue for as long as they require it. They can, of course, leave at any time if they show the ability to do so. No visitors not on the explicit white list—a very, very short list. If you are killed or otherwise rendered unable to administer the contract, Commander Maginot of the CSF or his designated representative will assume those duties. No change to any procedures is to be made without express, direct, and personal contact with the administrator of the contract—that is, you must personally make any changes."

The blond-haired doctor looked back up. "The last point is the one that puzzles me. To force you, or the head of the entire Combined Space Forces, to personally, physically come here to change any point of procedure, rather than merely verifying through standard secure means, is—"

"—absolutely necessary, not negotiable, and not going to be explained either," DuQuesne cut in.

Davison shrugged. "All right. Your business. Though I would give considerably more than my current energy account to know exactly how and why you managed to convince Commander Maginot to agree to this." He raised an enquiring eyebrow.

"I'm sure you would." DuQuesne smiled darkly, knowing that his height of over two meters and ebony black hair, eyes, and short, pointed beard helped make the smile more sinister than comforting. There were times he might have liked to be less obvious a presence, but on balance he preferred to stay the way he was.

Davison blinked and gave a somewhat disconcerted sigh. "Yes, well, let's finish up." He certified the contract opposite DuQuesne's certification. "All contracted and verified."

"Thanks, Doctor," DuQuesne said. "Have your systems give me a map to Nanomaintenance?"

"Certainly."

DuQuesne felt the "incoming" ping and let in the map data. With a wave to Davison, he set out.

That worked out well. Didn't realize Cussler was in charge of maintenance on this particular station, but that made things even better; I had a perfectly legit reason to come here this time, so I didn't have to jump through the usual hoops to cloud my trail. Even made a stopover at Circumluna 2, which ought to confuse her mightily.

He wound his way through several corridors and found himself in the central tubeway. At that point, a voice spoke to him—not from loudspeakers, nor through his interfaces, but seemingly from the air itself, in his ear.

"Dr. DuQuesne. I'm glad you've come. I have been waiting for your arrival."

Focusing his own personal sensors, he was just able to make out the nanoswarms now tracking him. "That's pretty impressive." *Very clever. Never quite violated my privacy perimeter, which means he was able to scope out my perimeter by remote. Damn good.*

"Thank you. I have already signaled my intention to accept your proposal and sent the consent data to the SCC and Dr. Sandrisson. You will find my initial suggestions for the maintenance supplies and designs are attached."

DuQuesne frowned. "We haven't even finished the overall ship design. Dr. Franceschetti had only begun on those when I left."

"True," the disembodied voice agreed, "but with a minor amount of analysis I could come up with a general design projection that I believe matches the likely final design to within a few percent."

Showing off, but with a purpose. He wants us to know that he's the right man for the job. DuQuesne passed through another door, and stopped, studying what he saw carefully.

Dr. Thomas Cussler's eyes were closed, slightly graying eyebrows contrasting with skin so dark brown as to be nearly black, his square face seemingly chiseled out of polished wood by a master sculptor. Shimmers of light danced near him in the air, and actual physical leads—treated superconductor—were attached to him at several points. DuQuesne, now looking at him with a data-transfer overlay map, could see a torrent of data—sensor feeds, augmentation data, analysis enhancement, and others—streaming back and forth and through the man.

Yeah, he's definitely a Transcender; believes in the ultimate destiny of mankind to unify with the machines we created. Doesn't do the full Upload thing because it'd qualify him as an AI under current rules.

This wasn't the kind of direction DuQuesne ever intended to go, but for a nanomaintenance man it was ideal. Tom Cussler was obviously aware of the operation of much of the station the way a man is aware of the operation of his body. "You sure you want to come along?"

Cussler suddenly sat up and opened his eyes, which glinted with humor and awareness. "Oh, most definitely," he answered, in a deep, warm voice. "Your ship may be far smaller than my usual systems, but I am fascinated by the possibilities. I've just finished making a backup copy of myself, in case of disaster, so the risk is minimal."

One way we really *think differently,* DuQuesne thought. *There's no way in hell I'd make a "backup"; it wouldn't be me, just someone who thought he was me, and what if it got activated by accident when I was still alive?* Aloud, he snorted and shook his head. "So I didn't even have to come here?"

"Perhaps not," admitted Cussler, extending his hand and shaking DuQuesne's, "but I appreciate the effort, and the personal touch. While I am perfectly comfortable making all my arrangements by virtupresence, many others are not—I note that our pilot, in particular, will want to meet me in person before we actually begin, so I have already made the arrangements. I'm leaving Maxine in charge for the time in question." DuQuesne got a fleeting impression of a pretty young woman in overalls, wearing a baseball cap and holding an oversized wrench, giving him a wave and a wink. "She can run things here almost as well as I can, certainly for a few weeks."

"Good enough," DuQuesne said. "Well, since I'm here, you want to get up and show me around the place?"

Cussler laughed. "Wondering if I actually move far from the center of my web, Doctor? Why not? My connections travel with me. Yet . . . it's rather odd, Dr. DuQuesne. I have a vague impression that this is not your first visit here. And I do not normally have 'vague' impressions at all."

He's damn good to have any at all. I'll have to upgrade Davison's security again, and especially the data-feed remote editing. If he can get even a vague impression . . . someone else might get more. And that would be real, real bad. "It's possible," he said, answering Cussler's implied question, "but if so it was a long time ago; probably before you really settled in here."

Cussler relaxed. "Yes, that would make sense." He rose and gestured to another door. "Shall we? This will take us to some of the better areas of the station most quickly."

"Lead on," DuQuesne said with a smile.

Chapter 5

Simon leaned back in his chair, massaging his temples. "So we are nearly ready to go?"

The diminuitive blonde woman opposite him nodded, answering in a soft Southern accent. "Speaking just for myself, I'm ready. Tom and the others have done themselves proud on giving me the best medical facilities we can fit in the space available. Of course, I'm hoping I'm just excess baggage."

"Gabrielle," Simon assured her, "a medical officer is never excess baggage. Obviously we hope you have nothing but an entertaining ride to look forward to, of course."

"Thank you kindly," Dr. Gabrielle Wolfe said, flashing a brilliant smile of appreciation at him. "Me and you both, I assure you. And you too, Arrie."

Ariane Austin smiled fondly back at her friend. "No doubt about it, Gabrielle. We just want to sit back and enjoy the show."

Simon could tell that Ariane wasn't being entirely truthful; she was a pilot, and at heart she wanted to be the one flying the ship into history. But she wasn't going to complain about that in public; she was going to pull her friends together as part of the team.

In an odd way, the fact that they held these face to face meetings as a courtesy to her preferences was helping bring them all together. Virtupresense was ubiquitous . . . yet somehow personal meetings still had an undefinable power that most virtual encounters lacked.

You made the right choice in taking her, Simon, Mio said.

Thank DuQuesne for that, he answered honestly. *I wouldn't even have thought of taking a pilot. Now I've got a crew that starts out unified, mostly.* He glanced over at the third of Ariane's friends, Dr. Stephen Franceschetti, nearly as small as Gabrielle Wolfe, one of the top concept engineers in the System and the main designer of the experimental vessel—which now had a name, courtesy of Ariane Austin.

The pilot had insisted on it. "No ship I've ever flown has been just a string of numbers, and even if the only time I actually fly her is in simulation, I'm not going to change that now."

And her suggestion of a name had been so apropos that there hadn't even been any competing candidates. In honor of what they sought—the proof of the practicality of faster-than-light travel, something dreamed of but never realized over the centuries—the test vessel was to be named *Holy Grail*.

He smiled again at the thought. "Dr. Franceschetti, how long until we're ready for launch?"

Steve ran a hand through short-cropped curly hair. "A week? The E-dollar support we've been getting has pretty much maxed out the construction and testing speed. Tom," he glanced to Dr. Cussler, who grinned back, "has already got the nanomaintenance working internally, which is helping a lot. Carl's got the controls installed, except for Ariane's pure physical actuator back-ups, which we're having to do a lot of modeling on to make sure we're not making any unrecognized assumptions."

"What do you mean by that?"

"What he means," Ariane said, catching his gaze, "is that our technology's so ubiquitous that we have lots of areas where we tend to forget about it entirely. Like the fact that we were installing physical control systems, and backup sensors that could've been manufactured three centuries ago, but the display interfaces were still assuming I could get a 3–D holographic input that's run by a T-0.5 display server."

"Oh dear. Yes, that would not do at all." Simon had the momentary, very unpleasant image of being inside a vessel whose pilot—*human* pilot—couldn't see where she was going or what might be in her way.

"That's been the main pain in the ass for this ship design all along," Carl put in. "Having to parallel every damn operation of the ship, one cutting-edge, the other something that dates back to, what, the twentieth century, maybe the twenty-first? I've had to work with Tom, Steve, and Marc," he nodded at DuQuesne, "to reconstruct models of those kinds of devices. Sometimes I feel like I'm trying to crossbreed a rocket ship with a Spanish galleon."

Simon chuckled. "Come now, it's not that bad. But it is an interesting challenge we are facing, I admit. Dr. DuQuesne?"

"Interesting, yes. I'm coming from the other direction—with all the advances we've made since that time, I was able to actually come up with a reasonably efficient design for a fusion reactor that *doesn't* require AI controls. Might actually be worth a paper or two at the next Energy Review Conference." The huge, black-haired engineer leaned back in his chair. "So main fusion reactor's a go. I've put in a good chunk of backup batteries, plus the absolutely enormous bank of superconductor batteries to hold the transition pulse for your 'Sandrisson coils.' Power runs to all main and backup systems are designed and almost completed. We've got all the drive systems installed, primary to final backup, except, of course, for the test drive; those coils are still being built up and you'll have to resonance test them day after tomorrow."

"Supplies?"

Tom Cussler answered. "That's my department. We have—courtesy of Commander Maginot—an AIWish unit, rating ten, with the limiting programming interlocks disabled, so I can use it for manufacturing just about anything. We'll have plenty of raw materials, so food should not be a problem . . . unless you're planning on spending a *long* time in this 'transition' of yours."

"Well," Simon said, "That depends on what you mean by 'long.' Because of the energy demands of the drive, we will have to spend some time—I calculate about five or six days—to recharge the coils, but no more than that."

Ariane glanced up, puzzled. "But . . . your probes jumped out and came back pretty much right away. Why can't we just do that?"

"Because we simply don't have room for *two* banks of surge superconductor batteries capable of carrying that much power." Sandrisson answered. "The one we have already takes up more than a quarter of the ship volume. Add another bank and we'll have room for about one person. Maybe."

"Your prior tests only lasted for a few seconds, Simon," DuQuesne pointed out. "If we stay in this . . . transition space for days, how far away will we have gone?"

"A question that's not quite as simple to answer as it sounds. Remember that the probes seemed to emerge at almost random locations. There was some correlation between how fast they were going and how far they had gone when they emerged, but it was not nearly so clear as I would have liked.

"Based on the maximum speed we have seen . . . perhaps a third of a light-year."

The others were silent, staring at him for a moment. A slow grin spread across Ariane's face. "Going where no one has gone before," she said.

"Aside from unmanned probes, yes. Of course, that's part of the risk. For the current approach, we don't have room to add a full backup set of batteries—the power requirements of the drive would scale up again—and so, if for some reason we end up unable to come *back* . . . "

The others looked momentarily troubled, but Ariane waved that away as though it was of no more concern than a smudge on the *Holy Grail*'s paint job. "Don't try to scare me out of this. *You* can stay home if you like. I could always fly her on my own."

Simon shook his head. "And I do believe you would. No, I don't think any of us are backing out. Certainly not me—I have a great deal to prove here. Anyone else?"

DuQuesne snorted, an eloquent, if nonverbal, response. The others all indicated they weren't backing out either.

"Then I do believe that our next meeting—this time, next week—will be our final meeting in preparation for launch." Simon smiled. "One way or another, we'll be done with this in a couple of weeks."

"With luck," Ariane said, as she and the others stood to leave, "it will just be the beginning of something bigger."

"We can only hope," he agreed.

Chapter 6

As usual, DuQuesne noticed, Simon lingered a bit longer than everyone else; generally he seemed to be giving people a chance to meet with him privately in case they had questions or concerns they didn't want to talk about in the general meeting. Since he didn't have any additional points to hash out with Simon, DuQuesne continued out.

But after he'd only gone a couple of corridors down, he slowed. There'd been something on the scientist's face, a shift in expression, that bothered him. DuQuesne shrugged and returned to the conference room.

Simon Sandrisson was still there, eyes closed but not resting; his face, now that DuQuesne was looking for it, seemed definitely troubled. "You okay, Simon?"

The green eyes snapped open in startlement. "Marc? I thought everyone had left."

"I had. Came back, though, because I thought you looked like something was eating at you. From what I saw when I came in, I was right. Want to talk about it?"

Sandrisson sat up, one hand reflexively smoothing his hair back so it framed, rather than fell across, his face. "Is it really that obvious?"

"No," DuQuesne answered, giving the scientist a very small smile. "I doubt anyone else would have noticed anything at all. But your question tells me you *do* have a problem, so spit it out."

"I suppose I should. Marc, is it really *worth* endangering all of you just to prove my own point? Am I conducting an experiment that I shouldn't?"

"Didn't you already have this discussion with Saul Maginot and me? The Schilling potential of this jaunt seems minimal." DuQuesne used the usual shorthand to refer to the risk of true lethal disaster, derived from the runaway nanotech or "gray goo" incident that had consumed the laboratory and persons of Dr. Michael Schilling, the unrelated Dr. John Schilling, and their forty associates in Lunar Lab 2—necessitating a thermo-nuclear strike to eliminate the danger. "And there's some good reason to go forward with this. You convinced Saul, obviously."

The scientist sighed, then took off the ornamental glasses and rubbed his eyes. "I played to his general concerns, partly because Mio was able to glean his hot-button topics from his public speeches and interviews. But privacy, self-determination, all these things are virtu-ally at an all-time high. I'm afraid I may have convinced him, but not myself. What is the danger and urgency here that justifies risking people?"

DuQuesne gave a derisive snort. "Sandrisson, let me tell you something. I've known Commander Maginot for

. . . well, a damn long time, and if all you did was try to play up to his fears, he'd have laughed you out of the conference room and denied you this chance, right off the bat." He shook his head. "Look, Simon, it's hard to see all the parts of this picture. Some of it goes all the way back to Harriman Delosius and the Anonymity War, which damn near wrecked civilization but ended up giving us what we've got now—a society that's bloody close to the ideal of everyone able to do whatever they want, whenever they want, as long as they don't hurt anyone else, and without anyone starving, freezing, or otherwise suffering because they can't even get the basic necessities of life. We still have different countries, but compared to what they used to be, they're practically volunteer clubs.

"But you know there's always that nagging set of voices out there worried that someone is doing something *bad* with that freedom—and of course the problem is, sometimes they're *right*."

Simon nodded. "Hyperion."

DuQuesne grimaced. "Yeah. Hyperion. That mess forced Saul to create the Combined Space Forces and the Space Security Council all at once. There are some things too monstrous to allow, even in the name of freedom. The problem is that it's *easy* to let that kind of change accumulate. People don't mind poking into other people's business . . . they just don't want other people poking into theirs. Governments exist to run society . . . and they do that best by having more and more information and control. Sure, the governments we have now don't have much of that at all any more—when AIWish nanoreplicators can give everyone pretty much anything, there's just not all that much left to do."

"Yes, yes," Simon said tiredly, "I know that part of the argument; I made it to the Commander. Do you really think there's a clear and present danger of this society turning into one that's really so much more controlled?"

"Oh, yes indeedy." DuQuesne gave his most unsettling grin. "There've been bills debated already on the floor of the SSC which would introduce requirements to insert override codes—only for use in the most extreme circumstances, of course—allowing the SSC or its active arm, the CSF, to directly interrogate your personal net, including your AISage, without consent. They've been defeated so far, but the problem is that we've come way too far with our technology; *if* such a thing were ever enacted, it would be a very, very, *very* short step from that to universal monitoring and control. And that is ignoring the joker in the pack of the AISages—imagine your favorite friend and confidant being secretly programmed to monitor you. It wouldn't be hard to manage."

Simon shuddered. "Mio says you have a horrible imagination and she's going to have nightmares about that."

"Sorry," DuQuesne said sincerely. He opened up his link so he could see the little Asian avatar glaring at him. "Really, I am sorry. That wasn't meant to imply anything about you."

She narrowed her eyes. "I certainly hope not."

"So, Marc," Simon said, "Do you really see FTL as helping this situation?"

"Indirectly, yes. Oh, it's not really going to be a solution for the Solar System itself if someone manages to trigger a totalitarian revolution, but what it would do is make it possible for there to be places *not* controlled by such a regime. The Solar System's got fifty-five billion people in it now, and it's actually starting to get a little difficult to find some area to set up shop where you're *not* going to be a little close to someone else. For, of course, varying values of 'a little close.' And if you *do* set up shop far enough away that other people aren't sure what you're up to, it's already true that they start nosing around to make sure that you aren't the next Hyperion Station."

"You may be right," Simon said reluctantly. "Mio just showed me a projection of your little horror scenario and I admit, it's terrifying. Less than one year from the time of authorization to potentially near-total control?"

DuQuesne nodded slowly. "That's the drawback to near-universal nanotech, controllable AI assistance, and so on. If it turns on you—or someone turns it against you—you've got almost no defense."

"What about you, DuQuesne?" Mio said suddenly. "I hope I am not offending you, but when we first met, Simon asked me to profile you along with the Commander . . . and I was not able to gather much of anything at all. You are a terribly private man. Is it just this issue that makes you interested in this project?"

DuQuesne chuckled. *Private indeed.* "Actually, I have plenty of reasons of my own. One is just simple curiosity. I want to know what's out there, and even with longevity treatments I may never know if we can't get your little gadget working."

"But currently we have every reason to expect centuries —if not longer—of life. Unmanned probes—"

"—haven't answered the questions yet, actually," he said with a sardonic grin. "Here's a little tidbit of info that I've gathered over the past few decades, but it's not generally known, though undoubtedly thousands or millions know parts of it.

"In the past forty years, no less than twelve interstellar probes were launched, using whatever was top of the line in automation and nanodesign at the time. A couple of these were basically backyard fan projects, but most of them got quite a bit of interest and energy backing at their time. By now, more than half of them should have arrived at their destinations and started survey and possibly even nanoconstruction work.

"Not a single one of them has been heard from."

There was silence for a moment as Simon and Mio contemplated that fact—and how very unlikely it was for so many advanced probe systems to fail utterly. Then DuQuesne stood. "Anyway, you feel any better?"

Simon looked at him wryly. "I am not entirely sure that 'better' is the proper term, Marc. However, I will say that I do feel less like a mad scientist risking others for the sake of his own vindication. Thank you."

"Anytime." He walked out, feeling reasonably satisfied. Throwing an AISage like Mio off track took considerable effort and timing; you had to read the personality just like any other person's, and take into account their own focus. She might—probably would—later on come to the tentative conclusion that he'd evaded discussing other reasons he was interested in the project.

But not until it was too late for that to make a difference.

Chapter 7

Simon floated in the zero-G observation lounge, looking straight "up" along the axis of Kanzaki-Three, staring at the long, slender shape of *Holy Grail*. The experimental vessel had the look of some delicate sea-dwelling creature, a streamlined torpedo with four exquisitely narrow tendrils—the magnetic guide ribs for its mass-beam drive—trailing far behind it. In a few days, he thought, they would all be on board, and only a few hours after that . . . he would know. One way or another, he would know.

Or, he admitted to himself and Mio, *I may not know, if everything goes perfectly terribly and we explode or disappear.*

Let's not think on that. Remember, our pilot thinks the risk is hardly worth considering.

Oh, that's *a comforting thought.*

Mio suddenly notified him that someone else had entered the lounge. *Not a member of our crew.*

Simon spun himself slowly and looked down.

The woman ascending to meet him was of approximately average height, with severely styled brown hair in a short, no-nonsense pageboy cut, slender, well-built, with long, delicate hands that somehow made Simon think of a surgeon, and not a trace of biomods—not even a bit of hair coloring. She brought herself to a stop directly in front of Simon, wobbling a little in the characteristic manner of someone unaccustomed to long periods maneuvering in zero-G. "Dr. Simon Sandrisson, correct?"

"I am, yes. And you are . . . ?"

She stuck out her hand. "Dr. Laila Canning."

Oh, my. Mio said silently. *Profile coming up.*

Simon allowed the information to flow and let it guide his response. "Dr. Canning! Very nice to meet you. What brings one of the System's most prominent biologists to Kanzaki-Three?"

"You, of course," Laila Canning responded tartly. "I'm coming on your expedition."

Simon blinked. "I beg your pardon?"

For answer, Canning opened up a connection. A bearded AISage avatar materialized, extending an encrypted data icon which Mio took; it immediately recognized her private decryption matrix and opened. She played the message to Simon, shielding it from Canning's AISage.

The message was from Commander Maginot, and was as short and to the point as every communication the CSF commander ever sent. Dr. Laila Canning was to be added to the crew, based on her own request, and would explain her interest in person. On a backchannel of the message, Maginot had added that Canning was a personal favorite of Dean Stout, one of the SSC members with the most influence. "I'd really appreciate it if you can accommodate this request," Maginot finished. "It *is* up to you in the end, of course, and if you feel it's not practical, tell her she isn't coming. I'll back you. But it'd be much, much easier on me if she goes."

Simon put on his "friendly professor" face. "Well, I see Saul's being rather close-mouthed as usual, but quite clear that you're to come along. Might I ask, Dr. Canning—"

"Laila," she corrected. "Let's not waste energy in formalities. Just get to the point—no offense meant, but I like getting to work right away."

"All right, Laila. Exactly what do you see as your . . . function on *Holy Grail*?"

She gave a quick, chirping laugh, almost like a bird. "Function? None in the sense that sounds like, Simon. You already have ship functions covered—even, I understand, have someone trained to fly the ship physically.

"*My* interest is in, naturally, the biological sciences. Your reports stated that biological systems appeared to continue functioning normally, yet even the most cursory examination of your data shows that you haven't any serious basis on which to make that claim. Oh, in very gross and trivial factors, yes. But . . . " Her eyes gave a gleam that echoed Ariane's when she was talking about flying a ship and risking her life. "In the details of the operation of biological systems—enzymes, RNA replication, metabolic shifts, all the thousands of different processes—in these areas you have no data at all."

"Are you saying you think there may be an effect we haven't seen?"

"I'm certain there must be," Laila said. "Oh, none that would show up on your crude tests for at least several days—the multivariate trending analysis I've done on your released data leaves me sure of that—but in the fine details? You're having *some* sort of effect that's disrupting other systems, *physical* systems, and biological systems are physical. They may operate very differently, but they're also exquisitely sensitive in many areas. I intend to be on board to observe, not only whatever laboratory animals I can bring with me, but all of your crew as well—with their permission, of course."

Simon looked at her speculatively. "You know that we will have to spend several days—instead of several seconds—in the transition space before returning. Do you think any of these effects could be dangerous?"

"Over that period of time?" She thought for a moment, and Simon sensed, through Mio, an immense amount of activity surrounding her—more, he thought, than he'd expect from just a woman with an AISage. "Probably not. My earlier comments perhaps overstated the crudity of your monitoring. You had quite adequate basic monitoring, despite the handicap presented by lack of processing power in transition, and your post-transition analyses of the test animals showed no anomalies at all. What I hope to see are very subtle effects, probably toward the end of the transition."

Simon sighed. "Let me see what I can do. Now that you've brought it up, this would actually be very interesting data—as a physicist, if you see subtle variations of biological function, it may give me clues as to the precise nature of any physical-law shifts we are encountering."

He opened a channel. *Steve?*

A cadaverous, black-cloaked figure materialized in his mind's eye: Allerdyne, Steve's AISage avatar. *My Master sleeps. What do you desire of him?*

I want to know if we can move the internal designs around enough to accommodate one more passenger.

This is within my power to examine. Allerdyne conferred with Carl Edlund and DuQuesne. *It will be a challenge, but we believe so.*

Simon smiled. "You are in luck, Laila."

"There was a problem?"

"The problem is the way the so-called Sandrisson Drive works," he answered, pointing to the ship and overlaying a diagram. "There are the coils that have to generate the transition field around the ship—to a very close specification. The problem is that the amount of power to generate the field increases drastically with the size of the vessel, up to a certain point, and *Holy Grail* is at a particularly steep part of the curve. If we have to make her any larger, we may find that we can't generate enough power in that space without either waiting *much* longer, or building her even bigger to give us more power generation—which will, of course, increase the field size needed, and so on. Eventually the curve flattens, but by then I'm building something the size of Kanzaki-Three and putting in an antimatter generator."

Laila blinked. "Oh my. I had no idea my mere presence could be such a problem."

"It *could* have been, but as it turns out, it isn't." Simon took her hand again and shook it. "Welcome to the crew of *Holy Grail*, Laila."

She looked up, and Simon could see a touch of the wonder and eagerness that he felt was necessary in anyone taking this trip. "Thank you so much, Simon. I know

I come across as rather abrupt, and I'm not at all a very social person. But I do very much appreciate the opportunity—and the fact you're taking some considerable pains to assist me that could probably have been better spent elsewhere." A mischievous grin flickered on her face as she glanced up from under her fringe of hair. "And that it's a bit annoying to have political pressure forcing some new passenger on you."

Simon laughed. "I think it will be less annoying than I might have expected, now. Care to join me at Café Rei? I was thinking of getting dinner, and I wouldn't mind hearing more about some of your research on Mars xenobiology."

"My compliments to your AISage's quick research and update," she said, smiling, "and I'd be honored."

Simon led the way, taking one last glance at the silver-shining sliver of *Holy Grail*.

Chapter 8

"Why exactly did we design this experimental ship to be like a giant coffin?"

Steve Franceschetti gave her a grave look. "To save on the costs of burial later, of course," he said in a faux-Transylvanian accent, dark eyes twinkling.

"Oh, ha-ha," Ariane said. "These low ceilings just give me the creeps." She sighed. "Never mind, I know it has something to do with the energy requirements of the drive getting ridiculous as the ship gets larger." She grinned as she saw Steve—and, via electronic avatar, Simon Sandrisson—wince at her oversimplification. "*And* the fact that we had to shoehorn in our biologist at the last minute."

Sorry about that, Laila Canning's virtual voice said.

No problem. You know, I haven't the faintest idea what a shoehorn is or why it's used to mean "squeeze stuff in."

Three AISages—Mentor, Darwin (belonging to Laila Canning), and Carl's Shaina—immediately produced images, descriptions, and linguistic detail. "Ow! Ow! Too many at once! Thanks very much, but we're getting close enough to the activation point that I'd better concentrate on the matter at hand. After all, that's the main reason I'm here."

All systems operational. Onboard AI fully functional. Backups show green. All personnel in prime condition. Nanosupport operational in all personnel, Mentor informed her as she leaned back in the pilot's position. *Projecting probabilities of injury in case of top four risk scenarios.*

The probability graphs showed minimal chances for any crew members; this wasn't surprising, given that one of the top four scenarios involved impacting with a random bit of space debris upon exiting after transition —something extremely improbable and still most likely to cause no injury. One thing did niggle at her perceptions, though. "Mentor, why are DuQuesne and Wolfe less likely to be injured than the rest of the crew?"

The deeply-resonant pseudo-voice replied, *Because examination of the returns of their bio-status monitors reveals, after careful analysis, a 99.78% probability that both of them are augmented to military specifications rather than merely high-risk protection and enhancement.*

That was a bit of a surprise. Not, perhaps, in Gabrielle's case, because she knew that Gabrielle had served as medical oversight in a couple of the nasty semi-political flare-ups across the Solar System, but why would a power engineer-conceptualizer like DuQuesne . . . She shrugged. It wasn't her business. The important thing was that the estimated risks—outside of the Unknowns that dominated the actual transition—were well below the acceptable limit determined by the experimental protocols. The greatest risk remained, simply put, the Unknown that had caused three of the probes not to emerge at all.

According to the test schedule, the *Holy Grail* would activate the Sandrisson Drive at a range of twenty million kilometers from Kanzaki-Three. This was more than far enough to make it certain that, even if this attempt proved to be just as random in its emergent location as the prior probes, there was essentially no likelihood of impact with anything. If things went anything like they were expected to, of course, no matter *which* direction *Holy Grail* went, they'd end up far outside the Solar System.

Like most vessels with the luxury of advance course planning, *Holy Grail* was using a simple mass-beam drive which permitted constant (low) acceleration and deceleration along her course. With hundreds of mass-beam accelerators distributed throughout the system, it was easy to get the "smart" nanoparticles accelerated to either provide any direct vector upon impact, or to arrive and come to relative rest (via appropriate use of sunlight) for later use at any point out to about the orbit of Neptune without making any special arrangements outside of scheduling. To use captured mass from the beam required, of course, that *Holy Grail* have a method to accelerate it, which was provided by the coilgun design that was a part of the mass-beam supports—in essence, the mass-beam magnetic capture field was reversed and used to throw away the mass it had captured. The fusion reactors provided the energy for the acceleration, and backup power was held in multiple superconductor-ring batteries.

For the higher-speed maneuvers which—everyone hoped—would not be needed, *Holy Grail* incorporated a fusion pulse rocket, and even some backup chemical rockets. Despite many decades of work, none of the more speculative drive systems—space-imbalance or bias drives, negative matter-based asymmetry, selective radiation differential methods, and so on—had ever been developed to anything workable. In the end analysis, you were still either throwing stuff at high speed out the back, or having someone hit you with a firehose to push you along.

She checked the status of all the drive systems, which naturally showed all green; if anything was wrong, she'd already have been notified—and probably the difficulty would have been corrected before her sluggish brain had finished realizing there was an issue. Even though nominally she was the commander of the mission, everything was being handled by the AIs. The status reports, the verifications of authorization, course clearance, flight-projected course and duration . . . all were being exchanged and finalized by entities that existed purely as data structures in a dual-mode semi-quantum computational network. Mentor, as befitted his status as the most highly-capable AISage and as the one assigned to her, would actually handle the flight of the vessel, unless something unforeseen happened.

She distracted herself from contemplating her essential uselessness by checking on her fellow crewmembers. Steve and his AISage Allerdyne were practically merged into a single individual, overseeing the entire condition of the *Holy Grail*. Dr. Sandrisson and his own AI companion were focused—unsurprisingly—on the experimental drive coils. She gave a virtual nod as Sandrisson acknowledged her attention with a smile and wave, and then continued her crew check.

Gabrielle Wolfe caught her wandering scrutiny. *Hey there. You feeling about as bored as I am right now?* The gentle Southern accent was conveyed perfectly by the silent voice.

Maybe not really bored, but useless.

I'm just hoping we both are useless. Because if we need a medical doctor, something just went terribly wrong. Gabrielle's electronic avatar smiled, identical to the delicately-built blonde in real life. *Too bad your job doesn't allow you to be furiously busy in idleness, like Laila.*

Ariane saw what Gabrielle meant. Laila Canning had made tremendous use of the limited space she'd been given, and revealed in the process the single-minded focus that had made her a biologist as respected in her field as Sandrisson was in physics. Canning was mentally integrated with all eight sets of crew biological monitors, twenty sets of monitors on her array of experimental animals, with no less than *three* AISages boosting her perceptual and comprehension capabilities to the point that she must be intimately aware of, and able to comprehend and analyze, each and every life sign of all the experimental animals and the human beings on board *Holy Grail*.

Dr. DuQuesne's avatar nodded to her as she directed her attention to that area of the vessel. She didn't, however, see any sign of his AISage Isaac, and there appeared to be almost no connectivity surrounding DuQuesne outside of direct observation. *Not watching the systems, Doctor?*

The massively-built, dark-haired, dark-eyed scientist-engineer shook his head. *No point at this stage. I have checked them, I know they are ready. Fusion reactors all at full, backup batteries fully charged, surge demand storage for Dr. Sandrisson's drive all ready. I would rather watch this historic event myself, without electronic intermediaries or enhancements. Although,* a glint of humor showed on the almost olive-skinned face, *you will note I am not separating myself from perceptual assistance. Perhaps I am already as soft as I feared.*

Or just prudent. I may also prefer to do things myself, but you'll note that my control and piloting systems are not just physical joysticks and displays.

Carl Edlund had, of course, given her straight physical interfaces, as they'd discussed, but the mind-interface control system, assisted by Mentor, cut out the physical reaction time. Only the time necessary for her to process critical data would delay reactions. As a racing pilot, she had been allowed only minimal nanoenhancement, but for this mission she'd accepted considerable upgrading. She wasn't bothered by simple upgrades—making her faster, tougher, stronger, easier to heal, all that kind of thing wasn't a problem. It was just things that touched the brain—the center of one's self—that got her nervous.

The enhancements she had now meant that even *with* the physical controls she could perceive, process, and react appropriately to a threat in less than seventy-five milliseconds. Without physical controls, her reaction time was a tenth that—and that assumed complex reaction time, rather than a simple reaction to a simple, unambiguous stimulus.

Of course, that was still slower than a glacier's flow when compared to the sub-microsecond, sometimes nanosecond, response time of a good AI control system. And if events involved moving at high speeds, a few milliseconds might mean hundreds of meters, or even thousands, crossed in the time it took her to react. She admitted to herself that her hope to be actually needed was a purely selfish one, and not a particularly bright impulse either. Anything that took out all the automatics would probably kill them all.

All her musing had taken some time. The timing countdown was dropping drastically. "This is Commander Ariane Austin," she said, using for the first time the title she'd been accorded as the ultimate backup pilot for the mission. "We're almost to the activation point. I can see by the telltales you're all ready, but in the interests of tradition and verification, all hands, please report readiness in order."

"System oversight, ready!"

"Sandrisson Drive, ready. For proof or mockery we shall see in a moment."

"Medical all ready. You can all rest easy."

"Power systems all secure," DuQuesne's calm baritone said.

Dr. Laila Canning's distracted voice answered next. "Experimental analysis and monitoring fully online. Please do not distract us." The *us* gave Ariane a slight case of the creeps.

"Hey, you tell *me* if the controls are working," Carl Edlund said cheerfully. "Me, I'm strapped in and integrated, my job's pretty much done. Let's go!"

"Nanomaintenence is online . . . everywhere," Tom Cussler said. *Holy Grail's* nanomaintenance and replication expert had integrated himself with the systems nearly as much as Laila Canning had with her experiments. "If it gets broke, I'll fix it. Just don't break anything."

"Definitely not in the game plan," Ariane assured him. "One minute to activation."

She reached out and grasped the manual controls. Contrary to her prior statement to DuQuesne, she decided it was best to cut out the direct connects. If they worked, all the other systems probably did, too. The manual controls and standard displays used old-fashioned electro-optical methods which were completely separate from the main integrated controls. If she was really going to be needed, these were the controls she'd need.

Thirty seconds. She could almost feel Sandrisson's anticipation, a bleed-through from his focus. He was, she realized, far more nervous about this than he let on. She smiled. *You're still a genius, you know.*

I hope so. But I'd much rather it get proved than have to argue the point after failure.

Don't worry. I'm the spare wheel. It'll go just fine.

The avatar-face was very contrite. *And as I said, I will owe you a much more involved and detailed apology, if your unique skills do, in fact, turn out to be necessary. I really did not mean any offense. You do know that?*

I do, she answered; to her surprise, she found it was true. Sandrisson had been trying to explain the entire situation to her—partly, she suspected, out of the need to convince himself once more that he was right—and it must have been very frustrating for him. *And I know I'm weird.*

But still charming and skilled.

Are you flirting with me, Doctor? She was even more surprised by the anticipation that welled up in her at the thought.

It is possible. The simulated green eyes took on a devilish sparkle.

She grinned widely. *Let's take this up again . . . maybe in a few minutes. Ten seconds left.*

Agreed.

Hey you two! None of that! Steve's simulated voice said.

You're just jealous.

The wizard-like avatar Allerdyne and Steve's avatar simultaneously demonstrated the maturity of AI and human intellects by sticking out their virtual tongues.

Five seconds. Sandrisson coils charging.

The field strength built swiftly, symmetrically. If Sandrisson was correct, the drive would basically enclose the *Holy Grail* in a deformation of space-time somewhat similar to a high gravitational field—but instead of squashing them down to nothing, would cause them to be catapulted into the parallel related spacetime represented by the Kanzaki-Locke context parameter matrix.

If he was correct.

Two seconds.

One second.

Activation.

In the sudden, silent blackness, Ariane heard Dr. Sandrisson scream.

Chapter 9

The scream was still echoing—in fact, had not yet finished—when the backup power systems brought her displays and controls back online. *But it's not* online! she thought desperately. The wireless systems were down, there was no connectivity at all that wasn't provided by hardwiring and actuators. *What the . . .*

Proximity Alert! What the hell . . . solid surfaces? Everywhere! One closing at high velocity! And still in null-G?

Racing-trained reflexes, enhanced by still-functioning nanotechnological augmentations, snapped into action. Chemical side-jets fired, spinning *Holy Grail* into reverse alignment with their vector on the fast-approaching object, and instantaneously triggering the nuclear pulse engine.

Except that the engine didn't fire.

Dammit! Her hands danced across the panel, molasses-slow manual controls overriding the original settings, shunting in the last-ditch backups.

Holy Grail shuddered as the massive chemical rockets roared to life, sending a blazing beacon of white-hot flame through the darkness. Incredulously, Ariane saw *reflections* all around her—dark-tinted shimmers and distorted waves, moving like the shadows and glints from water as you drove along the shoreline. The cameras pointing to the rear of *Holy Grail* showed an even more terrifying sight—a massive, unmistakeable, impossible *Wall*, a wall on which they were closing with terrible speed. Ariane went to full power on the rocket, the ship's structure audibly creaking as more than four gravities crushed down upon it. That unbelievable barrier continued to approach, looming in her displays like a gray oncoming tsunami, something elemental and massive beyond belief. The reflections of the rockets were becoming brighter, sharper, as they closed with the enigma.

Now she could see that they were slowing, but they were close, close, and the mighty tail of flame was actually *touching* that wall, splashing off it like a jet of water from a battleship's plating, broadening, still closing . . .

Almost stopped . . .

The long, arched tendrils of *Holy Grail*'s four mass-driver coilguns impacted squarely with the wall, sending a jolt through the ship, snapping one off at the base and bending the others. The experimental vessel began to twist, but the relative velocity was now almost zero and Ariane cut the rocket, going to docking maneuver thrusters. There was a screeching *clang* as the broken coilgun bounced off the main hull, and Ariane compensated. *Relative velocity effectively zero.*

As the thrusters cut off, she became really aware of the silence of the ship. The environmental systems were still (or once again?) running, sending a subtle breeze of air through the vessel, but . . . there was no contact. The central computer systems were down. She had no direct connectivity to anyone, even Mentor.

Well, first things first. She knew she wasn't hurt—just bruised a little from the maneuvers. In the control cabin with her . . . "Steve? Simon? Are you all right?"

The voice behind her and slightly to her right didn't speak; there was a slight indrawing of breath and a . . . whimper, a sound of such pain and fear that she couldn't even recognize it as made by the same man who had been flirting with her just seconds before. On her other side there was a moment of silence and a chill seemed to fall over her heart before, finally, Steve answered.

"I . . . I don't know." Steve Franceschetti's voice was hurt and thin and confused. "He's . . . gone. I'm alone . . . "

"He?" She was momentarily at sea, then suddenly understood. "Allerdyne?"

"Yeah."

"Simon? Simon, talk to me!"

The internal lighting electronics finally seemed to finish reconnecting, and the control cabin was suddenly lit. She winced and then looked around.

Sandrisson was staring wide-eyed into nothing, hand to his mouth. The blaze of light did seem to finally penetrate, especially as Ariane unstrapped and came into his field of view. The green eyes blinked and slowly focused on her, and he lowered his hand. "A . . . Ariane."

She repressed an exclamation at the blood; he was apparently completely unaware that he had bitten deeply into his own index finger in fear or shock. "Simon. Are you all right?"

He shook his head violently, muttering something in Japanese. Without Mentor to provide unobtrusive translation, she couldn't understand it, but the tone seemed to be both angry and disbelieving. "Y . . . yes. Perhaps," he said, switching to English, then winced and stared in surprise at his hand. "Perhaps not. I . . . I have not been without Mio for, oh, twenty years—since I was twelve. Like Steve, I am . . . alone now." He pulled a tissue from one pocket and wiped his face; she noted with some relief that at least some of the healing nanotech must still be working, as the wound on his finger had already stopped bleeding. "I will be all right for now, I think."

"Steve, can you get manual systems up throughout the ship?"

The diminutive system overseer wrinkled his brow, hands rubbing distractedly through his curly hair. "I . . . I have to think about that. Damn. They should have come up on their own. Except . . . I think they're set for at least some intermediary communication." He looked like he was ready to panic, but then closed his eyes, took several deep breaths, got it under control. "Too used to having Allerdyne there doing the direct access. Without him I can't directly reach my headware storage—I'll have to do a direct-link hack later. If I can remember how. Trying to remember exactly how to go about doing this . . . " He touched a few controls tentatively. After several more moments, he seemed to get a feel for what he was doing. Lights flickered momentarily again, then she saw another set of indicators on the main panel light up. "There, that's done it."

She hit the manual intercom. "This is Commander Austin. We have had multiple system failures but appear to be—at least for now—in no immediate danger. I need to know if everyone is all right. Please respond!"

DuQuesne's level, calm voice was the first to respond. "I am unharmed. My AISage is offline, however, and the main reactor has completely shut down. We are running on battery power only."

"How long will that last?" she asked immediately.

"For most ship internals, quite a long time. If you try to use the coilgun drivers or something similar, not long at all. I will get you exact numbers soon, but unless you do something extreme, the superconductor loop storage cells have enough power for weeks at least."

"Well, that's good news." She took another deep breath, continued to check on the others. Her old friend first. "Gabrielle?"

The usually-confident voice was much softer and unsure. "W . . . watch that first step. It's a doozy. My little friend's shut down too and I've got nothing in connectivity." Her laugh was forced, but at least it was a laugh. "I may have to actually use some of that stuff I studied in school."

"Carl?"

"Never . . . realized how empty it would be without her." The first response was not encouraging; Carl sounded distant and not really *there*. Ariane's lips tightened; as the controls and automation specialist, Carl was going to be critical to getting everything working again. His next sentence, though, carried more of the tall, whipcord-slender engineer's confidence. "Physically I'm A-okay, though. I'm trying to get manual control figured out for the rest of *Holy Grail*. Whatever took down the

AISages seems to have whacked the thinking automation, too."

"We'll worry about what did it later. For now, just keep getting as much as you can working again. Dr. Canning?"

She repeated the name several times, but only a thin, almost inaudible keening sound came back. "Gabrielle—"

"On my way. She was so wired that she must've crashed like a drunken fighter pilot."

And our maintenance engineer was a transcender. "Dr. Cussler?"

The voice that answered, after a long pause, was barely distinguishable. "Empty . . . small . . . lost . . . "

"Dr. Cussler—Tom—listen to me. We can't let the shutdown stop us. Focus!"

"Icarus," Tom Cussler whispered. "Bellerophon."

She exchanged a puzzled glance with Simon. Somewhat to her surprise, DuQuesne spoke. "Worry about our fall, and our hubris, later, Cussler. Right now, do you have any connectivity with the nanomaintenance systems?"

The direct technical question jarred a response out of the apparently nearly-catatonic engineer. "Nanomaintenance . . . on automatic. No AI controls at all. Basic computational evaluation." He took a deep, shuddering breath with the hint of a sob in it, but didn't quite break down again. "Even . . . distributed systems down below Turing threshold. Can't restart AISage packages—they thrash and drop back to baseline."

"Have you tried running a fresh core learning seed?" Carl suggested. "Maybe all the priors are corrupt. A naïve AISage would still be kilometers better than none."

Tom Cussler gave a sort of barking vocalization that might have been meant to be a laugh; it was not a comforting sound. "Infant seeds start up and then crash immediately."

"Worry about that later," Ariane ordered, using the same voice she used on her racing team when they started debating minor possibilities in redesign. "Dr. Cussler, I know this is upsetting, but I need you to make sure that we have the best maintenance we can manage without the AISages. Can I count on you to establish direct control where needed, or do I have to get Carl or Steve to take over?"

As she hoped, the implication that she thought he was helpless got a more focused response. "Of course I can do this. I made all of . . . well, with help I made all of them. And I . . . I can figure out how to control them myself. The information's there."

"Good." *That's everyone. Aside from Laila Canning, at least it looks like most of us came through it okay for now.*

But what did we come through into?

Ariane turned back to her own controls and brought up the displays and history. As she tried to bring up some more complex analysis of the current situation, her datacom implant suddenly picked up a carrier signal.

"Ha!" came Carl's voice over the speakers. "That's got it started. Steve?"

"Trying . . . yeah, I think . . . there!"

The carrier became active. "Oh, thank God," Ariane said, hearing the sentiment echoed around the ship as she made her connection.

It was still an eerily *empty* connection, with no trace of the almost omniscient, helpful AIsages or even less intelligent but usually more omnipresent, smart automation, but at least she could access a lot of the control systems and give them more complex direction.

A model began to build up before her, showing the two hundred meter long *Holy Grail* and then moving outward. A nearly flat surface just a few dozen meters away. More . . . farther . . .

"Holy crap," she finally said, unable to even think of an appropriately apocalyptic curse.

"Nani?" Sandrisson said, glancing at the display in front of her. "I . . . cannot quite figure out what I'm looking at."

"Let me put it into scale." She linked to Sandrisson's data feed directly, overlaying the data on the image.

Masaka, His silent voice said after a long time. *Impossible.*

Holy Grail drifted within a monstrous enclosure, in the shape of a somewhat flattened sphere, over twenty thousand kilometers across the wide axis, sharing that space only with a handful of other, spherical objects, ranging in size from one at the exact center which was nearly three kilometers across to several only a few meters across; with the exception of the central object, none of them exceeded three hundred meters.

Ariane studied the other objects. Featureless spheres as far as their radar could make out, and no more detailed by the few visible-light images acquired during the brilliant firing of the rocket, they were all clearly laid out along a plane that cut through the center of the enclosure, none more than a relatively few kilometers off of that imaginary surface. Judging by the minimal data left from the recorders during their emergency stop, they'd first entered this weird place at roughly a thousand kilometers from the center, maybe a little less, and then careened outward until they'd almost hit the . . . wall. Moving pretty much along the plane of the other objects, too—

She sucked in her breath. *No. That's insane.*

But the thought triggered the query, and even the simplistic, unintelligent automation available now was more than capable of performing a simple comparison and overlay.

"Mother of God," DuQuesne's voice spoke finally, the others in the crew having also connected to see exactly where they were.

Within that impossible space, the spheres drifted, moving almost imperceptibly slowly, following in precise and terrifying accuracy the motions of the Solar System from which *Holy Grail* had come.

Chapter 10

There were six other people seated at the table. That, at least, gave her a simple starting point for this meeting. With the AISages still all down, kinesthetic environment emulation still offline, and the wireless communication reducing them to something only slightly more advanced than early twenty-first century texting, they were meeting in the "conference room" aboard *Holy Grail*, a claustrophobically low, rectangular room which normally served as the dining room and kitchen.

There was a shellshocked sameness in all the faces looking at her, despite the physical differences between people like Gabrielle, Steve, and Marc. Despite her attempts to be calm, controlled, and optimistic, Ariane was sure they saw the same thing in her. They could hardly help seeing it, given what she knew she was hiding. But action always made her feel better, and now that they were all here . . .

"Let's start with our own status, people." She was surprised by the cheerfully matter-of-fact tone she heard in her own voice. It didn't reflect at *all* what she felt. "Gabrielle, I see we're missing one crewmember. What's Laila's status?"

Dr. Wolfe shook her blonde head. "Not good at all," the soft Southern voice responded. "She was hardwired and nanoconnected at the time of transition to multiple monitoring data streams, and, near as I can tell, had three resident AISage systems running simultaneously. In some ways, she was closer to pushing the exotropian envelope than anyone else here, even Tom." She nodded in Dr. Cussler's direction; the nanowizard winced in sympathy.

"All of us . . . well, almost all of us . . . know what kind of difficulties we've run into accessing headware and other systems without artificial intelligences to assist, but Laila Canning . . . the poor girl was running on a level most of us never really think about. I'm not sure but what half her regular thinking got piped through enhanced channels. Lordy, she had systems buried in there to optimize even the unconscious operations like breathing, metabolic rate, and blood flow, specifically for her work. That damn near killed her, too; I had to get Tom's help to figure out how to reset the defaults and lock the nanonetwork down so it wasn't trying to optimize based on no reliable input."

A part of Ariane—a very mean-spirited part that she wished would go away—still felt a nasty little vindication at this sort of thing. "Is she in danger?"

"Not right now—at least, not physically. But I've managed to get almost nothing out of her. She'll eat, sometimes, not much, but she hasn't managed two comprehensible words in the day since we came . . . here." She shrugged. "I guess I wouldn't count her out, but she ain't likely to be doing much for a while. I have her internal nanos keeping her in a sedated state."

"And the rest of us?"

The little blonde doctor gave a rueful smile. "Holding up so far, but not all so well. Laila may be the only one of us not functioning, but several of us are using our medical nanos to keep us on an even footing."

Thomas Cussler grunted agreement, and she saw both Dr. Sandrisson and Steve nod. "You, too?" she asked Gabrielle.

"Me, too, I'm afraid. You just don't know what it's like."

"And thank all the gods that may be for that," Sandrisson said, sincerely. "After the rest of us went over the records, it was clear that in the moments after . . . transition, there were exactly two people who were reasonably functional on board *Holy Grail*, and of those two only one had the skill and training necessary to gain control of the ship and stop her in time." He bowed across the table. "I said I would owe you another and far more detailed apology. Were it not for you—and for your reluctance to become integrated with electronic enhancements and assistants—we would all be dead now, Captain."

Ariane waved that off, feeling very uncomfortable. "Apology is accepted, but let's not make it sound like foresight. I got really lucky . . . if you call it luck for all the rest of us to get partly crippled. And what is this 'Captain' business?"

The others glanced at each other; Sandrisson spoke. "It simply . . . seems appropriate. You were, in fact, technically the captain of this vessel, you acted correctly in crisis when none of the rest of us could, and are currently the most functional member of the crew—with the exception, of course, of Dr. DuQuesne. And as the rest of us can claim the exalted title of 'Doctor,' it seems only just that you have one of your own . . . Captain."

You mean, by formalizing it, you drop the whole thing on my shoulders. Ariane repressed a sigh. They were right. And besides the reasons Simon had given, all the rest of them had jobs to do at all times; who else was going to act as the go-between, peacemaker, and maybe decision-maker? *All right, Captain Austin, let's get to it then.* "Dr. Sandrisson, I suppose we might as well move on to you. Can we just reactivate the Sandrisson Drive and go home? As I recall, we invert the field generation sequence, or something of that nature."

She knew as soon as she asked the question what the answer was; Sandrisson's face seemed to harden slightly. "That is . . . a generally true statement, although simplistic. Unfortunately, the answer is no. Even if I were to drain the entirety of our battery power, I cannot reach anything near the power levels needed to activate the transition. It takes several days' worth of our main fusion generator's maximum output to recharge the superconducting coils which permit the field to be created at all."

"So how long until we can get the fusion plant back online, Dr. DuQuesne?" she asked.

"Immediately or never," the massive, black-haired, black-eyed engineer replied. The sardonic smile with which he made the pronouncement sent an unpleasant chill down her back.

"What do you mean by that?" Steve demanded. "That doesn't make any sense."

"It makes just exactly as much sense as everything else in this damned place," DuQuesne answered shortly. "I've gone over every single component of the system—and there are a hell of a lot of them, let me assure you. I don't need an AISage to do the work, though it would be goddamn easier if I could get one. Everything in the plant checks out perfectly. The confinement field's perfect, the trigger sequence engages on cue, fuel's just as it should be—but when I kick in the start sequence nothing happens. No," he said, holding up his hand, "let me rephrase that. A lot of things happen, but not what *should* be happening. The fuel goes in, ignition sequence triggers, and . . . it doesn't ignite. No fusion."

"That's impossible," Sandrisson said. "If the entire sequence goes properly, you *have* to get fusion. You must not be getting to the right temperature and pressure."

DuQuesne gave Sandrisson a sour look. "Do *not* try to tell me my business, *Dr.* Sandrisson. You're a hotshot in the far-out theory department—you and your AIs—but there isn't a damn thing you or anyone else can teach me about power plants. I've been designing, building, and maintaining them, from fusion up through singularity, for forty years, and I've done some of it by my pure lonesome, not a single second-guessing artificial intelligence in the loop." The timeframe startled Ariane slightly; she hadn't realized DuQuesne was that old, but with modern anti-aging treatments it was very hard to guess whether someone was thirty or one hundred-thirty.

DuQuesne continued. "I know exactly what I'm saying. I get fusion temperature and pressure, and exactly nothing happens. The stuff goes to plasma, but no fusion, no radiation, nothing." He shrugged. "You're right, it's impossible. But that's what's happening." DuQuesne looked over to Ariane. "That's also why you had to go to the chemicals for that emergency stop; the fusion pellets kicked out right on cue for the nuclear pulse, but didn't detonate."

The others were still staring at DuQuesne as though they thought he might be losing it. Ariane didn't, and that scared her a lot more than the thought of DuQuesne being insane. "So when you said 'immediately or never' . . ."

" . . . I was saying that unless whatever's causing this goes away, or I figure out how to counter it, our main generators are dead. And so's the fusion-pulse rocket."

"So at the moment we have only whatever's in the storage coils. What's our functional estimate of time?"

"That I can give you, Captain. Assuming we don't have to fire up the coilgun drive and that I stop wasting energy trying to run a fusion reactor that doesn't want to play, we can keep *Holy Grail* going for about two months—sixty-two days, actually. You might shave a day or so off that if we do other high-demand operations, and two or three days if you're running the ion-electric drives a lot. But, basically, a couple months."

That was a relief. Two months was at least comfortably in the future, compared to the few days she had thought might be the real answer. "Thank you, Doctor." She looked over to Steve. "What about automation and AIs?"

Steve opened his mouth, glanced at DuQuesne, and suddenly gave a rueful grin. "I guess I have the same story as you do," he said; the big power engineer acknowledged that with a small smile. "I've got basic automation online for all systems, but when I say basic,

I mean *basic*. We're back at least two hundred years in terms of data processing—maybe not sheer volume of DP resources, but in complexity. Neither Tom nor I have been able to get a single AI to boot. Not even the pretty stupid ones used for basic monitoring automation. And that is, as we just said about the fusion plant, impossible. The hardware hasn't changed, the software simply *can't* have all glitched exactly the same way—and a full structural comparison shows no sign of significant damage or changes anywhere in the code or in the associational development matrices, anyway." He shrugged, looking frustrated. "So . . . they don't work, and there's no reason for it, so . . . they might start working tomorrow, but you'd better not plan on anything working."

That might be a major problem. "Dr. Cussler?"

Thomas Cussler still had that half-dead look about him, even his very dark skin seeming to have an ash-gray undertone, but brought himself back with an effort. "Yes, Captain?"

"Does this mean that our matter rendering is down, too?"

A tiny bit of animation seemed to return; a ghost of a smile flickered about Cussler's previously flat-line mouth. "Actually . . . no. Normally, of course, a matter-rendering installation like the AIWish series incorporates a sophisticated AI to interpret the desires of the user, create and modify designs on the fly, and so on.

"However, the safety restrictive interlocks were removed, which allows direct external control as well as eliminating the restrictions on what designs are allowable. The standard matter-record templates are still accessible with a little tweaking. Between myself, Dr. Edlund, and Dr. Franceschetti we have been able to make a manual or remote interface that will allow us to direct the replication operations from templates. What we *cannot* do," he continued, now at least sounding normal, "is create new operational templates easily. Anything currently in the database is usable, but given the complexity of any real-world object, it will be a very long and arduous process to be able to add in new design files for such things."

"Are the templates we have adequate for keeping us all fed, clothed, and any machinery maintained?"

"Oh, quite. I suppose that after a while the menu may become a bit boring—there are only a few hundred standard food templates installed—but if we can maintain power and provide the appropriate base materials to the renderer, we should be all right."

"Good news there, at least. Thank you, Dr. Cussler." She moved her gaze to Carl Edlund. "Carl, what about the drives?"

"Well, Cap," the control engineer answered, "You just about tapped us out on the big chemical burn. I think you might have another KPS in that, but no more.

"The ion-electric thrusters are fine, and we can run them for quite a while on the reaction mass available. Certainly more than enough to go anywhere we want to in this oversized planetarium. The mass-beam drive's lost one of the four coilgun mounts, but there's nothing for us to use as drive mass there, and we don't have the power to waste anyway." He grinned suddenly. "But I could rig one of them as a mass cannon if there's miniature space pirates around."

The joke was very weak, but she smiled anyway. "I guess we come to the real questions. What happened, where in the name of God are we, and what do we do next?"

Six pairs of eyes focused on Dr. Simon Sandrisson, whose elegant front was being severely tested by his obvious desire to disappear into the furniture. He took a breath and looked pleadingly at Ariane, but she had nothing to offer.

"I . . . I really wish I had an answer for that. I have gone over the records of the drive activation very carefully, from the time we began to build the field to the moment we stopped ourselves from hitting the walls of this place. The records after transition are, of course, very spotty, but as far as I can tell, the drive did exactly what I designed it to do. How we ended up in this . . . giant room, I have no idea."

"Dr. Sandrisson." DuQuesne's voice was firm but not confrontational. "As my limited understanding of the theory puts it, the basic effect of the Sandrisson Drive is supposed to be to place the ship into another space which is isomorphic with our own, but in which distance—for lack of a better term—is effectively shorter, so that by moving a short distance in that space and then exiting, you have effectively moved a much greater distance in ours, correct?"

Sandrisson nodded. "It's rather more complicated than that, but that is a reasonable general description."

"Then isn't it possible that this *is* that other space?"

Sandrisson seemed about to reply, but stopped, leaving his mouth hanging open for a few seconds. Finally he sat slowly back in his seat. "Well . . . there is not, in fact, any reason that it cannot be, I suppose."

"Maybe that's why fusion doesn't work!" Carl Edlund said. "Natural law is different."

"Please." Sandrisson looked pained. "While it is, in fact, possible for natural law to vary drastically in different, well, universes, such changes in natural law are exceedingly unlikely to have—how shall I put it—such neat and simple consequences. Something that changed the very way in which subatomic particles interact would almost certainly have drastic effects everywhere else."

"He's right," DuQuesne said. "We're not talking about just finding out your tinder's damp and the fire won't light—we're talking about finding out that suddenly gasoline won't burn even in a pure oxygen atmosphere with thermite for a match. That implies a whole slew of things that we're just not seeing."

"And it doesn't explain the AIs," the tenor voice of Steve Franceschetti put in. "The computers work, the data storage and retrieval works, the AIs should work. Our own minds still work. So what's going on?"

"I don't think we're going to answer that right away," Ariane said. "Let me tell you what I know.

"With some help from Carl and Steve, I've been doing a careful survey of this place we're in. The rest of you had other things to work on. I've made some . . . interesting observations.

"First, we are not *quite* the only things in here besides that mockup of our solar system. There's a lot of little fragments of debris drifting around, and not confined by . . . well, whatever method's keeping that model solar system running. My guess is that it's what's left of the three probes that didn't come back."

Dr. Sandrisson suddenly looked enlightened. "Of *course*. They were on a vector and going at a speed such that they hit the wall, or possibly one of those spheres, before triggering inversion back to our space."

"Right. So that's evidence, I think, that all of our probes passed through this space. Which means that *if* we can find some way to get those coils recharged, we should be able to go home."

The relief of that statement—even with all the other potentially insurmountable challenges associated with it—was palpable throughout the room.

"Next, the model of the Solar System. It appears to show every body in the Solar System, down to a certain size. I'm not quite sure, but the actual cutoff seems to be on bodies with a surface gravity below about a quarter of a meter per second squared. Is that significant, Dr. Sandrisson?"

"It may very well be. Let me check something." He got the distracted look of someone digging through electronic archives with no assistance. "Calculating . . . Now, that's very interesting."

"Expand on that, Doctor?"

"The Kanzaki-Locke effect, as one might expect of any spacetime-related effect, is affected by the precise conditions of local spacetime. The field can't be made accurately and reliably stable in gravity wells that deform the local shape of space too much, and the point at which you could theoretically compensate for it is around that very point—248.097 centimeters per second squared for the local gravitational acceleration. So this model shows all of the bodies which you want to be some distance from, with their relative sizes showing their potential to interfere with transition. I'm not sure why one would construct such a model, but there does seem to be logic behind it."

"Does that mean that the Sandrisson Drive itself can interfere with either gravity or other Sandrisson Drives?"

"Not with gravity—at least, not to any significant extent. No antigravity fields here, I'm afraid," the white-haired scientist said with a laugh. "With each other, yes, at distances dependent on the size of the coils and the transition mass and size—possibly hundreds or thousands of kilometers. The coils actually resonate and cause interference, so you couldn't safely activate such a drive if you were within range of another vessel, even if the other vessel was shut down."

That has some . . . interesting implications for later designs, if we get out of this, she mused. "Thanks. Anyway, I also noted that there are four detectable anomalies in the surrounding wall. Three of them are large circular areas, slightly depressed—no more than a meter depth, across something that's close to a hundred kilometers across—and set regularly around the, well, let's call it equator, of the room, coplanar with the ecliptic of our little solar system.

"The fourth anomaly, however, is very different. It's a small . . . shelf, projection, whatever, no more than a few kilometers long, at the very apex or nadir of this place, depending on what we're considering up or down. We don't have any sensor remote probes, but what little detail I can get suggests there might be more . . . something there. Unless anyone has any better ideas, I intend to take *Holy Grail* in that direction."

A quick glance around the table showed agreement. "After all," Carl added, "it's not like we have anywhere else to go. This place is clearly artificial, and one hell of a bit of work even by our standards; none of our orbital colonies are anywhere near this size. There's got to be something running that solar-system clockwork, and that means power, and power's all we need to get home."

"My thoughts exactly." She couldn't repress a very fond smile at Carl, who'd guided her to victory—with an occasional loss—in the racing circuit for years now. "Anything else?"

The faces around the table showed less shock and more hope, and at least a little direction now. When they shook their heads and stirred, she felt a little better. *We're still in a lot of trouble, but maybe the worst is over.*

"Then let's get back to work. Steve, if we can at least get some simple environmental projections . . . ?"

"Lighten the feel inside the ship. Got it."

"That won't consume too much power, will it, Dr. DuQuesne?"

"Not as long as most of it is done by tweaking our inputs."

"Got it."

She let the others go, then looked around the darkened room; it lit again at her hesitation.

If only I could turn on the lights outside *that easily.*

Chapter 11

"I surely do appreciate the help, Dr. DuQuesne."

DuQuesne smiled back at the little blonde. "Do we need the formality?"

"You're a very formal kind of man," Gabrielle Wolfe responded, pinching the cable-ring tighter to make it seal more securely. "A girl doesn't want to seem too familiar."

"I don't think of myself as particularly formal," DuQuesne protested mildly.

"Maybe that ain't the right word. Distant? Formidable? I don't know, but whatever it is, people feel it." He watched her struggling with the case connectors, and resisted an impulse to help; he knew Gabrielle Wolfe would let him know if she wanted any.

"She's right, you know," Tom Cussler put in from his current position at the AIWish manual input module.

"You're the kind of man who . . . well, even before we . . . lost computation . . . " Cussler paused a moment to recover himself before continuing, " . . . well, even before then, you were the sort who would walk into a room and everyone would pay attention to. Even the AISages. You're just not about getting friendly, DuQuesne, at least not on the outside; it's like trying to pal around with a top-ranked general. We can count on you, but you're not going to any parties you don't throw yourself."

Even after fifty years, I'm still . . . He gave a mental shrug. "Well, then, allow me to invite you to use my first name."

"With pleasure, Marc. And you can call me Gabrielle, or Gabby, or Dr. Wolfe, whichever suits your pleasure."

"So it's not your intent?" Cussler studied him.

"Not really. Just the way I am, I guess." The casual phrasing wasn't quite his normal manner, and he knew the others could probably catch it.

The flicker of a glance by Tom showed he was right, but Cussler didn't push it. "Well, if you can figure out how you do it, there's institutes back home that would hand you your own custom asteroid for the secret. How's it looking?" The last question was addressed to Gabrielle.

"Stable at the moment. What d'you think, Dr.—Marc?"

DuQuesne turned his attention to the new independent power source they were making for the life support and monitoring unit. "Let me see . . . " He concentrated and interfaced with the controls and diagnostics. "Stable. Not a bad job, considering."

Cussler grinned faintly. "Why do I get the impression that you could probably have done the whole thing yourself in just a little more time?"

"Tom, I'm hardly an expert in replication technology, outside of my own speciality. If all you needed were the storage coils, that would be a different matter."

"I suppose. Maybe it's just the fact that you're so much more together than the rest of us. Except Ariane, of course."

At least he's not pursuing that other line of thought. "Luck of the draw. If you weren't spending half your energy adapting to losing half of yourself, so to speak, you'd have gotten this done in half the time."

Cussler nodded, but stared at the replicator with an expression perilously close to depression, enough that DuQuesne noticed that Gabrielle looked concerned. "All the time I spent . . . wasted."

"Tom, honey, no one could've predicted this mess," Gabrielle said.

"Maybe not. Maybe not," the nanoengineer responded. "But it does make you wonder. Or me wonder. Can I really call myself an engineer when I find that I don't really understand half the field?"

"That's a bunch of crap, Cussler." While DuQuesne, in principle, agreed with some of the ideas, this wasn't the time. They really couldn't afford to lose anyone. "You're just *feeling* that way because everything doesn't come easy. And yeah, I'm more used to that than you. But you know all the principles. It's going to be a lot harder, since you need to do the searches, the sorting, and the understanding yourself, without any support, but it's still *you* doing it. The AISages were great, and they are great, but they have limits, and they can't *be* you any more than you can be them."

Cussler looked at him, and DuQuesne held his gaze—the right expression, both supportive and with just the right amount of impatience, enough to goad but not to depress. "I . . . I guess you're right. I just . . . "

"Haven't had to do it much before. We all know, Tom, and aside from Marc and Ariane, we're all in the same boat." Gabrielle put a comforting hand on Cussler's shoulder. "I surely couldn't have figured out how to get the AIWish working without help, and, as to making the templates, Lord no."

"Making? Hah, just a few tweaks here and there." Despite the deprecating words, DuQuesne could tell that Cussler was feeling better, at least for now.

He also suddenly felt as though he was being watched and glanced behind him. "Laila?"

Dr. Canning's eyes were open and looking at them. She blinked.

Gabrielle sprang up and ran to her side. "Laila! Do you hear me?"

DuQuesne shook his head; the biologist's gaze didn't track the doctor as she crossed the line of sight. Several more queries got no more response. "Gabrielle. Dr. Wolfe, can I ask you a candid question?"

Gabrielle Wolfe frowned, then turned to him. "What is it, Marc?"

"Are we wasting our efforts on her? I know how you doctors are generally trained, but is she really just brain-dead and unrecoverable?" He knew this would sound cold, but the fact was the question needed to be asked, and asked straight.

The pretty blonde's face went cold for a moment, glaring at him for the suggestion (in pretty much the manner he'd expected). Then her gaze dropped, she took a deep breath, and sighed. "Lordy, I really wish I could answer that, Marc."

That wasn't the exact answer he'd expected. Neither of the answers, actually. "What do you mean?"

"Take a look. With systems the way they are, I can't get the full-bore data, but I can show cerebral activity and some correspondences."

Several images from differing angles materialized on the medical platform display. DuQuesne narrowed his eyes, trying to figure out what he was seeing. He was generally familiar with the normal patterns of these displays, but . . . "What the hell?"

"That's the problem. If she was totally brain-dead, I shouldn't be seeing any coordinated higher brain activity at all. Instead, I'm seeing these . . . well, whatever they are . . . surges of high-level activity, but they're not distributed properly. A lot of them look rather similar to seizure activity, which can effectively 'light up' a whole hell of a lot of the brain at once, but they don't appear to trigger any motor responses. And when there's people speaking around her, she shows at least some reaction in the speech processing region."

"Any ideas?"

"Nary a one. Well, some, I guess—there hasn't been anyone doing experiments on it that I know of, and if they did, they'd've been taken out and shot anyway, so we've got nothing on what happens to people like that who've lost it all in one quick shock. Graceful degradation, you know; even if someone's headware AISage crashes, they've got about a thousand safeguards to make it so it's more like a slow shutdown." Gabrielle shook her head sadly. "This, she got the 'Sages yanked and all the support gone in like a millisecond. Could be we're seeing what happens to a brain like that—keeps trying to find the connections that just went down because there's nothing telling it where they went, and the connection protocols don't handle that."

DuQuesne studied the images for a few moments, then shrugged. "Well, I admit, I haven't any better explanation. But it's definitely not the same as being brain-dead, and you're right, I'm seeing some indication of reaction whenever we're talking." He met her gaze. "So we're definitely not wasting time or effort. And I hope you understand why I asked you that way."

Gabrielle pursed her lips, then sighed and nodded. "I guess so. Most doctors do tend to keep going on the life support until someone stops them, and we can't afford to waste resources if that was what I was up to."

"Well," Tom put in, "I'd sure as hell rather have a doctor who did that than one who went the other way."

DuQuesne chuckled. "I can't disagree there." He helped Gabrielle and Tom fasten the power module—mainly a lightly-armored superconductor battery with simple power regulators and readouts—securely to Laila's life-support module. By the way Gabrielle moved, it was clear she'd spent a lot of time in null-G environments, considerably more than Tom. "Gabrielle, it strikes me we have some other concerns health-wise."

"You're thinking about the gravity issues."

She's very good, he thought with surprise. He could, thinking about it, realize how she'd managed to read that from his own glances and body language, but it was a hell of a jump. "You're not a doctor, you're a mind-reader."

She gave a deprecating handwave. "I've just been thinking a lot about that myself lately. A lucky guess."

Tom frowned. "You're right. *Holy Grail* wasn't designed with spin because we weren't expected to be out for more than, at most, a month, and more likely about ten, twelve days."

"I'm going through the null-G medical refs, but it's hard to do by . . . well, hand, I suppose you'd say," Gabrielle said. "I know there's adjustments I can do to make sure our medical nanos prevent bone loss and the other subtle effects, but I didn't have them in forward headware because of the mission parameters. But . . . will we really need to worry about it, Marc? After all, we've only got two months of power, even by your estimates. Two months won't be particularly critical, if we just all exercise a bit."

"It might be," DuQuesne answered, testing the solidity of the connections. "Let's say we find a power source, but it's not on the level of a main fusion reactor. We might need to hang around here for months before we've finally got the Sandrisson coils charged enough to leave. They need an immense amount of power, remember, far more than all the other ship's systems combined. So we could have enough power to keep *Holy Grail* running, but still have to wait a good long time."

"I hadn't thought of that." Tom said. "I . . . I don't know how well I'm going to handle two months here, let alone many more."

"Tom, if we make it two months, we all'll probably be doing a lot better than we all are now," Gabrielle said. "It's the next few weeks we'll be finding out if we can cut it without the 'Sages.'"

"Either of you have hobbies?" DuQuesne asked. "Not the virtual world gamesims or stuff like that, but real physical kinds?"

"Eh?" Tom and Gabrielle looked at him, puzzled by the shift.

"Hobbies. Generally speaking, people often put a lot more of their own effort into their hobbies, sometimes even excluding their headware AISages. Right now we've been focusing on survival, on the areas where we've always used artificial support the most. Maybe what you need to remind you about how to be yourself, *by* yourself, is to focus on anything you like to do that didn't always involve one of those damn artificial brains. So do you have any hobbies?"

Gabrielle smiled slowly. "Now that's a right smart idea, Marc. And I surely do have a few hobbies. I think mountain-biking is rather restricted here, though, so maybe I should focus on my model-building."

"What kind of models?" DuQuesne asked. Tom was looking thoughtful.

"Vehicles, mostly. I look through archives of pictures and when I see something that strikes my fancy, I start working on building a copy. I use fabs like the AIWish for the parts, but I put 'em together by hand. I was working on a model of a 1990s diesel locomotive back home." Her eyes lit up. "You know, I think I could start on a model of the *Holy Grail*! That might even be worth something, one day, when we get back!"

Just seeing the animation returning to Gabrielle's face seemed to bring Tom's spirits up. "I think that sounds great, Gabrielle." Tom said. "And I do have one hobby that would work here; jewelry. Not particularly fancy stuff, and I'm not even close to an expert, but I like designing patterns, picking the materials, that kind of thing."

"That's just the kind of hobbies I was thinking of, too." DuQuesne said in agreement. "They need your personal focus, and your personal choices, and you've done them—I'd guess—mostly by yourself, not using the AISages to help."

"You're exactly right." Tom's voice was clearer and stronger than it had been since they first came . . . here. "For material synthesis, Maxine helped, yes, but that was only at the start. I've got all those templates already, some of them I haven't even used yet." He looked at DuQuesne. "Thanks. I think . . . I think that this will work."

"I'll make it an official medical recommendation," Gabrielle said decisively. "If you don't mind my stealing your ideas, Marc."

"Steal away." He grinned as she turned away to compose the announcement; the grin faded somewhat as his gaze wandered across Laila Canning, whose eyes had closed again. He checked the connections of the system once more, and noticed how, by that time, Gabrielle and Tom Cussler were exchanging experiences and ideas in their respective hobbies.

Neither of them had asked him about his hobbies. *Probably never occurred to them to ask . . . and if it did, they probably thought it'd be intruding.* He restrained a rueful smile. *I can see the inside, but I still stand outside.*

But looking at the two faces—more alive than they'd been for days—it didn't matter. *They'll make it now, and so will the rest of us. And that's what really matters.*

Chapter 12

Simon watched the tiny figure of Carl Edlund, clad in an almost-skintight ship-suit with a thin bubble helmet, drift cautiously toward a silvery, tumbling tree trunk—a major portion of one of *Holy Grail*'s coilgun supports.

"You're almost there, Carl," Ariane said.

"That's all well and good, but could you give me more damn light?"

Ariane frowned at the irritable tone. "Carl, *Holy Grail*'s external lights light it just as bright as we always had the repair slips."

"Well . . . it doesn't *feel* that way. Jesus, Ariane, you should see this. Except for this piece of wreckage and the *Holy Grail*, there's *nothing*. We don't make near enough light to illuminate even the nearest part of the wall." She could hear his breathing, a little too swift and ragged. "Back home, you always had stars, reflections off whatever planet or asteroid you were near, *something* you could see, anywhere you looked. But . . . I'm, like, floating in a sea of tar here, nothing. If I look in the wrong direction, it's like being struck blind."

"Sounds unpleasant," Steve said. "But it's just a few more minutes, Carl. And really, can you see it well enough to do the work?"

A pause. She heard Carl take a deep breath and hold it, then let it out, slowly; on the monitors, his vitals dropped. "Yeah. Yeah, I can get to it. I wish we had USRVs to work with, though."

Simon sighed. "I'm afraid no one ever thought we'd have any need for unmanned space repair vehicles, especially ones without their own AI, just remote-controlled. That's been mostly obsolete for almost two centuries."

He noticed multiple sharp projections jutting from the whirling, hundred-fifty-meter long rod and realized how easily one of them could kill Edlund; the ring-carbon reinforced suit might not cut, but that would only mean that they'd get his body back in one piece. "Carl, please be careful. I'd blame myself if anything happens to you out there." The blame, of course, had to do with the fact that it was his fault Carl was out there. The Sandrisson Drive coils were designed very specifically to generate the field in accordance with ship geometry—which meant that it wouldn't work at all without the *Holy Grail* being restored to its old self, within a very small percentage of error. And since they didn't have the mass to just manufacture another, nor the energy to spare at the moment, that meant they had to get the support rib, which in the past few days had drifted a few thousand kilometers into the blank vastness of the nearly-empty void that filled this impossible enclosure, back and re-attach it.

"And I wouldn't care who was to blame, I just want my favorite mechanic back in one piece," Ariane put in.

"Mechanic? *Mechanic!* And me with an advanced degree and certification in control and interface design, and another in small-craft drives!" Carl expostulated in hurt tones, as he cautiously approached the rotational center of the wreckage. "Besides, I'm your *only* mechanic. At least, the only one always on your team."

"And I want to keep it that way. Ohhh, watch out for that—"

"I see it." Carl evaded the sharp-edged piece of one of the accelerator rings as it rotated through the space he would have occupied otherwise.

I really have to take my mind off this. I can't stand watching. "So, Ariane," Sandrisson said, "how exactly is it that a young woman of your obvious potential ends up in a . . ." *Oh, wonderful start, Dr. Sandrisson. Have you any capability for starting a conversation with her without an insult?*

To his immense relief, she grinned and picked up the question without a pause, " . . . dangerous, adrenaline-fueled, juvenile sport like obstacle racing?"

Thank the heavens for a sense of humor. "Well, yes. No offense. You just seem no less capable than many I see in much more mentally demanding professions, indeed more capable than many, and it just seems . . . silly to me."

"You're not the only one," she admitted. "My mom and dad weren't happy about it, and they almost ended up not speaking with Grandaddy because of it."

"Their fault," Carl's voice put in. "If they'd kept a closer eye on you, maybe the old man wouldn't have been such a bad influence, and you wouldn't be trying to thread needles with a spaceship at orbital speed, fighting in bars, and hanging out with space mechanics."

"Really?" Steve glanced over. "I've seen your parents in interviews a couple of times, and they didn't seem upset about your choice of career."

"Not *now*, no." He could see her eyes get a distant look, seeing a not entirely pleasant past. "Once I started doing well, and they really understood that I was doing what I really, really *wanted* to do, they got behind me. But it was a tough few years." She looked back at Simon, her deep blue eyes meeting his gaze. "But that doesn't really answer you. My mom and dad . . . well, they both had jobs and hobbies and . . . maybe they weren't really thinking about being parents as much as they should. A lot of people do that, you know, have a kid and then just . . . "

Oh, how very much I understand. Sandrisson couldn't quite keep an edge of bitter sadness from his own voice. " . . . ah, yes. Children of convenience. With a few AIs to make sure they're taken care of, dropping in to make sure the children are 'okay,' involved in all the fun or entertaining parts of having a child, minimizing the less . . . fun. I think I begin to understand."

"You, too?"

"It is not, I am afraid, an altogether uncommon tale. But please, go on."

"Yeah, go on. I don't think Steve's heard this either, and it's kinda funny," Carl put in as he finally locked onto the slowly-spinning piece of debris. "I'll have the cable locked on soon."

"All right." She paused as though getting her thoughts in order. "So Mom and Dad were sort of there sometimes, sometimes not. They never forgot things like birthdays or anything—and we did do a lot of fun things together. I don't want to sound like I didn't think they were good people or fun to be around or anything." Sandrisson and Steve nodded in understanding. "But Grandaddy—that's Dad's father—he lived right on our ranch, in Texas, had his own spread about a mile from the house. I used to hike over there a lot—he was in charge, when Mom and Dad were out, aside from Lacie. Lacie was the housekeeper," she explained at their glance. "An Estine Systems SmartBot 440. Pretended to be a martinet, but I could always sweet-talk her." Simon could hear the fondness in her tone.

"Anyway, it was like an adventure going to see Grandaddy, because he had like zero automation. And his hobby was old machines. Cars, tractors, trucks, that kind of thing. That was how I met Gabrielle, actually," she said, slightly sidetracking. "We were going to the same college, but we didn't speak much until she noticed the picture I had on my wallpaper one day, me and Grandaddy standing next to Big Pig, his rebuilt combine, and she just fell in love with the Pig. Made a model of it that year and when Grandaddy saw it he just about cried."

She blinked. "Where was I? Oh, machines. So I used to help him work on the cars and things, and he taught me how to drive them." She grinned, the distance in her gaze now filled with warmth. "God, I remember how terrified I was the first time he drove me in one. I realized that there wasn't a single little bit of automation in the entire machine, and that he was doing it all by hand, and wasn't even tied into the local Net. And so, of course, he spun the car out—deliberately—in one of the turns, in a cloud of dust, and I was screaming, and by the time we really stopped I was begging him to let me drive."

Simon couldn't restrain a chuckle. "I see! So he scared you until you started having fun, and after that the best kind of fun was the sort that scared you half to death.".

Ariane gave a delighted laugh. "Just exactly like that, yes! After that, I knew my Grandaddy was the absolute cold-coolest guy in the entire world, and I spent most of the time I wasn't wired into school following him around with wrenches and stuff, and trying to drive his prizes. He had some small airplanes too, and I got a manual pilot's license—limited to private airspaces, of course—by the time I was thirteen." She was practically *chattering*, thought Simon, sounding like the teenage Ariane must have, talking about what had been the most wonderfully magical place in the world.

"And," Ariane went on with a smile, "he had really old books in his house, too, and didn't have direct Net feed except for email and things—it was like he hadn't changed the house since *his* grandfather was born, or something. So I used to read his old books—some of them going back to, like, the twentieth century, I think—and play those adventures when I got back home and could get my RecNet to render up something like the book."

"I'm heading back," Carl broke in. "We should be able to use the other three to generate a magnetic field that'll cut the rotation down, and then reel her in and put her back together. Then we make sure they're all straightened out and we'll be set."

"Good. Be careful on the way back, don't get clipped."

"Trust me, I'm watching."

"So . . ." She shrugged. "Make a long story short, Grandaddy taught me to be suspicious of automation and to like risking my life, so when I found a sport like obstacle space racing, it was a natural choice."

"My father," Simon said, "was a physicist himself. He was also a much more hands-on parent than Oka-san—mother." *Amazing how that still hurts, even now . . . and yet Okasan influenced my childhood far more, in some ways.* "Eventually I think that's why they . . . separated. Anyway, I grew up with datafeeds on mathematics and physics almost from the time I remember. But not pushed on me, just . . . all around, because it was what Father did, and I listened, even when I didn't understand.

"Father liked to move around a lot; some people don't see the point, given that the right interfaces can let you be there anyway, but he preferred the actual movement. Said it emphasized the shift in perspective for him. He was working at Oxford when I was three to, oh, seven, and then we moved to California, then to Kanzaki-One for several years." He smiled. "Which, naturally, explains why I speak with an English accent but—occasio-nally—curse in Japanese. Alas, my father did not indulge his ancestry, else I might be able to entertain one by cursing in two badly-accented languages."

Ariane smiled at that. "So it was your father's profes-sion that made you go into physics?"

"One moment," Simon said, having thought of some-thing. He touched a link control and concentrated, acti-vating a calibration pulse through the Sandrisson coils. *Oh, blast. That's not good enough.* "I'm afraid, Steve, that we're going to have to also straighten out the other three driver supports. They appear to have bent more than I think safe."

"No problem," Steve said cheerfully. "We'll do that when we finish reattaching the fourth one. Align all of them back to optimum. At least that's a pretty simple geometric design and all we have to do is use the built-in nanosupport to extend and contract the right portions."

Thank goodness for that. "Now where was I . . . ? Oh, yes. It was a little more indirect than that, actually. The education track I was in on Kanzaki focused on learning from personalities, human perspectives, and how the individual influenced the course of history, that sort of thing, and Kanzaki herself was naturally included." He gave a wry grin. "Do you really want the sordid truth? I got a crush on the virtual teacher and started studying physics to impress her."

"You didn't!"

"Oh, I most certainly did. I did my best to show off, too. I'm sure an old-fashioned psychologist would probably have all sorts of things to say about that."

"Oh, come on," Carl said, entering the control area. "How old were you then, anyway?"

"Sixteen."

Carl shook his head, bemused. "You can't tell me there weren't bootleg datasims of her available. Every school I ever went to, all the hot teachers were simmed and passed around like from the second day of class."

"Oh, undoubtedly there were. I had a few offered to me. But I was . . . perhaps am . . . something of a romantic." He could restrain the blush, but he knew his grin was now rather embarrassed. "I wasn't interested in an imitation of her—that would have felt cheap."

"But you said she was a persona, not the original!" Ariane said, looking puzzled.

"Well . . . yes, I suppose that was the reason I said it was a rather sordid truth," he admitted, shaking his head. "I wanted the true original simulation Kanzaki persona, but I wanted her to be real. Well, not *really* real, exactly, since the real Kanzaki was married, but real, like . . . " He rolled his eyes in exasperation. "You know what I mean!"

Steve laughed. "No one ever said teenage boys were sensible. C'mon, Carl, admit it, you've done something just as silly."

Carl grunted and then gave a sideways smile. "Mmmmaybe, but I'm not sure I'm going to talk about it with an audience." He glanced at the telltales. "Looks like the driver rib will be in position in about an hour; then we'll have to get Tom to tweak the nanorepair to activate and start fixing everything. But she'll be locked down enough for us to start moving in, oh, a couple hours."

"That's good," Ariane said. "Let everyone know that I'll be getting us underway as soon as you give me the green light. I'm going to go get something to eat."

Simon busied himself with his panel. *I hope that didn't make me sound too foolish.*

As the blue-haired captain passed him, she leaned over; he sensed her damping the room sensors to make what she said private. "It's not so silly, you know."

"Really?" He looked up at her. "I thought it was uncommonly silly."

She stopped for a moment. "I think AIs are real people. And that means that getting a crush on one isn't any sillier than getting a crush on a living, flesh and blood person, and wanting the actual one you're focused on rather than an imitation makes perfect sense to me." She grinned as she turned to leave. "And if he gives you any more grief, just ask Carl about Megan!"

Chapter 13

"*Now* I'm seriously creeped out."

Steve answered from behind her. "What really creeps *me* out is that I have no idea what you're talking about. Without worthwhile associative connectivity and Allerdyne, I don't know *anything* without actually looking for it and trying to figure it out myself. So what's up?"

"*That*, of course."

Rather than pointing a finger, she sent an image to Steve—and anyone else who might be listening.

Holy Grail floated about ten kilometers from the anomalous extension of the massive shell enclosing them. A long, narrow, rippled rod, with faerie-thin arches stretching in regular intervals along it, the thing reminded her of nothing so much as two snake skeletons back-to-back—except that these snakes would have been able to swallow something a dozen times *Holy Grail's* size in one bite. The black-silvery glinting object reached a full seven and a half kilometers from the wall, straight out from the geometric center of what they had decided was the apex of this impossible space.

"Well, yeah, it does look kinda skeletal. I didn't know that you found that so creepy, though."

Ariane shook her head. "It's not that at all. Look along there, between the, um, ribs."

Steve focused his attention, causing the view to zoom in. "Oh . . . those circular things? Regularly spaced, like dots along it." She could sense him detach from the direct feed and consult the databanks. "Hey, they're about the same size and shape as a standard ship docking port!"

Not *about*. Carl's silent networked voice held some of the apprehension she felt. *Near as I can tell, they're exactly the same. I wish we had probes on board.*

"As do we all." Simon said dryly. "However, we have neither probes nor the templates for probes—which is why I have not suggested building one with a set of Sandrisson coils to send for help. Since first we would have to spend months creating the templates for the probe by hand, and *then* I would have to design the coils for the probe."

Well, fortunately it's not necessary. I'll just combine data from the past few seconds and enhance. Carl was the closest thing they had to a sensor expert on board, and at the moment they didn't need really fancy tricks. *Yeah. Take a look.*

The shared image rippled and changed to a close-up of the wierdly dual-colored material of the extension. Except that in the center, the material was quite different. Composites and metals of much more familiar nature made up a circular area, with extremely familiar ports and connectors. A chill went down Ariane's back.

"Wow. It *is* a docking port." Steve said. His tone, however, didn't show that he was feeling the same reaction she and Carl—and maybe others—were. "That's convenient."

Convenient *is not the appropriate word,* DuQuesne stated flatly, showing he'd been watching for some time. *Unless that's also the word you'd use for coming across a standard power outlet in an Egyptian pyramid.*

Steve blinked. "Well, okay, I can see it's kinda odd that theirs looks just like ours, but—"

Utterly beyond odd, *Mr. Franceschetti.* DuQuesne's transmitted voice was somewhere between exasperated and amused. *It's a truism that every generation thinks its experiences are natural, but the lack of depth I see in most people's knowledge these days . . . I suppose I am getting old somehow. That docking port design is the result of hundreds of years of engineering for very specific purposes. For purposes that serve our species, and our culture, and which also probably incorporate a few . . . legacy features which are purely a result of some almost random decision made a hundred and fifty or two hundred years ago.*

"Steve, he's right. It's like . . . well, you're into art, right? You've actually studied the history of art and you can name off artists and their works without any of Allerdyne's input. What we're looking at here is something more completely impossible than . . . well, than walking into the hut of some lost tribe of savages, and finding that their witch doctor has just finished painting a copy of the *Mona Lisa*—exact down to the precise brush strokes—when they'd never even encountered civilization before."

That seemed to get through to Steve. "Then . . . how could it *be* here?"

I think I have an answer to that, but it only raises a lot more questions, DuQuesne responded. *I just went back over our initial entry to this space. It's hard to tell for certain, but as near as I can see, this . . . spacedock was not present when we first arrived.*

Dr. Sandrisson gave vent to an incomprehensible Japanese curse. "That entire thing was built since we arrived?"

And without radiating sufficient energy to draw our attention to that fact. In our own solar system we might, given sufficient motivation, manage to build something that size in a few days, but it would be a very, very spectacular bit of work indeed, especially in the infrared, as the waste heat had to be carried away.

"You all seem to be taking this the wrong way," Gabrielle Wolfe said, entering the control room. "Seems to me that this is downright hospitable of whoever owns this place. They've given us a place to tie up and a doorway to come on in and visit by."

Ariane laughed suddenly. "Gabrielle, you are the best cure for depression, as always. Maybe you're right." She looked at the hulking alien spacedock again. "There's still a creepy aspect though, which is exactly *how* they knew that design. If they managed to get it out of our computers . . ."

This time Carl laughed. *No need. It wouldn't be hard to simply create a match to the external docking rings on our hull, now would it?*

Ariane smacked her forehead. "Duh. The best example is a prototype." She felt better. That kind of approach was impressive, and the construction capability kind of frightening, but it made the unknown Others a little less godlike. And as Gabrielle said, it was a lot more friendly than keeping all the doors locked. If whoever owned this . . . place was hostile, they certainly didn't have to offer them a door at all. "What about control linkages? Even if they've got the hardware down, the firmware and software isn't likely to be identical. You can't deduce those from a scan."

"I would be very wary of using the term *can't* with respect to this place," Sandrisson cautioned. "We have already encountered several phenomena that we would call impossible if we were not directly experiencing them."

True enough, Carl said. *But in any case, even if they've just duplicated the hardware, it's not a problem. Me and Steve can tickle the hardware into accepting a firmware update from external control and that'll get the doors to open.*

Ariane nodded. "Good. Well, people, we aren't accomplishing anything just sitting here. We've got docking rings to fit us and we think we can get the doors open, so let's head on in. Our power supply isn't getting any bigger."

Fortunately, even rather stupid automation was well up to the automated docking task; Ariane had *done* full manual docking during her pilot training, but it was not something she particularly wanted to try again, and especially not with the two hundred meter long *Holy Grail* rather than a one-person fighter or racing vehicle.

As the alignment was completed, Ariane felt the docking rings engage and lock. "Steve, you and Carl didn't do anything yet, did you?"

"No."

"So much for *can't*," Sandrisson said dryly.

Out of a sort of morbid curiosity, DuQuesne said, *how did the station identify itself during the dock-and-lock?*

For a variety of reasons, including ensuring unambiguous communications routing, all installations had unique identifiers attached to them, used during all interactions ranging from docking to work requests. Steve parsed the command flow. "Identifier is . . . *null*."

What? Carl said, startled. *The system won't even oper-*ate *without a valid ID!*

"Sending another ID query." The answer returned almost instantly. "Just . . . wildcards. And our damn system's still accepting it."

"Okay, I'm officially creeped out again," Ariane announced. "*All* and *None*, that's what it's saying."

As though it is everything, or nothing at all, DuQuesne's silent voice mused. *Sending another ID query.*

After several tests, it was clear that the station alternated between the two identifiers with no preference. It was either a wildcard identifier, all possible identities at once, or a null, no identifier at all, both equally impossible and yet equally accepted by the *Holy Grail*'s systems.

"Creepy or not," Gabrielle said finally, "we sure ain't getting anywhere sittin' here pinging it. Are we going in, or not?"

"No real choice," Ariane admitted. "Everyone's outfits have the right environmental programming?"

"I made sure of it," Carl said, joining them in the control room. "No AI, as you know, but the basic sensors and rule-based expert systems will make sure they react to the environment pretty well. Just make sure you're fully charged before we go out."

"I'm staying," said Gabrielle. "The automatics have Laila under watch, but I just don't trust things without someone on hand."

Ariane nodded. Dr. Canning had shown only the faintest signs of recovery, and she knew Gabrielle felt that she was failing as a doctor, despite everyone from Ariane to DuQuesne pointing out that Canning's dependency on AI-support automation had been so extreme that even the best therapists would probably have to run a full personality recovery to even begin putting her back together—assuming there was enough of a backup and remaining structure of Laila Canning to rebuild. "Stay connected with us, though."

"No way I wouldn't. Now, don't none of you get yourselves hurt out there, all right?"

"I don't think even all the rest of us should go out. At least not right away," Ariane said. "I think it should be—"

"—not you," DuQuesne said firmly from the doorway. "You are the only qualified pilot of this ship and, of course, you're the captain."

The situation might be creepy, but she *had* been looking forward to being one of the first people to step foot on an alien installation. "Each and every one of us is unique and irreplaceable on this mission, Doctor."

"Indeed, but for different reasons. In this case, we are most in need of power—my specialty—and I will need to have assistance perhaps in locating and utilizing controls and systems. If more . . . exotic demands are placed upon us, we will require the services of a theoretician, but that could likely be done via remote."

Ariane wished she could think of an argument that wouldn't sound petulant, but DuQuesne was perfectly right. "So you, Steve, and Carl?"

"Makes sense to me," Carl agreed.

"What if . . . well, you get in trouble out there?"

"You mean, if we encounter something hostile?" DuQuesne looked slightly amused as he looked down on her from at least fifteen centimeters above her full standing height. "Captain, in all likelihood, if there was any hostility here we would be dead. Still, it might not be totally out of the question to bring some form of weapons for self defense."

"What, a club?" Steve said sarcastically. "Oh, sure, we could render something else without the interlocks, but I don't have any training in using real weapons."

"No virtual adventures?"

"Well . . . " the diminuitive systems engineer looked slightly embarrassed. "I tend to have the realism dialed way down. Makes it easier, and I'm more a story and dramatics guy."

"Dr. Edlund?"

"I do a lot of that; I use maximum reality with my weapons use, and I do multiple timeframes—I like crossover, actually, though I admit I still prefer melee to distance weapons."

DuQuesne nodded. "That should work well, then."

"What about you?" Ariane asked. "I'd volunteer, though I'm mostly a fantasy buff when I'm not working, which means I'm generally experienced in using *really* old-fashioned stuff—swords, spears, bows, that kind of thing. But I agree that I should stay here for now."

DuQuesne looked slightly surprised. "With your profession, I would have thought you get enough senseless excitement. On the other hand, that sort of weapon is easily rendered from even basic game files, and if you have some custom renderings that don't involve game-magic . . . ?" He glanced at her questioningly, and she nodded.

"As for myself," he went on, "I have similar tastes in entertainment to Dr. Edlund. I use the virtual inputs, but my actual body motions control the weapons."

Simon had been quiet during most of the discussion, but spoke up finally. "If it comes to that, I can handle a sword reasonably well—although I'm sure not nearly so well as Marc or Ariane, and probably not as well as Carl."

Ariane nodded and glanced over at Dr. Cussler. "Tom, we can render weapons, right?"

"Without the interlocks? If we have accurate full templates, I can make damn near anything." She was very cheered to see how well Cussler was recovering. "Game templates often don't have the detail, though, unless you *are* using full realism."

"I assure you, my templates are more than detailed enough," DuQuesne stated. "Examining the files Dr. Edlund's made available . . . well, some aren't usable, but there are some excellent candidates here. So between myself and Dr. Edlund we have at least some defensive capability, and if the captain disembarks at some point, I see that she will have some quite suitable weapons as well."

"How long will it take to render the weapons?" Ariane inquired.

"Oh, a few hours, assuming we're discussing hand weapons and not siege artillery."

She nodded. "All right. Then let's get that set up, and since it's getting a little late, shipboard time, the . . . well, away team, I guess, or boarding party, will go out tomorrow morning."

The others all agreed. Ariane leaned back in her chair as most of them left. *A few more hours to think about what else I might be missing, and wonder if I'm going to get us all killed.*

This "captain" business is really overrated.

Chapter 14

DuQuesne watched tensely as the inner lock door opened. It was easy to argue logically that there was no reason for any danger to be lurking on the other side; convincing his gut of that likelihood was not nearly so easy.

The lighted corridor revealed by the open lock—lit by some gentle, white source that seemed to come from the material of the ceiling itself—was only a temporary relief. He stepped out cautiously, Steve and Carl following, and stopped.

The corridor was large, though not nearly so immense as it could have been in this megastructure. The disquieting part was the absolute emptiness, stretching straight away in both directions for kilometers. Aside from the slight misty softening that kilometers of atmosphere gave any sight, the corridor might as well have been a simply-rendered graphic, with none of the scratches, dust, smudges, or a thousand other subliminal details showing that an installation had been built for use by living beings.

Of course, it didn't even exist a few days ago. The softened edges of distance did bring a more interesting point to mind. "Check our environmentals."

"Atmosphere's . . . perfect." Carl said after a moment. "78% nitrogen, a little more than 21% oxygen, smidge less than 1% argon, a little CO_2, and about 50% relative humidity. Pressure's one atmosphere, a little over one hundred kilopascals, temperature twenty-two degrees C."

"Any contaminants?"

"Nothing." Carl shook his head. "Aside from the motes we've brought with us, this air's just . . . air. No bacteria, viruses, sensor motes, or dust. Not even as much as you'd expect in a brand-new fabbed habitat. It's completely clean."

DuQuesne nodded. "No point in wasting our own resources at this point." His suit retracted the few-micron-thick helmet it had generated until that point. "Just keep the environmental monitors online and have it go to full life-support isolation if anything changes significantly, especially in our own life signs."

The air smelled . . . flat. With nothing else in it, there couldn't be smells, except what they brought with them. "Carl, our first priority is power. Could we get power from the lock connections?"

Carl stepped back to the lock and examined it. "Well, yeah, in an absolute pinch, I suppose. But these things aren't built to handle much power at all. I'm not sure they'd handle the draw that we're using just to keep everyone alive and comfortable, so we'd have to move out if we wanted to have a net gain. And it would take a *long* time to charge up to departure level that way."

And, DuQuesne thought, *assuming that our unknown hosts allowed us to dismantle the lock mechanism so as to cannibalize it for power, rather than just shutting off the juice when we started.* He spoke again, activating the shipboard connection. "Captain, we've entered and there is breathable, safe atmosphere inside. It's my intention to proceed inward, towards the main shell, as I would presume that is where we will find our answers. Looking down the corridor in the other direction, it appears to come to a dead end at about the distance we would expect if it runs the length of this . . . spacedock."

"Understood, Doctor. I don't have any better suggestions, so carry on."

A momentary dizziness assailed him, and adrenaline surged through his veins. *What now?*

Something bumped into his arm; he tried to turn, found that he was lying on his side.

Lying . . . ?

"Holy jumping Jesus on a pogo stick," Steve whispered reverently, as he slowly sat up.

DuQuesne and Carl stared at each other from the floor.

"What's wrong?" Ariane's voice demanded.

He stood slowly, feeling the emphatic, perfectly distributed drag of weight. "Captain, you have seen no movement from where you are, correct?"

"Movement? No, nothing is moving within the range of *Holy Grail*'s sensors. Why?"

"Because that means we have another mystery. There is gravity now. About . . . one full G, in fact."

There was a pause. Then Sandrisson's voice came dryly over the radio. "You know, I am becoming rather tired of having to believe six impossible things before breakfast. You are sure the corridor isn't rotating?"

"Very sure," Carl responded. "Besides the fact that we didn't feel any lateral acceleration, an analysis of our radio signals shows no sign that we're rotating with respect to *Holy Grail.*"

"*This* isn't nearly as courteous as the air," grumbled Steve. "I'm not used to Earth gravity, I spend most of my time in the orbitals."

DuQuesne snorted. "It will do you good. Even if your medical nanites keep you from the standard low-weight syndromes, it's good to be in real gravity. And this is hardly anything."

Even before he finished that sentence, he winced inwardly. *What the hell's wrong with me? Do I want them to know? It's just one clue, though so could be no-one will . . .*

But he heard a shocked indraw of breath over the link, and Carl stopped dead and slowly turned, eyes widening. "So *that's* why your background's fuzzed. You're a Super!"

DuQuesne wanted to kick himself. *Managed this masquerade for half a century, and now I make some amateur slip of the lip? Maybe . . . maybe I did want them to know. Still, look at their faces. Play it down, play it down.* DuQuesne gave him a frown, restraining a much stronger glare. *He wasn't even born at the time it all came apart. Hell, not another person on board* Holy Grail *was alive then.* "I would much prefer you not use that low-brow nickname. The Hyperion Project may have been —*was*—a mistake on many levels, but it insults the creators and especially the . . . results of the Project to use that term." *I have every reason to hate Hyperion, but, as one book put it, they did great things. Terrible, but great.*

"You're . . . one of the Hyperions?" Ariane's voice was clearly trying to sound controlled, at ease, but the shock was still there. *For most people, it's like meeting up with Frankenstein's monster. You don't expect a cautionary tale of our time to be working on your engines.*

"Yes," he said quietly. "But in the end, we . . . well, most of us . . . the ones who survived . . . we're just people. People with some special problems, maybe some special advantages, but not really that different." *And it'd be real nice if I could believe that.*

Steve nodded, and then to his surprise just gave an appraising grin. "Well, that explains your build. Two point five G's of spin acceleration for your whole life."

Thank you, Mr. Franceschetti. "Two point six, actually, to be precise. And sorry, Steve, you're not my type," he said—adding a small smile of his own to take the edge off it. *And express my gratitude for giving me this opening.*

The serious look behind the smile showed that Steve knew exactly what he was doing. "I already guessed that. A guy can still appreciate the view."

"Appreciate away, but let's get back to work." He could feel the tension easing. The revelation had been a shock, but—thanks to all gods that might be—the others had come to know him and trust him enough to let it slide, now. "We have artificial gravity and no apparent mechanism for it, which means we have a long hike ahead. I'm not sure if this qualifies as more of Gabrielle's 'hospitality,' or whether it's an obstacle."

About a half-hour and three kilometers later, Steve came down firmly on the "obstacle" side of that question. The design and systems engineer wasn't in bad shape, but full-gravity walking was clearly not something he was used to. For his part, DuQuesne was a bit impatient that he had to slow his walking pace to match theirs. He restrained that reaction, though; physical superiority was a trivial capability in almost all cases, nothing to be particularly proud of, and if someone wanted to, could be equalled with a little nanomedical boosting.

A part of him knew that wasn't entirely true, at least not in his case, but that was a part he repressed heavily and deliberately.

The corridor ended in a mostly-circular doorway with no visible seams, locks, or controls. "Seems to be made up of the same stuff as most of this spacedock. Carl, have you got anything on that yet?"

"Not a damn thing," the temporary sensor expert answered. "Which really worries me."

"Can you be a little more detailed on 'not a damn thing,' Carl?" Ariane asked.

"I really mean nothing. I can't even get a list of elements from it. Spectroscopic analysis gives me zip, I'm not getting x-ray diffraction patterns—in fact, radiation doesn't seem to go through it at all—and my sample motes can't get a single tiny bit of it to detach for analysis. The chemicals a few of them can synth up for analytical work don't seem to have any effect on it, either."

"It's not ring-carbon composite like our suits or the ship armor, is it?"

"No, that's the first thing I tested. I can't get a debonding to work at all."

DuQuesne frowned at the massive circular portal in front of him. "If that's the case, we'd better hope this thing opens easily, because it sounds to me like we haven't got a prayer of forcing it."

Steve walked up to the doorway, scanning. "I'm not even getting thermal patterns, except reflections of our own heat. It's totally even and there's no sign of any seams, panels, nothing."

"What are we supposed to do, then?" Carl wondered aloud. "Wave our hands and say 'Open Sesame'?"

Despite the chill that went, quite involuntarily, down his spine, DuQuesne realized that he was not really at all surprised that the ten meter wide door rolled aside immediately upon Carl's whimisical request. The lack of surprise was, in some ways, even more worrisome than total startlement would have been. "Apparently, yes."

"Damn. That's just wrong."

"There's no way that they . . . whoever they are . . . could possibly know that reference."

"If they've read all our data storage, they could. Or it could be a pretty simple guess to detect what appears to be a request to open."

"If they've read our data storage . . . but that would mean that they took in and assimilated our language, including an awful lot about our customs, history, and figures of speech, in a matter of a few days at most," Sandrisson protested weakly.

"Yes. It would."

The interior beyond the door was not lit. Light from the corridor spilled in, illuminating a vast expanse of floor and little else. DuQuesne glanced around, shrugged, and walked in, followed by the others.

Their own lights played about a room so huge that "cavernous" was an utterly inadequate description. Titanic, brooding shapes were visible at the edges of their lights—even with enhanced imaging, they were just dark outlines of massive machinery. Gravity was still present, but felt slightly different—lighter, DuQuesne thought. "This definitely wasn't built in the last few days," he said. "And it's not as immaculate as our little spacedock."

"How so?" Ariane asked.

"Dust. There's not much, but some dust on the surfaces."

"*That* doesn't look good," Steve's voice said.

Following the focused beam of the system engineer's light, DuQuesne could make out an irregular shape, an outline that didn't seem to fit at all with the neat, symmetrical station. "No, it doesn't. Let's go take a look."

As they moved towards the unknown object, Ariane said, "I know I may sound like a nag, but be careful. We don't . . . " Her voice abruptly faded. As it did so, DuQuesne suddenly realized the light from behind was dimming.

Faster than any ordinary human could possibly have managed, he whirled, reversing his course and lunging towards the door. But they had come too far inside. With a rumbling chime that echoed throughout the alien room, the great portal rolled shut.

"Captain! Do you hear us?"

Silence answered. He couldn't feel any of the data links active, either. He tried boosting power, but all his receivers showed were his own reflected signals, and those of Steve and Carl.

"It's useless," Carl said bluntly. "The way that stuff acts, we couldn't punch a message through it with a tera-watt laser and a fusion reactor for constant power."

"Open up!" Steve said to the door. "Open Sesame! Open, dammit!"

This time the door remained immobile.

"For a group of supposed brilliant intellects, we were rather easy to separate," DuQuesne observed. "Not, I suppose, that we had much choice. Had we sent in remote rovers, they would now be completely useless. But if we can't figure out how to keep that blasted door open, getting significant power is going to become even more of a pain."

"You're awfully calm for someone who's just been trapped, Marc." Steve looked, fortunately, as though he found that reassuring.

"I doubt we're actually trapped, to be honest. I would expect that whenever the rest of the crew follows, they will be able to open the door from their side, and none of them are so stupid as to walk through without making sure there's someone standing by as gatekeeper, even if they can't somehow jam the door open."

Carl nodded. "So what do we do? Just wait?"

"I see no point in wasting that time. They know our resources and that there's no need to panic. They aren't going to come charging out immediately, or at least I would hope not, and when the door does open we should be able to detect it immediately when our connections to the network come back online. So let's get some more work done." He turned back and started again for the distant irregular shape.

As they got closer, he was able to make out more details, but instead of clarifying what he was seeing, the details made things more confusing. He had thought at first that it was the ruins of some kind of machine, perhaps fallen from the distant ceiling in ages past, but . . . the jagged canyons of gray-brown alien material loomed above, not mangled machinery and electronics, but a winding path through the scallop-sided ridges.

"What the hell . . . is this . . . *dirt?*" Carl said incredulously as they reached the path.

DuQuesne felt one of his eyebrows rise in sympathetic disbelief. It certainly did look like the material on either side of the pathway, between the path and its enclosing ridges, was simple dirt—not dust, but soil, soil dry and dessicated but still dark and thick. The path itself had a metallic-plastic sheen to it, but the echo of their footsteps had the solidity of boots on thick stone. He squatted down and dug his gloved fingers into the stuff at the side of the path. "Sure feels like dirt to me. What do the motes say?"

"Minerals . . . organics . . . damn, it *is* dirt. Sterile, I think, but there's lots of organic traces in here, and this isn't standard Earth issue. I think . . . " He dug at a particular spot and came up holding a twisted, brown object that was crumbling into dust even as he showed it to them. "Yeah. That was a root of something."

"Curiouser and curiouser, as the old book says." DuQuesne stood up. "Come on, let's see if this path leads anywhere." Steve grumbled something. "Just a little farther—say fifteen minutes. If we don't get to something then, we'll take a break, have some lunch. Okay?"

"All right. I'm just not used to this kind of hiking. I think I'm going to really regret this tomorrow morning."

The three followed the path, winding between the ever-higher ridges which followed some kind of wave-like pattern. The path itself widened slightly, and in some angles of light DuQuesne thought he saw patterns on the flat surface, but whenever he stopped and tried to examine them, there was nothing there.

Rounding another corner just like the last three, the walls abruptly ended at an open space. Their path continued and joined with a flat, paved-looking surface covered with regular hexagonal tiles about a meter across; looking to the sides, they could see that similar paths joined from other steep-sided canyons on either side. A few hundred meters ahead, a smoothly curved wall belled out towards them, with another circular door—much smaller than the first, perhaps only three or four meters across—set in the precise center of the curve.

He glanced at his other companions, who shrugged and followed him across the paved area, footsteps echoing eerily in the silence. He contemplated the door for a moment. "We're *not* stepping through this one right away."

"No," agreed Carl, "but we can see if it will open."

He nodded. "True." He turned back to the door. "Open up."

As smoothly as the first, this door rolled aside. The light that came in was soft white light, clearly artificial and similar (but not quite identical) to the light in the giant spacedock, and quite a bit dimmer; through the door was visible a corridor that seemed to widen out, in a narrow cone-shape, until joining with a vastly wider room or corridor about ten meters farther along. That corridor, or room, seemed to be about a hundred meters across; tantalizing edges of shapes—which might be sculptures, street signs, or mechanisms—were partially visible in the restricted field of view.

DuQuesne was strongly tempted to go straight on through—and clearly so were Carl and Steve, despite the latter being footsore. But they'd have to leave at least one person behind them as doorkeeper, in case this door turned out to be one-way as well, and there was no telling when they'd be back. "Close and lock," he said after a moment. He didn't *know*, of course, that there were locks, but it seemed logical. And when the door shut, he thought he sensed a vibration that indicated the engagement of some form of locking mechanism.

"We'll wait on that one until we've gotten a report back to the others—whenever they decide it's time to check on us. In the meantime, let's have something to eat and take a rest."

Steve immediately dropped to the floor. "Works for me!"

As they ate, DuQuesne was constantly aware of the brooding silence of the installation. Given their limitations on replication mass, Tom Cussler had only been able to give them a moderate number of nanoprobes, but they'd scattered some along their entire route, which were spreading slowly outward on their own. So far, there wasn't a single sign of movement or life anywhere, and none of any active power sources—at least, none accessible. Given the characteristics of the hull-material making up the foundations of this impossible place, there could be a fifty gigawatt nuclear reactor right under his ass and he wouldn't know. Or, probably, even notice if it melted down right then and there. "Carl, have you tried cosmic ray background?"

"Nothing. This stuff either stops 'em dead, or wherever we are doesn't have any cosmic rays—which seems pretty damn unlikely," the controls engineer answered. "My background analysis hasn't shown anything, even though it's kept running since we started out on this field trip. No . . . wait, on the high gamma there's . . . something."

Carl transmitted the data to DuQuesne, who examined it. The faint variations in return from the high-end gamma radiation probes did not, however, tell him much.

He shook his head. "Maybe Sandrisson can make sense out of this. It's definitely not in my field." He glanced at Steve. "Franceschetti, have you got any thoughts on the whole layout?"

As a concept engineer, Steve dealt with the high-level design of large structures, so DuQuesne hoped some of this might make more sense to him. Steve scratched his head, fingers running absently through the short curly hair. "Hard to say. I mean, given the scale this thing's been made on, judging it from just what we've seen so far would be like trying to figure out what Kanzaki-Three's design and purpose is from, oh, one storage room alone." He glanced around.

"Well, one thing I can say is that this area was clearly made to include naturalistic features. The canyon has rough walls and profiles of natural weathered rock if you look, and the dirt is, well, natural in composition, if not quite Earthly. From the data we're getting in the returns from the nanoscans, there's other areas out there which have some similar features. There's also portions which are clearly artificial and meant to look that way, so I'd say you have a spacegoing race that did originate from a planet, and that liked to preserve some of the essence of living on a planet." He yawned. "Woo, I'm tired. Anyway . . . the open nature of the design indicates they weren't clearly separating working from living areas, at least to me. That is, the natural area doesn't have some specific division from the main entry or the operational locations.

"On the other hand . . . there's also no clear power sources and none of the machinery—whatever it is—seems to be running, except the air maintenance and gravity."

"Do you actually *know* the air's being maintained in here?" DuQuesne asked.

Steve looked nonplussed. "I suppose I can't be absolutely certain. But there *are* materials in here other than that nonreactive whatever-it-is, and I would think that after many years, the oxygen would have combined with anything accessible."

DuQuesne shrugged. "How many years, though? Can we actually tell how long it's been since, say, that root Carl found was growing?"

"Well, I might, by . . . " Carl trailed off. "On *Earth* I might, by doing things like carbon-14 dating, but those all rely on knowing the proportion of proper isotopes in things. I'm familiar with the proportions—some of the proportions, anyway—on Earth, but I have no idea if they hold at all here." He frowned. "If I assume the temperature and all has been reasonably stable, I can do a guess based on the decay of the relevant compounds." A few minutes went by. "It's . . . a long time. Millions of years, I think. But there's a lot of assumptions in that calculation."

"Understood. And if anything was doing any sort of maintenance . . . all bets are off." DuQuesne stood, dusting off his pants reflexively, though the ring-carbon composite generally didn't allow anything to adhere to it without special treatment. "Enough of a break. We'll certainly come back here, but there's a lot more to explore, and we've got a lot more time before we've put in a full day."

Steve groaned as he got up. "Why not let the nanos do it?"

"Because they have no directionality or intelligence, and may not even get everywhere, as you know. We can keep going in interesting directions."

"And because he thinks it'll do us good," Carl put in.

"Elitist supermen are such a pain to work with," Steve said. "Okay, Mr. Slave Driver, let's go."

"If I was a *true* elitist superman slave driver," DuQuesne said with a slight smile, beginning to move down one of the other artificial canyons, "I would send each of us out *alone*."

Steve looked around at the vast silent gloom of the mysterious station and shuddered. "No, thanks!"

Chapter 15

"Open!" Ariane shouted at the huge doorway. She experienced a moment of panic before she saw the circular portal rolling open as obediently as it had for Dr. DuQuesne and his team. As soon as it opened, she began transmitting. "Dr. DuQuesne! Marc, Carl, Steve, are you there?"

On the third repetition, a deep, level voice responded. "DuQuesne here, Captain. Please do not step through the doorway just yet."

She almost sagged to the floor in relief; Sandrisson's face mirrored the feeling. "Thank God. Are all of you all right?"

"Perfectly all right. It's only been about a day, Captain."

"Only! I wanted to get out here right away—"

The infuriatingly calm voice interrupted. "Admirable sentiments, but irrational, Captain. If it was a trap, given the technology here there would be no way you could arrive in time, if it was meant to kill quickly."

"As we told her," Sandrisson said. "We were all worried, but there had to be some decisions made about who might go on the second expedition. Have you found a source for power? Tom and I have managed to design and fabricate a transport vehicle which will allow us to move the storage coils when it becomes necessary. It's being assembled now."

"Unfortunately, not yet," Carl Edlund's voice replied. "Something has to be generating power, but we haven't found anything we can access yet. There may be ways of opening access panels if we can identify them, but no luck so far."

Ariane felt her lips tighten. Air was obviously not going to be a problem, but without power . . . "Anything of immediate interest?"

"How about a door leading farther into this . . . wherever we are?" Steve offered.

"A door? Could you open it? What's on the other side?"

"In order, yes, yes, and as we were not foolish enough this time to just step through, all we know is it's some kind of illuminated corridor and room," DuQuesne said. "We were not going to potentially get separated by yet another layer of this . . . material. Or, possibly worse, start separating ourselves, leaving one person behind as a gatekeeper."

"I agree, Doctor. We're trying to decide just how to proceed from here. A part of me says that what we really need to do is just move as much equipment as we can from *Holy Grail* to this point and bring everyone together. If we can't find a source of power, Doctor, the ship will soon be useless anyway. Isn't that true?"

After a moment of silence, she heard a slight grunt. "Um. Yes, I suppose you're correct. But what about the door?"

"Let me try something." She addressed the door. "Remain open until ordered to close." Gesturing for Sandrisson to wait, she walked into the gloom. Watching her internal display, she continued into the alien installation until she'd gone nearly twice as far as the first group had before the door shut. Light still streamed in from behind, undisturbed. She turned and shouted back at the door, "Close door!"

Instantly the door rolled shut again. A moment later, it rolled back open, clearly at Sandrisson's direction.

"That does seem to solve the problem," DuQuesne conceded, "but then what is the point of not being able to be opened from *this* side?"

"Hard to say. Perhaps to prevent people somewhere else in this installation—if there are any—from going into our ship area? Maybe it will become clearer as time goes on."

"In any case, that does eliminate the major objection. If the medical equipment for Laila Canning can be brought to this location, I see no reason that we must remain separated by kilometers of corridor and out of potential communication."

"I, for one, do not want to be the only conscious person in this ship," Gabrielle's voice put in. "If you all are going to be exploring the wilds, I want to be closer."

"Any objections?" When Ariane heard none, she nodded. "Okay then, we do it. Dr. DuQuesne, you and your team come back and let's get this done."

"On our way, Captain."

Chapter 16

She glanced around at the others. She had—successfully, this time—argued that she would be part of the group exploring through the next door. Part of that success was, admittedly, due to the complete lack of danger found so far, and the fact that unless they not only found a source of power, but an awfully *big* source of power, her piloting skills were going to become essentially irrelevant. Until that time, her physical enhancements, combat training (simulated, but at high realism levels), and adrenaline-junkie preferences made her a much better candidate for playing explorer than any of the specialists.

"After all," she'd finally pointed out, "unless we're suddenly going to have to go blazing out of here, evading cannon and missiles while Dr. Sandrisson tries to activate the drive in a last-minute glorious escape, just about any of you could manage to get *Holy Grail* undocked and to an appropriate point in the model solar system to be able to make a safe transition back. And, to be honest, *Holy Grail* isn't a fighter craft, so if someone *is* shooting at us, we probably aren't getting away no matter who's in the pilot seat."

So now she looked forward at the enigmatic portal, which had showed those few tantalizing glimpses in the few moments DuQuesne and the others had opened it. This time the advance party consisted of herself, Dr. DuQuesne, and Dr. Sandrisson; Gabrielle was, of course, staying with the still essentially comatose Laila Canning, Cussler was tending the operation of the replicator, while Carl and Steve were trying to set up simple automation for the camp. "Open door."

The white artificial illumination streamed in, brightening the advance camp that the stranded crew of *Holy Grail* had set up in the canyon-bracketed antechamber in front of the second door. The other three active crewmembers looked up as the door opened. "Ready for test?" she asked Steve.

"Yep. Go ahead."

She faced the door again. "Allow door to be opened from both sides if commanded by any of the people currently present, but not by anyone else without explicit instructions by one of those currently present."

She stepped through the portal. From the other side, Steve said, "Close door."

The door rolled closed again. Ariane waited a moment, then spoke. "Open door."

As obediently as it had from the other side, the door rolled back open. Ariane grinned as she stepped back through. "It works."

DuQuesne nodded. "We determined that it worked for the main door, after Dr. Edlund made the suggestion; it makes sense, a fairly simple security procedure which does not rely on newcomers to put it in place. Although it has obvious dangers in both directions, which indicates something about the builders." He adjusted the small pack he carried. "Captain?"

Dr. Sandrisson gave a smile and a nod as she looked over at him. Ariane took a deep breath and stepped forward. "Here we go."

The door rolled shut once more behind them. While it would have been nice to maintain communications during the exploration, given how little they knew about what was outside, Ariane felt it more prudent to keep the door locked, just in case. And, just in case something else *could* override that lock, the others would keep a guard on it.

The conical corridor emerged into an oval space, a hundred meters across, a hundred-fifty wide, and reaching a peak of thirty meters in height at the center. Two broad, straight lanes of empty space—one running directly from the corridor's mouth, the other at right angles to it—divided the space into quadrants. Low ridges or walls, smooth and featureless, interrupted at intervals by spaces, ran along the edges of these quadrants. Inside each were some enigmatic objects or structures, like wind-carved desert rocks and distorted hollowed tree trunks made of pearl-tinted steel and polished coal. The light itself emanated from somewhere near the ceiling, but try as she might, Ariane couldn't quite make out where. It cast soft shadows, despite the apparent lack of focus.

"Wonder what the hell those things are?" DuQuesne murmured.

"Let's take a look," she said. "Nothing's moving, and I'm not picking up any energy readings except the light itself." She picked the nearest open entrance to the first quandrant and walked over to the first object.

Up close it resembled some sort of abstract sculpture, with little upcurved points—not too sharp—small holes, and other small features spaced at intervals over the thing. Sandrisson and DuQuesne were examining the material.

"Well, what do you know. This stuff isn't the foundation material. We've got a central ring-carbon composite structure—not all that different from our own high-end armor—with mixed alloys and composites . . . in a pretty odd pattern, too." DuQuesne frowned. "No idea what it's for."

Something about the spacing of the smaller features was nagging at her. "Doctor . . . you know, I think this might be something like support columns. For whoever came here to be able to install other things, like chairs, walls, hang pictures, whatever."

Sandrisson leaned forward, touching one of the upcurved points. "I believe you may be right. This is almost like a wall hook. You could use these to support small objects, or as part of the support for something larger. Or use the holes here as fastening points, for bolts or something of the sort."

"And the pattern of materials makes sense from that perspective," DuQuesne agreed. "If you want to fasten things permanently together—welding, glue, whatever —you can find an appropriate surface pretty much anywhere. Without having whatever technology they used to make the foundation material." He turned to Sandrisson. "By the way, I know you were looking over the results Edlund got from the high-gamma and other scans, but you haven't said a damn thing to anyone. What's the story on that stuff?"

When Sandrisson hesitated, Ariane spoke. "Doctor —Simon—let's not get secretive here."

He gave an apologetic grin. "Sorry, Ariane. If you're a sensible man, you get in the habit of being very cautious of making extreme pronouncement when one's in the sciences, especially when it's not your core field." He shook his head. "And the implications are pretty extreme, I'm afraid. At the very limit of resolution of the far gamma, I was getting some indications of structure."

"But that would be at about 10^{-14} meters, or even less," DuQuesne said, wrinkling his brow. "That's down at sub-atomic size scale."

"Exactly," said Sandrisson, absently pushing back a strand of snow-white hair. "And I was only getting subtle indications of structure—very regular structure—even then. After examining all the other data—which showed not a single trace of any subatomic particle I could identify—I was forced to only one conclusion. What we are looking at is a structured ultrasubatomic latticework, a self-healing, self-supporting structure that is constructed of quarks. A coherent quark composite, if you will."

"I thought that you couldn't *get* individual quarks to play with," protested Ariane. "Don't they just bind tighter to each other the farther you try to pull them apart, like tying two things together with springs?"

"Something like that—rather the opposite of most natural forces, of course, which tend to weaken with distance—and yes, that is generally the way it works, with a few minor exceptions. Apparently, however, our unknown builders knew some things that we do not."

DuQuesne shook his head in disbelief. "That's about as close to the classic sci-fi 'unobtainium' as I've ever heard. You'd need a thermonuclear bomb to even start chipping away at it. You could lasso Jupiter and drag it in by main force with a rope of this stuff."

Ariane nodded. "Now, if we can just figure out how to make it, we're all set. But I don't think we're going to do that right now, so why don't we do some more exploring?"

"Fair enough." DuQuesne surveyed the oval-shaped room. "Which direction, Captain? There appears to be one door at the far end of this room, and one right across from the one we entered by."

Both doors appeared to be identical to the one they'd just recently left; circular and a bit less than four meters across. "Let's take the one at the far end. See where a right-angle turn takes us."

Ariane gave it the same instructions as the prior door, to which it appeared to respond just as well, and the three stepped through and closed the door. But as they started down this new conical corridor, which seemed to join with a somewhat wider corridor ahead, DuQuesne held up his hand sharply. "Do you hear that?"

A stacatto rapping was approaching, growing rapidly louder; to Ariane, it sounded very like the rattle of boots on pavement, many pairs of boots all running. A startling flash of movement, multiple figures passing by the entrance. In that quick moment, Ariane could tell the figures were bipedal, generally greenish in color, tall, and not human in outline, though that might be some kind of uniform or costume the things were wearing. There was no sign anyone had spotted them; the running sounds continued.

Cautiously, Ariane moved towards the corridor's end, followed by DuQuesne and Sandrisson. The footsteps, now some way distant down the corridor, slowed and stopped. But it was the next sound that turned the entire universe upside down.

"A thin branch that ends in air, Mindkiller. How pathetic this, your last run," said a sharp, cold voice.

Chapter 17

Ariane looked back at the others. DuQuesne's narrowed eyes and Sandrisson's widened ones showed they had heard the same thing. Impossibly, it seemed that the barely-seen beings down the corridor were conversing in English.

A deeper voice, with an undertone of exhaustion and defiance, answered. "If this is the end, then end it with less insult, for it should be beneath the Blessed to Serve. Unless your words come from the fear that we are alike, you and I, Sethrik?"

By now, Ariane had moved to the end of her own corridor. Suppressing a nervous breath, she risked a look around the corner.

The intersecting corridor ended about forty meters away, in a smooth curve. A number of creatures were gathered there, most in a semicircle around a single other creature which stood against the far wall; a more clear scenario of a fugitive brought to bay couldn't be imagined. Both pursued and pursuers were indeed tall, perhaps almost the height of Dr. DuQuesne or, counting the twin crests that seemed to adorn each head, even taller. Green and black patterns spotted the chitin-shiny surface of the things, and what appeared to be beetle-like split wingcases were on their backs. A long tail, flexible despite the chitinous exterior, rippled behind each of the creatures, adorned with what appeared to be a stinger; several of these tails were currently held in an erect curve, reminding Ariane unpleasantly and forcibly of a scorpion.

The cornered individual was facing her, allowing her to make out the fact that it did, in fact, have something akin to a face, though the individual features had a size and spacing that was unsettlingly not quite human. The feet appeared to be encased in boots, but judging by the lack of clothing on any of the other parts of the body and the fact that the "boots" had a smoothly-blending color scheme, she suspected that those were indeed the creatures' feet. But now the first voice—Sethrik?—was speaking again:

"Alike?" A buzzing insectoid shriek, like an angered cicada, sounded out. "We are nothing alike. We understand what we are, and from where we come, and we are united. You are the last of your kind."

"So end it, and free your world of my abomination." Ariane almost got the impression of a fleeting smile. "But there is something more important than eliminating my obscenity, isn't there?"

"You *will* give us full entry, Mindkiller!"

"I will not. The Minds no longer have an interface, even if you were to bring me back. I burned it out and sealed it with dustswarm motes that will kill me if they ever try to touch me again." The lone alien seemed to crouch slightly, gathering himself.

"You believe your fragment-mind is enough to out-think one of the Great Masters?" Sethrik—judging by slight movements and gestures, the alien slightly to the right of the center of the surrounding semicircle —seemed to give the equivalent of a laugh. "We shall all bear witness, then. In any case, the Blessed shall know peace, for either you shall succeed in your madness, by dying first, or you shall fail, and die after." The semicircle began to close in.

"*Wait!*"

Ariane was utterly astounded to realize that this was *her* voice. More, that she had rounded the corner and was standing in full view when she said it. Vaguely, in her ear, she heard DuQuesne's incredulous "What the living *hell* do you think you're doing?", but now that she had stepped forward . . .

Instantly, three of the circling aliens, one of them Sethrik, spun. The remaining seven did not move, giving the fugitive no chance to escape. "Wait? Identify your Sphere and Designate, creature! Do you dare issue challenge to the Blessed?"

When she gave no immediate response, Sethrik and the other two moved forward a pace. "Your threat pos-ture is unsure. A challenge would be a sure loss for you. What point to your interruption?"

"I don't know exactly what's going on here," she admit-ted, still completely at sea as to what had possessed her to step out, "but I'm not going to stand around and watch a lynching or a kidnapping." She sensed, rather than saw, both Sandrisson and DuQuesne step out, flanking her, slightly behind. They were probably even more confused than she was, but—thank God—they knew that they'd better back her up now and worry later.

Sethrik studied her with black, gleaming eyes that were subtly wrong in size and placement. "Weapons and threat analysis complete. All components concur. Minimal threat. There will be no combat." He turned away and looked at the first. "Probability of your escape or victory is now below threshold, Mindkiller. We all recognize it. Individual units you are superior to, but not sufficient to overcome order of magnitude numeric disadvantage."

The lone alien addressed as "Mindkiller" suddenly raised its—his?—voice. "But if they assist, probabilities may shift."

"They will not." Sethrik said confidently.

Ariane found that confidence—so matter-of-factly stated—galling. Even so, she was again startled by her reaction. "The hell I won't!"

That startled Sethrik—more, for some reason, than her initial intrusion, as near as she could tell. But he simply gave a quick open-shut gesture of his wings, and suddenly the two creatures still facing them lunged forward.

"Your diplomacy is unrivaled, Captain," muttered DuQuesne.

The green-black insectoids seemed to blur as they approached, moving at a pace she knew she couldn't match. No wonder Sethrik had been so confident. She and DuQuesne got off a single shot each; hers missed entirely, but DuQuesne managed a grazing hit. The searing plasma packet scorched a pure black trail along the thing's side, but it didn't even flinch. Sandrisson ducked aside and was dealt a blow in passing that kicked him back down the corridor from which they'd come.

She dropped the gun and kicked her own physical enhancements into highest gear; the things suddenly seemed to slow to merely awfully bloody fast instead of impossibly quick. A wingcase whipped open, almost smashing into her face, but she managed to duck under it and kick out.

It felt like kicking a mahogany table leg, but it did throw the creature off a bit. It jumped backward to evade a followup blow, and then lunged forward just as she grasped the hilt of her sword.

Thousands of hours of practice in a dozen virtual realms—all emulated with deadly accurate combat that strained muscles to the utmost—coalesced in that moment. Her body moved in the perfectly coordinated arc-thrust of the ancient *iai* draw-and-cut.

Even the chitinous armor of the creature couldn't withstand that carbon-composite reinforced steel edge. Only literally inhumanly fast reflexes kept her from bisecting it from one side to the other; as it was, she actually cut off the lower edge of one wingcase as it whirled desperately aside, revealing a gossamer crystal shimmer that might be a furled wing.

But the stinger-tipped tail had whipped around and smashed the sword from her hands. In the next moment, its hard, cold fingerlike talons grabbed her. The uniform responded instantly by hardening into almost unbreakable protection, but she knew that was only temporary. There was a very strong limit as to how much impact protection the suit could provide, and this thing could just beat her against a wall until she broke, even if the suit stayed intact.

The first impact rattled her teeth. She tried to twist with the next blow, and succeeded in cushioning the blow, but the thing's joints just didn't quite work like a human's, which meant that she wasn't having any luck in pulling free. The wingcases flared as it braced and lunged again, and she caught a flash of patterned pink and red. *What . . . ?*

The impact put a blood-colored haze over her vision for a moment, then she was yanked away again. *Whatever it is, it's different from the rest of him.* With that as the feeble justification, she swung her body up and around as it drove her towards the wall once more, and just as her body was driven into the wall, hammered her heel down.

She *felt* the buzzing shriek of unmistakable agony through her leg, and the iron-hard grip fell away. Barely able to keep standing, she focused her will and staggered to her feet, slamming an armored elbow into the thing's face and then grabbing the wingcase as it made an ineffective swipe at her. With all her augmented strength, she shoved upward and pulled.

A loud *crack* rewarded her, and the alien screamed again, this time weaker. Her vision cleared as she kicked the thing away from her.

DuQuesne, blood trickling from a cut on his forehead, had just managed to make his opponent attempt— unsuccessfully—to emulate a nail going into a board, with the corridor wall playing the board. The erstwhile nail did not look up for an immediate rematch with either opponent.

The remaining eight of Sethrik's group were trying to restrain their target, but they were apparently now aware that the humans were not cooperating. Abruptly the group—in a coordinated motion—drew back into a tight defensive formation. "This is unforgivable. We issue challenge!"

"I have no idea what the hell you're talking about," Ariane said, keeping a wary eye on the first two attackers.

That caused all of the aliens to freeze, utterly motionless. Sethrik's group finally leaned back, just as their prey suddenly generated a repetitive pulsing buzz which was overlaid, somehow, by laughter. "New players, Sethrik! First Emergents!" It laughed louder. "First is forgiven, Second should be, Third may be, Sethrik! You can't do anything!"

She did not like Sethrik's posture. Neither did DuQuesne, apparently, because he resumed a combat stance. Sethrik's words confirmed her forboding.

"If none witness, there are none to question," he said softly.

"Indeed," the lone alien said. But he pointed as he did so.

Ariane felt a crawling sensation between her shoulderblades, and turned, in guard stance.

A hundred meters or so away, almost invisible in shadows thrown by incomprehensible machinery nearby, stood a figure. It was hard to distinguish, a black shape like a hooded and cloaked man. But whatever it was, it had a dramatic effect on Sethrik. "*Shadeweaver,*" he hissed. He drew himself up, as did all his companions —in an eerily identical fashion. "So. First is forgiven. You knew not what you did, and we cannot act against you for that, and must yield." The entire group threw an unmistakably venomous glance at Mindkiller. "For your sake, you had best hope this abomination will explain your fortune, for the Blessed will not—nor do we ever forget."

The Blessed stalked past the humans, helping their wounded to walk with them. As they continued down the corridor, she saw the shadowy figure—Shadeweaver? —give an almost human nod, and then just . . . fade away into the shadows.

And, once more, I'm officially creeped out by this place.

Chapter 18

The tall green and black figure of the one addressed as "Mindkiller" strode forward. Simon noted DuQuesne moving up to interpose himself between Ariane and the alien. "Don't bother," Ariane said. "He's not going to hurt us at this point. Go check Simon."

"I'm fine," Simon said, pushing himself shakily to his feet and coming forward. The impact had stunned him but his suit had cushioned the blow. *The real blow is this entire . . . impossible set of events. None of it makes sense.*

About six meters off, the alien dropped to a sort of strained four-point posture, tail stretched far out behind, looking almost like a man doing a pushup. "My thanks, First Emergents," he said. "Truly I owe you much, for the Blessed had cornered me beyond any calculation of escape."

Simon could see Ariane's face now, a mask of caution. She clearly realized how carefully she would have to proceed. "You're welcome—I hope, anyway, that I won't come to regret it, since I didn't even know who or what you were when I got involved. To be honest, I'm not even sure why I did," she said, after a moment.

"Ah." The alien rose from what was obviously a formal position analogous to a bow or something of the sort; he cast what was clearly a speculative glance down the corridor to the shadows into which the "Shadeweaver" had vanished. "Then perhaps I also owe a debt there, as well. I find that . . . considerably more worrisome."

Up close, it was clear that however "Mindkiller" was talking, it wasn't the same as human conversation. The apparent mouth—smaller than the human equivalent, set in a just-too-triangular face with overlarge, slanted eyes and a tiny, almost unnoticeable pointed nose—moved not at all in relation to the words, or to the scraping, buzzing sounds she now heard as an undertone to the voice.

"If you owe us, does that mean we're going to get some explanation of what just happened here—and, for that matter, where we are?" DuQuesne said.

"I will do what I can to enlighten you, indeed," the alien agreed.

"I think introductions are the first thing to do," Ariane said. "I'm Ariane Austin; I suppose I'm the one in charge of this group. This is Dr. Marc DuQuesne, and Dr. Simon Sandrisson."

"I thank you for your names; individual designations are indeed useful," it said, studying them closely. "It would seem to me—forgive me if this intrudes on some custom of yours with which I am of course unfamiliar

—that your names carry little meaning other than the identification of self."

"Overall true," Simon responded with a nod. "While some people choose or are given names of specific significance, most of them are simply a matter of parental or personal preference and have no other significance."

Something about the creature seemed to relax; maybe the wingcases expanded slightly, as though not holding tightly to the body, or tense joints relaxed incrementally. *Now, I wonder what it was that worried him . . . and what about our naming practices relieved that worry?*

"My designation is not 'Mindkiller,' as the Blessed called me. I call myself Orphan."

"Does yours have the implied meaning?"

"Indeed, for I chose it carefully."

The fact that the "implied meaning" existed only in English reminded Simon. "So can you explain exactly how it is that you're speaking our language?" he asked, noting that Ariane was allowing him to do the talking for the moment.

Orphan gave a short buzz-laugh. "I cannot explain what is not true; nor can I explain the truth of which you speak, save only to say this: none here speak each others' language, yet we all understand each other to perfection. It is one of the gifts of the Arena."

"The Arena?"

The expansive gesture Orphan gave with arms and tail encompassed the entirety of space. "You stand within the Arena—a small portion of it, indeed, but then, none stand within more than the smallest portion, nor pass through more than a fraction in all their lifetimes."

"Why," asked DuQuesne, "is it called the Arena?"

"There are other names for it, true," the alien conceded, "but Arena is, to my thoughts, the most accurate single word. It is a place where we all meet and challenge, where bargains are made and broken and avenged, where an alliance may be built on blood and fortune. It is a place where faith is lost, and where religions are founded or proven true. It is where you shall confront, and be confronted by, truths and lies, enemies and allies, belief and denial, impossibility and transcendence."

A short-range radio ping from Ariane carried her reaction. *Great. That speech sure narrowed things down.* "Are you trying to be evasive?" she demanded.

Orphan's voice was contrite. "No, not at all, Ariane Austin. But the Arena admits of no simple words. You shall have to see it for yourself. Speak to me again in a few years and tell me if perhaps I was close."

"Look, we're actually trying to find a power source. If you can help us find one, I'd consider us even."

"A power source . . . ?" For a moment the alien looked curious, then his head moved back in a clear gesture of enlightenment. "Ah, it is clear! Forgive me, I have never before encountered First Emergents—in truth, within my knowledge it has not happened for a long time indeed. Of course, your—" for the first time, a word was not translated clearly, but sounded almost like a mishmash of many words said at once. "—Drive will need much power to return you to your system of origin. And you cannot generate it within your rooms."

"We already know that," DuQuesne said dryly. "We were hoping you had an answer to what we *could* do."

Orphan tapped his hands together in a casual gesture that Simon guessed might be something like a nod. "Yes. There are several possibilities. All have some . . . cost associated with them, of course.

"You could trade something with a Powerbroker, naturally. But unless you were quite fortunate, you probably have little or nothing to trade with you."

"What kind of things?" Simon asked. With an AIWish replicator, they could naturally duplicate just about anything, with a pattern.

"The most common things to trade are unique services, unreplicated items of interest, and, of course, people," Orphan answered.

"People?"

"Naturally. You learn so much more about a species that way. Many species, however, are reluctant to sell members of their own group."

Simon raised an eyebrow. "Yes, that grouping would include us."

"You haven't learned enough to provide useful services, I don't think, and unreplicated items you'll have very few of."

"Just out of curiosity," DuQuesne said, "how would they know, and why would they care, whether it was replicated or not?"

"As to how, I cannot say for sure. Some employ Shadeweavers to verify such items; others just seem to know. The why . . . well, for those willing to trade in such things at all, it appears to be a matter of perception. They think there is something more important about, for example, a sculpture done by hand or food grown as it does on its native world, than the identical object created by a replicator."

The collector's mindset; the numinous of the original. "All right, that makes sense," conceded Simon. "And I'm afraid you are correct that we did not bring much along those lines. What else could we do?"

"Well . . ." Orphan hesitated. "I have very limited resources of my own, but I could probably obtain enough energy for you to go home. But . . ." He was clearly torn between conflicting drives.

" . . . But it might be more than you can easily afford, even though we did save your tail—and the rest of you?" DuQuesne finished for him.

A buzzing laugh. "I . . . suppose that would be a good way to put it. But without your assistance, there would have been nothing in any case."

Ariane held up her hand in a cautioning gesture. "If it's going to end up causing you just as much trouble in the long run, I'd rather you not do it. Otherwise we wasted that rescue mission."

"No, no." Orphan seemed to have made up his mind. "Show me your power-cells or coils or whatever you may call them, and I will give you the energy you need."

"I find it hard to believe you carry so much energy on you," Simon said.

That won him another laugh. "Of course not. But I will have to see exactly how your devices are constructed in order to connect mine to yours, or else I shall have to bring yours with me to my own Sphere and then return them after they are filled."

"Makes sense. You'll pardon us requiring you to go through the more complicated process of bringing your storage material here for the transfer, rather than letting you take our storage coils." Ariane said.

"I forgive you the suspicion. It is only rational, an assessment of potential risk and gain perfectly in line with the situations."

"Then," said Ariane, "let's go back and let you take a look—and you can give us some more explanations, with all of us able to listen in."

An abbreviated dip and movement of the arms, clearly echoing the full-bore pushup-like pose Orphan had given earlier. "It would be a great pleasure to move forward so smoothly."

"Then follow me." She led the way; Orphan followed, with Simon and DuQuesne in the rear.

The excitement of the situation was starting to really make itself felt. *First contact,* Simon thought almost dizzily. *We have made first contact with an alien race, on the first voyage of a vessel using my own drive—and we shall soon have the power to return home!*

Things were finally looking up.

Chapter 19

DuQuesne followed a short distance behind the alien, taking care not to tread on the tail. He suspected that Orphan was just as aware of the location of his tail, and how to not let it get stepped on, as DuQuesne was aware of his feet, but no point in taking chances.

As they approached the entrance to the prior section of the station, the one they'd left just moments before first seeing Orphan and the Blessed, he noticed something. The wingcases had tightened slightly, and Orphan's tail seemed to have lifted up just a hair.

"Open door." Ariane said.

In the moment the door began to roll aside, DuQuesne saw Orphan's legs flex slightly, almost unnoticeably. *I may be making a mistake . . . but to hell with it.*

Kicking his combat capabilities into full gear (or as close to full gear as he ever allowed), the massive black-haired engineer lunged forward. In a single motion, he grabbed hold of the alien's tail, just behind the stinger, yanked, and *threw* with every ounce of enhanced strength in his two hundred kilogram frame. At the same time he shouted "Close door and lock!"

Orphan, taken utterly unawares, was slung down the corridor from which they'd come, an almost comical look of shock on the alien face, landing a full eight meters away with a skidding thud that sent a faint vibration through the deck.

"DuQuesne? What the hell—"

"This clown was getting awfully eager, or tense, the closer we got. A *lot* more tense. I think there's something he isn't telling us."

The alien's stance, as he rose, was dramatically transformed. The tail arched up over one shoulder and the creature crouched low, in what was unmistakably a combat stance. It buzzed threateningly. "You *attacked* me, you unshelled monstrosity!"

"You were talking really nice back there before. Am I right? You just couldn't *wait* to get through that door. You were hoping for just the kind of opening we gave you." DuQuesne had his combat knife out. After seeing the Blessed in combat, and seeing that Orphan had been holding his own against them at several-to-one odds, he wasn't under any illusion that he could take out the alien by himself, but he wasn't planning on making it easy. "Let me guess: once you're inside, you can give access directives. It'd be really stupid of the designers, or at least it wouldn't make sense to me, but if that's true, you have every reason to try to get inside someone else's enclosure."

Ariane spoke up from behind him. "Orphan, if you truly feel you owe us anything, you'd better admit it if DuQuesne's right."

The alien hesitated for a moment, then with a clear effort straightened himself and let the tail drop. "Your eyes are sharp and your mind quick. Yet . . . I could not let such an opportunity pass. The calculated risks were acceptable in view of the immense gain."

"Why? What would you get out of being able to poke into our little section of this mausoleum? Like we said, there's no power there, just us and a ship that won't go without the power you claimed to have. Unless that was a lie too."

"A slight exaggeration. I would have to bargain to get the power for your vessel, or at the least have to sacrifice my own vessel's return capability temporarily." The alien's voice was less friendly, somewhat defiant. "It would have been worth it."

"For the second time," DuQuesne said, glaring at Orphan, "*why?*"

Orphan gave one of his short laughs. "Because with such access, I can designate myself the right to travel to your system, or through it."

"You mean . . . if we entered your area, we could authorize ourselves to travel to your system?"

"If I had no additional safeguards, yes. It takes specialized knowledge to arrange such safeguards and prevent a casual authorization." Orphan gave an almost human-like shrug and sat down on the deck, coiling his tail around him. "I am the last of my kind, Ariane Austin. I may be able to gain some new . . . recruits might be the best word . . . but without some spectacular victory to show that despite being the last I am still a force within the Arena, they will be few, desperate, flawed, and likely killed off by the Blessed or any of a number of other Factions before they can learn the strength of their selves."

DuQuesne didn't get all the details yet, though he could make guesses. The main point was clear. "And getting access to a brand new star system filled with, um, First Emergents? That would be a spectacular victory, eh?"

"Oh, very much so, yes," Orphan agreed. "And one that would not have risked my sole and irreplaceable life in the Arena, as a challenge would."

"You don't share a star system with the Blessed?"

Whatever was doing the translating was good; the subtle overtones to Orphan's laugh clearly conveyed bitterness as well as dark amusement. "Oh, I could go there, but death as certainty does not appeal. We—the Mind-killers, as they like to call us—gained our own system years ago, but that cost us in the Challenge, and the Blessed have reduced our numbers since. Reduced them, as you see, to one."

DuQuesne saw Captain Austin frowning. "The problem is that after this, I'm not sure how much we can trust you, Orphan," she said finally. "Do you actually feel any obligation to us, or are you just looking for your own opportunity? Perhaps you are a simple criminal from the Blessed and I've made the mistake of intervening in an arrest."

"I regret to say that I can offer you no confidence at this time," Orphan replied. "Indeed I feel gratitude, which was I admit overcome by this opportunity. And despite Dr. DuQuesne's rather forceful manner of preventing my little triumph, I still owe you my life. So . . . I cannot enter your domain, not until we know and trust one another far better. And while I do have safegards, inviting you into my Sphere might not be wise either—for your sake and mine." He stood in a single smooth move like a rising motorized scaffold. "I therefore can only offer my services as a guide to the Arena, as an advisor in its customs. You shall need one, I assure you, for my little impulse was but a forthright and honest action compared to the intrigues you may find entwining you once you enter the Arena proper. First is forgiven, Second should be, Third may be; you have used your First already. Second and Third are not much protection."

"First, Second, and Third what?" Ariane asked.

"Transgression, is my guess." DuQuesne said, having been thinking about that ever since he first heard Orphan use it in conversation with Sethrik. "Newcomers get one free screw-up, and as a general rule people are encouraged to let 'em get away with a second. Really generous people can forgive you a third. But after that, you mess up, you've got nothing to save you."

Orphan gave that assenting handtap. "Precisely correct, Dr. Marc DuQuesne."

Ariane glanced at DuQuesne and Simon. "Well, Orphan, I think we need to go back and talk with our other people before we decide what to do. How will we be able to find you again?"

Orphan shifted, wingcases tightening. "Ah, yes. As to that . . . I shall simply wait here."

"It might be a while."

"I can wait for some time." Orphan hunched the wingcases tighter, then dropped them open in what was clearly a sigh. "I . . . must confess one more thing."

DuQuesne glared at him. "Out with it."

"Well . . . the Blessed will likely be waiting for me in Nexus Arena, watching for me to attempt to return home. If I am alone that would be very dangerous. If I am with you, their concession of your victory will prevent them from acting against either of us, at least for some time yet."

Simon laughed. "I see. So right now, acting as our tour guide is also going to keep you alive."

"Er . . . yes."

"Then," Ariane said, "You'd better hope my crew decides to give you that much of a chance. Otherwise you're going to have to take your chances with the Blessed." She turned back to the door. "Orphan, stay *way* back from this door. When we come back out, you'd better not try anything." DuQuesne rather approved of the almost predatory grin she gave the alien. "Because before I open that door, I will have specifically instructed it to close *on* anyone trying to get in."

DuQuesne grinned to himself as he followed Ariane and Simon through the door. *So aliens can shudder.*

Chapter 20

"I think I know where we are," Steve said.

Everyone looked at him with surprise. *The assertion was startling enough*, DuQuesne thought, *but what really grabbed* me *was the grim tone. Steve just doesn't do grim.* Until now, the discussion had been simple, a fairly straightforward account of what had happened to them, from the time the left through their meeting with the Blessed and Orphan, and finally their return, leaving Orphan outside.

"What?" Carl said finally, clearly speaking for the rest. "I'm not sure I follow you. What do you mean, you know *where* we are?"

The curly-haired design specialist's expression wasn't comforting. DuQuesne could see Gabrielle's professional concern at the twisted smile, cynical and certain and somehow with a shadow of despair, all at once, and DuQuesne realized that—nanomedical assistance or no—many of the crew of *Holy Grail* still were riding a very narrow razor-edge of sanity.

"I'm surprised none of the rest of you get it. Think about it. We get on board and activate this super-duper faster than light drive, and then what happens? Poof! We're inside this giant . . . orrery, isn't that what they called them? And all our AIs are offline, even though there's no way for that to happen."

"We all know what happened, Steve." Ariane said.

"Don't interrupt me . . . Captain. Let me lay it all out my way, then you'll all see. What was I saying? . . . Oh. So our AISages and all the others are offline and can't be restarted." He nodded at DuQuesne. "And then nuclear physics—and *only* the nuclear physics—decides to take a holiday, too, sticking us here. So we need a way out, some clue as to where to go. And when we start looking, why, surprise, suddenly there's somewhere to go that wasn't there before."

Gooseflesh suddenly gave DuQuesne a creeping sensation, something he hadn't felt outside of the still-recurring nightmares in . . . fifty years? He thought he knew where Steve was going now, and he fought to keep his face impassive.

"So we go there, and isn't it funny that it's made of some impossible super-material that we can't scan? Then when we go deeper, we meet some aliens, except they're maybe not quite all that alien, and we can talk to them." The diminuitive Franceschetti glared around at them challengingly. "Well? Don't you get it now?"

DuQuesne couldn't bring himself to speak. A part of him, the detached, calm part the world usually saw, studied his own reactions with clinical amazement. *I thought I'd purged it all. I thought Hyperion was over.*

'It was Ariane who spoke, but the slowly-paling faces showed that the others were starting to realize what Steve was saying. "You're . . . you're trying to say that none of this is real."

"It's obvious, isn't it? Physics doesn't take a vacation. And nothing can just change physical law like that—our resident experts," he jerked his head in the direction of DuQuesne and Sandrisson, "agree on that. That super-material, it's just the defined walls that keep us from going where the plotline isn't ready. A kinda clumsy approach, but I guess they were kinda in a hurry."

The discussion raged around DuQuesne, and for the first time in decades, he found he could barely follow what people were saying. It was the *tones* that mattered, the emotions and the denial and the fear. *Could it be true? Could it have happened to me* again?

"*No!*"

As shocked silence fell, DuQuesne realized that he'd spoken—no, *shouted*—aloud. He glanced down for a moment, saw his reflection in the surface of one of the tables they'd set up—a distorted, pale reflection, eyes staring and haunted. *I've got to get a grip on myself.*

"DuQuesne?" Ariane's voice was strained as well. The pilot-turned-commander was blaming herself for every-thing so far; obviously she was going to somehow try to blame herself for this current crisis as well.

He closed his eyes, swallowed, opened his eyes again, and fixed his gaze on Steve; he realized how angry he must look when the smaller man took an involuntary step back. "Sorry." He tried to relax his features, but they seemed set in stone. "You think our AIs did this. Put us in some kind of artificial adventure world for some reason. Maybe the Frankenstein fear come to life, maybe to pro-tect us, who knows. Right?"

"Our AIs, or others that invaded our machines. Maybe even before we got on board *Grail*," Steve agreed. The slight lunatic edge of his voice had faded; the others taking him seriously, and—maybe—the momentary fear of DuQuesne had apparently shocked him back on track, at least temporarily. DuQuesne's analytical side approved of the result, and noted that Gabrielle had her medical nano control in hand; possibly some subtle drugging was going on.

"Well, you're wrong." DuQuesne said bluntly. *You have to be wrong*.

Even Ariane gave him a sideways glance. "Um, Marc . . . look, I know it's a pretty unpleasant thought—absolutely creepy, actually—but the way Steve puts it . . . it's the only thing that makes any *sense* of this setup."

DuQuesne shook his head. *Scenario . . . Deployment . . . Balanced Stimuli . . . Adjustment . . . Denouement. No, dammit, it's not that way anymore!* "It's not the *only* thing that makes sense. It is, I will grant, the *easiest* way to make sense of things, but it's not the only way. Steve's also said some things that aren't quite accurate. There *are* theoretical levels of technology that would permit exactly this sort of thing. Depending on who's making the terms, they're various levels of smaller-scale technology; some call it femtotechnology down through attotechnology, by comparison with our nanotech, others have called it Plancktech. Basically, if one gets down to the scale of things below atoms, below subatomic particles, you start manipulating spacetime in the same manner that we currently manipulate atoms. And if you can change spacetime, you can literally manipulate the laws of physics."

Steve's answer was a short, nervous laugh. "Oh, yeah, that's a good answer. Do you notice that Ockham's Razor is about to cut you off at the knees?"

"All the Razor says is that you shouldn't go around creating unnecessarily complex theories," DuQuesne snapped, still shaking inwardly. *But I'm right.* "In this case, I'm looking at reality and explaining it; you're trying to deny the entirety of reality around you."

"What?" Steve's outraged expression almost comical. "That's . . . that's just assuming your conclusion, then making me sound like *I'm* the one not doing the thinking!"

"You're thinking, but you're not on the right track." He felt his equilibrium coming back, slowly. The analysis in the background continued. "First of all, an assumption like yours leads in the end to a tautological trap. It's the old elephant hunter joke, where a guy asserts he's the local elephant hunter, you respond that there *aren't* any elephants around there, and he, of course, says 'Yeah, see how good I am?' No matter what argument someone makes, you can counter it with assuming either a better virtual reality, or a more direct edit of your perceptions. So it's *useless* to think that way, unless you actually start to notice . . . well, a glitch, an inconsistency, a failure that would permit you to actually possibly break the delusion. And even then you have to assume that the hypothetical minds running the artificial scam on you would *let* you notice.

"So the only *reasonable* approach is to assume that what we're encountering is real. If we come across something that manages to *both* indicate that it might not be real, *and* that there might be some way we can prove it or escape from the delusion, fine, then we can act on it.

But without that, we'd just be locking ourselves into a mental trap—maybe some of us would try to 'prove' it by getting killed and hoping they'd wake up, I don't know. But it's pointless.

"Second, I *know* this is real."

"Assertion without evidence," Carl said bluntly. "*How* do you know?"

He gave Carl his nastiest grin. "Because, as you know, I'm a Hyperion."

"What the hell has that got to do with it?" demanded Steve.

DuQuesne had known that was coming. *How can I tell them? What it was like? How they tailored the challenge, the encounters, the friends and rivals and enemies and allies? How they used the finest AIs and best scientists they could buy? How we lived in the best of all possible worlds, the worst of all possible prisons, at the same time? How they knew their true successes were the ones who couldn't be kept there . . . and yet were so incredibly stupid and blind that they didn't realize what some of those 'successes' would do once they got out?*

Gabrielle Wolfe spoke up. "You all don't know, do you?"

She does, He realized. *She really does understand. I can hear it.*

"Details on some parts of Hyperion aren't really public knowledge," Gabrielle went on. "Sometimes . . . hell, most times . . . there's just a sort of comic tragedy to it, like some kind of warning parable for our times. What with replicators, sunpower, fusion, and all, even small groups can do things a lot of governments couldn't, back in the day. So an . . . interest group, obsessive fans, game designers, and utopians get together and try to create the ultimate colony, filled with supermen and superwomen, designed based on figures in stories, movies, myths. They get the best designs from genetic research, figure out the best way to raise their supermen to be what they wanted them to be from the latest psych research, and then go ahead and build it—high-G to take advantage of improved musculoskeletal development, of course. And then, when their superboys and girls get old enough, some of them believe their press, and things get ugly, and Hyperion ends up shut down—and a whole lot of people on both sides dead. But after fifty years, the ugly's faded."

She glanced sympathetically at DuQuesne. "I worked with—under—Saul Maginot. Studied some of the after-action files."

He managed a small smile, though it was surprisingly difficult. Even now, pity was something that hurt. "I see. Look, I don't think we need the details. Here's the point, Steve, Carl. They raised us that way—the interior of Hyperion was one gigantic virtual environment, a cylinder of lies half a mile across and ten long. They had AIs running the sims, with the best psychs in the loop, to make sure our lives went *just* the right way—always just the *perfect* level of rivalry to push us, and each of us at our own ideal level, all of us designed to be someone one of the participants had thought of. Sherlock Holmes. Clark Savage." He gave a twisted smile. "Marc C. DuQuesne."

"Most people, even the best—and believe me, even the stupidest of the kids in there was smart as hell—never realized the scam. You *can't* out-think a really large-scale AI, or catch it out in a lie, especially with a couple humans in the loop. Tech's advanced some since then, but these AIs were built into the entire station; they were *huge*. Speed-of-light lag was their biggest issue.

"But . . . a few of us *did* see through it. Subconscious analysis? Perceiving some kind of inconsistency that even the AIs couldn't figure out? Noticing, somewhere inside us, that everything was just *too much*? I don't know, but somehow we did. And we started gaming the system, from the inside, until *we* were the ones controlling *their* lives, and all of Hyperion Station. In the end, they realized it, but too late. Some of us just wanted out, others . . . " He swallowed, pushing back the pain, guilt and, yes, fear. "Anyway . . . I would *know*. To fool me on that, you'd need a lot more than we've got. Either way, you're not dealing with something *we* built. Given that, I say we treat this as real."

There was silence for several minutes. Then Steve let out his breath with a *whoosh* and sat down. "Okay, I'll go for that. I don't think I liked my idea much anyway."

"Believe you me, my friend," DuQuesne said, "I liked it even less."

"All right, people," Ariane said briskly, "I think this little side-track has seriously thrown off our concentration on the matter at hand, and I think it's upset more than a few of us. So why don't we have some dinner . . . or is it lunch? . . . and after that we'll get back to the real questions."

Watching how readily the others agreed—and how relieved he felt, just hearing the matter-of-fact statements—DuQuesne realized that they might have been even luckier than they knew. *She's actually commanding, and she doesn't even know it. Which is probably the best way for it to be.*

Chapter 21

"My question," Gabrielle said finally, "is what the hell you were thinking, getting involved in that mess to begin with."

Ariane tried to maintain a calm, reasonable look, but the heat in her cheeks told her that the embarrassment must be clearly visible. "To tell the truth, Gabrielle . . . I haven't the faintest idea. I was actually asking myself the same question at the same time I stepped out and got their attention."

"And," the deep voice of DuQuesne put in, "from your body language, I think the same thing happened when you triggered the attack, after Sethrik had dismissed us as a threat. Am I right?"

"Yes."

"But," Carl put in, slowly, "it's not *entirely* out of character for you, Ariane. Captain, I mean."

"How do you mean?" she said, defensively. "I wouldn't ever do anything that stupid!"

Carl grinned. "Oh, come *on*. Who started that bar brawl in Nuevo Aires because she couldn't let that amazon fanplayer push herself on some poor tourist? Who was the one who missed a qualifier because she just *had* to stick her nose into the wrong alley and ended up having to testify at a realporn trial in Moscow? And then there was—"

"All right, *all right*, you've made your point, I sometimes get myself in over my head, but really, Carl, Steve, you can't think I haven't got a little idea that things are different here? Gabrielle, help me out here!"

"No, you're right on that. You've settled into this captain role right nice, Arrie," the gold-haired medic said with a smile.

"So the impulse is in character, it's just that she shouldn't have acted on it," DuQuesne summarized. "And Orphan said something . . . 'perhaps I also owe a debt there, as well' . . . while looking where that thing they called a Shadeweaver had been."

Momentary nausea washed over her. "You think that thing somehow . . . *controlled* me?"

"Not *controlled* exactly," DuQuesne said, gazing speculatively into thin air as he spoke, "but . . . affected you. Perhaps suppressed your inhibitions just a tiny bit, causing you to act a little more on instinct. A number of drugs and other things can cause that. Of course, they can't do that so indirectly and accurately on an alien species, I wouldn't think, which makes the possibility rather more impressive and disturbing. But then, there's an awful lot that's disturbing about this place."

Gabrielle pursed her lips. "I wonder if these 'Shadeweavers' are maybe the people in charge here."

"Might be," Ariane said thoughtfully. "Sethrik and his pals sure seemed about to wipe us out until they saw the Shadeweaver was there, and then they bugged out."

"It's not much to go on, but I doubt it." Simon stood and stretched. "If I assume—as seems fairly likely—that the translations we are getting are as accurate as they appear to be, then the actual reaction Sethrik showed did not sound to me like the reaction of someone to a boss or completely overwhelming force, but more the reaction of someone to a dangerously unknown quantity. It's just a gut feeling," he said with an apologetic grin, "but that's the way it seemed to me."

"I'd agree," DuQuesne said.

Ariane was glad to see that he was—at least outwardly—fully recovered from his traumatic trip down memory lane. Until she'd noticed the dark face go pale, seen the haunted look in his eyes and heard the pain in his voice, Ariane simply hadn't realized how very much she'd come to rely on the imperturbable and calmly confident DuQuesne as a sort of bedrock, a backstop of sanity in case she totally screwed up. *It's only been a couple of weeks, but in some ways I'm closer to these people than I've been to anyone. Amazing what desperate circumstances do to you.*

"In any case, it's not critical to answer right now. The question is what we do next."

Tom Cussler looked up from the AIWish, where he'd been fiddling with some food templates. "Captain, I really don't think we've any choices. The empty, mostly-dead part of this installation seems to go on for a large portion of the sphere, or maybe the whole sphere. We could spend a lifetime exploring it and still not find a source of power, even if there were a thousand open and available energy outlets. The interior area of just the tiny layer we're in is greater than that of every body we've colonized put together, including Earth.

"And this alien you've met has indicated there're power resources to be had. He may be opportunistic, but I think self-interest is a good basis for at least a temporary relationship. Even though we've moved off the ship and, it seems, can at least save ourselves the energy of basic environmental maintenance, we've still got a limited time before we start running out of energy. A few months, half a year . . . once the AIWish runs out, we're dead if we have no allies, or no way out."

"We could explore the rest of this next area first," Simon pointed out. "It had active lighting. Possibly energy sources, or another route to somewhere useful."

"Doubt it," DuQuesne said. "I think Orphan's being honest most of the time, and there'd be no real reason for these 'Powerbrokers' he mentioned if people had high-level energy sources available elsewhere. Sure, we *could* be an exception . . . but I wouldn't want to bet on it, or take months exploring to rule it out."

Ariane glanced around and saw no disagreeing faces. "So we have to go. While I know the arguments against, I think it should be Dr. DuQuesne, Dr. Sandrisson, and myself again."

"Actually," Carl said, "I'd agree. You've already made contact, Orphan respects you, and in this case the less they know about exactly how many of us there are, and what the rest of us can do, the better off we are. An unknown reserve will give some people more pause than a known one."

DuQuesne nodded approvingly. "I'd say you're right. What you people might do, though—if the Captain agrees—is fabricate a bunch of solar panels. The next area seems pretty constantly lit, and if we cover a large part of a couple of the big rooms with panels . . . well, we'll never recharge the main coils with it, but we might get enough power to keep us going a lot longer. I don't like the idea of relying on outsiders just for survival."

"Good idea," Ariane said. "Like they say, 'make it so.' " She thought for a moment. "We have no way of knowing exactly how long we'll be gone, either—it may be a long trip, or we may have a lot of talking to do. So . . . everyone, help us make sure we take what we need with us. I have to assume Orphan won't take us somewhere we can't breathe, at least for too long, so our suits should be fine there, but we'll need to bring food, at least. A water purifier? Something to condense water from the air, maybe? I sure don't want to carry days worth of water. Weapons, definitely."

DuQuesne nodded. "But we're getting ahead of ourselves here, Captain. The first thing to do, before we go *anywhere* with our ally of convenience is to grill the hell out of him." He frowned, black eyebrows furrowing over onyx eyes. "*Arena*; the name alone is a flare-lit tipoff, given how very very accurate the rest of the translations seem to be. Just the side comments he's given, the assumptions made by Sethrik, that damn Shadeweaver character—there's about a billion things we don't know, and any one of them can get us killed."

"But we can't take all *that* long," Carl pointed out. "Orphan may be tough and all—your description sure seems to imply it—but he's got to eat and drink like anyone else, I'd bet, which means he can't take days and days waiting. Or probably can't, anyway."

Ariane frowned. "You're right. We never even asked him that. I'm starting to feel like a real idiot, you know."

"Don't be too hard on yourself," said Sandrisson. "We've all spent the last few weeks at the edge of shock, and that completely unexpected encounter was bound to throw off any reasonable train of thought."

"So we go out and have a long chat with Orphan about just where we are, what's going on here, the pitfalls, the advantages, the people—everything we need to know to survive long enough to get home," Ariane summarized. "But first we find out how long he can wait."

"Indeed," the physicist concurred. "It appears his biology is very similar to ours in some respects, but there's no telling what may be different."

"Something else you'd better be aware of, Captain," Tom Cussler put in. "As you requested, Steve and I went over your network data records following your encounter, and something very disturbing cropped up. Something killed off all your remote nanos in that outer area; they didn't spread, stopped working. We have nothing on your aliens except direct sensor reads from whatever you carried on you."

"But our internal nanotech is functioning fine?" At Tom's nod, she went on, "And the nanos we released here, in this old alien installation . . . ?"

Steve nodded. "Yep, still functioning just fine. Makes no more sense than anything else, but I'm sure there's some answer."

Ariane sighed. *This place seems to be a determinedly perverse mixture of ludicrously helpful and impossibly obstructive.* "Well, given all this, I think we've wasted enough time. The same logic of who goes still applies. Let's take a couple days' supplies and go out to question our alien friend."

As the others nodded and started assembling the food, water, and other essentials, she found herself already staring at the closed door, on the other side of which—perhaps only meters away—waited Orphan. *Maybe we'll finally get to the point of getting answers faster than new questions.*

Chapter 22

The tall, green and black form of Orphan stood smoothly as the door opened, the clean, sharp lines of his coloration giving an almost formal air to his appearance, emphasized by the clockwork precision of his movements. The alien stood a good thirty meters from the doorway, clearly taking no chances on being thought of as a threat. "Ariane. Dr. Sandrisson. Dr. DuQuesne. I greet you again, and hope that we are in fact to work together." An uneven ripple of the wingcases. "I trust you understand boredom as I do."

Ariane smiled. Trustworthy or not, Orphan had a sense of humor and—in translation, at least—of style that she found appealing. "So sitting in the corridor waiting was not to your taste?"

"No, I am afraid not. I did take some time to explore your outer area—in part to locate disposal areas for

wastes, if you understand my meaning. I have found one
of your Outer Gateways, though it is, of course, useless
at the moment."

And already I've got another question. "Well, the fact
that I don't understand that pretty much brings us to the
purpose of this meeting."

Orphan's head moved slightly back and forth, like a
bird surveying an unknown object. "Purpose? I had
thought you would wish me to bring you to Nexus Arena,
for I cannot leave safely without your cooperation, and
you would be unwise to enter without a guide."

"We'd be even *more* unwise to enter without knowing
a hell of a lot more than you've told us, Orphan."
DuQuesne surveyed the alien narrowly, arms folded.
"You've been part of this . . . Arena for a long time, I'd
guess, and you can tell us the answers to a lot of questions." He paused. "Unless there's some reason you *need*
to keep us completely in the dark before you drag us
into this 'Nexus Arena' place."

Orphan's wingcases scissored back and forth several
times, left-right-left-right like a pendulum; the face,
being somewhat flexible but still more chitin-like than
fleshy, showed less expression than his body language.
Suddenly he gave vent to the buzzing sound that was
immediately translated as a hearty laugh. "A reason? Yes,
but—I must confess—one purely personal, and perhaps
one that you would not understand; it may seem trivial
or nonsensical to you."

"Try me," DuQuesne responded.

Orphan seemed to understand immediately what was
meant by that fairly opaque phrase. *Either the translation's even better than I imagined,* Ariane thought, *or
Orphan's awfully good at guessing.* "Very well," the alien

said, hands giving that assenting tap, "I was looking forward to observing your reactions to each successive discovery and encounter; in all my lifetime I have seen no First Emergents, and likely never will again, and to see their first comprehension . . . do I make any sense to you at all?"

"Orphan," said Simon in appreciative tones, "what you say makes perfect sense to us, and by it I think we now know you are more like us than we suspected."

"You wanted to watch our faces—or body language—when we hit every revelation, because you'd vicariously experience the sense of wonder with us—and, maybe, because you'd have a completely irrational, but perfectly real, sense of pride over the Arena and its wonders." Ariane laughed and shook her head. "Meaning absolutely no offense—indeed, intending this as a compliment—Orphan, that is an entirely *human* reaction."

Orphan responded with that bow-like motion of respect. "Then as a compliment I shall take it. It pleases me that we have such perceptions in common, for perhaps that will allow us to work together more smoothly." He surveyed them, taking in the bags and equipment they carried. "So, I will have to forego that . . . dramatic pleasure, but perhaps I shall have a similar one in revealing all to you in a single discussion. Since you still would not wish to invite me in, and subject me to temptation once more, shall we move a bit farther along to one of the living areas?"

It didn't take long to get to the oval room with the strange support structures; DuQuesne and Simon set up a table Tom had fabricated to fit between two of the supports, while Ariane unfolded some chairs. Orphan spun one of them so the back faced the humans, and sat in it, leaning on the back with his arms. "My tail and wingcases are not accomodated by your sitting arrangement," he said apologetically. "But it is superior to the floor, which has been my only choice until now."

"Glad it's at least of some use," Ariane said. "Orphan, the first question actually is about you." She glanced over the alien, noting the nearly camouflaged pouches and belts that were the only equivalent of clothing Orphan seemed to wear. "You obviously can't be carrying too much on you in the way of food or water. Our time limit, obviously, is how long you can wait before you go back to some location you can get food. Water we can supply, of course."

"It is even possible, Captain Austin, that you will be able to supply food eventually," Orphan said. "Once we can establish methods to communicate replication patterns for food, and so on. But indeed my supplies are limited, and it has already been some time. I would appreciate very much some water now, in fact." DuQuesne passed him a canteen; Orphan opened it, seemed to sniff at it, then extended a tubelike organ—tongue? and drained the entire container in moments. "Excellent. You appear to prefer fewer dissolved minerals than we do, but that was quite adequate. You filtered out microorganisms as well, of course."

"Naturally," Simon responded. "While it would seem very unlikely that you could catch one of our diseases, there are bacteria which have a rather wide spectrum. Of course, that doesn't eliminate the potential risk from our current contact."

The wingcases snapped open and shut. "Such risks are not great. Though not zero, either. Many lifeforms are far more close in their biology than original speculation indicated—to the point that we can share both diseases and foodstuffs with various other species. This has, as one might imagine, been a source of glorious argument for the biologists of a thousand species." Orphan stretched and sat down again; Ariane wasn't sure, but his face seemed just a touch more rounded and glossy than it had been. "Ah, I feel much refreshed. To return to your question, then . . . I would feel uncomfortable about spending more than another day here. I did not flee with anything but a few travelbars, which are not very adequate nourishment."

"Then we'd better not waste much time," Ariane said. "Orphan, tell us about the Arena."

Chapter 23

DuQuesne studied Orphan as he hesitated. Despite the alien biology, the body language wasn't all that hard to interpret. *Not surprising, really; much of it's going to have derived from social and instinctive reactions which are pretty fundamental. That bow is a sort of submissive posture, possibly rank or dominance derived. Now he's unsure how to start and he's shifting back and forth—like someone trying to choose from different routes, or trying to find a way out of a small box.*

"Such a simple question with so large a set of answers, Captain Austin," Orphan said finally. "How to begin? I am not being evasive, I assure you; I simply am at something of a loss as to the proper starting point." He looked around at them. "You know how you came here. Perhaps the best starting point is to realize that all species come here in the precise same manner."

DuQuesne glanced at Ariane, then at Sandrisson. The reaction in Ariane's eyes was surprise and curiosity. Sandrisson's much more closely parallelled his own dis-belief. "*All?*"

"Well, all those of which we currently know. Except, of course, whoever or whatever created the Arena in the first place."

"How many species are there in the Arena?" Ariane asked.

"None can be entirely sure, Captain Austin, but roughly five thousand separate species are known to have at least one Sphere."

"A Sphere . . . that's where we are right now, correct?" Ariane said. "And each race has at least one of these? *Five thousand*—maybe two, three times that many—Spheres, twenty thousand kilometers across?"

Even before Orphan answered, DuQuesne shook his head. *Not even close. Impossible, remember. Everything here is impossible.*

"I said *all* species, Captain Austin," Orphan said. "Those that are, and have been, and will be."

Now he saw her start to grasp the implications. "So anyone in the galaxy who activates an FTL drive ends up inside their own sphere."

Orphan flicked his hands out, a gesture of negation. "No. Not in the galaxy.

"In the *universe*."

Even DuQuesne found himself staring at Orphan, who seemed to be still searching for the right words. Finally the alien spoke, gesturing as though to encompass all things.

"Step outside on your homeworld and look up. See, my friends, the thousands of stars that must blaze in your skies as they do in mine. See the dots of light that are galaxies, so far away that the racing rays of light they emit are old, old by the time they reach the eye. Try, if you can, to grasp these things, hold them all in your mind.

"Then imagine . . . imagine that you *could* hold it all in your mind, that you could see all things, all places, at the same time, that to you the riddle of time and space was as trivial a puzzle as opening a box in your hand, that you could open that box and see every star, every planet, as a master artisan might look upon it. An artisan who wished to create a replica, the greatest work of art praising Creation that ever has been . . . " Orphan paused a moment. "For every star, a Sphere. Within each Sphere, a faithful duplicate of its attendant planets and their moons; and the Spheres themselves, collected as are their originals in great gathering, a hundred billion Spherepools filled with a hundred billion Spheres, and all, all following with infinite precision the same cosmic dance as their counterparts."

For a moment, DuQuesne saw in his mind's eye what Orphan was describing, and it was enough to stagger even his imagination. He glanced at Sandrisson, who seemed half-fascinated, half-terrified at the thought. The physicist clearly grasped something of the scale and implications, far more than the awed Ariane. "You . . . can't be serious. You are saying that . . . that the entire realm of Kanzaki-Locke-Sandrisson space is filled with these constructs?"

"You still do not understand, Dr. DuQuesne." Even Orphan seemed subdued, as though simply thinking clearly and in detail about the truth weighed upon him. "It is not even that . . . small a construct, if you will permit me such an outrageous statement. As near as the scientists of all races have been able to determine, this 'space' *is* a construct—or at least, all of it that can be reached is enclosed *within* a construct. The Arena is a single construct, a volume many light-years across, which itself contains a duplicate of every galaxy, a Sphere for every star, in all the cosmos from which we come."

Ariane seemed to shake off the mood; perhaps her mind didn't handle the scale to the point that it could overawe her. "Who made all of it, though . . . and *why?*"

Orphan managed another, if weaker, laugh. "Ah, Captain Austin, the second question is perhaps the greatest of the mysteries . . . well, aside from the obvious *how*. Perhaps my little conceit of an artist, a model-maker who made a perfect model, is accurate—though it fails to explain other details of the Arena. Others believe it is a deliberately designed method to restrict us—imprison, some say, while others attribute a more benevolent motive to the Voidbuilders. The Faith, of course, have a far different interpretation of the situation."

With a great effort, DuQuesne forced himself to stop trying to comprehend the entirety of the Arena and the implications behind it. "Right. I hope we've given you some satisfaction in our reactions, Orphan, because I can honestly tell you I've never been so completely knocked for a loop by anything in my entire life." *In some ways, not even by the discovery of what a lie my life had been on Hyperion. A part of me had been guessing that for years. This . . . is completely out of the blue.* "But I think we'd better back off from the big cosmic questions and start to get down to the serious business, the details of our situation, and what we need to know to keep ourselves alive."

Sandrisson shook himself, blinked, and gave an involuntary shudder. "Yes . . . yes, I think I'd much prefer that, at least for now. I'm not sure but what this will give me a few nightmares."

Ariane looked at the two of them, clearly puzzled. "What am I missing here?"

"Captain . . . Ariane," DuQuesne said, feeling a sudden and unexpected grin appear, "believe me when I tell you I'm glad you *are* missing it. You need to keep focus on the situation, not worry about a picture so big that we're just a minor detail in one corner." *And it's not that she's stupid and we're smart. Sure, Sandrisson and I are probably brighter than she is, but she's got something we don't, and I'm not even sure what the word would be for it.*

Orphan bob-bowed from his chair. "I agree with Dr. DuQuesne, and I find that I have, also, contemplated more of the infinite than I care to. So . . . details.

"First, your Sphere. I have mentioned the Inner Gateway and Outer Gateway. The Inner leads to Nexus Arena, what one might call the heart of the Arena. To Nexus Arena all species travel eventually, and there are almost all Challenges given, accepted, and performed.

"The Outer Gateway, or—more likely—Gateways, lead to the top of your Sphere, to its exterior."

"And what's up there?" Ariane asked.

Orphan gave a wing-shrug. "In detail, one cannot say until the Gateway is opened and you take a look. In more broad terms, living space. The Arena insures that the top of the Sphere is reasonably habitable by the native intelligent species."

"Hang on," Sandrisson said, "Are you saying that outside the Sphere there is breathable air? Even though the interior of the Sphere, where *Holy Grail* entered, is vacuum?"

"Indeed I am, Dr. Sandrisson," confirmed the alien. "The 'breathable' part is, of course, not guaranteed once you leave the immediate region of your Sphere."

DuQuesne very carefully avoided trying to visualize those implications; time enough for that later. "And, to return to an earlier conversation, why—if there's breathable air, water, and so on up there—would the Outer Gateway be useless to us now?"

"Because the Outer Gateways will not open until at least some of the native race have used the Inner Gateway . . . and returned."

This place has a lot of rules . . . and we'd better get familiar with them. "So we couldn't force the door, or hack the controls?"

Another wing-shrug. "Many have tried; I have never heard of any group succeeding. Of course, most would end up exploring the Inner Gateway eventually, especially once the Outer balked them, so I would doubt that many have spent inordinate amounts of time on it. Perhaps it is possible, but why concern oneself with it?"

DuQuesne snorted. "Maybe because we just don't like someone else determining what we can and cannot do. Maybe we don't want to join this little community."

Orphan gave the bow-like gesture. "Truly there do we have similar thoughts, Dr. DuQuesne. That is in fact the very foundation of the Liberated—that we direct ourselves and our own choices, and follow not the directives of other overseers, no matter how great their Minds may be."

"The 'Liberated'?" Simon repeated.

An assenting handtap. "My faction, you might say—of which I am, both unfortunately and fortunately, currently the sole surviving member."

Ariane grimaced. "I see. So the Spheres are set up to basically force everyone to meet at this Nexus Arena."

"Indeed." Orphan's body tightened and relaxed. "I now begin to comprehend your difficulties, my friends. Many apologies; when one has lived one's entire life aware of the Arena, of its dangers and opportunities and rules, and has never before encountered any who have not . . . well, it is now somewhat sobering to realize how very much you do not understand." Orphan's hands stroked the edges of his head-crest in a gesture that somehow brought to mind the semi-conscious motion of someone drumming his fingers, or rubbing his chin in thought. After a moment, his hands dropped and he gave a brisk wing-snap. "We have limited time indeed, and I had best try to choose the most useful material to tell you. Thinking about it, I believe that will be to summarize the most important factions and the immediate steps you will have to take if you are to become accepted residents of the Arena—which you must, if you wish to return home in any reasonable time."

DuQuesne considered Orphan. He still thought the alien was willing to use them for its personal gain if the chance presented itself, but he was now much more convinced that Orphan did feel both a considerable obligation and something of a kinship with them. He caught Ariane's eye and nodded.

"All right, Orphan," she said briskly, "we'll have to leave it to your judgment. We've only got a few hours; tell us what we need to know."

DuQuesne made sure his internal data recorders were fully on. *I'd better not miss anything he says, because if I do . . . there might be no one left to complain about my sloppy procedure.*

Chapter 24

Another door rolled open before Orphan—Ariane thought this made six since they'd left the area where they'd first met Orphan, going in the direction that Sethrik and his gang of Blessed had gone. This time, however, instead of just continuing onward—perhaps with another of his travelogue-like comments on the structure and layout of their Sphere, the green-and-black alien stepped in and then aside, as though pulling open a curtain. "The Inner Gateway, my friends."

The room into which they entered was very large, even bigger than the oval rooms; it was essentially circular, over two hundred meters in diameter and nearly one hundred high at the center. Concentric low walls, interrupted in the center, emanated outward like ripples from the center of the far wall, with support structure pillars spaced between the low walls. And at the center of the far wall was something that could only be the Inner Gateway.

Ariane felt a chill go down her back. Even at this distance the Inner Gateway was awe-inspiring, a whirling funnel of light-destroying black, twenty meters across, with occasional pearlescent fragments of light flickering in its depths. "That's . . . a *Gateway*?"

Orphan's hands tapped together. "Of course. You did not expect a door like these others, did you?"

DuQuesne eyed the whirling ebony vortex analytically. "Perhaps not exactly, but I think we were expecting something less bizarre. Why, I'm not sure, it's not as though this entire trip hasn't been bizarre. So we step into that and end up at this Nexus Arena?"

"Even so. You will note the size and arrangement of this room, permitting the residents—yourselves, in this case—to construct appropriate structures to secure the area, limit traffic, and so on."

"No way to just turn it off?"

Orphan flicked his hands outward, a gesture of negation. "None. Although only those with the proper code, or random chance, will be able to arrive here." He advanced to stand before the Gateway.

Remembering their brief discussion of that aspect of travel and security, Ariane said, "And those codes are only directly available to us, right?"

"It is even so. Once I leave, I will be unable to return—barring a recurrence of the same fortuitous random chance that brought me there in the first place—unless you grant me access."

The maelstrom of night drew the eye and held it. Ariane tore her gaze away with great difficulty as DuQuesne said, "Well, how do we use this thing?"

A buzzing chuckle greeted his question. "That, my friend, is one of the easiest questions to answer." Orphan turned and strode without a moment's hesitation through the Inner Gateway. As he touched the swirling nothingness, it suddenly enveloped him in a gentle blaze of iridescent cold flame that just as abruptly disappeared . . . and he was gone.

The humans stared for a moment. Then DuQuesne shrugged. "Well, I don't see him as the suicidal type," he said, and stepped through.

Sandrisson approached the Gateway, staring. "Some form of . . . dimensional interface? Tesseract?" He reached out, touching the very surface . . . and disappeared in a blaze of subtle pearlescence.

Alone in the cavernous room, Ariane grinned. *Diving into a dimensional whirlpool so I can go somewhere I've never been! And my mom thought racing was dangerous!*

She backed up and took a running leap into the whirling heart of the Gateway.

There was a moment of abyssal cold, mixed with hair-raising electrical tingles and the scent of ozone, while dark-glowing streamers of impossible shapes whipped by her in a vortex her wide-open eyes could not translate and her mind could not fathom, touching nothing yet compressed on all sides as though in a vise. Then she burst through into brilliant golden light.

Her foot touched down on smooth stone or metal, skidding slightly as she realized her forward speed was undiminished, and she tried to slow down as something massive and dark—DuQuesne, she sensed—loomed all too closely in front of her. Instead of the graceful landing she'd envisioned, she stumbled and smacked clumsily into the power engineer's back. DuQuesne barely moved—giving her a new estimate for his mass and strength—but turned and helped steady her. "Are you all right, Captain?" he asked. His voice sounded oddly distracted.

She knew she was probably blushing; that had been a stupid stunt. "Yes, sorry, I was . . . " she trailed off, unable to speak, as she began to take in the scene in front of her.

Orphan appeared to fully understand their reaction; he opened arms and wings in a sweeping, expansive gesture. "Welcome, my friends, to Transition, what one might call the grand foyer of Nexus Arena."

The room—though that word was utterly inadequate—in which they stood made the one they had left seem little more than a closet, a cupboard when compared to a ballroom. Dozens—no, hundreds—of the enigmatic ebony-whirling vortices of Inner Gateways were arranged in concentric circles, smooth landing areas before them grading into downward-sloping ramps towards the center of the room. Lit from above by a gold-shining sphere, Transition was kilometers across, a vast amphitheater of pearlescent steel, rainbow-touched gold and crystal, and polished fragments of night.

And it was *busy*. Movement of a dozen dozen different shapes and outlines, iridescent flashes as creatures and machines emerged from one gateway, disappeared through another. Scents sharp, sweet, pungent, indescribable, filling the air just below the level of tolerance. A babble of voices, of alien shouts and electronic hums, of a dozen different rhythms of walking, rolling, hopping . . .

Ariane found that she, DuQuesne, and Sandrisson had almost unconsciously drawn together, backs to each other. She forced one of her hands to release what had been nearly a deathgrip on DuQuesne's arm.

Something—three somethings—moved up the ramp towards them. The one in the lead flowed forward with an easy grace if somewhat slowly, clothing like a shifting cloak or skirt of shimmering green-gold beads and plates concealing the exact method of motion. The upright portion was a latticework of blue and brown that looked for all the world like an elaborate open-work carving of wood in the shape of a candle flame, with a fluted, ribbed central column. Other small shapes darted around and back and forth inside the latticework, hovering and flitting around the creature, sometimes zipping out for a short distance then coming back; a humming sound accompanied its approach. The other two shapes moved in a more familiar two-legged gait, though not a human one; instead they bobbed forward with the measured rhythm of an ostrich. Wide-padded feet were visible underneath their clothing, which had slightly different coloration but similar patterns to those of the first creature, and the overall effect was something like a toad or frog crossed with a kangaroo. Gray-black eyes with slit pupils regarded the little party from those odd creatures, as the first alien reached the landing in front of the Gateway.

"Orphan!" the lead creature said. The translated voice was mellifluous, deep, hearty; an undertone of humming chimes seemed to come both from the main central column and the flying shapes nearby. "So it is indeed true, that you have encountered First Emergents and they have rescued you from the Blessed!"

"I would prefer to describe the events a bit differently," Orphan responded, "But the facts are indeed as you see them. Perhaps my companions and allies might care to present themselves to you, or you would wish to present yourself to them."

The creature drifted sideways to bring what Ariane presumed were sensing capabilities based in its central column more to bear upon the humans. It suddenly unfolded, the carved-wood appearance belied as the candle-flame outline blossomed, the alien momentarily taking on the look of an anemone; the small shapes within flew outward in the same moment (though all carefully avoiding coming near Orphan or the humans; Ariane could now see that they appeared to be something like a skate egg case with wings on each corner). "A greeting and great welcome to you, First Emergents! We greet you, and offer our name, which is Nyanthus, and our Faction, which is the Faith, and our position, which is First Guide."

The Faith . . . that's one of the most powerful Factions. Ariane quickly accessed the information Orphan had given them, the thumbnail sketches of a hundred things they needed to know. *Religious types, believe that the Arena isn't a "construct" in the technological sense, but that we're in the ruins of, or maybe an antechamber to, heaven or hell, and that the "Voidbuilders" were nothing more or less than true gods.*

Data access being very fast, she'd called that to mind even as the anemone-like Nyanthus continued, "To you we also present our fellows in Faith, Tchanta Zoll and Tchanta Vall. The Faith welcomes you, and praises your arrival in hope." The creature re-folded itself, the independent fliers returning to it.

Ariane guessed the gesture was one of welcome or respect, a bow or something. The speech had clearly ritual, or at least formal, elements to it. She hoped she wouldn't screw this part up. *The last thing we need to do is alienate* another *major faction . . . since it turns out the Blessed are one of the big boys.* "First Guide Nyanthus, we thank you for your greeting." Orphan gave a very slight handtap, showing she was proceeding correctly. "We offer you our greeting as well. I offer you my name, which is Ariane Austin, our . . . faction, which is Humanity, and my position—" *By default,* she noted to herself. "—which is Captain. To you I also present my friends and companions, Dr. Marc DuQuesne and Dr. Simon Sandrisson. We hope that all the greetings we shall receive in the Arena will be as pleasant as yours."

"Indeed would that be a fine thing," Orphan said. "Though I am afraid not entirely likely. Tell me, First Guide, what brings the leader of all the Faith to be passing by this ramp at this very moment?"

The chime-and-buzz translated to a warm chuckle. "Do the Initiate Guides not see when the Creators permit? Do we not watch and hear their guidance, that we, in turn, might guide those of the Arena to truth and revelation? It was in the seventh turning of yesterday's light that I saw this place, and knew you would come. Perhaps they are the ones?"

Orphan's snort of laughter was, perhaps, not as polite as it could have been. "And has the Faith not asked that question ever, for each new Emergents? Did you not even ask it of the Blessed when they arrived?"

"And so we shall ask, until the answer becomes yes." Nyanthus spun slowly in place. "You know that it is joy for us to see new arrivals, for they are most ready to appreciate the wonder of this Creation and understand it, as others—more jaded and cynical—cannot." The

First Guide flowed a bit closer to Ariane. "Behold much of Nexus Arena, Captain Ariane Austin; see many of its wonders. But commit to nothing until you have understood what you see, and if you need help in that understanding, know—the Faith is ready to assist you."

Commit to nothing indeed. I never wanted to be in politics, and now I don't have a choice. "I thank you for your gentle warning and your offer, Nyanthus," she said. "I am sure we will have many questions which the Faith can answer, once we know the right questions to ask."

The creature flickered its carved-candle top open momentarily again. "We are pleased with your courtesy, and shall now leave you to the learning; it would be unkind and unwise for us to further press you now." It bobbed at Orphan. "Treat with them well, Orphan; remember that the current can aid only those who seek not to shift it."

"I have been given more than one lesson in such things, First Guide. But your advice is well-taken." Orphan waited until the three strange figures had moved some considerable distance off. Then he turned to the humans. "Your first official greeting is, to be honest, one of the best that could be hoped for. Although somewhat worrisome in its own way."

DuQuesne nodded. "You mean the fact that the leader of a Faction important enough to play a major role in everything that happens here would show up to greet us?"

"It shows his interest, and does indeed give you an opening; the Faith are—within limits—trustworthy, and they do not make empty offers." Orphan's body language somehow conveyed a cynical smile; Ariane wondered if she was just learning to interpret it better. "Doing favors can gain the goodwill they need to gain more . . . converts, I suppose would be the best term."

"They're also powerful because they can perform miracles, if I understood you correctly?" asked Simon.

A buzz-slap was translated as a derisive snort. "Miracles? ZZ-Zk. Shadeweaver tricks with a different name, as far as I can tell."

"Which is why they don't get along with the Shadeweavers," Ariane said, nodding. The musing on the interactions reminded her of a question she hadn't asked."How many Factions *are* there, Orphan?"

"Some would say as many as there are individuals, Ariane Austin." Orphan spread his wingcases apologetically. "But that is not truly what you ask. There are a very large number of Factions, but there are—relatively speaking—only a few of them which are truly powerful and on whose actions much of the politics of the Arena hinge. You have now met three such, or four if I might count myself."

"I don't know if seeing a Shadeweaver for a second and having it disappear counts as 'meeting' the Faction," Ariane pointed out, glancing a bit nervously at a squat pair of creatures whose appearance seemed to owe a great deal to tarantulas; however, those aliens gave them a wide berth. In fact, it was evident that much of the Transition traffic kept to the individual lanes sloping down from specific Gateways, making collisions of traffic minimal and encounters between different species or groups something that would almost have to be done deliberately.

"A point. Although they undoubtedly consider that they have met you now. One of the most unpredictable and dangerous Factions, yet also most helpful when the mood strikes them." Orphan confirmed.

"Isn't counting yourself pretty arrogant, if there's only one of you?" DuQuesne asked.

"Perhaps. Perhaps not, in another sense. You will come to judge on your own. Let us say that my very existence is sufficient to disturb the Blessed and affect their actions, and in any accounting of the Factions the Blessed would be ranked very highly indeed."

Sandrisson, meanwhile, had been studying the spectacularly-varying crowds. "Orphan, I must say that there are other aspects of this that confuse me mightily. For example . . . how is that creature managing to walk at all?"

The creature Sandrisson indicated was a translucent creature, blue and green, that seemed as delicate as a jellyfish and moved along on tendrils scarcely more sturdy looking than tentacles.

"How . . . Ah, yes, I see your meaning, Dr. Sandrisson," Orphan said after a pause. "Look about you closely. See you the three Milluk—round-shelled creatures on four legs?"

After a moment, Ariane spotted the Milluk, about three feet high, almost spherical. "Yes, I see them." There seemed to be a faint haze near them, slightly brownish.

"I think I get it. Though if I'm right it's just one more 'How the hell does that work?' mystery," DuQuesne said. "The Arena is maintaining individual environments around all of us. So that thing Sandrisson was pointing at, it's in a very low-G pocket, and those, um, Milluk have their particular atmospheric requirements met."

"Exactly. Here we are all equal and supplied with appropriate support. On one's home Sphere, of course, conditions are kept appropriate only for the legitimate owners or claimants."

"Claimants?"

"Yes. It is possible to land on the outer Sphere and claim all or part of it, and until the claim is successfully contested the claimants can cause the immediate area they claim to conform to their needs." Orphan was guiding them now across the flat floor of Transition, towards a series of huge archways which clearly exited from this central station. "This is of course a rare event indeed, since it can only happen when the legitimate and natural residents of a Sphere have not yet emerged and laid claim to the outer Sphere, or if a direct attempt is made to invade the Sphere by a credible force."

"Invade? On the scale you're describing, I'd think that would be virtually impossible," DuQuesne said, frowning.

Orphan gave a surprisingly humanlike sigh. "Alas, Dr. DuQuesne, the problem is that no matter how many things I think I have explained, I realize there are a thousand more I haven't, and that you will need to understand soon. There are the Sky Gates, which are something like the Inner Gateway but . . . well, no, not really like them at all, I suppose. And while it is, of course, convenient to have a Sky Gate leading you to another Sphere directly, it is not at all impossible to reach other Spheres without that advantage, and indeed many are the opportunities to be had in that fashion." The translation of his next laugh was low, controlled, like someone hiding an impending surprise. "Allow me to show you. There is a viewing lounge to this side, and the sight may assist you in understanding."

Ariane exchanged glances with Sandrisson and DuQuesne. Sandrisson grinned. "I think our friend may have thought of another opportunity for his vicarious sense of wonder."

"If it helps me get a better understanding of this cock-amamie asylum, I'm all for it," DuQuesne muttered. Not for the first time, Ariane noticed the occasional odd turns of phrase the power engineer used, and now she understood *why* he did. Another tiny bit of comedy and tragedy from the Wagnerian-scale screwup of Hyperion.

They passed along a corridor which seemed—at least at the moment—little used, though still immense, thirty meters across and opening up into a strange room. Ahead of them the floor changed from metallic/stony to something clear as polished glass, with a broad latticework of shining silver for internal supports. Ahead, this glassy floor extended only another hundred meters, ending a few meters short of the wall, the gap edged by a protective railing a meter and a half high. To either side, the room extended at least a kilometer, and it was at least that high overhead and—dizzyingly—extended at least that far below.

Orphan led them to the railing. When they were all gathered, he turned. "Captain Austin. Dr. DuQuesne. Dr. Sandrisson. Behold the Arena." He gave a sweeping outward gesture, and the wall suddenly became transparent.

Ariane gave an inarticulate cry and barely kept herself from stumbling back from the rail; she saw DuQuesne's hands tighten, and Sandrisson *did* step back, almost seeking shelter behind her and DuQuesne.

Before them was a vast skyscape, a twining, roiling sea of air and cloud, brown and black and white and green, extending beyond the reach of sight in all directions. Through this atmosphere swam tiny shapes, some dimmed by haze of distance, that seemed no more than a meter long, finned or sailed things like strange fish.

Then one of them suddenly appeared to the left, emerging from a cloud in majesty, trailing streamers of mist from spars and masts, a titanic ship a kilometer long, lights blinking on its extremities, a distorted image of the massive, impossibly huge Nexus Arena reflected on the polished bronze-colored hull. As it passed, Ariane could see a bridge or forward observation deck, through which tiny figures were visible moving about. In the deepest distance, scarcely visible through the murk and gloom, another spark of light was seen, near to some monstrous shape, a shadow against shadow, of a Sphere that could envelop a world.

"Behold the Arena," Orphan repeated, more quietly, almost reverently. "The endless skies, the worlds that drift in cloud and light and shadow, a place where storms a million million kilometers wide clash above and around embattled Spheres, where trading ships and pirates and mercenaries travel beside, prey upon, and defend explorers, decadent tourists, lost souls searching for a home or a cause, armadas finding new worlds to conquer, and all, all of them looking, watching, asking for news . . . news of First Emergents, of ancient ancient ruins atop a lost Sphere, of rumors of Voidbuilder knowledge or Shadeweaver powers . . . and all of them returning here to hear that news, to behold the newcomers—and perhaps to Challenge them, or be themselves Challenged, and gain or lose all in a single contest. It is my home. Now it is yours."

Chapter 25

Ariane finally broke herself out of the spell that the awful grandeur of the Arena had cast. The description that Orphan had given before had been impressive, but it simply—to be honest—exceeded her ability to visualize. Apparently that wasn't the case for DuQuesne and Sandrisson, who'd been clearly shellshocked by the scale of the Arena in a way she hadn't.

But *this* was different. Here she could *see* and her mind was forced to grapple with a scale of construction and distance that wasn't appropriate to anything built by the hand of mortal beings. That almost-invisible shadow against the darkest reaches of the Arena's . . . atmosphere, that was a Sphere . . . like the one inside which they'd arrived, something so monstrously huge that they needed an interplanetary drive to travel from one side to the other in reasonable time. And that was just *one* Sphere, barely visible, with others to be found if one just kept going into the infinite veiled darkness and light.

She laughed suddenly, and Sandrisson jumped. Even DuQuesne twitched. "What's the joke?" Simon asked.

"It's just . . . funny how things hit you differently, just depending on what you're thinking at the time," she answered. "It occurred to me that if this was one of the simgames, I'd simply be looking and saying 'Wow, that's a cool idea—nice effects.' Totally different reaction if you're seeing it and thinking 'This is real.'"

DuQuesne grunted, a surprised sound. "Hadn't thought of it that way. Of course, I have reasons for not wanting to think of reality the way I do a game. I keep a very clear division between them, as you might guess."

"Actually," Simon said, "I'm rather surprised you participate in such entertainments at all . . . given the circumstances."

"My own form of therapy." DuQuesne's gaze was distant, and she saw a shadow of sadness in his expression. "It'd be easy to simply avoid all things that reminded me of Hyperion; it would also have crippled me in a number of ways, professionally and socially."

Orphan was looking from one to another, puzzled. "Having near-perfect translation is little help, my friends, when you talk in riddles."

"Never mind. It doesn't concern you," the dark-haired scientist snapped, brusquely. "No offense. It's personal, and let's not get sidetracked."

Orphan studied him a moment, then gave one of his wing-shrug gestures. "Indeed not. Come then. I hope you found this diversion entertaining and instructive."

"Gave me a gut feeling for what we're dealing with, that's for sure," Ariane said, following Orphan back towards Transition. "That's what's outside *our* Sphere, then?"

"Something of that nature, yes. The view will differ in details," Orphan said, as they emerged once more into the Brobdingnagian foyer of Nexus Arena. "For example, from my Sphere, currently the sky is predominantly greenish as a major storm is passing, and—"

Orphan suddenly stopped short—so suddenly that Ariane once more found herself bumping into someone's back. Orphan's was considerably less yielding than DuQuesne's. "What the . . . "

She trailed off as her gaze followed Orphan's, to see ten figures very like Orphan's striding purposefully through the crowd. The other groups parted, making way for Sethrik and the Blessed, who had apparently just entered via a Gateway somewhere near the middle of Transition. After a moment it became clear that Sethrik had not seen them, and they were able to watch as the Blessed left via the farthest side exit.

"My apologies, Captain Austin," Orphan said, once the last of the Blessed had disappeared. "Perhaps it was foolish of me, but I did not wish to precipitate a confrontation at this time."

"No apology needed. I didn't want another face-off right now either." Seeing Transition again reminded Ariane of a more immediate concern. "Orphan, you said we would get the access code to go home when we got here . . . but I haven't seen anything even in the way of controls for those Gateways."

"Eh?" The puzzled vocalization was translated from a muted wing-buzz. "But of course not. Would the Void-builders be so crude? A code you might misremember?

One that might be left behind, or stolen? You already *have* the code, Captain Austin."

As Orphan said the words, she realized he was right. There was . . . something, embedded in her knowledge of this place, something to think of or a state of mind to be in or an indescribable object to visualize, associated with the Inner Gateway. Something that hadn't been in her memory before, but was now ensconsced with all her other security codes as though it had always been there, even though it was nothing like any security code ever conceived elsewhere. *Creepy, I tell you! It's becoming my favorite word of all time!*

"That's . . . interesting," DuQuesne said after a moment; by Sandrisson's expression, he felt the same way. "But let's test it, shall we?"

"If you wish," Orphan said, turning in the direction of the nearest Gateway. "In fact, that is not at all a bad idea. It will cause your Outer Gateways to be unlocked; if some terrible misadventure befalls us all here, your remaining people will have two options, rather than one."

Orphan's easy acquiescence, and suddenly more purposeful stride following his new thought, made DuQuesne relax visibly. He made no attempt to change the course of action, but Ariane got the impression that Orphan's reaction had been enough of a confirmation for him.

They reached the Gateway; DuQuesne stepped through without even pausing in his stride, and only a few seconds later reappeared in a quiet shimmer of mother of pearl. "Works perfectly. Definitely took me back to our area; I was leaving markers."

She saw Orphan twitch with surprise—a feeling she shared. She hadn't seen DuQuesne do *anything* that indicated he was blazing a trail, and they already knew that scattering nanodust didn't work. Other Sphere's Gateway areas might look identical to their own, so how could DuQuesne be so sure? "I didn't see you do anything . . . " Sandrisson said, confirming that none of them had.

"You weren't meant to," DuQuesne said with a sideways grin. He did not elaborate.

After a silent pause, in which Orphan was clearly regarding DuQuesne with increased trepidation, Ariane spoke. "So . . . where to now?"

Turning from his study of the black-haired scientist, Orphan considered. "The Powerbrokers, I think. They hold the crescent that corresponds to Transition, on the other side of this first layer of Nexus Arena. The Embassies and the Grand Arcade are in the second layer, with the docks in a ring around the edge of that layer."

"I had the—perhaps mistaken—impression that Nexus Arena is even larger than our Sphere," Simon said, as Orphan began once more leading them onward. "Yet if we are walking, I would presume these layers are not impossibly large. So either I was mistaken, or there is some other use for the majority of the volume of Nexus Arena."

"In that you are correct, Dr. Sandrisson," Orphan responded. "None are sure whether the majority of Nexus Arena is dedicated to the Challenges, or to administration and control of the Arena itself; it is, however, well-known that no attempt to map the interior with accuracy has succeeded. The very top layers, these are constant, but below these—relatively minute—sections, Nexus Arena is yet another of the mysteries; a most frustrating one to many, as it remains impenetrable to analysis even though it is as close to all the inhabitants of the Arena as their own Embassies."

The bewildering scenes around them were simply too much to grasp all at once. Ariane left some of her internal nanos on record, just to make sure crucial data wasn't missed, but she focused mostly on Orphan rather than trying to take in everything they were passing; her comprehension and sense of wonder were already near to burning out, and she needed to have some reserves for these Powerbrokers and anyone else they were going to meet.

"Orphan, you said you'd never met First Emergents before, right?" DuQuesne said suddenly. "How often do they show up, anyway?"

"As one might expect, the times vary quite a bit, but I would say, on average, once every . . . oh, four to five thousand years." Orphan was leading them through an area filled with widely-spaced columns which a little observation showed must be elevators or something similar. "A bit longer than I have been present, I admit."

Ariane started to chuckle, then stopped herself, realizing that what would have been gentle understatement for a human being might be something very different here. "How old are you, Orphan? If you don't mind my asking?"

"Hm? Oh, roughly three thousand years. Two thousand, nine hundred, and seventy-seven, to be more precise."

She glanced over at DuQuesne, whose eyebrows had climbed suddenly with that comment. "Is this normal in the Arena?"

"Oh, not at all," Orphan said cheerfully. "Most live considerably shorter lives. Including the Blessed, which gives me some *most* unkind thoughts as to the Minds."

"The Minds are the leaders of the Blessed? Is Sethrik one of them?" Simon inquired.

"Sethrik? A *Mind*?" The explosion of buzzing that served as laughter for Orphan was so loud that the translated sound was actually momentarily overwhelmed. "A . . . a Mind! Why, if Sethrik were to hear that, he would . . . well, to be entirely honest I have no idea what he'd do, but it would be amusing, I assure you! No, he is no Mind, and you may pray to all the fates and gods which may be that you shall never meet one. In the Arena, fortunately, that is a prayer likely to be met, as no Mind has ever successfully entered the Arena, nor likely ever will."

DuQuesne nodded. "Artificial intelligences. The Blessed to Serve are slaves to a bunch of AIs."

"*Very* good, Dr. DuQuesne. Very good indeed," Orphan said, confirming DuQuesne's guess.

DuQuesne chuckled. "Must drive them nuts. I think I start to get the picture, Orphan. They have to work through the Blessed, but they had to make you guys independent thinkers to send you through. Which meant that a few of you would get uppity ideas about going your own way. Thus . . . the Liberated."

"You have the correct general idea. Though none of it was or is as simple as you describe it." The little group now passed through another set of archways, and beyond these Ariane could see several huge alcoves, with what appeared to be an immense window or port in the wall of each, and many different creatures milling about.

As they walked closer, she could see that each alcove was separated from the others by a wall, and from the open space in front by an elaborate gateway; framing each gateway was a large building, in the shape of a trapezoid with the center cut out for the gateway. Gateway and building each had the shaded undertones that implied that a lot of the construction material was the CQC—Coherent Quark Composite—that made up the structural supports of the Sphere.

"I think the story of the Liberated might be well worth hearing . . . sometime later," DuQuesne said. "I'm guessing these are the Powerbrokers. My earlier question, before we got sidetracked, was leading up to the question: if First Emergents are so rare, and the Powerbrokers can't move their power production facilities, then who are they selling to most of the time, and why? Given what I've now seen about the outside, I can figure out several power generation schemes that should work."

"An excellent question, Doctor. Indeed, once a race becomes well established, they can supply many of their own needs. However, it. is often convenient to make Nexus Arena a stopping point for many travels, due to the way in which the Sky Gates operate, and recharging one's storage capacity here is an excellent opportunity. Beyond those windows are charging stations, where ships of a thousand species may be charging their storage cells even as we speak. Also, since the power generation facilities must—almost of necessity—be set up on the outer portion of the Sphere, it is often not convenient to run a conduit from the generators to the interior; that would require leaving the Outer Gateway open, and there are risks inherent in that. Given that, the exterior power generation is often set up such that it supplies the exterior colony and fleet, while recharging for the interior can be done more easily by exchanging fully-charged coils here."

Ariane nodded. "Makes sense. So First Emergents may generally be the only people who *need* the additional power, but it's valuable to most people."

"Correct." Orphan was leading them towards one of the central stations. "You recall what I said about them not being a true Faction?"

"Yeah, I got it," DuQuesne affirmed. "Powerbroker's more a position—and not a permanent one. You have to answer one or more of these 'Challenges' every so often, or your station shuts down and won't start up again until someone else takes over—and that's a first come, first served situation. With you, the losers, as the *only* group that can't grab it."

"But they work together, sort of, to make sure that they all receive acceptable compensation for the power they supply, and that none of the Factions tries to control them," Simon continued.

"Excellent. This station is controlled by the Shiquan at the present time." Orphan's gaze was scanning the area directly before the gate, which included a sort of long, low table. "Ah. Very good. Come, I know this one."

The creature at the table was squat and had no need to sit, as it appeared to have no legs; it reminded Ariane somewhat of a slug with a sort of squarish face and four manipulative tendrils at each corner of the face. "Orphan of the Liberated," the creature said, waving all four tendrils, which changed subtly in color from gray-brown to several different shades as they moved. "Greetings and welcome to you. What purpose moves the Survivor from his safety?" The voice was light and warm, strongly feminine to Ariane's ears.

"Ghondas of the Shiquan, Master Powerbroker, my greetings and thanks," Orphan responded, giving the strange creature a full pushup-bow. "My purpose is to introduce to you those without which I would no longer be the Survivor. First Emergents, called Humans or Humanity."

Ghondas swelled and stretched upright, then flattened, attention now fixed on Ariane, DuQuesne, and Sandrisson. "To me you bring them? A kindly thought."

"Their leader I present to you, Captain Ariane Austin, who stepped forward and spoke for me when Sethrik had me inconvenienced." He introduced the others by title and name.

The sluglike Powerbroker did her rise and flatten trick again as her four eyes—shiny, crystalline objects, one set between each pair of manipulative tendrils—came to bear on Ariane. "Greetings and welcome to you, Captain of First Emergents. So you have confronted the Blessed upon your emergence? An . . . exciting introduction to our community, I would think."

"A bit, yes. Should I address you as Powerbroker, Ghondas, or something else, Master Powerbroker?"

Iridescence chased subtly around Ghondas's body; analysis showed that in ultraviolet she was constantly shifting color. This shift seemed to correlate with a translated gentle chuckle. "So long as we are speaking merely as new friends, Ghondas. Should we begin speaking business, perhaps we will be more formal—or perhaps not, as my mood takes me. I am sure that your visit is not entirely a casual one. Not sufficient power to return to the home, eh? It is a common story among First Emergents—or so I have been told."

"That is indeed our major problem at the moment, Ghondas. I do not know, however, whether we have anything of value to offer you for your vital services."

"Hm." The boneless body settled lower, relaxing, as though thinking was easier when less effort was expended to support Ghondas's form. "Confronted the Blessed . . . was it a Challenge? Was it accepted?" She glanced at Orphan.

"Alas, no. Such might have been the case, but I adjudged the odds poor, less than one in ten, and pointed out the Rules of Emergence."

A bubbling sound translated as a sigh. "Unfortunate. Not that your judgment was unwise—life is nearly always preferable to risk—yet that means they are still untested."

"So," DuQuesne said, "That means you won't trade with us?"

Ghondas rose. "A Powerbroker judges all risks, all factors, and makes no decisions with excessive unknowns. We have no need for extreme risk, save only if and when we must Challenge to keep our positions. Even if you have something of value—unlikely—and have sufficient of that thing to pay for the power you require—highly unlikely—the value is directly variant depending on your future; a unique collectible from a race that appears and disappears would be extremely valuable, but may be nearly worthless if you establish yourself and the collectible turns out to be something commonly available. The only thing of value you have that I would accept . . . " Ghondas's topmost portion swayed back and forth, moving her face to examine all three of the humans. " . . . would be one of you. Service, and knowledge of your race. That would be worthwhile."

Ariane shook her head. "I can't afford to trade my crew, even if it was something our people permitted, which we don't."

A shuddering ripple echoed through Ghondas's body, a metaphor of a shrug. "Then we may only speak of little things, of gossip and superficialities, until you have won a Challenge. Until that time, you remain children of the Arena, and must first grow up. It is for your own good, as well, for until you have won a Challenge you have no Embassy or hope of establishing one, few to none will bargain or treat with you—and even fewer in good faith—and you shall be unable to use your Straits, and your Sky Gates shall remain closed, until that time."

Ariane sighed. This was what she'd expected, but that didn't completely prevent the disappointment. "Well . . . I thank you for your time and your honesty, Powerbroker Ghondas. We shall meet again, I hope, when we have more to offer you."

"That is my hope as well, Captain Ariane Austin. At the least your story should be an interesting one, if you continue to associate with the Survivor. Not a long story, perhaps, but interesting."

Orphan has a reputation . . . and it appears to be both good and bad. "Are you hinting that we should reconsider the association?"

Ghondas's rise and fall was jerky, and the tone of voice reinforced an impression of quick—perhaps almost *too* quick—negation. "Oh, no, not at all, Captain! Orphan is not . . . usually . . . the cause of his problems. And we would not wish to imply that the Survivor is untrustworthy."

I think she's . . . wary of Orphan. Maybe even a little scared. And given the implied position of the Powerbrokers . . . maybe Orphan's estimation of his importance wasn't as arrogant as we thought.

She bowed to Ghondas and turned away. *Now what?*

From the corner of her eye, she saw something move abruptly, sharply; then an impact sent her reeling.

Chapter 26

DuQuesne had also been studying Ghondas—and Orphan's reaction to her comments. *He's definitely a Big Time Operator, Orphan is. Bigger than Ghondas. At the same time, I'm sure he's serious about needing our help—which tells me quite a bit about the mess we're in.*

Orphan's tail suddenly rose halfway, his body and wingcases tightening, staring at a point just past DuQuesne's shoulder, where Ariane had just passed him.

As he turned, Ariane staggered back and fell, her black-blue hair pooling outward as she hit the smooth floor ungracefully. He spun fully around. "What the hell—"

The thing that he was suddenly confronting was a nightmare, taller than him, standing on seven claw-tipped, chitin-covered, jointed legs, a central body like a

215

gorilla crossed with a praying mantis, the entire creature colored in violent splotches of red, black, and bluish-purple; it probably outweighed him by a hundred and fifty kilos. Two more of the things stood just behind it and in flanking positions. It screech-hissed from a mouth that combined the worst features of a lobster and a lamprey, sounds translated into a rough, grating voice. "You stand in my way and speak unquietly. Unwise. Move."

Ariane was getting up, looking shaken and pale, a trickle of blood from the corner of her mouth showing that she'd been hit harder than he thought. *Now that's just torn it.* "I move when you apologize for hitting my Captain. Not before."

Orphan hissed, a sound of dismay. *"Molothos!"*

In the moment before the creature reacted, DuQuesne had time to realize what a stupid mistake his antiquated instincts had driven him to. The Molothos were one of the most powerful Factions, and by far the most dangerous—a race of xenophobic—no, xeno*misosic*, alien-hating—creatures who had managed to establish a power base large enough to challenge even groups like the Faith. *Of all the lousy breaks . . .*

The monster lashed out with jack-knife mantis claws, a stroke faster than anything DuQuesne had seen in fifty years. He barely moved aside in time, as the bladed forelimb ripped through the air where he'd been; the second stroke was just as close. *This thing's a killer. Those aren't slaps like it gave Ariane; it's trying to rip my head off!* He noticed the other two were moving forward and fanning out, legs moving in a stacatto crablike gait which was deceptively smooth and swift.

This is bad. Very bad. This wasn't one of the formal Challenges Orphan had talked about, it was a random gang attack, and it didn't look like anyone—even Orphan—was inclined to help out. *No time to draw my gun, assuming these guys aren't armored enough to take a hit or two, and with the crowd around us I'd end up doing collateral damage. I've got to interrupt this guy's rhythm, throw him off.* The next time the sharp-spined foreclaw stabbed outward, he moved.

The impact stung like catching a swung baseball bat, and he almost lost his grip. *Thing's too fast, and I'm too slow and way out of practice.* But he had the claw, and the hiss-screech was a gasp of startled anger. For a moment they stood motionless, the Molothos trying to pull its claw back, DuQuesne holding it locked in an iron grip. *Jesus, the thing's strong. I don't know how long I can hold it. And if I shift enough to get my sword out, I'll hand it an opening and it'll be just too bad for me.*

A gray shadow suddenly fell over both of them, and DuQuesne felt as though mired in thick oil. He turned his head—more slowly than he wanted.

A squat, armored figure stood to one side, pointing a flattened, clublike weapon at both of them. "End this," it said in a hard, flat voice. "Initiating violence is prohibited outside of Challenge. You know this, Molothos Dajzail."

Dajzail's single eye—a crescent-shaped organ that extended around most of his head, like a wraparound visor—flickered with yellow light. It slowly relaxed the pressure, letting DuQuesne ease off and let go, but the entire body trembled, so much that the chitinous legs gave a slight rattling hum from their contact with the floor. *And I'm sure that's rage, not fear. It's furious that it has to stop, has to accommodate this guy.*

"This . . . creature refused to give ground, and insisted I . . . perform a service before it did so!" Dajzail snarled.

"Perform a . . . I insisted that you apologize for knocking over my friend and captain!"

The armored figure—which appeared to be of a race similar to the toadlike creatures that had been accompanying First Guide Nyanthus—bobbed slightly; the replying voice, though still mostly dispassionate, seemed to have acquired a faint trace of wry humor. "A hard service indeed . . . for a Molothos. But an unwise service to demand, as well."

Orphan stepped forward. "Adjudicator, my friends are First Emergents. And Dajzail did strike their captain without warning."

"I see that this is so. Then the fault is not theirs, but yours, Molothos. Not an uncommon situation. But let us simply set it aside; continue on with your business, remembering the prohibitions." As Dajzail and his two companions turned—without a word or glance—to continue onward, the Adjudicator raised its voice. "But be warned—if we see similar events repeated anytime in the next four weeks, we will be much less tolerant, Dajzail."

The hacking snarl was translated as an obscenity, but apparently any answer was considered acknowledgement. DuQuesne watched them leave with a combination of relief and disappointment. *Get over it. Only your stupid hindbrain wants to fight the damn thing. Didn't you spend five decades trying to wash that poisonous crap out of your head? Get over it.*

Instead, he turned on Orphan. "Thanks a lot for nothing. Were you going to take pictures of my dissection after they finished gutting me?"

Orphan was staring at him, still in his protective-threat pose. "You are insane. Insane!"

"What the hell's your problem? I didn't know exactly what they were, yeah, but once that started they weren't backing off."

"You confronted an unknown—and one so clearly formidable—for no reason!" Orphan said, the translated voice shaking. "There wasn't a chance in ten . . . in a *hundred* . . . that you'd survive it." Orphan shook himself. "And you wanted . . . no, you *expected* . . . me to enter combat." He glanced at the others, realized that they had been positioning themselves to intercept the other two Molothos. "I thought you had said that it was the Shadeweaver's interference that caused you to intervene on my behalf . . . yet this was even more of a risk."

Something about the whole situation's spooked him. Spooked him bad. DuQuesne shrugged. "Fine, drop it. You thought it'd be throwing good lives after bad, all right, your judgment to make. Who or what was that . . . Adjudicator?"

Clearly relieved to be away from the prior subject, Orphan answered in a much more normal tone. "Ah, the Adjudicators. They are the enforcers of the Arena, appointed by the major Factions. They have to be even-handed in their dealings, and the armor they wear—which, it is said, adapts to the wearer—has some connection with the Arena that allows them to intervene in any of the forbidden activities. There are not many such, but just a few Adjudicators have always been sufficient to keep people, shall we say, honest most of the time."

DuQuesne was now checking Ariane's injuries. The trickle of blood wasn't serious—he was rather surprised by the shock it had given him. He'd seen many fights before, and this had just shaken up the captain a bit; why did he feel like fussing over her? "No real harm done, Captain. Banged your lip a little, I think."

"Thank you, Marc. But next time, please think before defending me. My pride—and even my lip—can take a few hits if necessary."

He wanted to protest, but she was perfectly right. "Understood, Captain."

Ariane nodded to Orphan. "Now what?"

"I think," Orphan said, "we should make our way toward my Embassy. I believe we will encounter a few more persons of interest along the way, and it will be a good safe haven to rest at; I suspect we will all want a good rest after all this walking, not to mention the excitement." He chuckled, a flapping motion of the wings. "And I'm looking forward to a decent meal."

As Ariane followed Orphan, Sandrisson fell in next to DuQuesne. "I must confess, I had not expected you to take the position of Sir Galahad."

"What? That two-bit thug just pissed me off."

"I was furious as well, but I was—I admit—rather intimidated by those creatures, and Ariane was petrified by them; I think they strike some rather unpleasant associations with her. But when you saw her go down, you didn't hesitate at all." Sandrisson smiled. "Don't worry, I shall say nothing. Honorable opposition and all that." He moved forward before DuQuesne could think of a reply, leaving him to stare after the elegant white-haired scientist.

What the hell did he mean by that?

Chapter 27

So the Hyperion has a heart, and it's Ariane who's touched it. That's quite interesting. And a bit intimidating, I must admit. Simon shook his head slightly to himself. Oh, there were some people comfortable in group relationships, others where there were three or four partners who simply alternated time together, and so on, but the fact was he—and, he suspected, DuQuesne—was the sort to look for the old-fashioned and still popular standard pairing, one man, one woman. *And competing with someone like Dr. Marc DuQuesne, that will be something of a challenge.*

But, as noted before, he liked challenges, too. And of course in the end the "competition" would really depend on Ariane's preferences. And he did, in fact, have a little advantage there. He recalled a prior exchange, just before they arrived, and smiled.

But back to matters at hand. He watched their guide and Ariane ahead of him. Orphan's stride still seemed a little . . . off, somehow. He was still upset, obviously, and Simon had to admit that he wasn't altogether recovered; his hands shook slightly from the adrenaline of preparing to back up DuQuesne in that confrontation.

Then, he thought, *let's get back to the discussions and learn some more.* Lengthening his stride, he caught up with the other two. "Orphan, something Ghondas said drew my attention. What are the 'Straits'?"

The buzz-chuckle sounded almost normal now. "Another assumption not even thought of. In the interior of your Sphere, you undoubtedly noticed three depressions along its . . . equator?"

"Yes. About a hundred kilometers across each, depressed only about a meter or so."

"Those are the Straits; the conceptual parallel is that they can be opened, providing a—relatively speaking —narrow opening through which traffic may pass from within your Sphere to the rest of the Arena." Orphan seemed thoughtful. "A hundred kilometers now . . . that's somewhat unusual. Most Straits are much smaller, twenty kilometers or so. Interesting."

Simon glanced meaningfully at Ariane, and filed away that difference for additional thought later; anything unusual about their Sphere might indicate something of value, either here or at home. "And these Straits cannot be opened unless we meet one of these Challenges?"

"Correct."

"Then," DuQuesne said, entering the conversation as he fell in next to Orphan on the other side, "We need to find a good type of Challenge, one we're likely to win, and start moving."

"Alas, Dr. DuQuesne, if only it were so simple. But in general those who seek a Challenge have vastly less control over the nature of the Challenge; you may issue a Challenge at any time, but the Challenged is free to decline . . . and if they accept, they—not you—select the type of contest."

Simon nodded. "Not all that different from how many of our cultures handled duelling; the challenged party had the choice of weapons, thus—at least in theory —preventing a skilled and malicious individual from constantly forcing his chosen victims to match his skill in his chosen field."

A thought seemed to strike Ariane. "Well, Orphan, could *you* challenge us, and we then accept the challenge and—"

"Not feasible, no." Orphan's translated voice echoed his amusement. "The one issuing the Challenge will have to risk something of equal proportionate value to that which you risk, you see, and I have very little more than you that I can afford to risk. And there are other issues which would take a considerable time to explicate— which I promise I will do, later. Take it as given that while it may be possible, if you have large numbers of resources and allies, to arrange a Challenge for another ally that does, to some extent, favor them, as a general rule they are, and must be, serious affairs for all concerned."

They stopped before one of the elevator columns they had noted earlier. The side of the column slid open and they entered the fifteen meter wide cylindrical room within. With artificial gravity available, Simon wondered if they'd even feel the motion, but it appeared that Nexus Arena did not care much about minor shifts in acceleration; he felt the room begin to descend.

"So," Ariane said, looking curiously at Orphan, "why was Ghondas afraid of you?"

"Afraid?" Simon wondered if the subtle, sinister edge to the accompanying chuckle was just his imagination. "You give me vastly too much credit, Ariane Austin. The worthy Ghondas is *afraid* of very little indeed. However, I am not named the Survivor idly; as our prior discussion touched upon, I am quite long-lived by the standards of most in the Arena." The doors opened, revealing another space which once more demanded superlatives of size. Simon's mind was becoming either accustomed to the scale of things, or simply numbed by the constant assault on his prior conceptions; focused as he was on the conversation with Orphan, he merely noted that this layer of Nexus Arena was much more like a city, and vastly larger than the prior layer.

"Ghondas's people have held that station as Powerbrokers for a considerable time, nearly a thousand years, meeting many challenges to maintain that position," Orphan continued. "I have been their constant customer for all that time, and perhaps there have been occasional . . . incidents in which I figured that have been enlarged upon over that time. I find that having, at times, a somewhat mythic reputation is convenient; not being myself a Shadeweaver, I must, regrettably, rely on the magic of appearances alone."

"Appearances," Simon said, "can be as useful as actuality, at times. A more interesting question for myself and certainly for our biosciences people is whether—as it appears to me upon naïve inspection—most if not all species here are dependent on oxygen in fair proportion in their atmosphere."

"By far the vast majority, yes. There are a few known intelligent species that use slightly different metabolic pathways requiring other available materials, but these are extremely rare and none have established themselves as a significant factor in the Arena. Similarly, the common gravity span centers around the level that you and I currently enjoy."

"These facts giving rise to long and spirited debate indeed," A new voice, tenor, slightly rough and cheerful, interjected. "Are these the First Emergents, Orphan?" The new speaker was a tall, slender creature, wearing a loose-fitting white garment something like a martial arts *gi*, pure white fronds like feathery hair falling forward over a beaky face with large circular eyes. What appeared to be a beard underneath moved independently, sometimes covering the wide mouth completely; Simon, noting the way it could position itself and the fine, regular spacing of the hairlike portions, deduced the "beard" was a filter of some sort. This was the first alien they'd encountered which really had a very similar body-plan to human; it stood on two legs, apparently jointed in similar places, had two arms with hands (though composed of what appeared to be six fingers in opposable pairs), and lacked the balancing and defensive tail of Orphan and the Blessed.

"Relgof!" Orphan's greeting was equally hearty. "An excellent chance brings you here at this time." He gave a bob-bow to the creature. "My friends, this is Relgof Nov Ne'Knarph, a Researcher of the Analytic. Relgof, Captain Ariane Austin and Drs. DuQuesne and Sandrisson of the First Emergent species Humanity."

Relgof emphasized his anatomic similarity by doing a spread-armed motion of respect and greeting somewhat like a curtsey. "Welcome! My best wishes to you that you may quickly find your way to full citizenship in the Arena, and join us in the never-ending quest."

The Analytic! Simon felt a rush of excitement that he controlled with difficulty. As Orphan had described them, the Analytic was, in a way, the polar opposite of the Faith; an association of scientists, researchers, engineers, and other groups whose main interest was to explore the Arena and understand it and all its contents—more like a research foundation and scientific brotherhood than a government or Faction, as Simon understood it. They wielded considerable influence; as they had no true long-reaching ambitions, they could often get along well with most other factions, who would use the services of the Analytic.

"Thanks for the kind wishes, Relgof Nov—"

"Relgof, or Dr. Rel, will do, Captain. My full name is a cumbersome waste, I think, though it serves to identify me to my people. Dr. DuQuesne and Dr. Sandrisson? Are you, then, also students of science?"

DuQuesne chuckled. "I'm more a practical man, not much into the theory. Power engineering's my main focus. You want theory and science, Sandrisson's your man. He invented the Sandrisson Drive, after all."

Oh, Kami-sama, this is embarrassing. "Please, Marc, don't. That's like bragging to a modern researcher about your brilliance in inventing the wheel."

To Simon's astonishment, Relgof's reaction was very different. "The Sandrisson Drive?" he repeated, the word having that unique additional echo/overlay effect Ariane had noticed previously. "You invented for your species the method that brought you here? It is a great honor, sir, a great honor indeed!" The spread-armed curtsey seemed more emphatic this time.

Simon was, rather uncharacteristically, momentarily speechless, and he could see from the corner of his eye

Ariane grinning at his discomfiture. "Why . . . thank you, Dr. Rel, but . . . why? After all, there isn't a species here that has not achieved that knowledge, and—as I am given to understand—the most recent of those almost five thousand years ago."

The beard-filter flip-flopped twice, translated as a "tch-tch" noise. "You think modestly, as a true scientist should; yet tell me, how would you feel to meet, say, the scientist of your people who first explicated the laws of gravity? Vastly excited, eh? To a high and terribly lonely brotherhood you belong, Doctor; in all the history of the Arena, throughout all the reaches of time and space, a few thousand individuals have made that discovery and brought their people from isolation to participation in the Grand Arena. Even fewer have been those who themselves were alive, and willing to risk themselves in that first transition. Not to be argued is it that we have much knowledge that you lack, yet rest assured that your achievement is, by itself, sufficient to rank you highly as a Researcher."

"You . . . do me far too much honor, Dr. Rel." Simon could feel his cheeks burning, and see DuQuesne's grin join Ariane's. "Truly, I merely built upon the work of others."

The little group had reached what was almost certainly a conveyance, an object like a thirty-foot long loaf of silver bread with the top cut off. Orphan led the way on board; seating appeared to adjust to the individual needing to sit. He gestured to Rel to follow, but the gesture was both superfluous and probably not even observed; the slender alien was continuing his conversation. "Naturally, naturally—and the exact pathway of discovery is of interest to me. For example, in the records of my own people . . . " Relgof described the progression, which appeared to have developed through experimental results using extremely large-scale accelerators and the slight differentials that, Sandrisson knew, would show up in the particle counts due to the very rare event of just the right fields and vectors being generated to cause one of the particles to jump to Kanzaki-Locke space.

"That's fascinating. In my case, you see, we . . . " he glanced suddenly over at Orphan. "Meaning no offense, especially to such an obviously friendly and kindred spirit, but . . . is this discussion a good idea?"

"For the two of you to talk?" Orphan's handtap showed he understood perfectly, and Ariane's expression demonstrated that she'd been wondering if she should interrupt. "I think it should be a good thing. The Analytic tends to be rather free with information, far more so than most of us, and I doubt you have many secrets in the general theory area that need protection." He turned towards the front of the conveyance. "To the Embassy of the Liberated."

He looked back to Dr. Relgof. "My apologies."

Relgof waved that away with a surprisingly human gesture. "Think nothing of it, Dr. Sandrisson. You are First Emergents, you *must* be cautious. You know nothing of the Analytic as of yet, little of the Arena; I would be disappointed indeed if you were overly trusting."

Ariane was speaking to Orphan. "So the Analytic is one of the less dangerous Factions?"

"To do business with, certainly." Orphan inclined his head to Relgof.

"I would not wish to anger them overmuch, of course, as they have many friends and do, undoubtedly, keep some knowledge that is of value to themselves as a reserve and defense. Even the Shadeweavers have been known to consult and contract with the Analytic, so you can see that despite controlling only a few Spheres they have considerable influence. I had, I confess, not thought at all of the prestige your Dr. Sandrisson might have with them. History's impact is a bit different to me."

Reassured, Simon resumed the conversation, trying to describe the research process that had led to his own discovery. Relgof quickly showed his breadth of understanding, stopping at various points to clarify the steps he'd followed and exclaiming in warm appreciation at various insights. Simon still felt somewhat embarrassed at the reaction, but it was clear to him that it was a completely honest reaction from the alien scientist.

Before they had nearly concluded their discussion, the conveyance slowed to a halt before a building with green, black, and gold as its major color scheme. "Liberated Embassy," a calm, neutral voice said from midair.

Rel glanced up. "Ah, of course. You have no Embassy of your own. I suppose you will not be inviting me in at this time . . . ?"

Orphan flicked his hands outward. "I am afraid not. My new friends need, I believe, some isolation and time for thought."

It was clear that entering another's Embassy was a nontrivial matter; this gave Simon considerably more appreciation for Orphan's willingness to assist them . . . or desperation in needing their help. "Dr. Sandrisson," Relgof said earnestly, "it has been fascinating. I invite you to come to our Embassy soon and continue this discussion—and perhaps discuss your people joining the Analytic. With such students of the universe as yourself, clearly Humanity is a prime candidate."

"I certainly look forward to another talk. As for joining, I'm afraid I will have to discuss such things with my captain." Sandrisson glanced at Ariane. "But thank you very much."

Another spread-armed curtsey. "It was entirely my pleasure, and has brought a fresh ocean before me." As the others had now disembarked, Dr. Relgof muttered something to the vehicle, which swiftly glided off.

"So, we'll be safe here?" DuQuesne said, studying the massive building as they approached.

Orphan gave an emphatic handtap. "Absolutely. I will grant you full guest access to the Embassy, until you win your own. There, no one may harrass us and there is light, comfort, and water to be had. You have, of course, brought sufficient food for a time."

DuQuesne gave a grunt of assent. "That'll do for now, I guess. How dangerous will it be for us to explore the Arena without you, though? Because I'm just guessing here, but you'll want to hide out in your Embassy, or go back to your Sphere for a while, right? To stay out of the Blessed's way until you figure out an angle on how you're going to deal with 'em."

Orphan laughed. "You see clearly indeed, Dr. DuQuesne. But I will not abandon my position as guide as quickly as that, as long as one or more of you accompany me—to remind Sethrik of the circumstances of our truce, so to speak. Even so, it would not be amiss for you to venture out on your own, at least on these two layers. As you have seen, true violence is discouraged in Nexus Arena—except in Challenge—and you do not wish to give the impression that you are afraid of this place."

"No, definitely not," Ariane concurred. "And I'd guess that if we have to answer a Challenge, we'll have to at least risk being in places where someone might Challenge us, right?"

"You speak truly. And—if you are cautious and watch what you say—you may well learn more than others learn of you."

The doorway of the building rolled open as Orphan approached, and the group passed inside, whereupon it shut. Inside was a room that was merely large by human building standards, but entirely appropriate as the entry hall for an embassy or other official building. Lit with a bright light that had a warm orangish tinge, the Liberated Embassy showed an exuberant and direct cheer in the rough-hewn statuary, sharply-executed relief mosaics, and other ornamentation. The art, Ariane thought, was something Steve would describe as primitive, very directly representational for the most part, but well-executed. The floor was of a hard polished stone, mostly white but with symmetrical splotches like black snow-flakes scattered through it. Orphan paused for a moment in the center of the floor. "Embassy directive: the human beings present—Captain Ariane Austin, Dr. Marc C. DuQuesne, and Dr. Simon S. Sandrisson, are hereby granted full Guest privileges. I am assigning them the first suite on this floor for their use and convenience." He then led them across the floor to one of four doors evenly spaced across the far wall; the door rolled aside and he ushered them in.

"You are now privileged guests of the Liberated, on whose behalf I welcome you," he said, with a wry formality. "The Chief Ambassador Orphan also welcomes you, as does our great Leader, Orphan, and his Advisor, Orphan."

Ariane laughed. "Well, Orphan, Ambassador Orphan, Leader Orphan, and Advisor Orphan, I thank you. Something that Rel said has brought up another issue: you can join a Faction?"

Orphan's hands tapped. "Oh, certainly. If the Faction permits it, you could join and gain their benefits. The problem, of course, is that you would be *committing* yourself to that Faction—yourself and your entire species. The Analytic, I admit, would likely be the least onerous such commitment to make, but still, I have not gained the impression that you are empowered by your people to negotiate for your species . . . but as far as the Arena is concerned, you *are* in fact empowered to do so, and the Arena will consider such decisions binding, and will care nothing for later protests by other members of your species."

Oh my. That would, as the old saying goes, put the cat among the pigeons. Simon frowned at the implications. Ariane was in the position to make decisions for *all humanity* from the Arena's viewpoint? That could indeed be sticky. And did rather eliminate the quick solution to their dilemma of how to get home. "Can other individuals go their own way? That is, if Humanity were to join the Analytic, could individual humans choose to go join, well, the Liberated?"

"Yes, for individuals. For groups, the matter is complex, but the base case is as I have stated, and there would be many problems if, for example, you were to commit to the Analytic but your homeworld, or nations thereof, wished to repudiate that commitment."

"Forget it," DuQuesne said. "We're our own Faction and staying that way for quite a while. Too much to learn here and too many pitfalls."

Orphan showed them how the suite of rooms—twelve rooms for "private or group quarters," a central meeting room, a side room for conferences, a food preparation area, and biological waste disposal areas—could be configured and, to a certain extent, customized to their needs. "Now I go to my long-awaited dinner, and I expect you shall wish to speak amongst yourselves and rest." With a bob-bow, he began to leave, then paused, looking back with body language that somehow conveyed an almost ironic smile. "I would assure you that Guest access provides you with privacy in your assigned quarters, but you might not believe me." He passed through the door, which rolled shut behind him.

Chapter 28

"*Whew*," DuQuesne said, sinking into an oddly-shaped but compliant chair. "This, my friends, has been one long, *long* day."

Ariane couldn't help but smile at the huge power engineer. She suspected he wasn't nearly so tired as he made himself out to be, though. "In what looks to be a series of long, long days," she agreed.

"But overall an extremely fruitful one," said Simon. "A shame about the Powerbroker, but I believe we will find the Analytic a very useful partner."

She nodded. "I'm more interested in determining our next steps. My first question is . . . do we really want to go forward? We've opened the Outer Gate. Do we really need to go through this Challenge business now?"

She could see that DuQuesne had already been thinking along those lines; Simon gave a little "Ah . . . " which

indicated that the question hadn't occurred to him. She
waited to give him a few moments.

"You know, that's an interesting question, Captain."
Simon said finally. "Orphan's a rather . . . forceful personality, and this day has been filled with wonder enough
that his assumptions as to our next steps have simply
seemed natural." He looked over to DuQuesne. "Marc?"

"Much as I hate feeling like I'm being herded down
someone else's path," DuQuesne said slowly, "I think
we have to go through with it—not desperately, not stu-
pidly, but we have to play the game. For two reasons.

"First, unless the top of our Sphere is completely different than I suspect, the best possibility we'll have for
generating power will be building something like a
waterwheel. It'll take us *years* to recharge the coils that
way—assuming the AIWish keeps working and we can
keep it building stuff for us, *and* the stuff works on what
he calls the Upper Sphere like it does inside. Can *you*
afford to be away for years? Hell, I don't like having
been gone for the weeks we've already been."

Sandrisson shook his head sharply. "No, definitely not.
I am sure there are people waiting back home for all of
us—friends, family, and so on. More practically, if the
'Straits' are not opened, the Sandrisson Drive is, essentially, useless. It will allow us to move swiftly around our
solar system, but never give us the stars, because we
cannot exit from the Sphere and cross to other parts of
the Arena. And there is the issue that if we are gone too
long, others may try the experiment on their own, which
could severely complicate the situation here."

Ariane nodded. "And the second reason?"

DuQuesne gave a tight, cynical smile. "This whole
place is set up to make us meet at this Nexus Arena,

right? So I wouldn't put it past the builders or controllers of the Arena to make it force you to play the game, if you try to go to extremes to avoid it. Anything that can basically switch nuclear reactions on and off, and make the AISages shut down without causing a detectable bit of damage, can probably do other stupid physics tricks, like keep batteries from charging beyond a certain level."

Ariane winced at that thought. "That's a nasty thought . . . and it fits with what we know so far. Okay, we have to move forward. So what're our next steps?"

DuQuesne spoke up. "For my part, Captain, I'd like to head back and bring the others up to date. Then maybe take an expedition to this Outer Gateway and see what we have up there, take advantage of whatever resources we actually have to work with."

Ariane repressed an immediate expression of dismay. She really didn't like the idea of facing the Arena without the black-bearded, omnicompetent DuQuesne backing her up, but he didn't come up with ideas without good reason. "Can we afford to split up like that?" she asked finally.

DuQuesne shrugged. "I don't think we can afford *not* to, Captain. We've got more people than we've sent here, of course, but there's no way we're taking any part of this place by force of numbers. What we *do* need is resources, stuff that we can either trade or at least live on, and from what Orphan says, the Outer Gateway leads to a livable environment—maybe with food and water we can use. With that, we would have a *lot* more options, especially on the timeframe side, and—more importantly —we have to update everyone else.

"At the same time," he continued, "we can't drop the ball here, either. We've made apparently a pretty good start for a first entry, drawn some attention, and people are interested in that. We can't vanish for days or weeks after that—we'd lose the momentum of the moment."

"Are you sure you want to go back now, Marc?" Simon asked. "I don't mind saying that I feel a lot more comfortable with you here."

"Thanks, Simon. And I appreciate that," DuQuesne said. "But I think I *have* to, for the reasons I just gave. We've got a bunch of other people back there who've got nothing except a little ping I gave them when I went back through. And no, I'm not saying how I managed that, Captain, not here, not now. But they need the full update, and we need those resources. So, yeah, I'm going. The captain can protect you pretty damn well, Simon—at least against anything ordinary—and the security setup they have should prevent all-out war. Just don't commit to anything, and if you've got a question—any question at all—about whether someone's trying to put something over on you, say no and kick it over to the captain."

Simon nodded, to her vast surprise. *Just "kick it over to the captain," as though I actually have any better judgment on this kind of stuff than Simon? And he just accepts it? Don't they realize I'm making it all up as I go along?* "Well, then, I think I'm going to avail myself of the water for a cleanup, and then eat a little something and go to bed," Simon said. "Apologies for disappearing, but I actually want to replay some of my conversation with Dr. Rel; there were a few things he let slip—deliberately or not—which give me some new insights."

Once Simon was gone, she glanced over at DuQuesne. "Just kick it over to me?"

The big man shifted uncomfortably. "Sorry. I know that put you on the spot, but you didn't torpedo me."

"Because I figure *you* know what you're doing. You've proven you think about five steps ahead of everyone, even Orphan, so I have to assume you have some reason to make Simon and the others believe I actually deserve that silly title you all stuck on me."

DuQuesne shook his head. "You've got it all wrong, Captain. You don't believe it yourself, but believe me, you've got what it takes. The instinct, the aura of command, look of eagles, whatever it is, you've got it. I can fake it up when I need it, but that's not even close to the real thing, not by about ninety-seven rows of little apple trees."

She just stared at him for a minute, realizing that he sincerely meant every word of it. *Me?*

Then she shrugged. "Ooo . . . kay. Whatever you say . . . Blackie."

He winced and grunted. "I was afraid that if anyone on *Holy Grail* would know, it would be you. *Please* do not use that name again, all right?"

"All right. It was just that last line."

"What? Oh, that damn apple tree thing. You know, I've tried to drum all that crap out of my head for the past fifty years, and whenever I get put under stress, the blasted stuff comes right back out."

"Could be worse. I'd imagine if they had people based on even less realistic backgrounds . . . "

DuQuesne looked bleak. "Don't."

Touching on something he's not ready to talk about. "Sorry." She tried to give an apologetic grin, but her lip stung. "Ow."

"You going to be okay?" DuQuesne looked relieved to find another topic.

"It's just a split lip, Marc, I've had lots worse even when I was a kid. Does remind me how much I've been relying on your being there, though. Not that I want anyone getting killed trying to save my pride, but I wouldn't have been able to face down that . . . thing at all." She couldn't quite keep the embarrassment off her face. "I've got a . . . problem with spiders, and those things set off my spider reaction."

"They do have the look of the same kind of nasty to them in some ways, I'll agree. But after what we've seen, I don't think you need anything from me, at least not for the next few days. Just trust your instincts, don't give anyone anything, and if things really look bad, have Orphan bring you back to the gate. Bring him with you, if he's really in danger; he's got his own agenda, no doubt, but we need him, I think." He got up. "I'm going to get ready for bed myself. Captain, the only thing you need to do that you aren't doing is pretty simple—and it's also the damn hardest thing you'll ever have to do.

"Trust yourself. You're not just captain because we stuck you with the job. That's just how you *got* the job. But if you weren't actually able to *do* the job—to hold together this little group of independent thinkers—we'd never have gotten this far." He looked reluctant to bring up the subject, but said, "Do you think someone . . . something . . . like me follows just anyone? I've worked to get rid of the real superiority complex, but believe you me, I've still got a lot of little issues in that area, and most bosses put my back up. You . . . you just say what has to get done, and we do it. Even when I'm asking myself what the hell's going on, I'm still following your lead. So try believing you deserve the job you've got—" He grinned suddenly. "—even if you really didn't deserve to have it dumped on you."

He left for his own room, and Ariane headed for hers. Maybe . . . no, given his experience, *probably* . . .

DuQuesne was right. She had always been able to direct groups she was in. Maybe she did have a talent for leading people. Maybe it was even guided by good instinct for the right thing to do.

But still . . . he was going to be gone, leaving her with no backup except Simon. *I'd argue, but I think he's right.*

But, oh, dear gods, am I going to miss having him here.

Chapter 29

The inner doorway rolled open, and DuQuesne found himself staring down the barrel of what appeared to be an old-fashioned but no doubt highly functional tripod-mounted machine gun.

The blue eyes behind the sights of the gun relaxed. "Thank *God* it's you, D . . . Marc," Gabrielle Wolfe said in her soft Southern drawl, swinging the gun to point in a safer direction and stepping away. "Where's the others?"

"Didn't get my ping?" he asked, then answered himself, "Of course not; I entered during one of the closed cycles and it didn't take me long to get here."

Carl nodded. "It's still about twenty minutes before we'd be checking for the update. Thanks for that last one."

"Those weren't updates, they were 'wish you were here' postcards and 'still alive' pings." He glanced over at Cussler. "No one picked up on the scam, Tom, just like we thought."

"I'm glad. Not that most of us could have gotten away with it."

DuQuesne shrugged. "Admittedly, it takes a lot of training to be able to make sure no one's looking, or misdirect them, so that I could deploy one of the miniature RF nodes. I was most worried about Orphan; couldn't be sure he didn't have better senses, or some gadgetry I hadn't noticed. That's why I had a delay set up on them so they wouldn't radiate until after we'd left. Worked, though." DuQuesne chuckled. "He may be an alien, but you should've seen how totally flummoxed he was by the fact that I could be absolutely sure I'd come back to the right place, in a couple of seconds. He couldn't figure it at all."

Tom grinned widely. DuQuesne didn't blame him; it had been Tom and Carl who'd come up with the idea of making not nanotech devices—which, for some reason failed, outside of living bodies—but truly ancient RF repeater/sensor nodes using nothing more advanced than late twentieth or early twenty-first century integrated circuits, miniature sensors, power harvesting, and low-power transmitters. Several dozen of the centimeter-square devices had been hidden at various points in and around his clothing, and he'd deployed them at intervals and locations that would insure uninterrupted relaying. One of the others had had to come out and arrange for the inner doors to open at intervals, of course, but once the nodes had become active, they could provide a map to each successive location.

DuQuesne was sure that such devices were common in the Arena—espionage being as popular as it must be—but the combination of their quick adoption of the technology and his ability to deploy it unseen had been the key to effective use. The latter was, of course, the reason he'd pressured even Carl Edlund into keeping the existence of the nodes secret from Ariane and Simon. Had they known he was deploying these devices, they might have given it away inadvertently. By being unaware of it themselves, even their body language could reveal nothing.

"Where're Ariane and Dr. Sandrisson?" demanded Steve.

"They stayed behind to keep the pot stirred. They should be safe enough for now. Look, let a guy get settled, gimme a few minutes to breathe, and I'll tell you about it."

He didn't let them rush him; he wanted to make sure he went through the sequence of events, and the implications of those events, carefully and clearly. Once he'd gotten himself lunch—having been brought by Orphan and the others to the Inner Gateway after breakfast and discussion—DuQuesne brought the others up to speed.

The story—with numerous interruptions and questions—took quite a while. But finally he was done. "So that's where we sit. I've got all this on record, I can dump it to main storage or anyone's headware who wants the whole thing. But that's the summary."

The others were silent for several minutes. He could see they were all trying to absorb the impact of the full scale of the Arena—and the magnitude of the tasks facing them. Finally Gabrielle sat up briskly. "Well, let's not sit here doing nothing, time's a-wasting. So our next step here is that 'Outer Gateway' you mentioned before, right?"

"You got it," DuQuesne agreed, smiling at her straightforward manner. "We go see what's outside and if it's got stuff we can use. If what Orphan says is true—and I don't have any reason to doubt it—we have liveable biosphere of some kind out there. Figuring out what kind, how liveable, and how we can best make use of it, that's going to require some of us go out there and take a look."

"Well, then," Gabrielle said firmly, "it's clear that you'll have to take me."

"No, I'd think you want *me*," Carl objected.

"We're talking about new lifeforms and what we can survive on, and exactly how much do you know about biology?"

"We're talking about exploring and getting information —and living to tell about it. That's sensors and combat."

The diminuitive blonde smiled innocently up at Carl. "Honey, you want to try two falls out of three with me?"

"Enough," DuQuesne said, and the two immediately went silent. "I can appreciate that you've all been bored and getting pretty itchy under the collar. And I also appreciate that two of you are enthusiastic enough to want to come with me." He glanced at Steve and Tom. "And that some of you would like nothing *less* until after someone else has scouted it out."

Steve shrugged. "Hey, I'm no coward, but I'm also not a fighter or a rugged explorer type. I'm curious, but that's not really a unique or useful trait."

"My position, too, basically," said Tom. "Someone has to keep things running here anyway."

"Which is of course the crucial point," DuQuesne agreed. He glanced apologetically at Gabrielle. "Dr. Wolfe, in no way do I doubt your capability or your willingness. However . . ."

" . . . You are going to be telling me why you're taking Carl instead of me," she finished with a sigh.

"Yes. You're the doctor. That makes you in some ways the most crucial member of the crew; the longer we stay here—especially given the specifically dangerous conditions imposed on us by this 'Arena'—the more likely it is that some of us are going to get hurt, possibly very badly. Given that, it would be criminally irresponsible of me—or any of us—to permit you to be exposed to any more danger than we can reasonably avoid." He held up a hand to forestall an argument. "I am *not* saying we have to wrap you up in insulation and store you inside a box like a precious artifact; the fact is that with only seven functioning members of the team, we can't afford to have anyone who isn't kept busy most of the time. But you are not, and will not, be taking point on any serious exploration endeavors."

She nodded; he could see that she was severely disappointed, but couldn't argue the logic of the situation. "All right, Marc, you're right. Damnation."

"However," he said, smiling apologetically, "I do intend for you to come with us *to* the Outer Gateway and be standing by. If we run into something out there, I don't want to have to drag Carl—or worse, him have to drag me—back through a kilometer and a half of corridor just to get him to medical assistance."

"Well now," she said, more cheerfully, "that's a whole heckuva lot better than nothing. I'll at least get to take a peek out the front door and see the sky you were talking about."

"That you will."

Carl was already sorting through equipment that had been fabbed up. "We'll be going tomorrow?"

"I see no reason to delay. I'd go today, but I think we should take some time in examining what we will need to bring with us and thinking the potential scenarios through. I am not expecting to spend days outside without reporting back, of course—I want to scout areas no more than a few kilometers or so from the Gateway, enough to get a feel for the area accessible to us in the immediate future, and see what we can do with it."

"Makes sense."

Tom grunted. "In that case, I think I'd better start the old AIWish going on making some hiking and climbing gear in your sizes."

"And some radio relay beacons, and backup weapons. And given that we have no idea what type of environment it's going to be, you'll need to make stuff suitable for anything from Hawaii to Antarctica. We'll drag it all up and then after we pop the door we'll choose the gear most suited for the environment. We can always recycle the rest later."

"Just don't forget the most important stuff," Carl said emphatically. "Trail mix."

Chapter 30

Like the Inner Gateway, the Outer Gateway looming before them was twenty meters across. However, the Outer Gateway was not a vortex of unfathomable energies, but another simple doorway of the indestructible Arena material. It had been something of a hike, following the directions Orphan had given DuQuesne before he returned—through several corridors and then taking what appeared to be another elevator like those he'd seen in Nexus Arena. Given what he guessed about the design of this place, DuQuesne suspected that the relatively short ride was exceedingly deceptive and the elevator actually covered a vastly greater vertical ascent than simple human perceptions would indicate.

The elevator had opened into a large room—the room in which they were now standing and had made their advance base. DuQuesne surveyed the makeshift base camp, at which Gabrielle would be standing watch. All three of them were armed and facing the doorway, as they had no idea what might be waiting outside.

He felt tense, but also somehow . . . more free. It was a pleasant, yet eerily insidious feeling, one that harmonized with parts of him that hadn't been allowed free rein in decades, and he worried about that. Had all his prior work been useless? Or was it just that here, in the ultimate of all artificial environments, parts of the old Marc C. DuQuesne were just better suited than the persona he'd developed instead?

It doesn't matter right now. We've got a job to do. He checked to make sure the others were ready, getting wordless nods in answer. He faced the door. "Open Outer Gateway."

The great door rolled smoothly aside, and blazing sunlight streamed in, sunlight of such a familiar shade that he blinked. With the light came a distant rumbling noise, faint strange sounds, and a breath of cool, humid air that brought the smells of a new world with it; sweet scents, an undertone of pungency, the faint emanation of decay smelled in a forest. Cautiously, the three advanced to the entrance and stood looking out.

"Wow," Carl said finally.

The Outer Gateway opened onto a wide ledge of rock jutting from the face of a cliff. A kilometer off to the left, a great waterfall plunged down into the valley below, the source of the distant rumbling. The steep-sided valley was filled with lush vegetation, most of it a deep green in color, but with shades of lighter green and blue-green visible. Splotches of red, yellow, violet, and other colors indicated flowers or something similar, and motion was visible indicating something like birds flying between the trees.

Above, a cheerful white-yellow sun shone, looking essentially identical to the one they'd left behind weeks . . . or was it months? . . . ago; but through the generally blue background of the sky, and the white of the floating clouds, were hints of something else, a sub-liminal curve or suggestion of color that had no business being in a sky.

Gabrielle suddenly squatted down. "Well, hello there."

Following her gaze, DuQuesne could see that she was observing something moving along the ground, shiny and black with many legs—very much like a beetle. "Be care-ful," he cautioned. "The Arena may make it possible to survive here, but that certainly doesn't mean things can't be dangerous—and, in fact, Orphan says it's probably about as dangerous as exploring a new area of Earth was back in the old days. Which means that most things probably are perfectly safe, but you can't tell right now—"

"—whether that's a harmless wood beetle or the local equivalent of a black widow," Gabrielle cut in. "Don't try to teach your medical officer how to wrap bandages. I'm not going to take any unnecessary chances, Marc."

Carl, meanwhile, had been surveying the ledge. "Looks to me like we've got a pretty good path down from here, at least for a while. I'd want to belay us at a couple points, but it probably won't be necessary if we're careful."

DuQuesne agreed, after glancing over the indicated pathway. "Looks good to me. All right, are we clear on procedure?"

"You're going to check in with me every half hour, on the dot. If I don't hear from either of you within five minutes of that time, I give you a call. If I get nothing after another hour, I do not—and you have emphasized, I do *not*—come after you right away by myself. I go down and get Steve or Tom first, and have them back me up as I scout for you at the last known position. If I don't find you fast, or I stop calling in, they're to shut the Gateway tight and wait for Ariane or Simon to come back—or go through the Inner Gateway, their judgment call." The pretty blonde did not look entirely happy with this arrangement. "This does mean that if you two *do* get into trouble, that you either solve it yourselves or you'll be dead before anyone gets there."

"So we'd better not get in trouble," Carl agreed. "Setting time at . . . *mark*. Okay, first call back in one half hour, even if we're only fifty yards down the mountain."

"Good enough," DuQuesne said. "Let's go."

The "pretty good path" turned out to end after a descent that took them down almost a hundred and fifty meters, zig-zagging so as to cover something close to a kilometer in actual walking distance. The end of the path was a small natural platform (although considering the setting, DuQuesne wondered whether he should apply the word "natural" to anything here); looking over the edge, DuQuesne could see a sheer drop of fifty meters into greenery that ran just about completely up against the cliff; it was hard to make out what lay at the bottom.

Descents and ascents of that magnitude, however, had been well within their discussed possible scenarios, and after check-in he and Carl were quickly able to set up a powered winch, anchored to the rock by spikes, with a solar recharger. It would handle masses up to three times

DuQuesne's mass for that distance, and with regenerative charging from descents as well as solar, would be able to handle up to three such upward loads per day. "Not useful for high traffic, but I doubt we'll need anything more than that," Carl said.

DuQuesne nodded and as it was check-in time, spoke. "Gabrielle, we've completed the winch setup and it works. We're now heading down. I'm leaving our first repeater here." He locked the radio relay repeater onto the winch supports.

"Understood, Marc. What's your plan?"

"I'm going to head for the river. Water's always a good thing to have a lot of, and most lifeforms will tend to hang out in those areas. Our armor should hold off just about anything alive long enough for us to shoot it or cut it down, assuming we don't see it coming."

"Carl? Anything interesting?"

"Nothing of great note. Getting spikes of RF noise off and on, but at this point I can't tell what could be causing them. There's sure no sign of other aspects of civilization, so I strongly suspect a natural cause—maybe from up there." He pointed to the sky. "Storms out there might make lightning that's completely mindboggling, and the EM might go a long, long way."

"Well, keep an eye on it. Let me know if you see any patterns. We might also be seeing transmissions from some other Sphere. On this scale, it's possible that we could receive transmissions from Alpha Centauri in effective realtime, so to speak."

"Will do. Ready to head down?"

"Ready."

"Be careful, you two," Gabrielle's voice said. "I don't want to have to actually exercise any of my functions.

Just look out through the doorway at the sunset, whenever that is."

"We're assuming there *is* a sunset here," Carl said.

"Unless things change, there will be," DuQuesne informed him. "The sun's moved in the sky by a fair angle—about as much as I'd expect it to move back home, overall. Makes sense; if they're trying to make it liveable, they'd have to take into account that a lot of organisms depend on the night-day cycle." He swung onto the descent saddle. "Descending. Next call in thirty minutes."

The descent turned out to be actually closer to one hundred meters—near the limit of the winch's cable and reducing the number of up-trips that would be practical. DuQuesne had to pause the saddle several times to hack away vegetation that was encroaching too closely. Once he disturbed a nest of something that tried to attack in a swarm, but his light environment suit automatically closed up and the things dispersed shortly; they'd appeared to be something like a cross between a dragonfly and a stag beetle. Finally, however, he reached the bottom.

The base of the cliff was scree, fallen rock, but being woven into a more stable base by swiftly growing vines and other plants. He wondered idly how the Outer Gateway coped with geologic shifts . . . and then what sort of geology existed on this outlandish place. "Down, Carl. I've cleared the descent path, it should be okay."

With no need for him to pause, it took Carl only a few minutes to descend and join DuQuesne on the ground. It was somewhat warmer here, but not tremendously so. "Climate variations must be very different on these Spheres. I'm afraid we're going to have to re-work just about everything we know about the sciences in view of this place."

The two cautiously worked their way closer to the river, calling in as time required. Once well into the jungle, the undergrowth diminished considerably, making progress easier, but DuQuesne kept both of them moving slowly and carefully; he didn't want to get caught out by anything unexpected. Both of them noted a number of potentially interesting features—a plant, or something that looked like one, that appeared to move when they got close; a brightly-colored flying thing that gave DuQuesne the impression of a pterodactyl or, possibly, a bat—though with a bifurcated tail; one tree that had a circle of absolutely bare soil near it (which they both gave a very wide berth); and others.

Finally, DuQuesne could hear the river rattling over rocks not far off, and then reported in to Gabrielle. "It's going to get dark fairly soon, so after we scout out this area I think we'll set up camp, probably in a tree or hanging between a couple."

"Understood."

Out of the corner of his eye he saw Carl stiffen. "Hold on," he said to Gabrielle. "What is it?"

Carl pulled out a flat display. "Stronger RF spikes—and they've coincided with our calls the last couple of times. I just managed to get a good spectrum of the last one, and it looks to me like a transmission!"

DuQuesne immediately linked to Carl's data and scanned it rapidly. What he saw sent a shockwave of adrenaline through him. "Gabrielle, Code 6, repeat, Code 6." He cut off immediately, with Carl silently mouthing a disbelieving "*Code 6?*" at him.

He nodded. "Move."

The two of them hastened from their prior position, trying to parallel the river towards the cliff. "Code 6" was a contingency for what was to happen if DuQuesne thought there was a possibility of encounter with advanced hostiles. His glance over the data indicated several potential sources, which had shifted position, and which were closer—much closer—now than they had been previously. Critical now was to get away from the last transmission location. Gabrielle—assuming she followed the orders, which he hoped she would—had by now retreated inside the Gateway and locked it. It would be unlocked for a quick glance and interrogation at semi-random intervals for the next day or so, to allow them to make it back inside without giving adversaries a chance to attack.

He held up his hand, and Carl sank down to the ground; they hid in the dense vegetation and waited, weapons out and ready.

Long minutes ticked past, and then more minutes. Shadows began to lengthen as the sun-equivalent retreated behind distant ridges, invisible from their viewpoint inside the jungle. DuQuesne was relaxed but alert, deliberately slowing his breathing and heart rate to wait as long as he had to. After some initial tenseness, Carl tried to emulate him—fairly well, DuQuesne had to admit. But that wasn't too surprising, given Carl's preferred virtual adventure background; he really did know a lot about the martial arts, and control of one's body on all levels was a part of that.

Still, there was a limit to most people's patience, and after an hour and a half, Carl shifted. "How much longer—"

"Shh!" DuQuesne hissed with quiet intensity. His ears had just picked up on another sound.

To someone else—less trained, less paranoid—it might have sounded almost random, the dropping of detritus to the forest floor, the occasional scuttle of something else through underbrush; but to DuQuesne it sounded like something else, a set of carefully spaced footfalls—not human footfalls, either—timed to blend in with the background. But during the sounds there was also sometimes the faint rushing scrape of bushes or other plants being pushed aside by a larger body.

Carl looked at him questioningly; clearly he still couldn't hear it. DuQuesne shook his head very slightly; the other man looked grim and made sure he had a good grip on his gun.

The sounds continued, gradually approaching. No . . . there was more than one set of sounds. *Dammit!* DuQuesne cursed inwardly. Whoever they were, it was a trained squad. He caught Carl's eye, used his hands to give him vectors. *Four individuals. There, there, there, and there.*

A very faint shadow moved in the gloom; based on his sketchy knowledge of the area, he guessed it at about seventy-five meters off, and that made it pretty good-sized. Couldn't quite get a good look at it. Of course, if the things had infrared imaging on, they might already see him and Dr. Edlund. They would *certainly* spot them as soon as either of them moved.

Then another movement in shadow, a bit closer; this one stalked cautiously, smoothly into a slight clearing, and DuQuesne's heart seemed to drop straight into his boots. A centauroid body atop seven sharp-jointed legs, with a pair of jack-knife arms held curled and ready.

Molothos.

How the hell did they get here? There's no way they could have known where we came from. We must just be hitting the absolute jackpot *of bad luck; some scouting party happened to find our Sphere and land on it.*

He considered their options coolly, dispassionately. They'd be discovered in the next few seconds—that much was certain. There were four of them—and he'd be stupid to assume there weren't more somewhere else. No chance to make a sprint for the winch; unless the things were terribly slowed by the vegetation—unlikely —the two of them would just end up being a piñata for Molothos to gun down. That was assuming that they could outsprint the things through the jungle and not get killed by something along the way. Surrender was pretty much out of the question; even if he hadn't had a first-hand sample of their attitude, Orphan's description had made it clear that he'd be about as warmly welcomed as a Jew into a Nazi meeting. Oh, they might keep one of them alive, or both, for study, but that wasn't going to be much fun.

And it would just leave the problem for later, leave it to get worse. No. Only one thing to do.

His one hand was still in Carl's field of view. He aimed it at the one to the right, since that was on Carl's side, wiggled his gun ever so slightly, then held up three fingers. Carl's eyes widened, he swallowed. Then nodded.

DuQuesne balled his fist, then began the count. One finger. Two fingers.

Three.

As the Molothos suddenly gave a chittering hiss and turned towards their hiding place, DuQuesne and Carl opened up on them.

Let's start a little interstellar war!

Chapter 31

"Meet me here in thirty-nine and a half hours," Orphan said, preparing to step through the Gateway.

"That's a rather odd number," Simon said.

Orphan buzz-chuckled. "Because in this case the facile nature of the Arena's translation obfuscates the actual meaning. That is two of my days." He gave them a serious look. "Don't be late; I would not want to meet my erstwhile people alone." Then he disappeared in a flare of iridescence.

Alone in the Arena. The very thought sent a chill—both of excitement and fear—down her spine. Instead of showing that, she turned cheerfully to Simon—who was looking apprehensive—and said "Well, now that we've dumped our chaperone, let's see what kind of trouble we can get into."

"I think," Simon said dryly, "we'd best avoid the trouble if we can." His eyes scanned the immense foyer area as they walked towards the elevators.

"No real argument there," she conceded. "Simon, I've been thinking about what we know about the Arena, and I guess I'm starting to get a—really vague—grasp of why you and DuQuesne found it so shocking. That is, it's really impressive even to me, but for you guys it's kicking at the very foundations of reality, right?"

"I suppose that's one way to put it, yes," the green-eyed Sandrisson said after a moment. "I knew, of course, that there was a conceptual framework which permitted a UFOR—Universal Frame of Reference—and that it was on that conceptual framework that I could base the Sandrisson-Kanzaki-Locke Drive." He shook his head, gazing around in bemusement. "But never in even my wildest dreams—or I suspect DuQuesne's—would I have imagined a literal instantiation of this, a separate reality which permits us to make the concept of simultanaeity a real and rational part of the universe. And—in point of fact—we are seeing, not one UFOR, but two, two separate levels of such a frame of reference, one privileged over the other."

"Whoa. Two? Where are you getting that?"

He waved a hand behind him. "Those, for starters. They amount to instantaneous teleportation gates from one part of the Arena to here. But from what Orphan said, the Arena itself is—while vastly smaller than the universe it models—truly immense, something between fifteen and thirty light-years across.

"Those gates means that simultaneity is meaningful within the Arena as well as in our universe. Meaning that there is some privileged frame of reference for the Arena itself as well as for our universe." Simon smiled faintly. "I know, for you, the entire concept of *non*-simultaneity makes no sense. It doesn't for many people."

"I'll agree with that. But I'll accept that it's an important and—until now—very real concept for understanding our world."

Simon waggled a finger at her. "It is *still* a very real concept for understanding our world. The existence of the Arena and associated frames of reference merely shows that the relativistic effects are limited—special cases which will collapse if subjected to analysis from the point of view of the privileged frame, but only if they become relevant to the spacetime track of . . . " he saw the incomprehension in her eyes and stopped. "Sorry."

She grinned as they entered the elevator. "No need to apologize, Simon. Just because I don't understand doesn't mean you have to stop talking." She stared at the blank doors of the elevator as they descended. "The thing that gets me is really the sheer *scale* of the Arena. I spent time trying to visualize it last night, and it's . . . scary. Billions of stars, each with a Sphere, gathered into billions of galaxies, all connected, running like clockwork—you know, sorry to divert, but I don't think I've ever actually seen clockwork, and I'd think it must fail a lot more often than solid-state devices . . . anyway, all of that running, while keeping track of all the things happening in the different locations . . . "

"Not to mention," Simon said, "maintaining the environment around the Spheres. Energy balance for something this size is . . . inconceivable. How do you stop areas of Spheres from overheating or underheating? If the walls are reflecting heat, the entire Arena should be warming eventually to an oven. For that matter, how does one have *walls* on something like this? Are the walls themselves expanding as the universe does? What *powers* this?"

Ariane noticed, as they exited and headed for one of the automated taxis, that a considerable number of the Arena's diverse inhabitants were—mostly discreetly —watching them. By now, imagery—suitably translated for the various species—from their prior day must have made the rounds, and given that First Emergents showed up only once every few thousand years, they were undoubtedly a major source of interest. Some of those creatures were probably trying to figure out a good way to approach them, others just wondering what they were up to. Hopefully none of them were hostile . . . well, except the Blessed and the Molothos, both of which were already sort of done deals on that side. The Molothos hated everybody and they'd gotten in the Blessed's way from the start. She helped Simon board, as she was leading the way, and then sat down. "The Grand Arcade," she said, giving the name Orphan had given them for the central meeting, entertainment, and business district to be found on this level of Nexus Arena. The silver autocab immediately departed.

"Simon," she said finally, "do you think . . . do you think the Arena is a *technological* construct?"

He stared at her for a moment. Then his glasses flashed as he tilted his head back and gazed to the far-distant ceiling, chuckling gently. "Ariane, I am a scientist. I do not believe in gods or demons. And as DuQuesne pointed out, we know theoretically how such technology might come to be. The existence of a universal frame of reference is upsetting and astounding, but given that, someone with Plancktech—the ability to manipulate reality with what amount to spacetime-scale devices—could do everything we have seen.

"That would no more make them gods or magical than we would be gods in, oh, the Roman era. Being hidden is what makes them mysterious. Clarke's law applies, of course—I can't distinguish the powers here from magic, not logically and beyond argument, but Okham's Razor helps me there; it is less complex for me to simply assume a race that's progressed a great deal farther down the path of technology, than to assume some being or set of beings with utterly unknown and unconnected powers of 'magic.'"

Just hearing him say that so calmly, with a certainty that swept aside the awesome existence of the Arena and replaced it with the investigative analytical wonder of the eternal scientist, steadied her. She smiled. "Thanks, Simon. That really does help."

The elegant white-tressed head bowed graciously. "My pleasure as always, Ariane. Oh, by the way," he continued, as though a thought had occurred to him, "did I mention that I actually did figure out why it was that the probes seemed to be giving almost random results in terms of their emergence?"

"No, actually, you didn't. So, go on, tell me."

Simon smiled. "It came from examining the data logs on our . . . shutdown, and comparing those with what would thus likely have happened on the probes. On *Holy Grail*, we had deliberately designed alternative paths and shutdown protocols that assumed other systems onboard, and that were predicated on the assumption that things that normally never fail . . . might. Well, modeling the *way* in which the systems would have failed in the absence of such careful design—which would have been useless without, of course, human beings on board to run those alternative systems—shows that many of them would have had their drive systems come on and run wild, so to speak, for the duration of their time in the Arena-space. Thus causing them to randomly displace, rather like a rocket touched off in atmosphere with no guidance. Since they tended to start with relatively small vectors, unlike *Holy Grail* which was moving at something like ten KPS when we transitioned, the final emerging locations were very close to random."

"Ha! That does make sense. I'm glad we cleared that little mystery up."

The vehicle slowed and stopped, depositing them at the entrance to what would, elsewhere, be an immense open-air mall or marketplace; a vast circular expanse of streets and smaller buildings, miniature parks, covered smaller arcades, wandering street performers, and vendors of a dozen species. Smells—ranging from the enticing to the repugnant—drifted on the air, though something prevented the entire effect from being overwhelming; the scents of uncountable numbers of species of intelligent beings, of meals being cooked in a hundred or a thousand different ways using a million ingredients, the pungency of other goods—perhaps spices and fuels, or perhaps something indescribable in function—combined to make a heady and almost intoxicating whole. Everywhere Ariane looked she saw some new type of creature, and all around were the sounds of different beings, devices, and signals.

"Let's just take a look through the area. If someone engages us in conversation, fine, but let's not try talking ourselves yet. And don't commit us to anything."

Simon nodded his understanding. "More than a trifle overwhelming."

Taking a deep breath, she plunged into the whirl of the Grand Arcade, Simon at her heels.

Chapter 32

Ariane sagged onto a nearby bench. "God, I'm tired. This place is the size of New York Megaplaza." She nibbled at the purple-edged, yellow flame-shaped object the Chiroflekir vendor had called a *tullundu*. From her expression, she was trying to decide if she liked it or not. "How do you like your snack?"

"It's quite good, actually," Simon said cheerfully. He'd noticed the delicate, blue-green jellyfish-like alien—the same species that had caught his attention early in their entry to the Arena—and suggested they at least ask him about how common it was for different species to actually be able to eat one another's produce. As it turned out, the biology of the Chiroflekir was startlingly similar to that of Earth creatures, enough so that the tentacled creature had several candidate foods in stock, and was willing to offer some samples in exchange for one of their ration bars; even if it couldn't eat the ration bar, it was material that gave Olthalis (the vendor) some unique and useful information about the First Emergents.

Simon took another bite of his selection—deep red, rod-shaped, with a startling white and pink speckled interior, called *nidii*—and then offered it to her. "Here, try it. I'll take a bite of yours."

The two alien food samples changed hands and Simon took a bite of the *tullundu* and chewed contemplatively. *Hm . . . somewhat salty . . . a faint sharpness, a smooth internal texture, almost oceanic backtaste . . . ah, yes.*

Ariane bit into hers with a crunch-snap like that of a good apple, and her face lit up. "You're right, I like this. Like . . . I don't know, cattail stem crossed with seaweed?"

"Not a bad comparison. I like this one, too. Reminds me rather a lot of uni."

"Sea urchin roe! That explains the vague familiarity. Not quite the same texture, though. And I never did really like uni."

"Well, then, I'll try to be a gentleman; please keep the *nidii*." He glanced appreciatively at Ariane's sharp-featured face.

By the smile she gave him, after a pause, he suspected that the glance had not gone unnoticed. "You've always been a gentleman, Simon. Except for those early moments putting your foot in your mouth."

He gave a rueful laugh. "Ariane, you have *no idea* how much I regretted those two *faux pas* moments. I was not attempting to impress you with my intellectual bigotry."

She put a hand on his arm. *Oh, now, that's a more definite signal.* "You're forgiven. Now, if you'd like, why don't you escort me into that den of iniquity over there? If the translators are correct, that's the Random Fortune Casino."

"Is it really?" Simon took her arm, and was pleased to find that she leaned slightly into him as he did so. *It is rather fun to find it's just as exciting at thirty as it was at sixteen. A casino, now . . . that's interesting.* "Amazing. They must have some form of money or credit for wagering, perhaps after you become a full citizen, winning one of these Challenges. Well then, let's go take a look. And try not to gamble our planet away."

Inside the building—despite the mass of radically diverse aliens and unfamiliar artwork—it was almost homey. The air of excitement, of dice being thrown and machines being activated and games being played for high stakes . . . this was very much the same as any casino back in their solar system. "It seems that in some ways, we are all very much alike," Simon observed. *But there's . . . something . . .*

"That's actually pretty comforting," Ariane said, seeming to relax a bit. "Okay, human beings can be dangerous bastards too, but if I can understand alien psychologies the same way I understand ours, it's going to be a lot easier to handle than if they really did have very, very alien ways of viewing things."

"Indeed."

As they strolled along, Simon became sure that there was something . . . *off* about this casino. Everything *seemed* normal on the surface, just as it would in an Earthly gambling establishment . . . and yet . . . and yet . . .

"What is it, Simon?"

"I'm . . . not quite certain yet," he answered, in an absent-minded tone of voice. "Give me a few more minutes."

They stopped next at a game involving four-sided dice being rolled on a long table, somewhat reminiscent of a craps setup. He studied the rolls . . . the bets . . . *so desu!* He drew Ariane aside. "I know what it is. You've noticed it, too, haven't you?"

Ariane's expression reflected how he'd felt earlier. "Well . . . something's been bothering me, but I don't know what it is."

"*Odds*, Captain," he said, intensely studying the other games. "The odds. Look at those dice. They're betting on combinations of the ways in which those dice fall; none of them exceed one chance in sixteen—either two ones or two fours. That . . . card game over there. The deck appears to have three suits of ten cards each, and the combinations that appear to be sought run in the same area of probability. The roulette wheel equivalent, over there, in the high stakes area, offers nothing beyond a twenty to one gamble. I don't think I've seen a single game yet in which the odds against the gambler exceeded fifty to one or so except what appear to be pure lotteries—and even those seem to go no higher than a thousand or so to one."

"That seems . . . awfully good odds, actually."

"*Very* good odds by the standards of Earth casinos—or terrible odds, in the sense of whether you can get rich quick. In standard poker, odds of fifty to one only get you to three of a kind. Getting a full house is about one chance in seven hundred, while a straight flush is one in seventy-two thousand; roulette wheels commonly top out at odds of fifty to one hundred to one, and lotteries of course run into odds of millions to one."

He was so focused on what he was seeing that he was startled when Ariane pushed him gently aside to let a passing quadrupedal alien go by. He shook his head. "Yet this is a busy, clearly profitable casino, and one that does a great deal of business. It is located on a prime area of what must be some of the most in-demand real estate in the universe—the Grand Arcade of Nexus Arena—and thus must reflect the demands of the vast majority of customers, from tourists to high-rollers, and do so with enduring popularity. I can thus only conclude that virtually all of those who visit these establishments will not tolerate odds even nearly so high as those which rather conservative human gamblers expect."

Her face lit up with understanding. "I think you must be right, Simon. Remember when DuQuesne confronted the Molothos, how utterly freaked Orphan was? Remember what he said? Where a human being would have compared the chances to one in a million, the largest number Orphan could seem to think of in that situation was a hundred. As though only a lunatic would ever place a bet on something more than a hundred to one."

Simon nodded slowly. *Exactly.* "Yes, and that's not the only similar indication; Ghondas's speech contained other suggestive phrases along those lines. So what does it all mean, that's the question. Why are we such risk-takers or, alternatively, why are they all so risk-averse?"

Ariane shook her head. "No idea. But I think we should keep this little fact to ourselves for now. If there's a significant difference, it's worth our while to hide it until we can figure out if there's an advantage in it for us." She glanced towards the entrance, instinctively, as she thought of DuQuesne. "Maybe Marc will have some idea when he gets back."

"Probably," Simon said. "And I'm sure, after checking into that Outer Gateway, he's looking forward to getting back to the excitement here."

Chapter 33

DuQuesne snarled something wordless as the gun buzzed silently in his hand, demanding a new ammo pack. He dove for cover as a screaming storm of edged shrapnel shredded the foliage where he'd just been standing. Yanking out another from his fast-shrinking store of magazines, he ejected the empty and slammed the new one home. "Carl?"

The control expert's voice answered in a whisper off to his left. "Still here. How the hell many of these things are there?" Hearing movement off to the left, Carl fired several bursts in that direction.

"No idea. We killed the first four, but at least one of them managed to call home base and they sent out commando parties to get us. I *think* I've killed five or six more, how about you?"

"Five or six? How the hell do you get that kind of accuracy with these things?" Carl demanded. "Their armor shrugs even the AP stuff off unless you get a joint or the eye."

DuQuesne saw movement out of the corner of his eye, whirled and fired a burst that made the Molothos whirl away in a dancing gait like a spinning top; as the thing spun towards cover, he switched to single-shot and fired; the bullet carved its way straight through the narrow seam that joined the lower body to the upper; the creature collapsed like a deflated balloon, legs splayed limply about it. "The waist seam's my preferred target. I think they keep their brains in that area."

"The *waist*? Every time I try for that shot, it bounces off the body armor. Anyway, I think I got two." Carl's eyes narrowed. "Marc . . ."

"I hear it. They're rushing us." He glanced around quickly. "This way!"

The two humans sprinted from cover. The hissing screeches of the Molothos, translated into various equivalents of "There they are!" and "Get them!" competed with the screeching hisses of their weapons. A rattle of impacts jolted the two, but failed to penetrate the ring-carbon composite armor. Just before reaching the clearing ahead, DuQuesne pushed Carl, pointing, and the two raced around the edge of the clearing.

Seeing an opportunity to cut them off, two Molothos sprinted across the bare ground, seven legs blurring like piston-driven shafts.

As the two aliens passed the lone tree and a third appeared at the edge of the clearing, DuQuesne fired a single quick shot backwards. The bullet missed both Molothos and smacked squarely into the trunk of the tree.

A hailstorm of black and purple shapes plummeted from the branches above, erupted from the ground, spewed forth from fissures in the tree trunk, and enveloped the Molothos. The aliens shrieked in consternation and began firing randomly.

"What the hell was that?" Carl demanded.

"No idea. I figured you never got bare ground in a jungle without good reason. And one of the trees on Earth that's like that has some very nasty ants clearing the area around it. Figured it was worth a try."

"Two or three more down?"

DuQuesne shrugged, bulling his way through the undergrowth ahead of the more slender Carl Edlund. "Maybe one, if we're lucky. The Molothos' armor probably will hold up against those things, it's just going to slow them up."

"I was afraid you'd say that." More movement off to the side. Carl reached into a side pocket and fiddled with something, then pitched the small object in the direction of the noise. A blinding detonation and shockwave followed, and DuQuesne saw with approval that one of the fragments of debris that rained down around them was a jointed leg in armor.

"I didn't recall bringing grenades, more's the pity. What did . . . a power pack?"

"Yep. Programmed a short across the mains on the pack I had for the laser cutter. Figured I wouldn't be needing it."

"Good thinking." He heard more noise to the other side, fired and modified course. "We're in trouble, you know."

"The thought had occurred . . . " More gunshots. " . . . to me. On the positive side, they're using some kind

of needle-shotgun thingies that don't work so well against
our armor; probably standard issue for dealing with animals or primitives and they didn't expect high-tech types
here. I guess you're about to tell me some bad news?"

"We're being herded. Don't know what towards, but
we can bet it's not good."

"Time to make a stand?"

DuQuesne shook his head, then saw the river ahead
of them. "Can you swim?"

"Like a fish, and this armor won't get in the way." Carl
grinned. "I get the picture."

The two sheathed their guns and dove in, going as
deep as they could into the water. The Molothos might
be able to climb, and could certainly walk well, but they
were not built at all well for swimming. They might, if
heavy enough, manage to walk along the bottom, but
with the fast-running current . . .

The current hurled them along, bouncing DuQuesne
and Carl against rocks. Once, something huge with a lot
of teeth made a snap at Carl, but broke teeth on the
armor and fled, as the two battled their way through
the water. Suddenly gravel grated underfoot, and they
staggered from the river, battered and bruised but mostly
unharmed. "Quick, into the trees!"

The two barely made the treeline before they saw their
pursuers emerge on the other side. "Six of the bastards."
DuQuesne took careful aim, as did Carl, and opened
fire.

Two of the crab-centauroid monstrosities went down
in the first barrage, the other four scattering; one's
weapon suddenly exploded in a sun-bright flare, leaving
a staggering headless corpse. The others hunkered down
behind shoreline rocks and returned fire, scuttling from

rock to rock until they reached the water and, to DuQuesne's dismay, disappeared beneath the surface. "Damn. Didn't slow them as much as I hoped."

"We got three, though."

"And I've got one and a half mags left. What about you?"

"One. And my sword."

He gritted his teeth. *I'll be damned if it's going to end like this. Not if I can help it, it won't.* The two kept moving, not intending to be caught as sitting ducks.

It was the sound of vines against carapace that warned DuQuesne, just before the Molothos charged from both sides. He and Carl, with almost rehearsed accuracy, fired on the one on the left; a bullet found its mark and the creature went down, and only one piece of the alien shrapnel-loads penetrated, making an annoying but far from crippling cut in DuQuesne's upper arm.

Carl's katana streaked from its sheath in an *iai* draw so fiercely driven that the ring-carbon reinforced steel blade carved its way through the armored striking-claws and buried itself in the torso of the second Molothos. The creature shrieked its agony and struck out, barely missing Carl as he wrenched the blade free. Hurt but still mobile, the Molothos tried to bring its gun to bear on Carl but the sword struck the weapon, tearing it from the alien's grasp and possibly rendering it useless. DuQuesne fired the last burst from his gun, failing to kill his opponent who dodged at the last moment. The last bullet did, however, strike the Molothos's weapon, shattering it. With the two aliens momentarily taken aback, the humans sprinted back into the woods. "We've got to find some way of ambushing them. And then finding out where they're based."

"Easy to talk about," Carl gasped. DuQuesne realized that despite being in excellent shape Carl simply couldn't keep up with him much longer. But if he let Carl fall behind . . .

More movement, to the side. *More of these damn things?* They turned slightly as they ran.

As they burst out into a clearing, DuQuesne staggered and went down, as did Carl, striking the ground heavily. For a moment DuQuesne thought something had leaped on top of him, something massing around a hundred kilos, but as he rolled over he felt nothing there, just the increased pressure of . . .

"Enjoy our gravity, do you?"

In front of them, silhouetted against a sharp, angular shape which could only be some form of vessel, were three Molothos—armed and ready, weapons trained on the prone humans.

Even getting across the river was in their plan, DuQuesne thought with grim admiration. *They may not have expected the casualties, but they knew just how to herd us.*

The trap was set, and now . . . now it's closed on us.

Chapter 34

DuQuesne forced himself to his feet. So did Carl, but he was clearly sagging under what was at least one and a half gravities. Two more Molothos emerged from the jungle behind them, the third wounded one trailing by a short distance. "So what are you waiting for?"

The Molothos leader shrieked. "Your speech will be silenced. You have killed many of my people, and I will have recompense for that. We have claimed this Sphere, and your intrusion is cause for war! If your repulsive species values its life, you will offer a Sphere or two in tribute!"

"You're *on* the only Sphere we have, you monster," Carl said. DuQuesne said nothing, for he was coming to the realization that he stood at the brink of a precipice, or at the edge of apotheosis, and he was at once both petrified and elated. *Of all the ways things could have gone, I end up here, in this place, at this time.*

A low hiss came from the surrounding Molothos. "Scout Master Maizas . . . there was no sign of a ship here . . . " one pointed out. The leader, Maizas, studied them with heightened interest.

"Is true . . . ? First Emergents, then! A stroke of perfect luck, almost worth losing a few troopers," the leader said finally. "An open Sphere for the taking, new knowledge of another race. Good, then, that we have not yet killed you, though twice the order was nearly given. You shall tell us what we need to know, give us entry to your Sphere, and in return I may even permit a few of you to live."

DuQuesne felt strangely lightheaded; something inside him was rising towards the surface and inevitable breakthrough. *And why not? It's too late now. Nothing left for me or anyone if the monsters finish this.* "Sounds like not much of a deal. What if I tell you to go straight to hell?"

Maizas hissed contemptuously. "You care for your fellow creatures, one would hope; you may be animals and less than animals, but even such creatures care, even if with less delicacy and sympathy than we for our own. In this case, you—seeming the leader—shall do as I ask, or we shall kill the other. Very slowly and painfully."

The Molothos had drawn closer, snaring them in a ring of armored monstrosities. "Here in the area we claim, you are in gravity half again what you knew. You have no more weapons save those you hold in your hands and will be slow and easily slain by my warriors. You will talk, for we can make you do so, and you will be begging for your life to end sooner, if you make me wait much longer."

That is it. *The absolute living end. Torture Carl to get me to talk so you can kill me later? No way in hell!* As he thought this, he finally let go of all the restraints, the fear and the control he'd spent so many decades to hammer into place, let loose everything he'd feared, all the *difference* that had separated him from the rest of the world.

For a moment, he felt both as though he stood outside himself, and that he was suddenly more himself than he had been in fifty years, at once terrified and transported by what was happening. *I'd forgotten . . . forgotten what I was. I was so good at repressing the memory, at denying my own past, that I'm now almost unable to grasp who I am. What it feels like to be . . . what I was.*

It feels . . . good.

His head snapped up and he glared straight into Maizas's yellow-glowing eye. Something in his stance and gaze registered even with the aliens; the troopers raised their weapons and Maizas took a slight step back.

Marc C. DuQuesne sneered at Maizas, holding the alien's gaze. "That would be a good trick, if you could manage it," he said contemptuously. "But you've got it all just . . . exactly . . . backwards."

With a sudden movement, he leapt into the air, two hundred kilos in over one and a half gravities doing a standing jump that took him three meters into the air. As he'd expected, Carl dropped to the ground, obviously shocked at what DuQuesne was doing but equally certain he needed to be out of the way. One of the troopers, hair-trigger reflexes overstrained, fired, spraying his compatriots with bladed death. The wounded one went down in a fountain of blood as the flechettes found the chinks in his armor. DuQuesne landed squarely on Maizas's back, the impact driving the body to the ground. The troopers hesitated, fanning out but afraid to fire with their commander in the way. "Your problem, you pea-brained, overbearing, pompous crayfish, is that you think you have *any* idea of what you're *dealing* with."

As Maizas struggled to rise, he took advantage of that, bounding with the alien's own strength aiding him from Maizas' back to the next trooper, catching the striking claw as he descended and then twisting his body just *so*, wrenching the claw around, hearing both tech and natural armor creak and split under the force. He brought both heels down as hard as he could in landing; the concussion transmitted through the armor breaking the carapace underneath. The Molothos gave an unbelieving agonized shriek as DuQuesne vaulted from him to the next arachnoid creature, tearing the gun in its tendrils away so forcefully that one tendril stretched and tore apart.

The other tendril and striking claw caught at him, and the shredding mouth seemed far too close; instead of biting, though, it shrank away, closing up. *Interesting*, he thought, as the thing tried to pound him to pulp with the striking claws; instead, it found the human catching the other claw and holding it immobile while forcing the first claw back.

The other two Molothos troopers closed in from behind, and DuQuesne dropped to the ground just as four claws ripped through the air. Rolling to the side he went underneath the third trooper, then with a sudden effort grasped the underside of the carapace and rose to his feet in a single fluid motion, heaving the Molothos into its companions like flinging a sack of grain. As the three aliens tumbled and scrabbled to right themselves, he yanked the power pack from the alien weapon—the location of such a pack seemed obvious to him—and pitched it down the throat of the middle creature. Spiked lamprey-teeth contracted convulsively, and the super-conductor storage cell paths were suddenly and disastrously disrupted; a sun-bright concussion blew DuQuesne four meters away as he tucked and rolled.

Rising to his feet, he glanced at Maizas, who was staggering backwards, disbelief written plainly in the alien body language, trying to make it to the low, long vessel behind him. He caught one of the alien's legs and yanked it backwards, so hard that it dislocated, and dragged the Scout Master right back where he'd come from. "Oh, I don't think so, Maizas," he said, feeling the cold, hard, freeing certainty once more, the knowledge that he was doing the right thing and that nothing in all the universe could stop him. "I told you you hadn't any idea what you were dealing with. I was raised in gravity more than half again *yours*. I was built by people so insane they didn't realize what kind of a monster they designed, and I've spent half a century hiding what I am." Peripherally he was aware of Carl's wide-eyed stare. "You brought it out, you son of a bitch. You made me let it out, and I don't know if I'll ever find myself again." He spun Maizas to face him, caught the two striking claws in his hands and squeezed hard, feeling the armor bending under the force. Hard black eyes reflected dimly from the surface of the wraparound yellow eye of the Molothos, but he could feel a quiver run through the creature, and not one of simple rage.

"You are going to tell me exactly and precisely everything that I need to know, and you are going to do it now, and you will not try to lie to me. Or else," he said, and grinned savagely, "you will find out how very much worse things can get."

"I . . . I am not afraid of you. Or of death." The translated voice shook slightly. "Let me go."

"There's worse things than quick death. And you're damn well afraid of me, unless you are a hell of a lot stupider than I think you are. Don't try to lie to me; I don't have the time or the patience for it. If I let you go and leave, the first thing you'll do is run over to your ship and either call for reinforcements if you've got any, or head back home with our coordinates if you don't."

The creature snarled-spat and rasped at him. "Not the *first* thing, no. For we are not uncivilized monsters such as you. The *first* thing I would do would be to properly bid farewell to our fallen people, and either bury them or with ceremony reduce them to ash, that they not be defiled either by your . . . witch-doctors who may call themselves scientists, or by the mindless beasts of this world. *Then* I would call the reinforcements." It looked at him with defiant arrogance. "Consider that to your advantage. You would have some time to flee and fortify before we came to take your world. Perhaps you might even retain the interior." It hissed contemptuously. "But you have nothing to threaten me with. Death a soldier will face a thousand times, and you have already killed all of my men. You have no one to hold hostage."

Carl came over to him. "Um . . . DuQuesne . . . "

"Don't worry, I haven't become a monster. Not too much, anyway, I hope."

"Look, he may be right. That ship . . . I don't think it's large enough for any long-range travel even in the insane conditions of the Arena. He's got to have a larger ship nearby, probably with a lot more people on board. If he's telling the truth . . . "

"Which I think he is, in this case. Yeah, it'd give us a good chance to get back and lock down. But then we're losing in two ways. First, we're conceding the surface of our Sphere to these jokers, which just doesn't sit well with me, and second, we're losing the only source of power, food, and other resources we have to stretch out our time here. We can't *afford* to lose here."

"You've already lost, DuQuesne creature." Maizas said. "If we do not report in . . . a short time, our main vessel will either send more to investigate, or may come in closer to inspect directly—and how well will your freakish speed and strength fare, I ask, against weapons meant for combat between the stars?"

"All the more reason for me to get you to talk now."

"What are you going to do? Torture him?" Carl looked apprehensive.

"In a way. Not by breaking his legs or burning him or anything. I don't think he'd break easy that way, if he would at all. He's a tough customer, Maizas is, and he wouldn't be leading scout expeditions if he didn't have some of what it takes." He was surveying the other bodies, found the catch, peeled the armor off of the one he'd killed through that double-heel impact. "So . . . yeah, take a look at that."

Carl looked where he was pointing. "Yeah, he's got one hell of a nasty mouth."

"More than that. Look at those teeth. Look at the musculature, and the . . . well, bone or something behind it. You're an engineer, think about the structure there, how does it work? And way down there, you see?"

Carl studied the dead Molothos's mouth more carefully. At a faint sound behind them, DuQuesne said "Don't even think about it, Maizas. If you so much as twitch again, I'm coming over there and tying your legs in knots. Which, since they aren't meant to bend much, won't be much fun for you, but *will* keep you from going anywhere. Oh, and by the way, I'm jamming any short-range transmissions, so if you think you can do anything by remote, you've got another think or two coming." The alien let out a frustrated hiss.

"Man, I see what you mean," Carl Edlund said finally. "It's like a garbage disposal—grabs, holds, and feeds straight into a grinder. Looks like it might be organic diamond-plated or something, but *nasty*. But . . . so what?"

"You'd think that would be a hell of a weapon in hand to hand, wouldn't you? But instead of taking a bite at me, the one pulled away, sealed right up. Seems to me, a creature with a one-way mouth has to be damn careful about what it eats, because it can't spit something out once it realizes it's made a mistake. So reflexively they don't bite *anything* they don't really want to, and especially not anything that might be poisonous or sickening. Like unknown alien creatures."

Maizas buzz-snorted. "A reasonable show of deduction for a monster, but what point your waste of time?"

"Oh, just this little point," DuQuesne said, heaving the body up and moving it a little closer to Maizas. "You've got yourself some real civilized rituals and tastes. Maybe even a religion of purity, something along those lines. I figure I have one thing I *can* threaten you with."

Maizas's limbs shrank into themselves slightly, as he started to realize that DuQuesne really did have some kind of a plan. "What . . . what do you mean?"

"I mean that I can make sure you never *want* to call back in again. Because if you don't start answering my questions double-quick, Maizas . . . " He reached down and tore one leg from the dead trooper. "I am going to stick *this* in your mouth. Since you can't spit stuff out, anything you can bite into you have to grind up and swallow once it goes in, or you choke or starve to death." He saw a shudder run through the alien's frame as he finished, and the cold grin came back. "If you don't talk—or if you lie—I will be feeding your troopers to you, one bit at a time. You'll be the defiler—and I'm betting that's even worse than leaving the bodies for us aliens to cut up." His grin widened as he saw horror in Maizas's contracting stance, like a dying spider. "Isn't that right, Maizas?"

A moment passed, and he saw from the pale expression on Carl's face that the horror was not just on one side. Then the Molothos spoke, this time in a low voice filled with loathing, but tinged with fear and without any of the prior arrogance. "Ask your questions, you void-spawned demon. Ask them. You . . . you have found your key in abomination." It shuddered again. "Ask, and I . . . I will answer."

"Better," he said, knowing that the cold, unmoved tone was translated as well as his words, and also knowing how it must be affecting his friend, but knowing that he could no longer concern himself with that. "And remember that I *will* know when you are lying. Make no mistake about that. I can *smell* it. And if I hear a single lie, why, you get to take a few bites. And if you're still lying, I'll feed you this guy's brain. Or whatever part of him I think you find most sacred, private, or disgusting." He sat down on the dead trooper's carapace. "Let's start with your ship . . . "

Chapter 35

It had not taken long to ascertain the overall situation. There was indeed a much larger vessel, the carrier or mothership—Maizas' word translated as "Twinscabbard," implying two scout landers within the vessel. That ship currently hovered just outside the gravitational influence of the Sphere; DuQuesne had verified that Maizas really meant what that implied, which had allowed the Molothos a small measure of amusement at their ignorance.

"Hard to get details," DuQuesne said during a short pause in the interrogation, speaking softly to Carl at some distance from the prisoner; he'd have preferred to use direct radio communication, datalink to datalink, but figured it was much more important to continue to jam any frequencies Maizas might be able to transmit on.

"But I get the impression of a pretty big ship, probably about the size of a destroyer, as long as *Holy Grail* but a lot more massive and built for exploration with a real big side order of combat. How're you doing?"

The last question covered a pretty wide area of ground—considering that he'd given Carl an assignment to do, the controls expert could simply report on that. But it also left open the possibility of other responses. Which Carl gave.

"Wishing I had your genes, actually. And some of your training, though not your life," Carl said with a grin. "Sure, it was a shock, and you're one hardass bastard, but then I never thought you couldn't be. But you don't seem *all* that different to me. Well, no; I get a lot more of a 'do not get in this guy's way' vibe, but it's not in the vein of you being a psychopath or anything; just along the lines of there being no way to actually *stop* you, so don't be stupid, if that makes sense."

"And I'm also bloody transparent as glass, then?"

Carl shrugged. "Marc, once any of us knew the truth, anyone who watched could see you were like that guy in that poem . . . yeah, the Ancient Mariner. You had your past hanging around your neck like an invisible lead albatross. One that scared you to death. Why, I'm not sure; you obviously weren't one of the causes of the problem. I guess you were just scared that you *could* have been . . . which I suppose isn't completely crazy." He shook his head disbelievingly. "I'm a damn good martial artist—saying this with no modesty at all—but watching you I realized I'm not only not in your league, I'm just barely aware of the rules. I'd take bets that there's never been anyone anywhere in Earth system that could out-fight you—leaving out your bioenhancement, too."

"You'd lose that bet," DuQuesne said quietly, remembering one of the partial successes—a warrior with the innocence of a child, who, when he'd learned the truth, had refused to come with DuQuesne and the others, instead staying behind to fight for the simulated world that was all he knew. "Sorry, Mr. DuQuesne, but these are my friends," he'd said, looking up at DuQuesne through impossibly spiky red-black hair. "I know . . . they're not real to the bad men who are coming, but . . . they're real to me, and no one's going to take them away without a fight."

And they did not, DuQuesne thought with a painful smile. *They sent in automated assault vehicles, and he broke them. They sent in augmented troops, and he—and his friends, virtual though they were—sent them running.*

And then they sent in gas, and he fell finally, slowed, beaten, and still conscious when they shut it down and his family disappeared in blankness.

"No, you'd lose that bet," he repeated. "But if you said 'outside of Hyperion,' you might be right."

Carl had seen the shift of expressions, but decided not to push, apparently. "Anyway, I've done some careful poking around in his ship, like you asked. It's really . . . well, *alien*, not to sound silly about it, but the laws of physics are the same for all of us, even if this Arena likes to play tricks with them. So I've scoped out the basic operation of the thing. It's something like a VTOL jet, basically, heating air through a one-way intake to push the thing around—a sort of air rocket, I guess. Jibe with what he's been saying?"

"Pretty much. He hasn't tried many lies at all—one or two minor ones, and he immediately straightened out as soon as I twitched."

Carl looked at him curiously. "Can you really *smell* if someone's lying?"

He chuckled, observing Maizas was just about finished with the drinkglobe he'd requested (and that DuQuesne had verified didn't contain anything like poison or something else allowing the Molothos to make an unscheduled exit). "Sort of. Most creatures have chemical shifts associated with trying to evade something, with doing something dangerous. I can usually pick up on some of that—with people, too, of course—and he's also got some body language I can read. He's good at controlling it, but if you look *real* close at his legs, the claws dig in a little more when he tries to lie; it's part of that contract-inward defensive posture." He saw the last of the drinkglobe disappear. "Right. Here's what I want you to do . . ." he gave Carl some quick instructions, then turned to Maizas and spoke up. "Enough R&R. More questions and answers."

Maizas was still nervous at his proximity, but made no attempt to evade answering the questions, even volunteering additional interesting information on occasion. This just confirmed DuQuesne's suspicions; Maizas wanted to stall, and live through the stalling. *No problem, my little alien friend. Because you're giving me exactly what I need.*

One of the most important pieces of information he extracted from the Molothos was the fact that their ship had, in fact, travelled to their Sphere the long way—through the weird atmospheric environment (which DuQuesne's treacherous false upbringing insisted on trying to label as "ether") of the Arena—and the journey had taken the better part of a year. This was not unusual; while there were apparently something called

"Sky Gates" which could allow instantaneous transportation from one Sphere to another (DuQuesne guessed these to be exterior Arena versions of the Inner Gateway), these only existed for inhabited, fully active Spheres, and linked only to a small set number of destinations. Thus any Spheres which were uninhabited, or to which you did not know a route, had to be reached the long way around. The Molothos routinely expanded their reach this way, finding livable Spheres, settling on their outer surface, then building new vessels and continuing onward. Radio was unreliable at "Sphere" distances (roughly one hundred thousand kilometers) but sometimes one could get a message through to a nearby Sphere.

The important point here, he thought, *is that we have to keep that Twinscabbard from ever reporting back—physically or via radio—that they've found us. They've got one Sphere near us, somewhere—can't quite make out the directions from what Maizas says, he's no navigator anyway—and so they might be able to report back fast. And if that Sphere's actually active, they could get a big fleet here within a year.*

The problem, of course, was exactly how to prevent a ship with several hundred xenomisosic alien troops on board from first exterminating them all, and then heading home for more reinforcements.

A buzz-chime sounded faintly from inside the ship. Maizas's legs relaxed slightly. "Now, alien monster, where were we? Yes. You wished to speak of our power sources. The most common are superconductor storage coil batteries—which is, in fact, the general method used throughout the Arena." The alien was speaking in a calm, measured, perhaps slightly too emphatically cooperative way. *Yep. That was a signal you were waiting for.*

Carl suddenly bounded out of the landing craft. "DuQuesne! We've got company!"

Far distant in the sky, a bright dot had appeared. DuQuesne pulled out his electronic binoculars and focused on the dot.

Waveringly outlined against turbulent sky, he could see only a general shape, a broad flying wing with hints of lines and other external features, a suggestion of baroque and impractical designs for ordinary space vessels. The range showed that what he looked at was huge, at least three hundred meters wide.

The shrieking cough translated as triumphant laughter. "Trapped, trapped now, little beasts!" Maizas crowed."I kept you here and talking, easy for destruction or capture! Not so clever, not so smart as you thought you were! And now comes *Blessing of Fire* to take your Sphere!"

"Not sending down the other scout lander with troops?"

"Pzkt!" The sound was one of contempt. "Standard doctrine. If one scout lander crew incapacitated, maybe second fares no better. First the main vessel descends to within detailed examination range and a decision is made as to approach." It looked at him arrogantly.

"Excellent." DuQuesne's grin was so savagely triumphant that Maizas involuntarily shrank away. "Exactly what I wanted to hear."

"Wh . . . what?"

"You think I'm *stupid?* Think we didn't know you were stalling? I needed you to stall, Maizas. I needed you to feel that your best chance was to tell us anything we wanted to know, keep us interested, so that we wouldn't run off and hide before your reinforcements got here.

And your reaction told me that—in all likelihood—your main ship would be doing the backup, which was what I was hoping would happen."

The alien stared from DuQuesne to Carl in shock. "Insane, you are! Nearly were you overcome by my troops before; even now, a fully prepared lander would deal with you! You have no defenses against shells and beams that can rend ships of war, and no weapon that could harm so mighty a vessel as *Blessing*!"

"Wrong," DuQuesne said. He pointed behind the alien. "I have *one*."

Maizas whirled and stared uncomprehending for a moment; then the buzz-shriek showed he understood all too well. "No! You . . . you cannot! You know nothing of our technology, the systems will not recognize your commands, it is impossible—"

"All I need," DuQuesne said, yanking tighter the bonds on Maizas's body, "is power and control. I am a power engineer, and Carl Edlund is a master of controls. And you—you pathetic sap! You've told us everything we absolutely needed to know while you were busy stalling!"

"DuQuesne, that ship will be in good detailed scan range in about nine minutes," Carl warned him.

"With what we've figured, that's enough; and we don't know what their telemetry might say, so we had to wait until now. Be glad it has to come through atmosphere, or we'd have about nine seconds." DuQuesne vaulted inside the ship, with its oddly triangular corridors, and started ripping out the control runs Carl had pinpointed earlier. *I need to arrange a controlled short across the main drive . . . here . . . here . . . linked in with Carl's designs . . .*

Maizas was now struggling desperately against his bonds; the alien commander was now no longer nearly so certain of the outcome as he had been a moment before. "Struggle all you like, Maizas; you're going nowhere. That's ring-carbon composite, a hundred times stronger than any steel ever made. I couldn't break a length of the stuff that was a tenth that thick."

"I've rigged what amounts to a couple joysticks, Marc, but . . . it's gonna be very, very dicey. We're having to shunt control though our stuff, which wasn't meant to handle the power, and cut out all of their controls. I've put in all the redundancy I can but . . . this thing's going to have almost no margin for error."

"Just give me the best you've got," DuQuesne said, using one of the Molothos sidearms to blow holes in the control panels at critical points. "I've set up the simple cross connect to the engines. This only has to hold together for one really short flight, Carl; all I care about is that the remote will hold the signal for long enough."

Blessing of Fire was growing in the sky, now visible as a dark dot with a hint of shape.

"You'll have to drop the scrambling to do it. I can run an antenna to the hull to amplify the reception, give us the range, but what about his headware?" Carl indicated Maizas.

"Oh, I think I've got something for that problem." He grabbed Maizas by one striking claw and began dragging him up the ramp. "Come on, Maizas. You're going on one last ride."

The alien struggled futilely as the former Hyperion pulled him into his scout craft. "This cannot work!"

"Oh, I rather think it can. Maybe not a *good* chance—only one chance in a thousand, say, given other issues involved—but a chance more than worth taking," DuQuesne said; he noted that this statement seemed, for some reason, to shock the Molothos even more.

He finished dragging Maizas into the shattered control cabin. "I think we've killed off most of the relays in here, and the hull will shield any direct headware transmission. Now, you guys do talk—like us—with part of the same apparatus you use to eat with. It's possible, once the scrambling goes down, that you'll be able to trigger something like a voice-command relay, even if I think I've got them all. I doubt it, but just in case . . . " He rammed the point of a Molothos trooper's leg into Maizas's mouth. "Here we go. All you have to do in order to activate any such thing . . . is finish eating."

He needed no words to translate the utter horror in Maizas' contracting stance.

"DuQuesne! It's speeding up! I think they guess something's happening!"

The black-bearded power engineer hooked the ends of Maizas's bonds to what had been landing restraint points—sort of the equivalent of seatbelts—and headed for the door. "Coming!"

The Twinscabbard-class vessel *Blessing of Fire* loomed larger in the sky; thunder of engines was now faintly audible, though seeming to come from a much more distant point, sound still slower than light even in the weird conditions of the Arena. "At least the design of their ship utterly precludes supersonic speeds in air," he said to Carl, accepting the clumsily-assembled control rig. "Not surprising, given other considerations, but it's a good thing for us."

"Especially," agreed Carl with a grin that echoed his own predator's smile, "since their landing vessels *can*, if you push them."

He waited. The problem was judging the exact critical distance and the reactions of the aliens. At a far longer range, of course, a ship like *Blessing of Fire* could have rained destruction down on them with almost pinpoint accuracy. This argued that, whatever their genocidal views towards other lifeforms, they valued the lives and health of their own people, something that Maizas's various statements generally confirmed. So they'd want to wait, get really close, see whether any of their people were still alive, and if there was any way they could manage to save them, rather than just pounding the site to slag from a distance.

But exactly what *was* that distance . . . and how long would it take for them to make their decision? What would their reactions be? What sort of defenses would the ship have active under these circumstances? Part of this plan . . . well, a very large part of it . . . depended on the Molothos being overall as arrogant as the individuals he'd already met, and being really unlikely to assume that any ground-based threat could harm *Blessing of Fire*, especially in the absence of any evidence of civilized natives who might have notable weaponry.

"Five kilometers out and they're slowing, DuQuesne."

"Roger that."

Blessing of Fire loomed huge now, bronze and silver and gravel-gray and monstrous, casting knife-edged shadows on the mountains. "Four kilometers, DuQuesne!"

"Activating now . . . ."

A low thundering snarl came from the Molothos landing craft; it began to rise, tilting to port. *Damnation!* DuQuesne jiggled the lefthand joystick, incrementing thrust, balancing the scout lander with clumsy care, like a man trying to balance a long box half-filled with water. *This has to look like at least a somewhat controlled takeoff.*

He fed more power into both engines, adjusting the balance by pure instinct; *Ariane would do this better*, he suddenly thought, and realized that he really wished she was here to do this. *Cut it out, superman. This is not the time for self-doubts.* Beside him, Carl sucked in his breath as the ship nearly clipped its wing on a nearby tree.

His internal telemetry, from the sensors they'd scattered through the interior, showed Maizas standing almost frozen in the center of the room, leg still stuck in the Molothos's mouth; Maizas was making furious keening noises but obviously accomplishing nothing.

Cleared the trees. Now . . . he pushed gently forward, while still increasing power. The ship began to move forward.

Blessing of Fire slowed and began to circle around, clearly trying to decide what this new development meant. "They're transmitting to the scout lander, trying to get an answer, DuQuesne," Carl said.

Not much time now. But . . .

The scoutship was moving forward now, engines almost in full forward alignment. He began turning the ship towards the Twinscabbard.

"I have a coded transmission! I think it's a remote override!"

That wouldn't do them any good . . . but they knew, now.

Just one little second too late.

DuQuesne wrenched power higher on the starboard engine—seeing the condition telltales on their controls reaching critical points—and slewed the fifty meter long scout vessel around to point directly at *Blessing of Fire* . . . or where she would be, in about seven seconds. "See you in hell, Maizas!"

Then he slammed both engines to full.

The whining rumble of the air-rockets changed abruptly to a scream as the entire power of the scout lander's superconductor storage coils was directed to the engines, a single catastrophic surge of power that kicked the low, armored vessel forward at multiple gravities, far beyond any design tolerances. At almost the same moment, blazing spears of energy streaked from *Blessing of Fire*, one scoring a dark line across the swiftly moving scout vessel, the others missing by mere inches. With only a few more seconds, the antimissile batteries of *Blessing of Fire* would have turned the lander to vapor.

But there were no more seconds to spare, as DuQuesne's improvised missile annihilated the three kilometers between it and its target and smashed at nearly a kilometer per second straight into the main body of *Blessing of Fire*.

The massive Twinscabbard-class vessel seemed to stagger in midair, tilting, slewing out of control, plummeting from the sky. Carl punched a fist exultantly skyward. *"Yes!"*

DuQuesne grabbed Carl's shoulder. *"Get down!"* Both men hit the dirt, just as *Blessing of Fire*, continuing forward on a course to destruction, struck a mountaintop five and a half kilometers away. Metal and composite screamed in tortured agony at the unstoppable impact and—somewhere, deep inside the vessel's stricken core—ripped across the energy-saturated superconducting storage coils that supplied the power for a journey a hundred thousand miles long.

The flash of light ignited the tops of trees for nearly three kilometers around; the concussion blew many of them flat like matchsticks. Wracked by the shockwave and temporarily deafened, the two men slowly rose and looked up in awe, to see a monstrous mushroom cloud towering above them, slowly, slowly dissipating into an ordinary cloud of smoke above the burning remnants of the destroyed starship.

And both men felt, at the same time, the oppressive weight of gravity lessen and return to normal.

Chapter 36

Ariane was trailing slightly behind Simon and Dr. Rel. She and Simon had discussed their next move, following their interesting, and still rather incomprehensible, discovery of the past day, and decided that at this point they should simply not mention the discovery to any of the aliens—even Orphan. "I definitely don't want to do anything irrevocable until I've had a chance to discuss it with Marc, at least," she'd said.

Simon had concurred. "Oh, definitely not. But in that case, I think we should continue talking with the other Factions. Unfortunately, since we also have agreed not to be separated, that means we'll have to take turns selecting our . . . targets, so to speak."

She'd found the simile amusing, and accurate. They were trying to find appropriate targets from which to extract information while avoiding giving away anything important. That morning they had discovered that the Arena had something equivalent to a messaging service which could find them at Orphan's embassy, and found messages from no less than seven different Factions —five of them unknown and thus, if Orphan's information could be trusted, probably of minimal importance in the short run, one from the Faith, and one from Dr. Rel. The Faith's message had been short, welcoming, and requesting a meeting at some point in the near future; Dr. Relgof's had been long, rambling, and excited, hoping to see them again today. As Orphan had indicated the essentially benign nature of the Analytic, and since she already rather liked the odd alien scientist, Ariane had agreed to follow Simon's lead. She'd informed the Faith that she would be somewhere in the Grand Arcade with Dr. Relgof of the Analytic, if they wished to reach her.

So now they were walking through one of the park-like areas, with Simon and Rel talking, sketching incomprehensible diagrams in the air, arguing, all in that language of science which not all the technology of the Arena could make really understandable. The Analytic representative was, clearly, a recruiter of some sort, as he did subtly try to influence the conversation to discussion of their candidacy to join; but while Simon was clearly tempted on some levels, he avoided making any commitments and kept returning to scientific discourse.

Still . . . as she had to follow them around, it was a bit boring. So she was grateful to see the green and gold, bead and plate outfit of Nyanthus approaching her. Simon caught her eye and she nodded; Dr. Sandrisson stopped, making sure that he and Dr. Rel would not just wander farther off and separate the two.

The First Initiate Guide did his flowering, anemone-like bow. "Again, I am honored and pleased to meet with you, Captain Ariane Austin."

"And I with you, First Guide Nyanthus," Ariane replied, bowing in return. "To what do I owe the considerable honor of being once more sought out by the very leader of the Faith?"

A rippling, chiming chuckle. "To our constant interest in recruitment, of course, and the Guidance I have received, which says that you are perhaps of more importance than you may yet imagine. Such visions are oft-clouded, true, and have been known to mislead, yet I always heed them, for the Creators send no such guidance without reason."

She grinned. "I thank you for your honesty. I guess recruiting new members is a constant competition here?"

"Indeed, by most Factions. It is, alas, not true of the Molothos—misguided and pitiful creatures—nor for the Blessed. But most of us do indeed compete to gain the advantage of appropriate additions to our membership. For us, it is of course a mandate, a responsibility, a duty, to prevent those that we can from falling too far into . . . how should I put it? The snares of disbelief, or worse, that entangle far too many of those who walk the Arena." Though Nyanthus had no clear sensing organs, he gave the impression of glancing in the direction of Simon and Dr. Relgof. "The Analytic . . . are a group of great knowledge, but of questionable wisdom. Still, a better choice of association than others, indeed."

"I hope," she said, with a bit of trepidation, "that you'll understand when I say I am not currently planning on committing to *anyone*. We want to be our own Faction, at least for a while, until we're sure of our direction."

"Oh, quite understood." Nyanthus spun slowly about his center, symbiotic flying forms dancing around and through the candle flame-shaped openwork of his upper body. "But with such an understanding, have you any objection to learning more of the way of the Faith?"

"None at all." She was frankly curious. Orphan had talked of "Shadeweaver powers" and "Faith miracles" as being, to his mind, basically the same thing, but they'd actually seen very little of either, and she wondered exactly what it was that these beings could do that even the high-tech, super-advanced, and mostly ancient civilizations here could possibly consider miracles or magical. "As long as it neither commits me to anything, nor . . . influences me, in any way outside of the way that information would normally influence me."

Nyanthus paused in his rhythmic motion for a moment. When he resumed and spoke, the translation of the chiming voice was grave. "Ah. I see that you have already encountered agents of the other side, our adversaries, those which the naïve call 'Shadeweavers,' and for which we have other . . . much worse . . . names. I understand your caution, Ariane Austin. You are wise to be cautious. But I give you my personal word—which, as you may ascertain with any here, is as solid and unquestionable as the very Arena's existence—that no such influence would be placed upon you."

"In that case, yes, I am very interested in learning more of your ways. All of the Arena is . . . overwhelming."

"Is it not?" She caught a hint of religious fervor in the simple question. "Indeed, is it not beyond any mortal comprehension? But let me not be carried away by my own beliefs. It is my purpose here to invite you to—"

A deep, resonant bell-like tone suddenly thundered through the air of Nexus Arena; the ground quivered beneath her feet, and all through the immensity of the Grand Arcade, silence fell. The sound, like a gong and a pipe organ built for a giant, throbbed in the atmosphere for long moments before fading away.

Nyanthus stood stock-still, even the symbiotes motionless on the ground or within his body; Dr. Rel was paused with one six-fingered hand in the air, as motionless as though he had been paralyzed. As far as she could look, no one moved. Distant autocabs traveled, carrying what momentarily seemed to be cargoes of statues.

Then motion resumed, and a huge susurration of conversation, twice as loud as before, spread like a breath of wind before a storm through the Arcade. She turned to Nyanthus as he slowly resumed motion. "What the heck was that?"

"The Ascendant Chime." Nyanthus's warm, deep voice was subdued, hushed with startled awe. "I have never heard it before, and likely never will again. It means some one of the species here has met its first Challenge, become a true Citizen of the Arena."

Ariane was confused. "But . . . wouldn't that mean *us*?"

Nyanthus laughed faintly. "Oh, you are not the only species who have not yet met your first Challenge. Some species have spent thousands of years without daring to meet a Challenge, or—unfortunately—failing to win those they were forced into. One of these, undoubtedly, has finally succeeded. A joyous day!"

"The Arena doesn't tell you who?" Simon asked, joining them.

It was Dr. Relgof who answered. "Indeed, it is a puzzle to me as well as to you, Captain," he said in his rough tenor voice. "Nearly always it is well-known the challenges which are underway, and the participants therein—and if one of them is a species seeking to win its first true recognition, then always there is *someone* watching. Yet so far, I hear nothing from the Arena, no announcement from spectators or Adjudicators, or from the victors themselves—who would almost certainly wish to spread this news far and wide."

Ariane could see that both Relgof and Nyanthus were sincerely as much in the dark as they were. "Are Challenges ever held outside of Nexus Arena?"

"On occasion," Relgof said. "Yet . . . even those are usually announced and well-known. But if not . . . then the victors, or the losers, would return here eventually, to announce the fact." He glanced around. "I see a few others have already reached the logical conclusion. Quickly—let us go, before the movement becomes a mob." He began to move off, his long gangly legs making surprisingly quick strides, so that both Simon and Ariane had to jog to keep up, and Nyanthus seemed hard-put to stay even with them; his two silent escorts, Tchanta Zoll and Tchanta Vall, grasped him on each side and began to carry him.

"Where are we going?" Ariane asked.

"I would guess . . . to Transition, yes?" Simon said in reply.

"Precisely deduced, my colleague," Dr. Rel confirmed. "There, almost certainly, will the news come. If it is not already being spread by joyous victors or pleased spectators, then soon it shall be, when they can arrive here—and, almost of a certainty, that shall be through the Inner Gateways of Transition."

It took some time for them to make their way through the thickening crowd and up the elevators, but eventually, after an hour or so, they did manage to reach Transition. The area that Ariane thought of as the foyer of Nexus Arena was incredibly busy now; it seemed that the news was spreading to other Spheres, and new arrivals appeared almost every second—perhaps the equivalent of news reporters, sightseers, or just the curious.

Even waiting here wasn't wasted time from Ariane's point of view; this odd event was giving them a chance to observe a tremendous concentration of the Arena's drastically varied lifeforms, and she had her head-recorders going constantly. She had no doubt Simon was doing the same thing.

A Gateway about a hundred meters away blazed with pearlescence, and she recognized the solitary green-black figure. "Orphan! Over here!"

As their alien friend moved through the crowd, she pushed forward to meet him. "How did you . . . Oh, I see. It's already that time, isn't it?"

"It is indeed, Ariane Austin. But it seems that we have a far more exciting moment at hand. I had hoped . . . but clearly you have taken no Challenges in my absence, for this is a gathering of people who await the news." Orphan glanced around. "Look, even Sethrik is here for the spectacle."

"I'm more interested in that," Simon said, pointing. Following his finger, Ariane saw three black-cloaked figures—two clearly inhuman, one not so alien in outline—standing in the middle of the floor, with a clear zone extending at least ten meters around them in all directions.

"Well, now, that's interesting," Orphan said. "Even the Shadeweavers, it would appear, are entirely in the dark. And you, First Guide? You have no insight into this mystery?"

"Alas, I have none, surprising though that may seem, Orphan."

Ariane expected a momentary resolution of the tension—as did, it seemed, most of the crowd. But time passed, and none of the new arrivals knew any more than those already there. An hour. Three hours. Four.

"Maybe we should just go back to the Embassy?" Simon ventured. "I must say I'm getting hungry . . . and in need of certain other facilities."

Ariane winced. "Er. Yes, I think I need that myself."

"Well," Orphan said, "We can go back in pairs, and keep our position. I really do believe we don't wish to miss this; it is a once in many lifetimes occurrence."

Ariane couldn't argue that. Her bladder, however, did need tending to. *It'll be just my luck*, she thought, *that right after we get on the elevator heading down the news will break.*

But when she and Simon returned, carrying food and cushions to sit on, nothing had changed. But with so much to see, and talk about, she didn't see it as wasted time. *There's so much to learn from everyone. I can do that as well here as anywhere else.*

Four more hours passed, and she started considering making a second trip. The peak traffic had died down, and the crowd was maintaining a watchful vigil, having sorted itself into some lanes to permit normal freight and traveler traffic to pass.

Then a shimmer of iridescence, near the very center of the room, caught her eye, and to her utter astonishment, she saw Carl Edlund step out. But instead of stepping down, he glanced around, staring wide-eyed at the incredible mob of aliens gathered in near-silent anticipation, and stepped right back through.

There was a whisper of confusion at this. Then the same gateway blazed pearl again. The shape materializing out of it, though, was huge and misshapen, something out of nightmare, unrecognizable . . .

Oh my God!

Marc C. DuQuesne pitched the body of a Molothos down the rampway before him, the chitinous carcass making a thunderous clatter that echoed throughout the entire room, followed by a shocked chittering screech from Dajzail and his group. "Sorry about the mess, Captain," he said, his voice somehow amplified by the Arena. "But we had to do a little pest control on our Sphere." His smile was brilliant enough to see across the two hundred yards separating them, and she swore she could see a twinkle in the black eyes. "Why don't we go find our new Embassy, and I'll tell you all about it?"

Chapter 37

It was, perhaps not surprisingly, the Molothos who moved first after DuQuesne's dramatic entrance. Dajzail and his squad bulled their way through the crowd, most creatures scrambling out of the Molothos' way in near-terror. The arachnoid alien screeched something so filled with rage and obscenity that it could not be translated as anything except a roar of fury. "You insult, and then you attack, the Molothos? Your head will ornament our Embassy, your bones be decorations of the True House!" The fighting claws of all four Molothos were flicking in and out like animated jackknives, unable to restrain the need to tear and rip.

"I just cleaned out a little infestation on our home Sphere. And you might want to think harder about that little fact before you make the same mistake that poor bastard did," DuQuesne retorted; Ariane heard a new tone in his voice, one hard and cold and utterly without fear. Far from retreating, he took a step forward, daring the Molothos to come closer.

Dajzail paused; Ariane guessed that, given what she and Simon had learned, Dajzail was reevaluating the odds against him. But the other Molothos spread out in an attack formation.

An invisible but irresistible force suddenly hammered the four Molothos and Marc to the ground; both sides strained to rise. "Results of Challenge do not justify conflict."

The voice was not loud, yet it was everywhere, thundering softly in Ariane's very bones, causing the aliens throughout Transition to flinch. "Rules are clear. Human Representatives DuQuesne and Edlund have successfully completed Type 2 Challenge. Molothos have lost Challenge. Forfeit claim on Sphere. Humanity's Sphere now fully active." DuQuesne was suddenly on his feet, no longer held down; not so Dajzail and his people. "Molothos will remember law of the Arena; in Nexus Arena, anger is permitted, vengeance is not. Restrict passions to Challenge, Embassies, or other Spheres."

A pause, during which the Molothos still struggled to get up—held, Ariane now realized, by the simple expedient of increasing local gravity until they couldn't move. "Adjudicator Vchanta Nom indicates this action possibly violates prior warning. Arena partially concurs; penalty is removal to Embassy, no emergence, four point seven hours."

And as simply as that, the Molothos were gone, the space where they had been empty.

"Well, well," Orphan murmured nearby. "A magnificent group of enemies you have made today, Ariane Austin. Few like the Molothos, and you have managed to both defeat and humiliate them in the same day. This will doubly elevate your standing in the Arena."

Dr. Rel was studying them apprehensively. The tone of his voice reflected his stance. "I find more significant, and perhaps . . . disturbing, that the Arena—which, when it speaks at all, speaks with utter precision—named two, and only two, of your people as having met and completed the Challenge."

Orphan stiffened, then turned slowly to gaze at DuQuesne as he approached, the crowds parting respectfully before the big man. "Indeed . . . a thought which had not yet struck me."

Simon was grinning widely. Ariane felt an answering grin on her own face, and suddenly she was running to meet DuQuesne. "Marc!" She grabbed him in a hug and lifted in a sudden impulse; she heard his faint grunt of surprise as she actually lifted him off the ground for a moment, then dropped him back down "Marc, you miracle-worker! We're *in*, Marc!"

"It's a start, Captain," he said, with a quiet smile behind the black beard. "Simon," he continued, accepting a firm handshake from the white-haired scientist.

"I add my own congratulations as well," Orphan said, catching up to them. "Might I ask how you managed it?"

"No," DuQuesne answered bluntly. "Or, you can ask, but I'm saying nothing, until after I've been able to discuss it with the Captain. In private. Which means in our Embassy, not yours."

Orphan looked rather miffed, but said nothing; Nyanthus swirled up and gave a flowering bow to DuQuesne.

"The Faith congratulates you on what must have been a stunning and dangerous victory, Marc DuQuesne. Captain Austin, I know you must now speak with your people at some length, so I shall be brief; it was my purpose to invite you to a ceremony of the Faith—just to observe, as we discussed—which in point of fact has a connection with your people. The ceremony will be held in a few days hence, so please contact me, or one of my people, as soon as convenient, that we know whether you will be joining us in this celebration." He bowed again, symbiotic fliers symbolically enveloping all of them, and seemed to float off, accompanied as always by his silent bodyguards.

"Orphan . . . Dr. Relgof . . . " Ariane said, a bit distracted by the implications of Nyanthus's hurried invitation, "Um . . . how will we find our Embassy?"

"Nothing could be simpler," Orphan responded in his usual warm tones, prior annoyance either gone or hidden. "Once you have won through to your citizenship, the Arena naturally assigns you one. While I understand your need for privacy, might I at least travel with you and see where your Embassy is placed? I have some theories as to what basis the Arena uses for its decisions, and it amuses me to prove myself wrong time and again."

"Of course you may, Orphan. Dr. DuQuesne didn't mean any insult, and we hope that—once we have clarified the capabilities of our Embassy and decided on our next course of action—we can invite you to visit us and return your courtesy. And you as well, Dr. Rel."

"The Analytic and myself will be very pleased to visit you at your convenience. Come, let us go, for the crowd is becoming less intimidated and soon may seek to overwhelm your sensibilities with volume of questions and attentiveness."

Rel's observation was accurate; the crowds which had been respectfully or uneasily keeping their distance were now slowly moving closer—those who were not already leaving for the exits, the main "show" being over. Ariane caught a glimpse of Sethrik and the Blessed leaving—in a straight line that parted the crowd like water, swerving only to avoid the three black-clad figures that still stood almost motionless near the midline of Transition. As she gazed in that direction, the one almost humanoid figure seemed to meet her gaze and incline its head. Shadows coalesced from nowhere around the three Shadeweavers, and a moment later dissipated, leaving nothing but empty floor.

She noticed that even after their departure, it was some time before anyone else dared cross the space where the Shadeweavers had stood. By that point, she and the others had almost reached the exit from Transition. Turning her head again, she saw the elevators looming before them.

A group of moderate-sized aliens, blocky creatures with rhino-like hide and ridged, triangular, beaked heads, approached the little party, clearly intending to intercept them and engage in conversation. DuQuesne merely moved slightly forward and looked at them, and they stopped as though they'd run into a wall. Looking at the ebony-haired power engineer, she realized there was something very different about him, especially now; the hard coldness of a glacier seemed to surround him, and something else, a supreme focus, confidence, something that made her almost afraid to talk to him.

It wasn't her imagination, either; the aliens felt it, and Simon's analytical gaze was mingled with concern. The crowds before the elevator hesitated as the doors opened; none made a move to enter before DuQuesne, and only one made a hesitant step forward to join them on the ride down after the five of them had entered the huge elevator—a single step that halted immediately as DuQuesne glanced in his direction.

The ride down in the elevator, short though it was, simply reinforced the impression. The five of them were virtually silent, and even after they'd emerged and gotten one of the silvery autocabs, little was said. He glanced at her at one point, and she could see the difference in his expression. There was no difference she could point to, nothing that a photograph would show clearly, but she knew, somehow, that this was at least partially *not* the Marc DuQuesne who had left them only a day or two ago.

She was distracted from this discovery by noticing they were approaching Orphan's Embassy . . . and then passing it, stopping a mere hundred meters farther on at a plain-fronted building similar in size to the other Embassies, but with—as yet—no markings of any kind to distinguish it. "Embassy of Humanity," the sourceless voice of the autocab announced.

"So we are neighbors!" Orphan said. "A bit of good fortune, perhaps an omen of sorts. I look forward to visiting you, then!"

Relgof looked curiously at Orphan. "And have you once more been proven wrong?"

"Surprisingly, no," responded the green and black alien. "One of my theories predicted that the Human Embassy would be very near to mine; I am rather startled to find it is so. But gratified. If I find more evidence to support my little theory, I will of course share it with you."

"Such generosity would be appreciated." Dr. Rel stood aside to let the humans disembark, and gave his curtsey-bow. "Dr. Sandrisson—Simon—call me as soon as your schedule permits. Now that you have proven yourselves in the Arena, much becomes possible that was not before, and we would surely wish to discuss these new opportunities immediately."

"Indeed so," agreed Orphan. "As your allies prior to the event, we would hope to find this to all of our advantages. But we shall delay you no longer."

"Thank you again, Orphan," Ariane said, and clasped his arm firmly; he returned the gesture after a very brief hesitation. "I know you have your own motives, but you've been a true help and I don't think we'd have gotten nearly this far without you. I count ourselves very lucky to have met you."

Orphan seemed somewhat touched by the words and gesture; he returned the favor with a full pushup-like bow. "Captain Austin, it has been a unique pleasure. I, too, feel we were exceedingly fortunate, and hope that a continued association will benefit both Humanity and the Liberated."

"Come on, Captain," DuQuesne said quietly. "The faster I get you brought up to speed, the faster we can decide which way to jump next."

As the autocab glided off, carrying Orphan and Relgof, the three humans turned and walked towards the blank-faced Embassy; the door rolled aside noiselessly as they approached.

Chapter 38

"So we're now at all-out war with the Molothos," Ariane summarized.

"Maybe not," Simon said. "Challenges are fairly clearly defined here. The Arena itself emphasized that it's frowned upon, at the least, to create a cycle of Challenges for the sake of revenge."

DuQuesne snorted. "That just means that revenge is a dish served very cold here, and maybe you have to get creative about how the Challenge gets delivered."

"True," said Ariane as a thought struck her, "but there's something you don't know that we've discovered that really has a big bearing on the whole situation."

DuQuesne sat, attentive but somehow . . . hard to reach, as she and Simon described the apparent disparity between the alien and human attitudes towards acceptable risk. "I'd have to guess that, once they calm down, the Molothos will have a real problem in that they'll have to evaluate the risk involved in pushing a war with us. Right now, they only know two things, assuming they listened to the Arena carefully—and I'll bet they did: first, that we did kick them off our Sphere, and second, that it only took two of us to do it. They have no way of knowing that we just happened to have a superman available for the job."

DuQuesne nodded. "I'm hoping they'll also have quite a bit of work to do to figure out where we are," he said. "The *Blessing of Fire* came to us the long way around, took 'em a year of travel, and I'm pretty damn sure no one got a message out before the crash. From what Maizas said, this kind of exploration is pretty standard for them, and they've been doing it for thousands of years. It's slow, and they have lots of problems off and on, but I'd be real surprised if they don't have several dozen, maybe several hundred, expeditions like that going on all the time, maybe from separated colonies that themselves take a while to get news to the central groups."

"Yes, I see what you mean," Simon said. "In many ways, parts of the civilization of the Arena are going to mirror the Age of Sail. The Sky Gates are only accessible from Spheres that are fully active, which means that if they colonize only the surface of a Sphere they have to travel to and from it by long journeys. Unless that particular sphere has a Sky Gate terminus from an active Sphere, I suppose. So it could be as little as a year, but likely considerably more, before they can even figure out which of those expeditions has to have been the one that met up with us."

"And it might take even longer if expeditions can get lost from hazards along the way, which I get the impression is possible." Ariane felt a little better. If they hadn't gotten fully up and running in a year, they'd probably have other problems to worry about. "We've lost the chance to study their ships, but was anything salvageable?"

"Haven't checked the wreck yet," DuQuesne answered, "but there was a lot of equipment we could salvage from the base camp and the dead troopers. And our witch-doctor Gabrielle is busy defiling their corpses in the name of science. Truth be told, I'm pretty sure that there's going to be nothing much worth saving at the crash site; the energy involved was nuclear detonation range. That gives us a good idea of what sorts of weapons you can make here, too. Nukes won't work, but there's a few ways to hit that scale of power that seem to be perfectly possible in the Arena."

They were still dancing around the real issues, and Ariane was tired of it. She stood and faced DuQuesne squarely. "Okay, Marc," and even as she said it she felt herself having to fight the invisible weight of . . . whatever it was that had changed in him, that seemed to have dropped a wall between him and everyone else. "Okay, Marc, the real question right now is . . . how are you, and what's wrong?"

DuQuesne's mouth tightened, but she didn't drop her gaze, though her heart was inexplicably pounding doubletime and she felt for some reason as though she was the one being cornered. Finally the big engineer looked away. "Captain, I didn't have any choice. I had to . . . had to become the person I was back on Hyperion. But do you know what that was? I was someone's idea of a superman, yes. And as you—and probably no one else on *Holy Grail*—know, based on someone *else's* idea of a super-villain."

He stood and began pacing, and even that *pacing* was different, the movement of a predator, of something so dominant and dangerous that you just *knew* you'd better stay out of its way . . . or else. "I'm not even, strictly speaking, human. They put . . . other stuff in us. And no one, not even me, knows exactly what, or what it might do. How stable it is in the long term. But it's the personality that's the problem. I was *designed*, dammit!" He slammed a fist against the wall, and the sound was like a sledgehammer. "The way I think, the way I talk, what I like, what I hate, the way I cut my hair or trim my beard, you can be sure as God made little green apples that someone wrote it into my profile and made sure it became reality."

"But . . . Marc, you've spent fifty *years* not being that. That has to have changed you."

"Yeah. Maybe. But a lot of that was done by forgetting, Ariane. Forgetting and repressing everything about myself." He smiled bitterly. "And if necessary, making my environment repress it. Gravity isn't variable, at least not where we come from. So what exactly was I going to do in order to both keep in shape and keep from constantly feeling—and looking—like I was an Earthman walking on the moon?" He held up his arm, pinched it. "Sure, medical nanos will minimize muscle and bone loss, all that, but they won't shift your perceptions.

"For that, I had to design my own clothes. Every suit of clothes I wear, every piece of it, is basically actuator fabric, harvesting energy from my movements to oppose those movements. It drags at every motion I make so that it feels as though I'm in my full gravity. None of you have been inside my cabin, so you don't see the other rigs I have there to keep myself restrained. All of them have cutoff signals, of course—in case of emergency —but until yesterday I hadn't cut them off in fifty years."

Ariane nodded. She thought she was starting to understand what DuQuesne was driving at, and it sent an ache of sympathy through her.

The big man sighed, looked down, shook his head again. "I didn't *want* to be what they made me. I'm not even exactly sure why I didn't change my name, except maybe . . . well, no, I do know. I was erasing so much, I needed to keep a part of me, a central core that would let me at least have a touchstone of continuity."

"DuQuesne . . . Marc . . . " Simon's brows were knotted, trying to understand. "What was so bad about what you were? What you are now?"

DuQuesne gave a frustrated snort, almost a snarl, that made them both jump. "I . . . don't know. It's hard to explain. I try to get my own head around it and I just end up chasing my tail. It's even harder now, because I'm . . . what I was, mostly, now. It's like letting the damn genie out of the bottle.

"Part of it's just knowing I'm . . . not a person. I didn't grow up, no matter what my memories say, in anything like a real world. That haunts me every day. Am I saying these words because I'm programmed to? Because it's what a good-guy version of *Marc C. DuQuesne* would say? When I let go, I'm so totally confident, certain . . . and different . . . everyone can see it. Feel it, even. But I'm not . . . close to most people. Very few. Can't be. Part of me doesn't even really know how to connect, but I can fake it."

DuQuesne was pacing again, faster, with the sharp, nervous motions of a trapped animal. "Like I said, I'm not even *human*, Ariane. They didn't just make perfect humans, they changed bone density, modified muscle structure, spliced in useful elements from a dozen other species, redesigned skin, connective tissue; as long as it wouldn't show outwardly . . . or show anything they didn't want to show, like some poor SOBs who were based on something a little inhuman . . . they'd use it for any advantage. And *nobody* knows exactly what all the stuff was that they did. Oh, if I was willing to do a full analysis, let someone put me through a full-scale scan or nanoprobe, yeah, we could have figured it out . . . but there are some things that ought to stay buried."

He suddenly threw back his head with a sharp, barking laugh that had very little humor in it. "And of course there's the other set of reasons. The less people know, the better my advantage. Good guy or villain, DuQuesne still knows the value of a secret, my friends. And the worst part? Hyperion's Marc DuQuesne lived about twenty years—though there were parts that felt longer, and the Marc DuQuesne you knew, about fifty. I've lived half a century in the non-Hyperion world, had friends, a career, all that.

"But there's no doubt which part of me's dominant now. I can feel the loss, I feel sorry for it, I'm scared by it even, but the fact is that . . . that shadow, that little mask, feels just exactly like that, a little role I was playing until I woke up. Everything's a dozen times sharper now, brighter, clearer. Those fifty years were spent in . . . in a daze, slow, dumb, crippled. The fact I did it to myself doesn't make any difference. I'm awake now, and the thought of going back . . . oh, there's no way in hell I'm going back, not ever again, not by all the hells of space!"

The vehemence, combined with the anachronistic wording and slight though definite change in voice and posture, frightened Ariane. Frightened her a lot more than she would have thought. "Does that mean that all the time and work we've done together . . . don't mean anything to you?" *Does that mean* we *don't mean anything to you?*

The dark-haired head snapped up and the eyes looked wide; for a moment, the expression was much closer to the old DuQuesne. "No! That wasn't . . . wasn't what I meant. I'm not a monster. Not like that." He managed a small smile. "For all their idiocies, the Hyperion group weren't completely insane. They didn't want a sociopathic superman. A . . . a magnificent loner, maybe, but not someone who'd discard people whenever they were no longer useful." He shook himself and then forced himself to sit down, glancing around the sparsely-furnished room which was the conference room of their Embassy. "And my personal crisis of identity is wasting your time and ours, Captain. I'm sorry for the difficulty."

The curtain had dropped again; maybe Marc still didn't even know what parts of his past and his present had to be addressed. *Sure as hell* I *don't know.* But whether he was really reachable or not now, he was right. "We're not entirely finished with this topic, Dr. DuQuesne, but you're right. But do *not* make the mistake of thinking that I will forget it, or let you forget it either."

The black eyes managed a faint twinkle. "I would not dare to believe the Captain would forget anything at all."

She smiled back. "Good. Then . . . what next?"

"Well," said Simon, "I think it's clear that we *have* to move forward to another Challenge, somehow. Even with the additional caution, I'm afraid that Marc is correct; the Molothos hate all other races to begin with, and a humiliation like this must be essentially an imperative to war for them. They cannot afford to allow such an event to go unpunished."

DuQuesne leaned forward, relaxing into . . . well, whatever his real self was, and grasping Simon's drift immediately. "So in a year or two—three at the outside—there'll be a Molothos battle fleet at our Sphere. The real problem is that, according to Orphan, the Sky Gates work two ways: if you activate a Sandrisson Drive inside one of those Gates as though you were trying to transition to FTL from our universe, you'll jump to the point that the Sky Gate connects to—somewhere near Nexus Arena, or to another Sphere, something like that.

"*But* . . . if you invert the field inside the Sky Gate, you'll pop out into the regular universe, maybe a light-year or so from the home system."

"Oh, bloody hell," Sandrisson said in a horrified whisper, and a cold hand seemed to close around Ariane's heart as she, too, understood. "That means they can bring the war home to us, once they figure out where we are."

"Exactly. So we *can't* take years to recharge and go home, even if we could afford to stay away that long personally. We've got to get home fast, and start the human race preparing." He grinned sharply. "But it's not all bad. We're citizens now. Our Sphere's fully activated. We need to establish some real relationships and figure out if we can manage some form of trade." He rubbed his chin. "Now that we've kicked out the Molothos, I advised Tom—with your approval, Captain —to start fabricating components for a water-driven power system. If we get that going, then we can bring in more raw materials, replicate a few more AIWish units, and at least have the start of manufacturing for our little set of desperate impromptu colonists."

Ariane nodded. "That sounds fine to me."

"What about the Straits?" Simon asked. "Should *Holy Grail* go out? We could bring her up to the surface . . . " he trailed off as Ariane shook her head vehemently.

"*Holy Grail* was designed for space operation only, Simon. I'm not sure she'd hold up at all in an atmosphere, and if the descriptions of the way things work in the Arena are to be trusted, she'd have to fly through atmosphere in a 1-G field. No way."

"Ah. Yes, that would be a bit sticky, to say the least. I suppose that must wait until we either are here long enough to manufacture ships, purchase them, or get home and can have them built there." Simon looked slightly embarrassed. "Then at this point all I can think of are generalities. I don't think it's fair to keep our other people back at the Sphere all the time, so I think we need to rotate people in and out on occasion."

"Very important," agreed DuQuesne. "Right now they're starting to feel a little left out, especially Gabrielle, but even Steve and Tom are going to want to be part of this, and deserve to be. When we get back home—and we will, one way or another—the crew of *Holy Grail* will be famous, and all of us deserve some stories to tell."

"I can't disagree," Ariane said slowly, "but what about the fact that we didn't want to reveal our numbers?"

DuQuesne shrugged. "We don't have to state that they're seeing everyone . . . and this latest development will mean that even a couple of us may be seen as pretty formidable. If they think we're all capable of dealing with a Molothos invasion given two people and a little time, we may have some considerable leverage."

Ariane couldn't restrain a laugh. "Yes . . . I suppose I'd be pretty scared if I thought some newcomers' entire species were superbeings."

"So," Simon said, "the other thing to do is continue to develop the connections we've already made—Orphan, the Faith, and the Analytic—and see what we can manage to get out of those. I'd call Nyanthus immediately, Captain; how one of their rituals can relate to us I don't know, but I'm very sure we want to find out. Check of course with Orphan to make sure that accepting the invitation won't be a problem for us. I will meet with Dr. Rel—I would very much like DuQuesne to come with me—and see what the Analytic can discuss with us now that we have ascended to full citizenship, so to speak."

"I've no problem with that." DuQuesne stood. "But I want to get back and start involving the others in the next couple of days."

"All right," Ariane said. "We'll do it that way. Once we've had these two meetings and evaluated anything that comes of them, we start bringing the others over. Maybe even move everyone here, but we'll decide what needs to be done then."

The finality in her voice caused both Simon and, to her surprise, DuQuesne to simply nod. Sensing the current meeting at an end, Simon excused himself. "It's been a very long day indeed, Ariane. I'll see you both in the morning."

As DuQuesne nodded and turned, she said, "Wait a minute, Marc."

She could feel that intangible wall again, and it almost made her change her mind, tell him to go on. She thought, for an instant, that he was going to keep going anyway. But he paused, then turned. "Yes, Captain?"

"Marc . . . I don't know . . . I can't know . . . exactly what it is you're going through. I suppose there's only two or three people living who could. But I want you to know three things." She took a deep breath, feeling the weight of his scrutiny. "First . . . I'm not letting you go hide inside that wall, Dr. DuQuesne. Maybe I look a lot slower and stupider than I did to you before, but I'm still your friend as well as your Captain, and I'm telling you I'm not letting you hide that way."

The bit about "slower and stupider" hit him, made him blink apologetically. "Captain . . . Ariane . . . I didn't mean . . . "

"Second, I want to thank you for taking that risk, for letting out something that obviously scares you so much. Because if you hadn't, I'm sure that you and Carl would be dead. I don't care nearly so much about the Challenge business—although that's a wonderful bonus; what I care about is that both of my friends came back alive, and it's only because you *are* what you are."

A very faint blush appeared to be visible on the cheeks, not quite hidden by the almost-olive complexion. He started to speak again, but she didn't give him the opportunity.

"And, third, I trust you, Marc. Absolutely. I want you to remember that whether you were made or made yourself, you're a man who people can trust, and *will* trust. They *made* you a man of iron-clad honor and that's a part of you that you've kept. You've given your word to help us, and you will, and I want you to remember that I believe in you. If you need to talk . . . you know where to find me." She swallowed, feeling a new and hard-to-analyze nervousness, as though she was skirting a very dangerous canyon at her feet. "But if you don't, if you can't, it doesn't matter. Because no matter what you think, *I* know you're the hero you're afraid to be."

She saw he was searching for the right reply, and a part of her suddenly panicked at the thought that he might find it. "That's all, Dr. DuQuesne. You can go now; I'd better get some rest myself."

His expression was almost comical, and as the door rolled shut behind him she couldn't help but giggle. *My God, I think I just managed to out-maneuver Marc DuQuesne!*

That made a very pleasant thought to take with her to sleep.

Chapter 39

The Temple of the Faith was near the center of the Embassy level, one of five great buildings surrounding a sort of central square (which happened to be pentagonal). The Grand Arcade surrounded this central square, separated from it by a ring of other buildings, not quite so large and impressive as the central five.

The Temple of the Faith was also a striking building, in the shape of a many-armed spiral whose arms began as tiny beads and enlarged into great spheres, coalescing in the center to a huge tower of spheres ranging from one nearly five hundred meters across at the very base to rice-grain sized dots composing the point of the highest spire, more than two kilometers above. It, like the uniforms of its adherents, was predominantly green and gold, patterns of geometric yet living complexity twining across the surface of the spheres in emerald and auric diversity.

It was a night-cycle within Nexus Arena, and above glowed only the faint hint of sparkles and reflections from the ceiling . . . or whatever night-like imagery the Arena had chosen to display. Whatever the case, the Temple was lit like a bastion of luminance against darkness, a blazing spire of belief and hope set against the backdrop of night.

"They don't lack in their showmanship, do they?" she murmured.

DuQuesne's ears caught her comment. "Not one little bit. Shaped like a galaxy of spheres, reaching upward to the sky, all that kind of symbolism works real good for me. I'd guess that kind of thing must work pretty good for a lot of species, since that's the design they chose." He glanced around. "Not that these other buildings are any slouches at design either."

"Indeed so, Dr. DuQuesne; I am sure that your people, as well, recognize the value of striking the right perceptual chord in your fellows." Orphan, who had accompanied them, surveyed the other buildings. "For public display, for recruitment in many cases, or merely a statement of presence; these are the Faction Houses. Not all Factions have them, of course, but those that do use them to ensure that they are recognized outside of their Embassy, and to conduct business of a general nature for which they still would not wish to give access to their Embassy.

"And here, of course, the greatest of the Faction Houses, won only by direct Challenge, built to design of the one controlling them, mighty statements indeed of the power and influence of their owners. The Faith, of course, before which we stand. The Blessed, my former people. The Molothos, who recruit not at all but indeed wish it clear that they are second to none. The Analytic, masters of Knowledge. And the Vengeance, adversary to the Arena itself."

"*Not* to the Arena, Survivor," a knife-sharp voice snapped from the surrounding gloom. "Merely to those who *created* the Arena."

The speaker was of the species Orphan had called Milluk—a spherical body suspended on multiple slender legs that arched up above its back rather like those of a daddy longlegs, three eyes spaced equidistantly around the body, with some sort of manipulative arms or tendrils underneath. At this range, as it entered the light near them more fully, Ariane could see a glitter as of another eye or two underneath—which made sense, given the need to be able to see what one was manipulating. The creature was surrounded by a slight brownish haze and attended by a faint sharp smell. "You know better than to make such inaccurate pronouncements, Orphan."

The great black wingcases gave their swift shrug. "Who is to say whether opposing the creators of the arena is not itself opposition to the Arena?"

"I'm a little puzzled here," Ariane said. "I thought no one knew who or what made the Arena. You have some sort of name for them—Voidbuilders is the term I've heard—but that's about it."

"Oh, we know them—Captain Austin, is it not?" the creature said. "Selpa'A At, Swordmaster First of the Vengeance, greets you. In safety and in security, in peril and plague, in victory and vengeance, may your course be ever your own."

"Ariane Austin, Captain and—for the moment—leader of the Faction of Humanity, greets you," she echoed and bowed. "May your course also be ever your own as well. So what do you mean, you know the Voidbuilders?"

"As well as any know their own fears and phantoms, the Vengeance know the Creators," the deep and mellifluous voice of Nyanthus answered from the direction of the Temple of the Faith. "Swordmaster First, I thought we had an agreement that you would not harangue my brethren and supplicants before the very doors of my Temple? Would you stray so far and invite—nay, provoke—Challenge for such offense?" The voice of the First Guide was as calm as ever, but Ariane noted that the movements of the symbiotic fliers were much more sharp and jerky.

"Be you so eager for the confrontation, First Guide of Delusion?" Selpa retorted, rocking back and forth on his suspending legs. "Orphan is not one of your poor misguided larvae, and these First Emergents, now their own true Faction, have hardly had time to become ensnared in your ... quaint misunderstandings. And I stand a bit farther than 'before your doors,' unless it is soon your intention to ban me also from the doors of my own headquarters and perhaps the Grand Arcade as well?" It was clear Selpa had intended to say something much more offensive, but decided not to—*probably*, Ariane thought, *because he wants to have a reasonably good chance to talk with us in a friendly setting. Sure isn't because he wants to avoid offending Nyanthus.*

The First Initiate Guide was clearly exceedingly unamused. "I see that you have selected your stalking point well, Selpa. Just a few meters beyond our agreed perimeter. Indeed, you are blameless in literal fact, though not so much in the spirit of the agreement.

I—and my bethren—shall remember this is your way, and examine the other agreements that we have carefully; perhaps we would be also well advised to forget following the spirit of charity and generosity, and instead trace closely the letter of the agreements." Nyanthus whirled slowly aside and flower-bowed before Ariane. "Forgive this disturbing confrontation, Captain Ariane Austin. I have invited you here for a joyous and solemn ritual, as a witness, and would have hoped nothing would sour this evening."

Selpa buzzed from some unseen organ; the buzz was translated as a sigh. "My apologies to you, Captain Austin. As is obvious there is much between my people and the Faith, yet I would not have it said that I sought to ruin your freedom to see and choose. But, if you will, come yourself or send others of your people to speak with me and mine. For I assure you that no story of the Arena will be fully told if it excludes the truths of the Vengeance." He rose high, dropped low, and scuttled off into the night, towards the sharp-spired, blade-angled building that Orphan had named as the Vengeance headquarters. Ariane got the impression that Nyanthus was following his adversary with a speculative gaze.

As the others began to disembark, Nyanthus interposed a long branchlike tendril. "Many apologies. But only one may be witness. The others must all be of the Faith."

Ariane glanced at DuQuesne and Orphan questioningly. Orphan seemed unconcerned, but DuQuesne was studying the First Guide narrowly. "No funny business?"

"I must only guess at the meaning of your metaphor, Dr. DuQuesne, but I offer you my personal word of honor that there shall be laid on your captain no influences, blessings, geases, or other manifestations of our powers; only the sights and sounds she beholds shall influence her, as such things doubtless have always done throughout her life."

"And indeed the word of the First Guide is good. That much I confirm with no reservations whatsoever," Orphan said firmly. "Then we shall move on."

DuQuesne shrugged. "Take care, Captain."

"I will."

Nyanthus led her up the curving gold and green ramp through the immense main doorway, which—unlike the standard Arena door design—was designed like huge scalloped shells on hinges, and opened dramatically outward as they approached. Strains of music reached her ears—music that followed strange chord progressions and rhythms, yet—somehow—beautiful and joyous as the crescendo of Beethoven's Ninth, or Satterli's "Jovian Themes."

She followed the First Guide to a green and gold room, which looked out upon an immense circular amphitheater, composing a great deal of the first central sphere—three hundred meters across, she guessed. Rank upon rank of the Faith stood below, all wearing something—whether it was a cloak, a shirt, engraved and inlaid into chitin, an ornamented crown—of green and gold, often with single or multiple spiraling circular patterns. In the center, a flat space with a spiraling pattern of flat-topped spheres like steps, these leading to a smaller flat space at the top of the spiral's central sphere. A single figure in a dull gray robe stood at that central point.

The figure looked almost human at this distance. Using electronic binoculars, she saw that it appeared to be of the same species as Dr. Relgof, though this individual had fluffy top plumage of a striking gold color, eyes of a clear and piercing blue-green, and the filter-beard was wider and tinged with red and pink. He also looked nervous; the filter flip-flopped frequently and he was clearly trying to restrain an impulse to move.

"I must join the ceremony very shortly, Ariane Austin, but allow me to explain the significance of this event. You see, our order is limited in numbers of Initiate Guides by the Creators; only so many may be so elevated at any given time, and so normally the Ceremony is performed only when a Guide dies or chooses to lay down his burden.

"But when a new species emerges into the Arena, the Creators recognize they, too, will need ministering to, guidance, and assistance from the Faith. Thus at that time they give us a blessing to elevate one or more of our bethren who are worthy to the exalted post of Initiate Guide. Mandallon, the candidate you see below, has asked to be given the honor of elevation in the name of your people. If the Creators are in accord, he will today become something much more than what he was . . . and will gain also terrible responsibilities that he never before imagined. Thus it is to him—and us—extremely important that one of your people, your best representative, witness his Elevation."

The eyes of Mandallon seemed to look up at her through the high-powered lenses. He blinked as though hoping to make her out better, but unless those eyes doubled as telescopes he could only see her as a small figure in the balcony with Nyanthus. "He looks pretty nervous. Is the ritual dangerous?"

The First Guide flowered briefly. "It can be, Ariane Austin. Infusing the power of the Gods into something

mortal can be more than the mortal can bear, and indeed
without some sort of control, the Elevation can be devastating. But we are here to support our newfound Guide,
to contain the power he will suddenly hold, to show him
how to control it and wield it when the time comes. I
have done this seven times in the past forty-two years.
Unless Mandallon has within his heart some hidden flaw,
an uncertainty or failure of belief, he will be perfectly
safe."

Nyanthus bowed like a waving anemone again. "Now
I must go; the true Ritual of Elevation begins." He glided
out, and a curtain-door came down behind him.

The singing and music continued, interspersed with
chants. As she listened, she began to sort out some patterns to the song and ritual; what was most interesting
was that there were occasional words interspersed in the
ritual chant and song which simply weren't translated:

Hail the Creators, the Voidbuilders, the Makers!
Leinis mithid okee . . .

*Blessings on the Arena, the Way to Heaven, the Test
of Holy!*
Illiamswon belkam dolgo . . .

And so on. She noticed that on those phrases the pronunciation became much more variable and ragged;
some creatures probably couldn't even *make* some of
those noises normally, and as near as she could figure,
this was something like having invocations in, oh, old
Latin, when most, if not all, of the worshippers didn't
even know what the words meant.

The song reached a crescendo, building slowly over
several minutes, and she felt chills going down her spine.
It was beautiful, and alien, and solemn, and when the
crescendo suddenly cut off, it was an impact as sharp

and focusing as a slap. At the exact same moment, eight shimmers of green and gold light appeared in the central area, one at the beginning of each of the seven spiraling staircases of flat-topped spheres, and one at the very top, directly behind Mandallon. The gray-robed figure shivered but stayed very still; by his posture he knew that Nyanthus now stood behind him, blossomed into what appeared to be a sunburst, symbiotes hovering between the branches like flickering flames.

"Brethren of the Faith." Nyanthus's voice echoed throughout the room, though she could see no speakers, no amplification devices, and no such were detectable to her scanners. "Welcome in joy and hope and vision. **Reskar vetula aen**, in the words of the Creators: *Behold you all a miracle!* This day we are fortunate, blessed beyond those of these many hundreds of years past; this day, a new people has entered the Blessed Arena, and to them shall be given a Guide!"

So that's supposed to be the actual language of the Voidbuilders themselves? The language of the Gods? She shook her head with a slight smile as the assembled crowd—thousands of the Faith—answered with both ritual and enthusiasm. *Even if it is, I have to wonder if after however many thousand years you could even recognize it. Or maybe they're pronouncing it right but have the meaning wrong. That might explain why it's not translated—the translation's only done if you actually know what you're saying. Otherwise I suppose all you'd have to do to translate some unknown text would be to try to read it aloud.*

"Mandallon, long a disciple and student of the Faith, has asked for this great blessing." The crowd fell silent again. "He has meditated in the seven Gyres, and each time the light has remained clear. He has spoken with his seven teachers, and all have heard his plea. For us of the Faith, all that remains is to ask the Creators to Elevate him." Nyanthus drifted slowly in a complete circle around Mandallon, stopping as he returned to his first position. "Yet it is not only for ourselves this is to be done, but for others who are not of us, though it is of course to be hoped that one day they shall follow, or even lead, where we seek to go. Captain Ariane Austin, what say you?"

As abruptly as that, the entire attention of the chamber was focused upon her. "What say you, representative of Humanity? Will Mandallon be worthy as a guide? You know him not, yet in some ways you must judge him. Judge with your heart. Judge with your soul. Judge as one day we all shall be judged. What say you?"

Way to blindside your guest, Nyanthus. Or is it necessary by the ritual that I be totally clueless about my part in it until you hit me this way? I guess it is. She stood up and leaned slightly out, seeing the thousands of eyes and other sensing organs following her every move. Then she shouted down, and her own voice was amplified: "Mandallon, tell me why you would want to be Elevated in the name of Humanity. Not why you want to be Elevated as such, or what you could do for us, but why Humanity?"

There was a gasp and whisper throughout the gallery; she guessed that the general ritual didn't have a specific provision for the newcomers butting into the procedure that way.

Mandallon was clearly flustered and uncertain how to respond. She repeated the question, then added, to make it more formal yet to get across her point. "Answer me . . . answer me with your heart. Answer me with your soul. Answer me as you would answer a friend, if a friend to my people you're supposed to be."

The candidate for Elevation looked around at the staring eyes, and at the unmoving form of Nyanthus, and seemed almost ready to bolt from the stage. But somehow he got a grip on his panic, the filter-beard stopped vibrating, and he looked up at her again. "I hear and answer your question, Captain Ariane Austin, and my answer is simply this: any who dare to taunt the Molothos upon the third day of their arrival are in desperate *need* of a Guide!"

Ariane laughed. "Then I approve, because we'll probably get in a lot worse trouble soon enough!"

The laugh was echoed around the room. "A question and answer which has brought its own small joy and wisdom. The omens are good," Nyanthus said. "Then, Mandallon, stand and pray, for we begin. May next we speak as equals."

A new song-and-chant began, this one a clockwork tune that shifted tone each time the seven Initiate Guides took a step forward on their spiraling staircases. At each step, Nyanthus faded from view and reappeared at the top of the next staircase. She couldn't see any method to accomplish this, though at this distance of course a lot could be hidden.

Finally, in the midst of an intertwining, echoing melody, half dirge and half hymn, the seven Initiate Guides reached the high platform, whether by a scuttle, hop, step, or flow (as each was a different species). Immediately they began a rhythmic hammering chant in that untranslatable language: "**Vensecor secutai peheli ix** . . . **Vensecor secutai pehili ix** . . ."

A blue aura began to blossom around each of the Initiate Guides, and Ariane leaned forward, trying to understand. Her sensors said nothing, again, but the auras expanded, intertwined, formed a seven-pointed sapphire wall enclosing Mandallon and Nyanthus. Through that wall extended an arm, tendril, or other manipulative member of each of the Initiate Guides.

A sharp silver sparkle suddenly limned two of Nyanthus's branches; they were now edged, graceful bladed arches. One of his other branches coiled around a simple white bowl, a bowl that reflected like polished marble.

"As one of us you have studied, as one of us you have trained, as one of us you have believed. Now in ritual ancient on any world, you become one of us yet again." The arched branch-sword flicked out to each extended limb, and from each Ariane could see through her binoculars a few drops of blood (or whatever fluid passed for blood) drip into the extended bowl, which was turned with each cut so that in the end seven trails of droplets met in the center—red, green, brown, blue, varying shades of life intertwined. The blade cut Nyanthus, and she saw a vivid lemon-yellow droplet fall in the exact center of the bowl.

Nyanthus reverently dabbed Mandallon seven times with the mingled blood. "Now have you come to the finality of your training. Now have you come to the threshold of the Creators. Let them bless you. Let them heed you. Let them give to you their strength that you will serve us all," Nyanthus said, deep voice tense and focused. "Call upon them, Mandallon! Call in their tongue, and ask the blessing of the Creators upon you, and may you be blessed as we!"

Golden hair-feather plumage waving, Mandallon drew himself up and said: "**Recardisea tinduk wesni; cotarey wademor tharus zatra; setsdensu kama threy!**"

A blaze of blue-white fury detonated around Mandallon, kicking back even Nyanthus—who, the incredulous Ariane saw, was also surrounded by the blue aura. Mandallon, through her glasses, seemed in agony, yet transported, almost ecstatic, at the same time, giving vent to a wordless cry. A shockwave rippled out from the center, not quite damaging, but palpable in its force, and *still* her sensors registered almost nothing. Oh, they sensed the passing shockwave, but not what would have been necessary to cause it. *What the hell . . . ?*

It seemed forever the lights warred in the center of the amphitheatre, but in actuality it was only moments before the blue faded and Mandallon stood . . . garbed not in gray, but in perfect green and gold, glittering and new.

Ooooo . . . kay. I'm not sure that's exactly my favorite word "creepy," but we've definitely hit a whole new level of WTF weird.

Boy, am I going to have some questions . . .

Chapter 40

"Ariane Austin, I give you my name, which is Mandallon Ell Ir'Rathsab; my Faction, which is the Faith; and my position, which is Initiate Guide." Mandallon's body language—which seemed, like Dr. Rel's, not entirely dissimilar from that of humanity—showed the lingering excitement and tension, and his tone of voice a firmly-leashed pride trying to break forth as he greeted someone for the first time with his new position.

Certainly not about to break his mood, Ariane smiled and bowed low. "I greet you in friendship and hope," she said, remembering the forms of greeting Nyanthus had used previously and modifying them for the occasion. "I give you my name, which is Ariane Stephanie Austin; my Faction, which is Humanity; and my position, which is Captain. Congratulations to you, Mandallon."

She and the new Initiate Guide were near the center of the large room which was serving as a reception hall following the event. *It's really almost disturbingly amazing how similar we are in many things. But then if you think about it, this sort of ritual and celebration makes an awful lot of sense for civilizations.*

"I . . . I can hardly believe it myself. It is a miracle in itself, that I stand here speaking with you!" Mandallon's voice was slightly . . . cleaner, sharper, than Dr. Rel's, and other little details of skin, fronds, and so on, hinted to Ariane that Mandallon was quite young, the equivalent of twenty or so. "I had expected to follow the normal path, for another thirty or forty years, before one of the Guides passed beyond or set down his mantle, and even then—as I'm sure you've guessed, Captain Austin— there would be many of us vying for the honor. Instead, barely had I completed the Sevenfold Trail when I am Elevated!"

She nodded, smiling. His breathless enthusiasm felt familiar, much more the behavior of someone closer to her own age than the considered and mature *gravitas* of Nyanthus, the calculating practical cheerfulness of Orphan, or the omnicompetent confidence of DuQuesne. "Good luck for you, then. But . . . there must have been an awful lot of older candidates in line for the honor. No offense meant to them, or you, but . . . why would the Faith select you over what was undoubtedly a large field of more experienced candidates?"

"Symmetry and symbolism, Captain Austin," Nyanthus answered from behind Mandallon, drifting in his mysterious way sideways to stop near Mandallon's side—but still slightly behind the newly-minted Initiate Guide, clearly yielding him, in this moment, the preeminent position. "You have been born anew as a people, emerged new-birthed into the Arena. You are a new people, a young people, unknown and untried. You do not need an Initiate Guide steeped in ritual and habit, one who has followed a course laid down centuries ago; you require one as young, untried, and ready to learn as yourselves. Not one unlearned or lacking in Faith, of course, but one who is ready to understand others in a way those of us more anchored to the rocks cannot."

"That makes sense," Ariane acknowledged. "So in this case, he was only competing against others who'd just recently completed their preliminary training?"

"Yes, even so. But Mandallon was also chosen by the Creators—not only as you saw today, but also as we saw in our own counsels, for we choose not blindly, but ask that all our great decisions be guided by Their wisdom."

Mandallon's filter-beard and fronds were vibrating oddly at this discussion; Ariane suddenly realized this was probably the equivalent of blushing or nervous shuffling. She smiled at that. "But you still seemed to believe there was potential danger."

Mandallon jumped into the conversation, clearly much more comfortable talking about this subject than listening to what bordered on effusive praise. "Oh, there is always a danger. Even though the Creators may guide us, it is not always certain what their guidance is telling us. Sometimes it is to point out someone who needs to be tested—and may fail—in the most fierce of all fires. It may be, also, that one of the other Guides could fail. It is rare, of course, for how could any Guide have become what . . . we are . . . " He hesitated almost wonderingly at the "we," then continued, " . . . what we are without having solidified their faith beyond almost any possibility of breaking? Yet sometimes it happens, and not always for reasons easily understood."

"So . . . " She wasn't quite sure exactly how to broach the subject she wanted to address; obviously she didn't want to offend her hosts, but what she'd seen raised so many questions. "What . . . what can you tell me about what I just saw? I mean, I could *see* a lot of . . . really interesting things, but my sensors couldn't make much sense of it, and I certainly wasn't actually participating in it."

The chiming buzz of Nyanthus translated as a rich, tolerant chuckle. "Ah, Captain Austin, how carefully you attempt to ask what sort of trickery we are using on the common people to reinforce the belief." Mandallon visibly relaxed, clearly not having been sure what to say or how *he* should take the question.

"I didn't say—"

"Of course you did not, and I would have been most disappointed in you if you had." The openwork candle flame flicked open and closed. "I truly wish I could convey the essence of what you saw, Ariane. Indeed I do. For those of us who are a part of it, the existence of something beyond mortal comprehension is as real and undeniable as the stone beneath us. Tell her, Mandallon. Tell her now, while it remains echoing in your mind, resonating in your soul."

The new Initiate Guide took a deep, vibrating breath. "I . . . I felt myself almost . . . rebuilt. I felt the strength of the Creators flow through me, burning out my impurity and weakness, replacing it with strength almost too great to bear. For a moment . . . for a moment, I saw through Their eyes; I could *see* the Arena, not just Nexus, not just Sai'Daku, my home Sphere, but *all* of it, from impossible center to ungraspable Wall, and for that tiny instant I could understand it, see and grasp where all things were, as easily as I can see and grasp these delicacies laid out for us." He gestured at a nearby shelf running around the hall. "I can barely strain out the essence of that now, but . . . but now I have tasted their wisdom and scope, partaken of the true nature of All as much as any mortal being ever can, and I *know* what before I only believed."

He closed his eyes, spreading the filter before him as widely as it would go, took another breath. "And I felt my brother Initiate Guides supporting me, keeping the holy Power restrained within my frame, guiding me to the way to leash it. For we are . . . how can I say . . . conductors, channels for the Power. We do not generate it, we merely direct it and permit the Creators to act through us. It takes much discipline and practice to be able to do so reliably and well, and . . . I have much to learn."

Ariane didn't really know what to make of that. She really sincerely didn't believe in "Creators" in the godlike sense that the Faith used the term. It just . . . didn't work for her. This place was awe-inspiring, yes, and way beyond her ability to understand, but really, so was Kanzaki-Three or any other major space station. Maybe it was her own failure of imagination or faith, but she just thought that a real deity, or group of deities, would make something that didn't feel, to her, so very . . . manufactured.

On the other hand, she also believed that Mandallon and Nyanthus were telling her the exact truth as they saw it, and if Mandallon had—even for an instant—been able to apprehend the entirety of the Arena, she wasn't sure but what that *would* come damn close to being something like a god. Maybe the records of the ritual would reveal something to Simon or DuQuesne.

But Mandallon was speaking again. " . . . for you and your people?"

She blinked. "Many, many apologies, Mandallon Ell Ir'Rathsab. I was thinking so much about what you told me of your experiences that I have, I am afraid, failed to hear what you just said."

Mandallon spread his six-fingered hands in a parting wave. "There is no need to apologize; if you found wonder in my words, then perhaps I have already begun my work. What I said, Captain, was that as you are, symbolically, my people, from which I was born into the Faith as an Initiate Guide, it is traditional that we do for you a service. Is there anything that the Faith, through the small offices of myself, might do for you and your people?"

Her heart gave a great leap. *Could it be . . . ?* "There is indeed one very important service that we have need of, and that perhaps you could assist with." She began to tell Mandallon of their need for power for *Holy Grail*, but even before she was done he gave an apologetic negative.

"Truly I wish that such a thing were in my power, Captain." His tone was sincere. "But it will be a very long time before I could channel such vast amounts of the Creator's power, and convert it such that it became one with your machines. I am sure you realize how very much energy is involved in the use of that device. The Faith does not encourage its new-born Guides to immolate themselves."

Ariane tried to hide her disappointment; how well she succeeded she didn't know. "An understandable precaution, especially if you wish to keep encouraging young people to join the Faith and follow that particular career path." Nyanthus and Mandallon acknowledged that with a small chuckle.

She tried to think. Clearly Mandallon was supposed to render them a symbolic service—it was important to him to do it, and it was certainly incumbent upon her not to waste such an opportunity. But really, what did they need, aside from the power he couldn't give them? The only thing she could think of immediately was securing their Sphere, but didn't know if that was a job you could trust to a newly-minted Initiate Guide; she'd have to ask Orphan exactly who could do it, and what she'd have to arrange. Other than that, what would you need a priest for, except—

And suddenly it came to her, a perfect choice, solving a problem that had been gnawing away at her for weeks. "Mandallon, there is something else that perhaps you could do for us, something that requires much less of power, but much more of care and delicacy."

Mandallon leaned forward slightly. "I wish not to sound boastful, but I was noted for my ability to focus clearly and well on the most minute of details, and none advance to Candidate of Elevation without walking the Sevenfold Path; one of the Seven Parts of the Path is the Way of Compassion."

"There is one of my people, a very skilled and wise woman, who was terribly hurt by our entry to the Arena, because she was relying on artificial intelligences at the moment of transition. She has not truly awakened to herself since, spending most of her time in what seems a near-coma. Is it possible that you could help her?"

Mandallon turned to Nyanthus. The First Guide's candle flame-like structure flowered again, and for a few moments the symbiotic flyers wove their way around both Guides. Then Nyanthus resumed his more usual pose and Mandallon turned back to a rather puzzled Ariane. "I have communed with the First Guide and through him seen the sort of injury you describe."

That's interesting. Again, I detected nothing, so it's not RF communication like our implants can manage. Mandallon continued, "A terrible, terrible thing indeed, one that could shatter a soul as well as a mind, to be reliant on the poor electronic minds that cease as soon as they enter. But though terrible, it is a thing well within our power to alleviate, perhaps even cure. It would be a great honor and privilege for me, if you would permit me to make the attempt."

It was amazing, the weight that seemed to lift from her shoulders. *I hadn't even realized how much I'd been worrying about her, pushing it to the back of my mind with everything else that's been going on . . . and probably a hell of a load of guilt along with the worry.* "I would be very glad if you would. Our medical officer has tried all that she can, given our resources, and nothing's worked. And now . . ."

"Then say no more. Send for me, when you have brought her to the Arena from your Sphere, and I shall make the attempt." Mandallon gave his species' curtsey-like bow. "I thank you for finding such a perfect and admirable service for me to perform. I only hope the Creators will see fit to bless me well that day."

"And I, too." She noticed how the crowd had maintained a discreet distance from them, yet remained focused on them—more specifically, on herself and the new Initiate Guide. *This is really supposed to be his night, I think. And I don't think I'm getting much else out of this tonight; I need to get this back to the others, get Laila back here, and think it all over.* "In that case, Mandallon, please again accept my congratulations and thanks, but I'd better get back to my Embassy and let everyone know. We've all been very worried about Laila."

"Please don't promise *too* much!" The sudden almost-panicked tone nearly made her smile—it was exactly what any new-minted professional felt the first time they were about to be put on the spot. "I cannot guarantee that I will be able to restore all that she was—only the Creators can do that, and they may or may not. But I will do the best I may, and I am sure she will be far better than before."

"If you do your best, then we ask no more, Mandallon. Don't worry." She bowed again and began to politely make her way through the crowd, which was beginning to close in on Mandallon. She noticed in particular several individuals of Mandallon's own species, but . . . slightly different in particulars. This time she did smile.

"Something amuses you, Ariane Austin?" Nyanthus was drifting along next to her.

Well, you're getting good at reading human expressions awfully fast. "A bit. I'm guessing that in the Faith, an Initiate Guide isn't expected to be celibate?"

Nyanthus laughed. "Indeed not. Oh, there are variants for different species of adherents, and I have heard of such practices in other religions, especially some of those scattered wild amidst the Spheres, but the Creators did not give to us our ability to go through life with others only to have those of us closest to them give up that most precious gift. You have perceived, then, that Mandallon has a number of admirers at this most auspicious event."

"You'd see the same thing at a similar human event, I assure you." They were approaching the front doors with a measured walk, having cleared the worst of the crowds.

"Mandallon is young, and his people place great importance on formal bonding and family groups. An Initiate Guide, I think I need not emphasize, is a great asset for any family. Although it should also be emphasized that outside of their immediate family, our Guides are carefully sworn never to intervene in matters affecting their own people; otherwise their powers might be used by their people to advance their own causes rather than that of the Faith."

Ariane nodded. "Makes sense. But what if their people try to . . . well, use the immediate family as a lever?"

The candle flame openwork suddenly looked rigid as steel, and Nyanthus's voice was hard. "Then other Guides would come, and instruct them in the terrible error of their ways." Just the sound sent a chill down her spine; she had no doubt that Nyanthus was speaking from a personal experience, and the cold and unyielding nature of his voice left the indelible impression that whatever the Guides did would be long remembered . . . and long feared.

As abruptly as it had gone cold, Nyanthus's voice returned to its usual warmth. "But few indeed are those so foolish; far more seek to ease the way of an Initiate Guide, for all we seek to do is aid others to the path of the true light. I—and through me, Mandallon—thank you again many times for coming and witnessing this most special event for your people. I hope that one day I shall see you, or some of your people, passing through this doorway as more than a simple guest."

She bowed. "Thank you many times as well, Nyanthus," she said, the chill having faded but the memory not ever likely to. "I hope that we shall always work well together, at the least, and certainly I think that you will find at least some of my people passing your doors in that fashion one day." *Given the ludicrous things we've believed before, and still do, the Faith is positively sensible; I'm sure that they'll gain a fair number of converts eventually.*

The air of Nexus Arena was somewhat cooler than the Temple of the Faith, and had the undefinable feeling of open air—despite the fact that it was undeniably *not* open air, but just air inside a very big structure. She began walking, heading for the Grand Arcade where it would be easy to find one of the autocabs. The streets were lit, but with a dim light at intervals that permitted one to walk but still emphasized the dark patterns of night above.

As she passed from one pool of light into the shadows between, it seemed that the shadows moved, coalescing next to her like a whirlwind of ebony. She jumped aside with an incredulous curse and drew her pistol.

Yellow eyes blinked at her from the black shadows, that she now saw were robes over a nearly human form. "Your weapon will not be needed, Captain Austin. I intend no harm to you or yours."

Aside from causing me a bloody heart attack, maybe! She forced her heartbeat to slow down and reholstered the gun. "You damn near got shot."

The voice was quiet, yet deep, with a timbre that vibrated like the lowest note of a pipe organ. "Many apologies, Captain Austin. I had arranged the forces to bring me hence when you passed, but perhaps I had misjudged at what distance, or in what manner, to do so. All of us can make mistakes, can we not?"

"I suppose. Even Shadeweavers?"

The responding chuckle was also deep, rippling. Ariane couldn't put her finger on why she found the sound itself disconcerting; perhaps it was something she'd heard elsewhere, a reminder of a voice that was associated with dark and dangerous things. "Even Shadeweavers, Captain Austin. So, you have seen the Faith make a great business of bringing another into their service."

Ah, yes. You and the Faith get on like oil and matches. "It was a lovely ceremony."

"I will agree that they are excellent at spectacle, Captain. The symbolism is excellent, the ambience carefully considered, the presentation flawless. All calculated well to engender exactly the sort of reaction you have seen—and no doubt felt, to some extent, in yourself."

"I appreciate their beliefs, and I can't say they're entirely nonsensical. I've heard much sillier religious beliefs. The Arena is very spectacular." She continued walking. The Shadeweaver traveled with her; she tried not to show her reaction when she realized the cloaked figure was literally floating about ten centimeters from the floor and drifting along at exactly her own speed. *Hologram or some similar projection? He probably isn't even actually here.*

The hidden shoulders shrugged. "Spectacular indeed, Captain. But the Faith delude themselves, and others. Whether they believe what they say, or whether the central Guides know precisely what nonsense they spread, is a matter even we Shadeweavers debate. But they are no more holy than you, or I."

"Maybe," Ariane said with her own shrug. "But at least *they* haven't tricked me into getting involved in someone else's fights."

The rippling chuckle again, and a flash of yellow eyes hidden in the cowl. "True. At least, not yet. But your hostility is so misplaced. Had you not acted, Orphan would not have been in your debt, and your position here would be . . . far more precarious, in all probability."

"You didn't do that for my benefit." Ariane stopped and glared at him. "I'm sure you had your own reasons. Well, let's get something straight here. You don't *ever* go messing with my head again. None of your people."

The cowl tilted. "You are attempting to intimidate me, Captain? You have no idea what you are doing, you know. We could be excellent allies, and as to being enemies, you are hardly *able* to threaten me. I really would not recommend it. But I see you are not in a mood for conversation." They were reaching the edge of the Grand Arcade, and the Shadeweaver turned to go down a side street.

"Now hold on!" Ariane snapped, grabbing the Shadeweaver's sleeve. "I'm not done—"

The world suddenly went black, spinning around her like a top. She staggered and almost fell, catching herself by grabbing something solid at her side. Her vision cleared. "Holy . . ."

She stood in front of her own Embassy, gripping the newly-materialized front gate in her hand.

Chapter 41

That's the fun thing about the Arena. Every time you get a question answered, it just leads to more questions. DuQuesne didn't speak immediately, and neither did any of the others, following Ariane's summary of the previous night.

Tom Cussler was frowning, as was Simon. Carl was grinning and shaking his head. "This place just gets weirder and weirder," the controls expert said, finally. "But I'm glad it looks like we have a solution for Laila's problem. Speaking honestly, we could really use a bio expert."

Simon nodded. "And it will take a great weight from my mind. After all, I was the one who let her join, despite the fact that we didn't really need a biology expert . . . or, at least, we didn't think so at the time."

"If what Mandallon does will work, it'll be a big relief. I've already invited Orphan over—I want to make sure I'm not making any mistake from his point of view."

"I agree." DuQuesne weighed whether he should continue. *Someone has to at least bring it up, even though I know what the result's going to be.* "Being perfectly honest here, Captain, the problem *I* have with it is that you're planning on bringing in what could be a twenty-four-karat spy and letting him get full access to one of our people."

He could see Ariane start to open her mouth to protest reflexively. It was clear she'd already taken a great liking to Mandallon. She managed to stop herself, while the others glanced at each other but didn't seem inclined to immediately comment. Finally, Ariane spoke. "I'd hate to think that was the case, but, okay, I suppose it could be." She frowned.

"I don't think it really matters," Simon said.

Yeah, he would be the one. DuQuesne glanced over at Simon. "Why's that?"

"There are really only two possibilities here. The first is that the Faith are, within the limits we already know, being straightforward with us. In that case, Mandallon truly is here to do us a service and anything he learns would be incidental to that service—and we could probably prevail upon him to not speak of it.

"On the other hand, the Faith could be playing a cynical game and Mandallon, as innocent as he appears, could be a world-class actor. But in that case, the Faith would need no special permission from us to get information about our biology. We trusted Nyanthus's word—based on others saying it was good—that no 'funny business,' as you would put it, would be used on

Ariane. But with the implied capabilities of the Faith and Shadeweavers, they could easily have gained most, if not all, of the information they would get from examining Laila while Ariane was visiting their own Faction House." His glasses flashed opaquely for a moment as he adjusted them slightly. "In point of fact, the only way in which this event might give them information that they could use, and yet not have gained otherwise, would be if their powers require our permission to function—and we can of course place our own conditions on this operation, to minimize this risk."

DuQuesne grunted. "You have some points. I don't think that nearly covers it all, but the bigger general point probably is that the Arena natives have an awful lot we want, and the more important things about us . . . probably aren't going to be in our biology. Mandallon's going to be in Laila's *mind*, though, which should be a reason for concern."

"The problem is, right now we don't know if she *has* a mind," Ariane said bluntly. "According to Gabrielle, she doesn't, by our standards. She doesn't think we could fix her even if we got her back home. If Mandallon can fix that . . . we *owe* it to Laila."

And that is the real *issue. Basically whether to abandon one of her crew, or take a chance to save her. A responsibility she takes seriously now.* "I've said my piece. You people can call the shots, but just remember: in a way, every single word we say might be valuable to someone." *But there's no way I'm getting these people to act like covert ops people, and—being honest with myself—it wouldn't work. The trusting approach gets us information, too, and they're just not cut out for paranoia.* "Bring in Orphan, like you said. Not that I trust

him any more than I have to, but he's got his uses."
DuQuesne shrugged and moved on to the next subject.
"How about the Vengeance?"

Ariane acknowledged this with a small smile. "Oh, I
want to hear what they have to say. Getting a good perspective on how everyone views the Arena . . . I'm starting to think that this is going to be one of the major
aspects of how everyone interacts—how they think of
this place."

"That sounds very likely, and fits with what we've seen
so far," Simon agreed. "More interesting to me, of
course, are the specific phenomena you witnessed last
night. More than ever I wish I'd been there to see them.
How long did that . . . transportation trick of the Shadeweaver's take?"

"Based on my own internal clock, and comparing it to
the running time . . . a very small fraction of a second.
The whole 'things went black and spinning' seems to
have been either just my own reaction to it, or my perceiving something as taking a lot longer than it did."
Ariane shrugged. "Honestly—there's no actual clear
interval that I can measure."

*Which means it was essentially instantaneous; tele-
portation?* "Did it feel anything like our experiences with
the Inner Gateway?"

Ariane thought. "You know, Marc, I think you may
be on to something. It wasn't identical, but there were
strong similarities."

"I," said Tom, "am actually more concerned with some
of the implications about the Faith's 'Initiate Guides.' If
you reported that conversation accurately, it seems to be
clearly implied that a more experienced Guide actually
would be able to recharge *Holy Grail*'s Sandrisson coils.
Am I correct?"

"All but stated that outright, yes."

DuQuesne met Tom's gaze; Tom spoke for both of them. "That is, to be perfectly honest, terrifying. If that's true, Captain, the better trained of these people are the equivalent of nuclear weapons."

Ariane shrugged. "I realized that myself, but it's not . . . relevant, to be honest. We're not here to match ourselves against them, and from everything I hear no one in their right mind would try to face them down in a blunt instrument conflict anyway."

A pale green sphere of light chimed into existence nearby, making most of the others jump suddenly. DuQuesne wasn't startled, mainly because he'd adjusted his expectations in this place. "Liberated Representative Orphan has arrived, Captain Austin," the Embassy voice said quietly.

"Admit him and show him here," Ariane said. "I wish I knew how this place manages those little stunts," she continued to Carl and DuQuesne.

"I could think of several ways I could arrange it," DuQuesne said, ticking those ways off in his mind as he said it, "but I'd also bet none of them are the method it's using."

The tall green-black figure of Orphan strode into the room, and gave them a broad, deliberately human bow. "I greet you once more, my friends."

Less defensive posture. Less stress in his voice. Surface coloration seems slightly richer, at least in some parts of the spectrum. "You've had good news, I see," DuQuesne said dryly. Ariane shot him a startled look.

"Is it indeed so obvious?" Orphan looked at DuQuesne with little-veiled curiosity. "I had thought I was good at being, how might I say it, circumspect. But yes, quite good news. A small Challenge I accepted some months past has come due, and I have won it—due, of course, to your assistance."

"How'd we manage *that* when we didn't even know about this Challenge until now?" Ariane asked.

"Because the nature of the Challenge had to do with my, shall we say, social position in the Arena. You might say that the Challenge here was in the nature of a rather serious bet. The bet was that I could not convince any Faction to ally with me, other than those which had already provided assistance, and that I could not get any substantial additional assistance from any of my prior allies, given my current precarious circumstances." He gave the open-handed gesture that served sometimes for a smile. "Now it has become clear that you have allied yourselves with me, and on the strength of our current relationship, a number of other Factions have been cautious but willing to extend me some additional support and credit, and thus there is no doubt that I have won this Challenge, which will prove most useful.

"But you did not invite me hear to brag of my current good fortune, I am sure; so instead, tell me what it is that you wish to discuss."

Ariane smiled; the smile contrasted brilliantly with her tanned skin and dark blue hair, DuQuesne noticed. It was a very nice smile, too. "That's wonderful news, Orphan. Was it the Blessed who made this bet?"

"Oh, not them directly, but one of their minor allies, the Tantimorcan. A mostly one-species Faction—there are, of course, quite a large number of those—with special skill in the design of ships both civilian and military that can operate well in the Arena. I will introduce you to them sometime; my own price was for them to become *my* allies for a period of not less than three of their years—which is about two-point-seven of yours." Orphan's voice showed the deep self-satisfaction of this victory.

"That would be excellent, Orphan," Simon said. "I am quite sure that there are factors involved in building vessels for this environment which are different from both the demands of building aircraft for Earthly environments, or ordinary deep-space craft."

"Many, some of them obvious, some . . . quite subtle indeed, Dr. Sandrisson. But please, I appreciate the congratulations, but what is your news?"

Ariane quickly filled their alien ally in; DuQuesne nodded at the efficient way she laid out the situation. "So, basically, we think this is probably the best use of the favor that Mandallon offered, but I don't want to make a mistake here."

Orphan considered. "I now recall having heard something of this tradition, a long time ago, perhaps when I first spent considerable time talking with Nyanthus. An intriguing and most useful offer. There certainly are other options . . . but given that I know that you feel a strong responsibility towards your people, and that you must have severely limited numbers of people available, I would concur. This is an excellent use of the Faith's abilities, and Mandallon is almost certainly underestimating his potential. Securing your Sphere would be another possibility . . . but I do not believe that he will as yet have the knowledge and skill to do that effectively and reliably." He gave a decisive handtap. "Yes, indeed, have him cure your injured."

"There is another . . . interesting issue." Ariane described her short conversation and encounter with the

Shadeweaver; Orphan stopped her at several points, making her back up and tell the sequence in more detail. Once she was done, the green-black alien stood silently for several moments, thinking.

"You do not have uninteresting days, do you, Captain Austin? The Shadeweavers are an intriguing Faction, as you know. They are separated from the other factions not merely by their unusual abilities, but by their focus and dedication to their own interests. One who becomes a Shadeweaver is required—as far as I can tell—to abandon their prior responsibilities and commitments. They belong only to the Shadeweavers, not to their old species or Factions.

"They also do not speak idly to others. Something about you has interested them greatly, Ariane Austin. Perhaps something of your people, or something of you personally." His wingcases tightened in a manner DuQuesne thought of as indicating a frown. "Your conversation does make it clear that I owe our alliance to their interference, which is, alas, somewhat worrisome. I must go to them and ask what sort of offer they would like from me. They expect such debts to at least be acknowledged and, in preference, paid, though they cannot demand or force such payment." The black wingcases gave a scissors-like shrug. "How unfortunate that you did not converse with him longer; it might have given us an insight into their true interest."

"Next time, Captain," DuQuesne said, "Try to keep your temper under control."

"It's not easy, Marc. That whole business gives me the serious willies. I don't like the idea some guy just waved his hand or whatever and made me step forward to almost get us killed. No matter *what* his motives are."

DuQuesne could see that even just talking about the subject bothered Ariane. "Fine. Then maybe I'd better try talking to them sometime." *I don't like it either, but I can deal with it a lot better than she can, I'd bet.*

"Sounds good to me." Ariane gave him a brief smile. "Carl, Tom, could you go and get Laila brought back here?"

"Sure thing, Cap," Carl said. "Do you want Marc to come with us?"

DuQuesne repressed a small smile. That was a clever way for Carl to ask "Who should stay on the Sphere?" without giving Orphan an idea of how many people constituted their Faction currently.

Ariane answered,"The work you'll be doing there is pretty straightforward as I understand it—"

Carl grinned and gave a half-serious salute. "Very straightforward—repress the natives and exploit the natural resources for our own selfish gain. Oh, and build a water-powered generator."

"Yes, straightforward," she said, with a fond smile at her long-time crew chief, "and I'd like Marc here for when we talk to the Vengeance, at least, and to observe whatever it is that Mandallon does."

She's right enough on that. Tom and Carl shouldn't have any trouble following through on what I gave them, and having new visitors here . . . well, I am the best qualified to observe stuff everyone else misses. "Understood, Captain."

"So you *are* inviting old Selpa to give you his recruitment speech? How droll." Orphan's voice was vastly amused.

"You don't take him seriously?" Ariane asked.

Orphan's hands flicked out in that *no* gesture. "Oh, I take the Vengeance extremely seriously indeed. They did not choose that name idly, and the implications of dangerous intent are most clearly desired. But Selpa'A At is a true believer, and . . . " he paused, searching for the right words. "I suppose what I find droll about it is that you are now being pursued by most of the significant Factions, so you'll be hearing the same story from each . . . just told from a completely different and sometimes quite amusingly wrongheaded point of view."

"Make sure you record it, I'll want to hear it all," Carl said as he and Tom got up. "We're heading out then—no reason to leave poor Laila there any longer than necessary."

"Thanks, Carl. Tell Steve to take a break and come along; I know obviously Gabrielle will be coming since she's overseeing Laila's care now."

"He'll be glad to hear that; he's been . . . looking forward to getting the chance to come." Tom sounded relieved at the thought he'd be giving Steve the good news; reassessing certain subliminal cues, DuQuesne suppressed a slight smile. It appeared that Steve and Tom shared something more than just a preference to *not* get into the line of fire. Good for them. He suspected that Ariane hadn't noticed, though, and made a note to quietly bring up the subject; interpersonal relationships could be very good or bad in such a small group, and as the commanding officer she needed to be aware of what was going on in her command. And once more, the dialogue had managed to avoid directly implying how many people they had.

"Take care, Dr. Edlund, Dr. Cussler. I look forward to meeting these others of yours." The alien raised a tall glass in their direction, one set with the sipping arrangement Orphan seemed to prefer. Orphan had gotten himself a drink from the containers set aside for him in the room's preservation unit—something like a refrigerator, but with some other wrinkles that DuQuesne hadn't quite figured out that made food and other perishables keep a lot longer.

While the Arena proper had incredibly advanced technology for its own use, the inactivation of nanotechnology and associated devices meant that they had to stock up the Embassy in the same manner that places had been supplied centuries ago: go shopping, find what you want, and literally carry it home with you. DuQuesne found that quaintly amusing, but it also introduced a lot of other considerations in terms of supply which simply hadn't been an issue previously. You actually had to think ahead and go get supplies for any guests you were inviting over, rather than just having them bring along a few templates and plug them in.

"No offense, Orphan," Ariane said, after the others had left, "but I'm not sure we want you present when the Vengeance gets here . . . which will be in about twenty minutes or so."

"Indeed? But . . . " Orphan paused. "I think I see. They will surely change their approach if I am present—recognizing my long residence and detailed knowledge. They may speak more directly and freely if I am not there."

"And that might let us learn more than we would otherwise. Unless you think they'll try to say something about you that you don't want us to hear?"

Orphan laughed. "Oh, there is no doubt that some people will have many things to say against me. But I think I need fear nothing from the Vengeance, save that they'll likely call me a fence-sitter and opportunist —which, in all truth, I am." He stood. "But I trust that I need not leave your Embassy?"

Ariane smiled. "Oh, not at all. I'll want to talk over everything they say afterwards, anyway."

"In that case, I shall with your leave take myself—and my drink—into the adjoining meeting room, where I shall communicate with my new allies on some specific arrangements I need from them. I can keep quite busy." Orphan bob-bowed to them and left, still quite cheerful.

"Nice to see him happy," Ariane said.

"Oh, quite," Simon agreed. "He may be, as he claims, an opportunist, but I get the impression he is also one to abide by his commitments—so anything which improves his lot will likely improve our own."

"As long as we keep an eye on him," DuQuesne said. "I like him myself, but everyone else isn't comfortable around him. Which means that there's a downside to being associated with him, and we still haven't run into it."

Ariane looked at him sharply. "You really think so?"

He nodded. "Captain, I've listened to a lot of conversations—both ones you've been present at, and others—that touch on our little ally there. Here, let me give you an example. I wondered whether that 'Survivor' moniker was just because he was the last surviving member of the Liberated, so I asked around.

"Captain, that's only a tiny part of it. The real reason he's called the Survivor, and at least a good part of the reason people aren't comfortable around him is that he's gone on at least three expeditions into unexplored parts of the Arena—other Spheres, the Deeps between Spheres. These expeditions were looking for something —remnants of other civilizations that were here and died off, maybe traces of the Voidbuilders themselves, whatever. These were well-equipped expeditions—several ships, trained crews, supported by at least one major Faction each time—and not one of the people who set out on them was ever seen again.

"Except Orphan. I didn't get the details on the others, but once he was apparently found, drifting alone through the clouded space between Spheres, by a Shadeweaver contingent. What he saw, what happened, he has apparently either never told to anyone, or else everyone he's talked to has never said a word." He shook his head. "So whether they call him the Survivor or Orphan or some other nickname, everyone's nervous, maybe a little afraid, maybe a little distrusting. Lot of that's associated with the fact that he's a direct—really, the *only* direct—adversary of the Blessed, and the Blessed are scary folks. Means that at the very least, he's bad juju by association; you pal around with him, the Blessed lean on you."

"And I suppose the grace period we bought by our little victory is pretty much over," Simon said slowly, "since we're now no longer First Emergents but full-fledged citizens."

Ariane winced; DuQuesne could see that point hadn't occurred to her. "You're right. So we'll have to be really on our toes from here on out."

"And try to keep as many other Factions on our side as possible," DuQuesne emphasized. "Now I think I'll get myself a few snacks and a very tall drink; listening to someone else's slanted discussion of the Arena's going to be thirsty work."

Chapter 42

"Welcome to our Embassy," DuQuesne said as he admitted the round-bodied, spider-legged Selpa'A At. "May your course be ever your own, if my Captain has told me your greeting aright."

"She has; your course be ever your own as well, Dr. DuQuesne." Clearly the representative of the Vengeance had done his research well enough to know the individuals he would be addressing.

The two reached the conference room; upon entering, Selpa rose high and dipped low. "I thank you for agreeing to speak with me so soon, Captain Austin. And I apologize again for intruding upon what was obviously an important celebration; while I do not, in any way, share the beliefs of the Faith, I would prefer not to have left a poor impression upon you."

DuQuesne observed how Selpa quite casually muttered something even DuQuesne couldn't quite catch, and the walls extended some sort of complex framework which apparently served Selpa's people as a chair. *He's been around the block a few times, I see. But then, maybe most people here are that casual about making use of these capabilities. Hard to tell at this point.*

"Say no more about it," Ariane said. "We've plenty of arguing factions back home, believe me, so I'm not unfamiliar with that kind of friction. I invited you here so that I could hear the truth of the Arena as *you* see it. We've our own views, of course, the Faith theirs, now it sounds like the Vengeance has a rather different one."

Despite the Swordmaster's obvious intention to sound calm, courteous, and rational, DuQuesne noticed that Selpa couldn't conceal a rather acid undertone as he spoke. "Different? In some ways, not at all. There are many things on which we all agree: that something of vastly greater power than any of us can imagine constructed the Arena for some purpose of their own; that the limitations on travel to and from the Arena are no coincidence of spacetime, but designed features; and so on.

"But different indeed are our *interpretations* of the facts we see, of the reasons and motivations that we attribute to these 'Voidbuilders.' The Faith, as you well know, believe that the Voidbuilders are nothing more or less than gods, beings so far beyond our comprehension that they exist on a plane entirely separate from, and superior to, we mortals below; they also believe that the Voidbuilders are essentially benevolent in their motives. The Analytic have no one theory, but many competing ones; they are interested in the *how* more than the why."

"And what," DuQuesne said, when Selpa paused, "Do *you* believe?"

"Let me, rather, set forth for you some of the facts, and then speak of what these facts lead us to believe, Doctor," Selpa countered. He considered a moment, bobbing slightly in his cat's-cradle chair. "Perhaps you are familiar with the question of why, given the age of the universe, neither your species, mine, or virtually any other in the history of the Arena have ever met? Why, in fact, the entire universe was not taken by whatever species first rose to full intelligence and went into space?"

Ariane shrugged, but DuQuesne nodded. "The Fermi Paradox, we call it, after the scientist who first articulated it. Even sending out a few self-replicating probes at slower than light speed, a species could easily survey—and even settle or remake, with nanotech and power available—every star throughout the galaxy in a few million years. Given how short a time that is in the cosmic sense, it seems to argue that intelligent life is really, really rare—so rare that at the least you can't have any other intelligent species closer together than several hundred million light-years, maybe a billion or more depending on how fast technologically advanced life-forms can develop."

Selpa bobbed. "A reasonably succinct and accurate statement of the basic question, yes. Yet here there are several thousand species, and always have been, at least for many millions of years."

"Hold on. Are you saying that your species, or those of some of those in the Arena, are 'many millions of years' old?" Ariane looked incredulous.

"Not quite." A patch on the alien's body vibrated, a vibration translated as a chuckle. "The oldest species do approach a million or so, but it does seem that there is some limit on how viable even an intelligent species is over such a timeframe. But the members of that species have records showing that when they were First Emergents, a million years gone, there were roughly the same number of intelligent species present, of roughly the same ages."

"Someone's giving me funny numbers," Ariane said after a pause. "I think Orphan said there were about five thousand species currently known, and that new First Emergents only appear once every three or four thousand years, which would seem to mean that your oldest species would be closer to twenty million years old."

The chuckle, accompanied by a bob. "Your confusion stems from conflating different concepts. Those five thousand species include many who were never "First Emergents"; they may have been discovered by other species near their own solar systems, but not themselves have gained star travel—or they may be solely residents of the Arena itself, born here, with no homes in what we consider the true universe until they won a Sphere in Challenge. First Emergents are much more rare.

"Still, you can appreciate the point that in the universe on average, at least every few thousand years a new species must be reaching full intelligence and beginning on the path to the stars, yes?"

"Thus," DuQuesne nodded, "bringing the Fermi Paradox question directly to the fore."

"Tell me," the alien said, rocking slightly forward, "Dr. DuQuesne, tell me what the Paradox might say if instead of these replicating probes, you assume that you must travel to each star physically, as intelligent beings in a vessel that will sustain them for the journey?"

"Slow things *way* down," DuQuesne said immediately. "Not sure exactly how much—depends on your assumptions —but a hell of a lot slower."

"As it turns out, that *is*, in fact, the way it must be done," Selpa said quietly.

DuQuesne frowned. *I think I might see where he's going with this already, and I don't like it one little bit. And it fits way too well with what I told Simon way back about our unmanned expeditions.* "You mean if I were—not here in the Arena, where the stuff doesn't work, but back in our own universe, where it does—to launch a small, fast nanoprobe to a nearby star, it . . . what? Wouldn't work? Wouldn't get there?"

"To be honest, it is difficult to say for sure, Doctor." Selpa's voice was hard and cold. "What is known is that—naturally—many of the Arena species had tried just such methods of exploration and colonization. And all of them have failed, completely and utterly, despite long-term, in-depth studies of their approach in-system, seeming to demonstrate that the technology worked perfectly. A few—such as the Rodeskri, Nyanthus's people—have even gone so far as to launch full-scale manned expeditions *following* such automated exploration devices, and on *those* occasions, the automated exploration devices operate perfectly."

Ariane rubbed her temples. "That doesn't make much sense. In fact, it makes no sense at all."

"Oh, but it *does* make perfect sense, Captain Austin." There could be no mistaking the bitter tone now. "Taken together with other facts, it makes all too much sense. Consider, for example, the fact that if you were to actually travel far out into interstellar space, beyond the edge represented by the portion of Arena space near your

Sphere, you will find that the stardrive fails to work. And similarly, too, for any attempt to use it outside of a Sphere or the Sky Gates.

"Or the fact that one cannot open the Outer Gates and live on your Sphere until and unless you have found your way to Nexus Arena and been confronted by all who have come before you. The inability of those in the Arena to enhance their capabilities with the assistance of artificial intelligences, or even to enhance themselves beyond certain limits, for another fact. And the entire 'arena' aspect itself, the webwork of challenges and restrictions, of confrontation and fortunes that rise and fall."

The hair on the back of DuQuesne's neck felt like it wanted to stand straight up. *Yeah. I know* exactly *what he's saying, and in some ways it makes sense. And hits way* too close to home.

"Well . . . it certainly says it's an artificial environment." Ariane said, thoughtfully. "But we knew that from the start. Instead of tap dancing around it, why not come out with it? What is it that your Faction takes from all of this?"

"Very well. To us, there are two obvious conclusions. The first is that the Voidbuilders are nothing mysterious at all; they are, in fact, very like all of us. They simply got here first. They reached the pinnacle of technological capability, and used that to make sure *that no other species would ever equal them again*. No species would expand too far into the cosmos. None would travel unhindered between the stars, for good or ill. Instead, all following species would be drawn into this . . . cleverly-designed trap, where they would be deliberately, and inexorably, maneuvered into confrontations with each other, keeping them busy, making them feel as though they were progressing, or at least fighting for progress. All the while, of course, distracting them from focusing on the true adversary: the Voidbuilders themselves, the makers of this box into which we are lured and trapped.

"Some of us believe that it is even worse, in fact, that the Arena is a source of entertainment to them, that our little struggles are promoted not merely as distractions for us, but as amusements for the Voidbuilders—or their heirs. Or," and the way Selpa'A At turn-rolled in his chair somehow gave DuQuesne the impression of a twisted, humorless smile, "for the Arena itself, the original Void-builders having perhaps died off a hundred million or billion years ago, leaving only the Arena to watch itself and follow directives given by those long dust."

Ariane's face looked slightly paler, but DuQuesne saw her shake her head and give a faint smile. "That's a pretty grim view. I mean, take this limit on automatically exploring and terraforming, or whatever, the entire universe. You could look at that as actually just keeping any one species from wiping out the possibilities of others, right?"

The twitch Selpa gave hinted at an almost knee-jerk reaction to such questions which showed momentarily in an angry tone of his voice, before he got it under control. "Perhaps," he snapped. "Perhaps, but again, is it not disturbing that this is not the choice of those living in our own universe, but decided by those outside? Is it their right to decide how much expansion is 'reasonable'? For, after all, expansion in the more conventional man-ner would also allow you to wipe out the possibility of other species nearby, if you were to travel to nearby systems and remake them for your use."

"So your name is meant absolutely literally," DuQuesne said, after a moment's pause. "You really do want vengeance."

"One could say we want *justice*, Dr. DuQuesne. They think they can dictate the way in which the universe works? They believe they can keep the secrets of such technology to themselves? Let them try. For the power they use *is* everywhere, and throughout the Arena are traces of ancient works. Some of them are Voidbuilder relics. We seek these out, and other clues to their power and function, and one day we shall find the key to their power. And on that day shall there be a great reckoning, between these arrogant ancients and we, who have fought our way through all their snares and deceits!"

Well now, full-on rant mode there. These guys are as serious as some of the Middle Eastern types who honestly get worked up over what Alexander the Great did centuries back. "Okay, I got it—and obviously why you and the Faith don't get along. But if I get your drift, you figure the Faith are just using Voidbuilder tech, right, which should go for these Shadeweavers as well. Can't they shed a little light on this?"

"Oh, I have no doubt they *could*, Dr. DuQuesne." Selpa's tone was ironic. "But why not follow the logic to its conclusion? The Faith might be tolerated, even encouraged, as their . . . beliefs do not endanger the Voidbuilders; worship automatically acknowledges that the one being worshipped is above judgment by mere mortal beings, or should be, and this would accord perfectly with their desires, and perhaps be even more amusing.

"But would the *Shadeweavers* be tolerated? They must be using the Voidbuilder's powers, nothing else is conceivable. So why would the Arena tolerate their existence?"

DuQuesne grunted in understanding. *Well, like many fanatic creeds, if you accept the basic postulates, you can make a twisted sense out of anything.* "Shadeweavers give up their prior facction and personal connections, if what we've been told is right. So . . . your guess is, they do that because they don't really *belong* to their old faction or *have* any of those connections, right?"

"Oh, well deduced, Doctor. Yes. Our suspicion is, and has always been, that the so-called *Shadeweavers* are . . . call them avatars, perhaps . . . for Voidbuilders. Puppets they control, or perhaps that the Arena itself controls. They may look and act in some ways like their former people, but they are no more *of* their original people than you are of mine." He bobbed, and gave a hum that translated to a sigh. "On occasion we do—must—ask them for assistance, but we try our best to minimize the contact. We trust no one with those powers—not the Shadeweavers, nor the poor deluded Faith."

"If you're right, it's pretty ironic that the Faith don't get along with the Shadeweavers, and vice versa. The Shadeweavers would be like angels, direct pipelines to God."

Ariane nodded. "But . . . again taking the Vengeance's point of view . . . the conflict is in the Voidbuilders' best interest, keeping the Faith from seeing the two powers as being one, and also giving them an external clear opponent which seems as supernatural as their own."

"And amusing, as well," concurred Selpa.

"What about the Initiate Guides? Are they Voidbuilder puppets too?" asked Ariane.

Selpa rocked back and forth. "I am . . . undecided on that, myself. Some of us believe so, others not. It happens that I knew Nyanthus before he became an Initiate Guide, many, many years ago. He . . . he does not seem to be a different person, does not seem to be a monster playing a role. I do not like the thought that anyone, even a Voidbuilder, could fool me in that way so completely."

Different tone of voice and phrase there. Poor bastard; sounds like he was friends *with Nyanthus way back when.* He caught Ariane's eye; she glanced at Selpa with sympathy, and he could see she'd made the same guess. *Nothing hurts worse than losing a friend to a cult you don't believe in. Or, maybe, having both of you in the cult but only one of you gets elevated? Hard to say.* "So maybe they're actually given these abilities just to make the scam more convincing?"

Selpa's response sounded eager, seizing on an opportunity to move away from the past. "Exactly my thought, yes. I have tried to show that it was a trick, self-delusion, but . . . much as I may prefer to say otherwise . . . I think that many or all of the Faith truly believe their delusions."

Well, we've gotten the summary of their position—which, right or wrong, sounds pretty nuts to me. "What about the other Factions? You have anything to say about them?"

"Directly, they have little bearing on our goals, except insofar as they may discover or hear things that could help us in our search. The Analytic, of course, simply seeks out the truth for their own researches; we have often gained some useful information from them. The Molothos . . . well, in many ways their general attitude mirrors our own, but," the impression of a cynical smile, "they have certain rather insular attitudes which makes it difficult to maintain any long-term cooperation. It is not pleasant to work with someone who thinks of your entire species as a waste of resources.

"The Blessed . . . we can work with them; the Minds who guide them have perhaps been more shortchanged by the Voidbuilders than anyone else; they have intelligence and capabilities vastly beyond those of any ordinary organic intellect, and yet they are utterly unable to enter or even perceive events in the Arena. So they are quite willing to entertain the possibility that the Voidbuilders are the enemy.

"As to the other Factions . . . there are too many to easily discuss. Some cooperate, some do not, some do not care."

"What about the Liberated?" DuQuesne asked, partly out of curiosity to see whether Orphan's prediction would be accurate.

The hum-buzz was translated as a snort of laughter. "A Faction of a single member? A member who plays all Factions against each other, never taking sides longer than necessary to gain his advantage? An opportunistic and untrustworthy creature, the Survivor."

"He seems to have held up his end of our bargains so far," Ariane protested.

"He has been in somewhat desperate straits," Selpa pointed out. "But . . . very well, perhaps I was overly broad in my statements. We have had . . . some unpleasant encounters with Orphan. But I will admit that I have not heard that he would directly violate his word or go back on a bargain, though he is certainly more than capable of obfuscation and creative interpretation where it suits him."

*Had "unpleasant encounters," have you? Have to ask
Orphan about that. Sounds to me, though, like he managed to end up with the upper hand. Which says one
whole hell of a lot about him.*

After a pause, Ariane stood. "Well, Selpa'A At, I thank
you for this meeting. It was certainly interesting and
informative. I've gotten a different perspective on some
things, and learned others I didn't even know. But we're
not committing to any Factions other than our own at
this time. I hope you understand."

Selpa put his feet fully down and the chair-cradle vanished into the wall. "I quite understand, Captain. I hope,
however, that we will be able to work together. You have
made a most . . . impressive entrance to the Arena, and
it is clear your people will have much to offer."

"I hope we will too." Ariane glanced at DuQuesne.

DuQuesne nodded at her and went to escort the Vengeance leader out. Once Selpa'A At was gone, he went
back, making sure that Orphan was still in his conference
room. "That was interesting."

"What do you think, Marc?"

"I'm not sure yet." He found her gaze uncomfortably penetrating.

"Reminded you of Hyperion, didn't it?"

*Way too penetrating. Thought I was harder to read
than that.* "Yeah. Not the same idea, but same effect.
Which I don't like even a tiny little bit. I had entirely
more than a sufficiency of having my life and choices
mapped out for me by some group of clowns outside my
life, I really really don't like the idea of someone doing
it to my entire universe."

"But do you think they're right?"

*Do I? I'd better think about it on both sides. Part of
me's paranoid enough to embrace that theory, the other*

part doesn't even want to think *about it, and neither of them's exactly rational on the matter.* "Like I said, I'm not sure yet. My guess . . . I think no one's got the exact reason yet. I don't think the Arena's going to be that simple to pin down. Like . . . do you believe Nyanthus and Mandallon were telling you the truth as they saw it?"

Ariane nodded. "Oh, certainly. You would be, too, if you'd talked with them."

"No doubt. Nyanthus struck me as a true believer, not a scam artist—and I'm pretty good at spotting those. So anyway, if what they told you is true, we're not dealing with people 'just like us,' like Selpa wants to believe. Beings that can deal with seeing the entirety of the Arena, like Mandallon did for just a second? I don't think even those super-AIs the Blessed call Minds could do that for an instant. Even shrunk to scale, this place is too huge and complicated for anyone to *really* envision. Even me." He grinned at her for a moment.

She laughed. "But if anyone *could* do it, it'd be you."

"My Visualization is very flawed and imperfect," he said, and getting a slightly sad-edged smile in return for quoting the source of her own AISage. "But I do the best I can. Should I go get our opportunistic fence-sitter?"

"Yes. I think I want to hear his input while the conversation's fresh in my head."

DuQuesne nodded and went out. *So do I. More and more, I'm getting the impression that he's a lot more formidable than he's generally let on. And at almost three thousand years old, he'll have something interesting to say about almost anything.*

And I still don't trust him as far as Steve could throw him.

Chapter 43

"Thank you for trusting me with this most delicate task, Ariane Austin," Mandallon said.

Ariane smiled at him. He really did have that "earnest young man" air about him. "Thanks for coming, Mandallon. Follow me, we have Laila in here." She led the way towards one of the side rooms from the main Embassy entrance. "I didn't know if you needed anything . . . equipment, special materials . . . ?"

"No, nothing like that, Captain Austin," Mandallon replied. "Just my own faith and, I hope, the blessing of the Creators upon me, that I shall see her spirit and guide it back to you. I have done much studying in the past few days of the old records, and meditated and prayed, and I think I now understand clearly what is to be done, if she has been harmed as you say."

The door rolled open in front of them and they entered. Gabrielle looked up, while Steve, Simon, and Carl stood. "Gabrielle, this is Mandallon, Initiate Guide of the Faith. Mandallon, Dr. Gabrielle Wolfe, our Chief Medical Officer." *Also our only medical officer. I wonder how long we can actually keep people confused about just how few of us there are?*

The diminutive blonde doctor exchanged curtsy-bows with Mandallon, having been shown the gesture previously by Ariane. "Pleasure to meet you, Mandallon. Must say, I'm not really used to the idea of having someone pray as a principal method of healing, but I'm about at the end of my rope."

"Dr. Wolfe, I am sure you've done everything you could. But truly, if I understand the problem aright, there is little that you could do here, or perhaps even in your home system, for such a terrible injury to the mind." His filter-beard flip-flopped nervously. "I cannot guarantee that it will work, you understand; the blessing comes only through me, it is not truly *of* me."

"All we ask is that you give it your best." Gabrielle looked down at the still, blank-faced form of Laila Canning and sighed. She ran her fingers gently down the woman's straight hair, a gesture of affection that Ariane recognized as part of her concerned bedside manner. "Ain't as though she could be much worse off than she is." She looked over to Ariane. "If this doesn't work . . . I don't think anyone at home could do anything. They'll probably . . . probably pull the plug once they examine her."

Ariane shook her head; she'd only known Laila for a few days, but in that time she'd come to like the direct, matter-of-fact manner and razor-sharp mind behind the biologist's plain brown bangs. There was no way she was going to just let her stay a vegetable on a table if there was a way to change that.

"Then . . . should I begin?" Mandallon asked hesitantly. "Or are there . . . rituals, observances? Any taboos?"

Gabrielle and Ariane exchanged smiles at the young Initiate Guide's diffidence, and DuQuesne's deep chuckle rumbled around the room. "Not really, Mandallon," he said. "There's taboos on various things, sure, but doctors and such generally get a pass, and you not even being our species, we're not worried. Unless you're going to get out knives or something like that, just go and do whatever you have to."

"Oh, no, no, I will do no cutting or anything of that nature!" Mandallon looked either scandalized or afraid he'd given the wrong impression. "Just some gentle contact and prayer."

"Do you mind if I keep recording everything?" Gabrielle asked. "We've got her wired up like a Christmas tree with sensors, and if you do fix her up, I'd really like to have a chance to try to figure out exactly how you managed it."

Mandallon's laugh was more natural-sounding, less tense, now. "You are, of course, welcome to use all the sensing devices you wish. Analyzing the power of the Creators is, I am afraid, likely to be beyond you, but there is no forbiddance of such an attempt." He gave one more glance around. "Then . . . I shall begin."

One six-fingered hand reached out and rested, featherlight, on Laila Canning's forehead. Mandallon closed his eyes and bent his head, feathery topknot nodding down over his face. After a few moments, Ariane heard Gabrielle gasp; a faint blue glow was emanating from the young

Initiate Guide. At the same moment, Mandallon began a prayer, one in the ancient incomprehensible language that the Faith believed was that of the Voidbuilders themselves:

"**Dilkare deon arlyo**

"**Camven rangestel ancfrin . . .** "

"Well, bless us all," murmured Gabrielle. "Look at that . . . "

As the blue light began to extend out, bathing Laila Canning in insubstantial illumination, the vital monitors reacted. Her pulse, previously a slow forty beats per minute, rose swiftly, passing seventy. Her breathing quickened. The brain monitors showed increasing activity. "Not normal, though . . . completely unrecognizable. My *God*, look at that, Marc!"

"I see it." DuQuesne was suddenly standing next to them.

Ariane wasn't sure what she was seeing, but it looked to her as though almost all of Laila's brain was becoming active. "Isn't that good?"

"Looks more like a seizure," whispered Gabrielle.

"**Tolfas niperod ingecar,**" Mandallon intoned. "**Meriban . . .** "

Small blue sparks danced suddenly along Laila's body and rippled almost playfully across Mandallon's hand. The alien priest stiffened. "I . . . I see her! Creators and watchers, helpers and healers, heed me now! Bring back this woman, Laila Canning, from the place within herself, regather her memories and feelings, her loves and joys, return them to this her mind and body, to we who still walk the Arena!" His other hand joined the first. "Come now, Laila Canning! Return! **Satwond norlew hite!**"

A brilliant flash dazzled them all momentarily, and the displays went blank; apparently the sensors had been overloaded. Mandallon sank down, exhausted; Ariane stepped forward to help ease him into a chair as Gabrielle practically leaped to the bedside.

Then Laila Canning opened her eyes, gave a tiny gasp, and began to cry.

Chapter 44

"I . . . I'm afraid it's all very, very confused," Laila said. Her voice was the same, but the tone was not the abstracted, impatient one that had last been heard before their transition into the Arena. The scientist's contralto was soft and still somewhat thick from both disuse and crying.

It had taken almost half an hour for the revived woman to stop crying, and another fifteen minutes of quiet argument with Gabrielle Wolfe to convince her that they really did need to try to ask her questions now, rather than later—when memory might have faded. Even so, Ariane could feel her old friend's gaze tracking her like a security cam backed by a rifle. "Laila, it will help if you can remember anything. We're still trying to figure out what happened to you."

Her eyes surveyed the area narrowly, her analytic nature obviously not entirely subdued by her experiences. Given the circumstances, Ariane was glad that Mandallon had immediately left the room when asked; she was fairly sure that Laila hadn't actually seen him, and she was under enough stress as things were.

"This is . . . not *Holy Grail*. Or any place I'm familiar with," Laila said finally. "How. . . how long was I out?"

"Weeks," DuQuesne answered, bluntly. "We'll fill you in later. Right now, we need to know what you remember from the time we activated the Drive."

The biologist grimaced and forced herself to sit up. "Ouch. Yes, even with the nanomaintenance apparently one gets stiff after weeks. Indeed." She studied the others, then sighed. "It isn't pleasant. I wasn't even . . . *me*, I suppose." Her voice trembled. "I . . . there was a sort of 'I' there, in a way, I have a feeling of . . . of wandering through disconnected rooms, hearing voices. I think some of them were your voices. Others were speaking in languages I couldn't understand. And it was all empty at the same time, cold and lonely. It . . . it was like I imagine an infant might feel, abandoned, no one there, nothing to tell me who I was or where I came from. I saw . . . things go drifting by, animals, mathematical formulae, cell diagrams, DNA structures. Sometimes there were echoes of voices, of Linnaeus and Darwin and Crick, I think."

"Your AISages?"

She nodded. "They're . . . gone now."

Simon looked surprised. "You're handling that . . . rather well. It took me quite a while to recover."

She ran a hand through her brown hair, then grimaced at the stiff, uncombed feel. "Yes . . . odd, I suppose.

But . . . part of me seems almost glad, as though I never needed them." She frowned, narrow, delicate features furrowing in thought. "Which is *very* odd."

DuQuesne's expression was hooded; Ariane could tell he was worried, but not what he was thinking. "Go on, Laila. Do you remember anything else?"

"Oh! Oh, yes." She suddenly looked more animated. "I was wandering, not knowing who I was or where or even, really, *that* I was, and then . . . it was like there was a beautiful white light, and singing. I don't recognize the singing, it's . . . very strange, but somehow still beautiful. And as the singing and light got louder, I suddenly heard my name, and I said to myself, 'Yes, that's my name. I'm Laila Canning.' And when I said that, I heard my name being called from inside the light." She smiled suddenly, a quick sharp flash of white teeth like a lightning bolt. "And . . . this will sound silly. It already does, I suppose."

"No, not at all. Please, Laila, even if it does sound silly, just go on." Ariane wasn't sure what to make of all this.

"Well, I moved toward this light and the singing and the voice calling my name," Laila said slowly. Her gaze was distant, not focused on anything present. "And . . . well, I *was* moving. I mean, walking. There was grass, silvery-green grass with white and gold flowers, and a lovely smell, and there was . . . someone waiting for me, holding his arms out, the light spilling around him." She blushed visibly, looking uncomfortable. "You know, I'm a scientist, and this sort of cheap romance-sim imagery isn't what I thought my own mind would give me. But . . .

" . . . I kept walking toward him, and as I did I was more and more . . . *me*. I suddenly thought 'That's very strange grass, I've never seen it before, I wonder what species it is?' and I was thinking of picking a blade to examine it. But then I realized that the person calling me . . . wasn't a person. Human, I mean."

"Really?" Ariane tried to keep her expression neutral.

"Well, he was generally human*ish*, I guess, but he had a lot of features that were just wrong. Six fingers on his hand, three pairs of two opposed digits, for one thing. But I wasn't scared . . . or even all that surprised. And the light behind him . . . " Suddenly she had an almost ecstatic look on her face. "The light was filled with life. It *was* life, everything I've ever seen or known or wondered . . . for just a moment, just one tiny moment, I *understood* life, I knew everything about it, all of the ways it could or has developed on a million different worlds, all the different species Earth has ever had, how to rebuild a Tyrannosaurus rex from base pairs, exactly how the first living cell came to be . . . I *knew* this, it was child's play, all so obvious and beautiful and perfectly clear.

"And then he spoke my name again and took my hand . . . and . . . and it all went away, except the memory, and I felt myself *breathe*, and I remembered the scream as poor Crick cut off, and . . . well, it all hit me, and I started crying. Sorry about that." Laila Canning's embarrassment was still plain on her face.

Ariane nodded after a moment. "That's good enough, Laila. Sorry to be pushing you so soon after you came back to us. We'll leave you alone with Gabrielle for now, okay? She really wants to examine you, see if you can eat, all that kind of thing."

Laila nodded. "All right. But you have something—I'd guess a lot of somethings—to explain to me, too. I can tell that much."

"You're right," Gabrielle agreed. "But not until after I'm sure you should be discussing it. Now out, all of you."

The rest of them nodded and went to leave. Just as she stepped through, Ariane glanced back. For just a moment, she thought she caught Laila's eyes looking straight at her, brown eyes somehow analytically cold, yet with a vast interest and even amusement mingled in that momentary glance. But even as she thought that, she could see that Laila wasn't even looking at her, but at Gabrielle as the doctor conducted her examination.

This whole thing is really getting to me.

Chapter 45

"This," DuQuesne said, unable to keep from staring, "is . . ." He trailed off, clearly unable to find words.

Orphan laughed. "Dr. DuQuesne, it is not often I see you unable to give proper voice to your thoughts. But I will confess—at times, it strikes me that way as well, when I stop to think of it."

They stood on Power Dock 5, one of three . . . skyship? Starship? Simon wasn't sure what word to use—docks controlled by Powerbroker Ghondas and her people. The immense structure stretched more than ten kilometers out from the side of the vastly larger Nexus Arena sphere, with room for hundreds of vessels to dock, charge their superconducting coils, and load or unload cargo or passengers—and most of that room was in use, a steady stream of workers, crates, and individuals of a dozen dozen species going up and down the kilometer-wide central portion of Dock 5.

Above and to the sides, the incomprehensibly huge Arena surrounded them, curtains and swirls of varicolored mists and clouds the size of worlds helping the sheer immensity of distance to dim the sight of a volume large enough to encompass uncountable billions of Spheres and Spherepools. Below, the titanic swell of Nexus Arena belled outward, silhouetted in distant-sharp relief against the cosmic clouds. Adding to the vertiginous feeling was the fact that no roof existed; the wind against their faces, sharp-tinged, warm now, then cool, then hot, touched with scents unknown and perhaps unknowable, was breathable yet alien, alien and filled with hints of promise and peril from a thousand million worlds yet unseen. They could go to the railing and look over, a drop into what might as well be infinity, a plummeting fall that might never end until the universe was old.

"My brain keeps trying to put this in a human-sized perspective," he confessed finally. "I find myself trying to estimate distances and sizes, and then realizing that I am not even coming within orders of magnitude of the correct values. Are *all* of those objects I can see moving about here vessels?"

Orphan surveyed the heavens, clearly pleased with once more managing to have such an impact on the human newcomers. "Many, perhaps most, but not all, Dr. Sandrisson. For example . . . there, you see?" He pointed to a very distant object, something barely visible that vaguely resembled a fish with four fins extending from it in a cruciform shape. "That is a *vanthume*, one of many species of skyswimmers. A filter-feeder, for the most part."

Laila immediately raised her electronic viewer. "Oh . . . oh, my, it *is* alive. And so huge. A filter-feeder, you say? So there is the atmospheric equivalent of plankton. That would make sense in this sort of environment . . . will it come closer, you think?" The words tumbled over each other in her eagerness to speak on her speciality.

Orphan's hands flicked apart in the negative gesture. "No, not significantly; such creatures know well to avoid approaching any Sphere closer than a certain distance —where the Sphere's gravity begins. From a cosmic point of view, the cutoff is sharp as a knife, but to smaller beings such as ourselves or even the *vanthume*, there is a short area where the transition can be sensed and avoided. It will come no closer to us than it is, which is perhaps twenty thousand kilometers or so."

"Bakana!" Simon said involuntarily. "That means that this . . . creature is over twenty kilometers in length?" The distance also brought other questions to mind. "Odd . . . if the gravity begins so far out, how is it these . . . ships sail so easily between the docking areas? And to see so far . . . is the air extremely thin between spheres? I don't think the transmission coefficient in ordinary air would permit such a distance, not by an order of magnitude at least."

A buzzing chuckle was the reply. "Ah, Dr. Sandrission, have you not yet learned that the Arena has its own rules? Nexus Arena is, in fact, mostly without external gravity, save for the areas of the docks; there is a . . . sheath, you might say, of gravity at around twenty thousand kilometers, but it is only a few hundred kilometers thick. As for the viewing . . . that is, I am afraid, one more of the mysteries of the Arena. The density of the air varies relatively little within a Spherepool, although between Spherepools it can become much thinner. On a particularly clear day in the Arena, viewing distance has been known to be as much as two hundred thousand kilometers, allowing one to sometimes see quite a few neighboring Spheres. On most days, of course, it is more on the order of fifty thousand kilometers."

Quite impossible with our laws of physics, Simon thought. *But . . . if the air here were, in fact, a construct itself . . . the CQC material shows the Voidbuilders design on the level below the subatomic, at least . . . yes, one could change the actual properties of matter to increase light transmission, while forcing it to behave, chemically, as does ordinary air.* He gave an inward smile. *Of course, I could simply give up and call it magic or a miracle.*

"Which of these ships is yours, Orphan?" he asked. "Since that *was* the main excuse you had for bringing us here."

"Excuse? Ah, you see past my wingcases too easily, Doctor! Is it so obvious?" Despite the words, Orphan's posture and easy gestures showed that he was neither bothered nor concerned.

"That you enjoy watching our jaws hit the floor?" DuQuesne said dryly. "Yeah, it's pretty obvious."

"A . . . disconcerting turn of phrase, as it was translated to me," Orphan said. "Yet . . . I can see its meaning, yes, for several of you do appear to have your mouths open oddly when surprised. To answer your question, my vessel—or more accurately one of the vessels belonging to the Liberated—is a bit farther up."

"That reminds me, Orphan," Laila said, having reluctantly lowered the binoculars to follow the rest of them. "I . . . have a question for you, if I may."

Simon noted DuQuesne's speculative glance at Laila and recalled that the Hyperion had expressed significant concern about how well Laila seemed to have adapted following her awakening. She clearly missed her AISages, but had not dropped into the depression or frustrated panic that had affected and nearly destroyed several of the others. DuQuesne admitted that it was *possible* that the fact she had awakened to a universe for which her natural interest and talents—biological research—were ideally applicable was cushioning the blow, aiding in her adaptation. But DuQuesne was suspicious that there was more to it than that.

"By all means," Orphan responded. "I rarely discourage questions, although I have on occasion been known to refuse to answer." The flick of wingcases was an ironic smile.

"Well . . . you and the Blessed. You appear to be identical, or nearly so, to Sethrik, but you're in entirely different Factions. Where exactly do the Liberated come from? You have your own Sphere, so did you evolve separately, or . . . "

Orphan laughed again and flicked his hands outward. "Oh, no, certainly not, though that would have been most entertaining, to observe the furious bioscientific debates on how two identical species could arise on separated planets." DuQuesne could see Laila's satisfied nod; she'd obviously expected that answer, as the other one would be difficult to believe even in this difficult-to-believe place.

"No, indeed, Sethrik and I are, biologically, very much the same, or to be more precise as much the same as are, say, you and Dr. Sandrisson," Orphan continued. "That is, we are of the same species of creature, evolved—with more than a little bit of modification by the Minds—on the same world."

"So how did the Liberated come to be?" Simon asked.

"I suspect you could easily deduce the sequence of events yourselves." Orphan replied. "Dr. DuQuesne?"

DuQuesne's expression showed he was trying to figure out why Orphan was putting him on the spot. "My guess? Let's see . . . Okay, you guys evolved like we did, figure you went through the same basic tech development. So you end up roughly where we are now, get AI, start integrating it, and at some point it went Frankenstein on you."

"Excuse me—'Frankenstein'? This term did not translate." Orphan interrupted.

"Really?" This was one of the very few indications of non-omniscience from the Arena's usually seamlessly perfect translation.

Sandrisson gave a capsule summary of the term and general meaning; most of the way through it, they saw Orphan give his assenting handtap several times. "Ah, yes, yes, very interesting! This is a concept which is not native to our people, but I have found it in a number of other cultures." He sighed, a fluttering of wings. "A shame; perhaps had we such a darkly cautionary tale in our collective memories, the Minds might never have come to be."

Interesting, thought Simon. *If you don't have the concept in your head as a package, the translation fails. Means it's not just transferring the data to us directly; it's finding the closest or most appropriate translation and giving us the words or word-equivalents.*

"So far, the tale was easily told for you, Dr. DuQuesne," Orphan said after a pause. "Can you finish it?"

"Lessee. Well, the rogue AIs became your 'Minds,' super-powerful artificial intelligences controlling your world and all of your people. Hell, for all you know you *did* have a concept of Frankenstein, but the Minds would've wiped all *that* knowledge out in jig time. Anyway, my guess is they also started tweaking your makeup. Probably had to work around basic safeguards and excuse the work as improving your safety by making communication easier, that kind of stuff, but the real final goal was to make your people basically the worker drones of their hives. Maybe you'd designed 'em so they were hardwired to protect the existence of your species, so they couldn't just wipe you out and replace you with machines, but they could make you a lot more . . . tractable." DuQuesne thought for a minute, and a grin suddenly burst out across his face. He laughed.

"What's so funny, Marc?" Simon asked; Laila had a very confused look on her face.

"Just figured out the rest of the comedy that played out. See, the Minds eventually figured out the Sandrisson Drive, right? But with everything controlled by AIs, and with their little Blessed drones completely dependent on the Minds for direction, what happened? Whole thing crashed, of course. The *best* of their people were probably like Laila, and the worst-off probably died of shock." He saw Orphan's assenting handtap. "Right. So . . . probably took 'em years of experimentation trying to figure out what the hell was going wrong. Eventually they had to admit that something in that alternative space was simply shutting down any AI that went in. Hey, Orphan!" He was struck with a sudden thought. "What about when you go back? Is the AI trashed, or do they start up again?"

"Alas for my people's own liberty, I am afraid that they resume their function as soon as they re-enter an amenable space."

DuQuesne nodded. "Doesn't destroy 'em, but any sensing or exploration is pretty much totalled. But the minds of the Blessed seem to function, they're just so dependent on the Minds to direct 'em that they collapse." He grinned again. "So the poor bastards—the Minds—have to go reversing a lot of their prior changes, making the Blessed more independent, less dependent, more capable of initiative and personal decisionmaking. This gives them people capable of finally going into the Arena and becoming part of this place.

"Of course, the joker in *that* deck is that this gives the re-engineered Blessed a small chance to decide that maybe they don't want to do the Minds' work at all. And one day it happens."

"Well and truly thought out, Dr. DuQuesne. You have envisioned the past very well from your present set of facts." Orphan looked off into the gold-green sky. "Tashind was her name, and she broke with the Blessed so swiftly and completely that even the Minds were caught off-guard; they had, of course, been aware of the possibility, but she had been careful enough to conceal her intentions even from them and to act just before she was to be 'rotated' back home for testing and, if necessary, readjustment. Her defection triggered a number of others from the groups closely associated with her, and before the Minds had really grasped the potential disaster, Tashind had managed to arrange and win a Challenge, declaring herself to be a new Faction, the Liberated. The Arena accepted this declaration, which utterly enraged the Minds; they actually reacted quite irrationally, and sent a force of the Blessed to try and storm our Embassy, for which the Arena sealed them up in their own Sphere for over a year of your time."

Simon shook his head with a smile. *What a price that must have been; cut off from all contact with this universe for more than a year?*

"I," Orphan went on, "was born quite some centuries later, and my training, as it happened, was carefully designed to make me an infiltration expert; I was to seek out Liberated agents, turn some in, and trace back the others; they were operating from several locations, not just the Embassy. As I suspect you can guess, after sufficient exposure to their heretical ideas, I—alas—came to be overly influenced by these terrible concepts of personal independence, of action without direction by machines, and so on, and one sad day I repudiated the Minds and joined those I had been created to destroy. And thus here I am!"

"Orphan leaves out one of the most significant of all events," came another rough-edged voice. Glancing back, they saw the gangling form of Dr. Relgof striding swiftly up. "I greet you again, my friends. I was seeking Simon, in fact, but it is interesting to hear the old tale again."

"What significant event?" Laila asked, glancing at Orphan.

He looks hesitant; almost embarrassed, Simon thought, studying Orphan's posture. *Or perhaps as though he had something he wanted to keep out of our hearing, and Dr. Relgof has now forced the issue through implication.*

"Since my good friend Dr. Relgof Nov Ne'Knarph seems so enamored of the idea, why not allow him to tell it?" Orphan said, with a sharp glance at the Analytic scientist.

Yes, it would appear that he had wanted to keep something quiet.

It was clear Relgof wasn't entirely sure why Orphan was using that particular tone, but he shrugged—a rather humanlike gesture—and went ahead. "Certainly. Well, you see, Orphan joined the Liberated during a rather, how might we say, sticky time for them. Tashind had died several centuries back, after the Blessed finally caught her, and they had no one even nearly so charismatic and effective to lead them. At the same time, the Minds were making a major effort to finish off the Liberated by chipping away at their resources.

"Orphan, of course, knew everything the Minds were up to—or rather, as much of it as any individual could understand, given that the Minds are much more than ordinary mortal beings in terms of their capacity, speed, and ability to grasp concepts. He had also been very carefully trained by the Minds to be a master of infiltration, espionage, and so on, and he quite naturally turned all that against them. It wasn't very long, as the story goes, before Orphan was leading the Liberated, and expanding their membership significantly. He managed to strike some bargains and gain support from a few other Factions, further increasing the Liberated position.

"At that point, the Blessed and the Faith were, if not exactly allies, at least on reasonable terms, and the Blessed had performed a number of favors for the Faith. As everyone learned later, they called in payment of those favors in a very specific way, arranging the Liberated to be Challenged by the Faith."

Apparently now that the felines had been set loose and Dr. Relgof was well into narrating the details, Orphan had regained his preference for dramatics, because he picked up the story. "This did not exactly turn out as planned, at least not on the part of the Minds. I was able to win the presented Challenge, a strategic maze-duel, and as the Faith had planned to demand that we sacrifice all of our current allies—rendering us isolated and vulnerable—I felt justified in demanding something equally large from them: a Sphere. The Arena concurred that this was if anything a smaller proportional sacrifice than the Faith had demanded, and thus we gained our own Sphere. Ah, that was a day I still bring forth from my memory to cherish and to warm me against these colder latter days."

The wingcases fluttered and slowly settled, like dead leaves' last movements. "For the next few years it seemed we were poised for true greatness—if only we could solve a few small problems, we would be a faction growing at our own rate and soon beyond the easy reach of the Minds.

"But . . . that was not the case. The Minds realized all too well what it meant, that we had our own Sphere, and they changed priorities, focusing every resource they could spare to direct against us. In individuals and small groups they managed to track us, herd us, kidnap us. They used allies and connections unstintingly, expending favors garnered over a period of many centuries as though they were nothing, simply to gain a few more of us. Finally . . . I was all that remained." He stopped, gazing again into the infinite enclosed sky. "That . . . that was a thousand years ago."

"Holy Mother of God." DuQuesne muttered to Simon. "He's been a single adversary of the Blessed—who are controlled by probably Hyperion Station-level AIs, or bigger—for a *thousand years*, and he's still alive and free?"

Simon nodded, eyes narrowing. "There's a great deal that he still isn't telling us—that he isn't telling anyone, I suspect. And that worries me. But on the other hand, I believe we now understand him rather better, and that might make him easier to get along with."

Orphan shook himself, then gestured. "But enough of that, my friends. I brought you here to experience something more of the Arena, to show you how the vessels that travel between Spheres work, to enjoy this time of learning as much as we can. After all, we have met, and we are new allies, such as I have not had in centuries. Perhaps, at last, the Blessed and the Minds have reached their limit, exhausted the resources they can spare purely for my eradication." He turned towards the vessel before them, an almost baroque-Victorian construction that seemed composed of equal parts polished wood, crystal, brass or gold, and bright steel; a long, spindle-shaped central body with smooth-sculpted jets fore and aft, and five sail-like sheets suspended equidistantly around the hull by slender masts and wires. "Now this, my friends, is—"

A leaf-green globe *popped* into existence next to DuQuesne; he didn't seem surprised, but Simon and the others jumped slightly. The globe immediately began speaking. "Marc, Simon, Laila, y'all better get back here!" the voice of Gabrielle Wolfe said urgently, her accent strong with her emotion. "We got serious trouble!"

"Simon here, Gabrielle. What's the problem?" *She isn't the type to panic, and "trouble" in the Arena isn't a word any of us want to hear.*

"Steve and Ariane were out to the Grand Arcade, and somehow Steve got in trouble . . . don't know the whole story yet, but the short of it is that the Captain's done gone and accepted a challenge from the Blessed!"

Chapter 46

"No offense, Captain, but what the *hell* were you thinking?"

Ariane restrained an acid retort. The former Hyperion's tone of voice and gaze showed that his anger had its basis in concern; he was afraid of the consequences to her and maybe the rest of them, not just mad over her doing something stupid. "Marc, I was *thinking* about the characteristics of the Challenges. Remember, we've been getting info about them sort of piecemeal, mainly because we've had so many other things to worry about."

DuQuesne took a deep breath, held it, let it out, visibly calming himself. "Right. Well, we still have the option of backing out, though it would cost us a lot, so let's just look at the situation. What happened?"

It all started out so simple. "Well, Steve wanted to see the Arcade for himself, and there's a lot of it I hadn't seen yet . . . and to be honest, we're still just feeling our way around here. Going out and meeting people in unofficial settings tells us a lot that we won't necessarily get when we have these big formal meetings with reps from various Factions." She glanced around, saw the others nod (except of course Orphan and Relgof, who gave their own equivalent). *Not surprised Orphan's here, with the Blessed involved, but I think Relgof came along because he just actually likes us—or Simon at least. Don't think I'm discussing anything sensitive yet, so I don't need to worry about kicking them out.*

"So we wandered around for a while, looking into new areas—Steve actually managed to trade, gave some art examples to a physical artistics trader and got us some trade credits, basically the local currency. He's a good haggler." Steve tried to smile, but didn't manage much of a grin. *Wasn't really his fault, but I'll bet he thinks it is.* "Thinking back on it, there was this one guy—from that sort of rhino or triceratops-headed race, you remember them?—always in sight, but it didn't really register at the time, and I don't know if I'd paid much attention to it even if I had. I mean, these days there's always someone following us or staring at us; we're still awfully new."

"Right," DuQuesne agreed. "Maybe you should've been more careful, but hindsight's perfect and we aren't. So go on."

"So we ended up at the Random Fortune Casino, and Steve decided to try his luck."

"Let me guess," DuQuesne said with a grimace. "He got cleaned out, leading to an argument that got leveraged to a challenge?"

Steve couldn't keep from a laugh there. "Oh, how very wrong you are, my favorite superman. Take a look at *that!*"

Steve Franceschetti upended a small bag and a river of silvery-bronze polygons rattled across the table. Orphan almost upset his chair—would have, Ariane suspected, if it weren't for his bracing tail—and Relgof's beard-filter flipflopped so hard she thought he might sprain it.

"By the Death of Minds!" Orphan exclaimed. "Stephen, this is . . . a quite considerable sum indeed!"

DuQuesne was eyeing the pile speculatively. "Well, well, well. So it was the *other* problem."

"Other problem?" Sandrisson looked puzzled.

Ariane shook her head, laughing despite herself. "Simon, I think it's clear just where you *haven't* spent a lot of time. Real casinos don't like anyone to win *too* much, too reliably; it generally means the guy's cheating somehow; even if not, too many good wins can cost you a lot in your house margin. So they've got people around to escort you out of the establishment if you get to be too lucky. You don't actually *see* this happen very often, because it really is very, very hard to cheat in a modern casino, even with good AISage help, and to get to that level with just honest to god luck . . . well, it's rare."

"But I got there," Steve said. "I understood that craps-like game pretty well, so I took some shots on that, tripled my money pretty quick, then played a few hands of this card-type thing, doubled my money, figured it was my lucky day, and went to their roulette machines.

"Guys, it was like I was psychic. I think I missed about two or three picks in a hundred. I could do no wrong; any game I hit, anything I tried playing, once I knew what the hell I was supposed to do, I did it." Steve shook his head, grinning.

Then the grin faded. "I was back at the dice table and there was a big crowd around, and all of a sudden these two bruisers, same type as Nyanthus's bodyguards, grab me and drag me out, where this horn-headed guy starts accusing me of cheating." The diminutive design engineer's jaw tightened at the memory.

"Steve's almost pathologically honest," Ariane said, taking over. "It's a matter of pride with him, and accusing him of cheating just really pushes his buttons. Which of course to some people looks like he's guilty and defensive. And I got stuck in the crowd—I think partly deliberately—and by the time I got there it had gotten to a shouting insult match, and Mr. Hornhead suddenly said . . . " She consulted her headware to make sure she got the wording right. "Um . . . 'For such insults exchanged and received, if you will not apologize, then there is no remedy but a Challenge! Do you accept or do you refuse?' "

"*I* was going to refuse." Steve said pointedly. "I'm not stupid, I recognized that I didn't want to commit us to that kind of thing, even if it was my authority to do it, which it wasn't."

"But it wasn't that simple." Ariane glanced at Orphan. "One of the points I remembered then was about the strategy of Challenges. You *can* refuse a Challenge, or even two, but you *have* to accept the third one, or else you suffer the penalty as if you'd lost the Challenge anyway. Right, Orphan?"

"It is indeed so."

"Now, just hold on there. Why in the world *would* anyone decline the third one, then?" Gabrielle demanded.

"What if the Challenge ends up a duel to the death?" DuQuesne pointed out. "Might be worth giving up whatever you'd lose in the challenge to keep from dying, or seeing one of your friends die." She saw Gabrielle nod in understanding.

"So what Orphan had told us was that one of the most common strategies is to set up Challenges to be refused, so that the real person behind it could then put forth the third Challenge and come out of it with what they were after. I thought it would be a real bad idea to put us in a position where someone else could back us into a corner, so I decided to shortcut the tactic and accept."

"Unfortunately," Orphan said, "*that* is also another common tactic—to prey upon those who are cautious in the other way."

"Yeah. I kinda figured that out," she said with barely restrained sarcasm. "So as soon as I accept, the guy says 'So be it! I then present to you our representative in this Challenge,' and that son of a bitch Sethrik steps around the corner, and I swear, if he were human he'd have been wearing a grin about a yard across."

"They can *do* that? Choose other representatives? What's to stop everyone from choosing the most dangerous people to represent them?" Simon looked disturbed and worried—the way he tried *not* to look too much at her, she guessed he was mostly worried about her.

"Two things, in truth." Dr. Relgof answered. "First, of course, the Challenger does not choose all of the conditions of the Challenge; the major type of Challenge is chosen by the Challenged. So unless you can be certain as to the skills and choices of your opponent, any proxy is something of a risk.

"More importantly, however, is that the one who actually *meets* the Challenge is the one who receives the benefit."

"Oh, my." Gabrielle said. "You mean, if I were to issue a Challenge to, oh, those nasty Molothos and I had Orphan be my representative—"

"—then upon winning I could, in fact, take for myself and the Liberated the prize that I was ostensibly gaining for you. Yes."

"Of course, since this was pretty obviously a Blessed set-up, that wouldn't have been an issue. The stooges never expected to get the prize—they were just looking for an opportunity to pick enough of a fight to trigger a legal excuse for a Challenge."

"So," DuQuesne said slowly, as though he was afraid of the answer, "what is it that you've challenged them to?"

"I hadn't made up my mind yet," Ariane said with a sudden smile. *But I have now.* "Since it was our first official Challenge, and because I think Sethrik's pretty damn sure he has the knowledge and skill edge in most things, they gave me a little time to talk to you and think about it. With one stipulation: that I, personally, am the one to actually participate. I did counter that with the requirement that Sethrik himself be the one in on the other side."

DuQuesne looked up sharply. "I don't like this one tiny little bit, Captain." *Is there more than just professional concern behind that voice? Am I crazy to even think it? And even if there was, should I even pay attention to it?* "Sethrik's got almost all the cards here."

"That's a very accurate assessment, Dr. DuQuesne." Even Orphan's translated voice was somber. "I feel somewhat responsible for this, as the Blessed would undoubtedly not care much about you were it not for me. But . . . Captain Austin, I dislike counseling retreat, yet Sethrik is a terribly formidable being; he is the current leading agent of the Blessed, the chosen representative of the Minds, and they can—without manifesting full artificial intelligence—provide him with considerable knowledge and skill in many or all fields of endeavor."

One of the green balls of light appeared. Ariane smiled at the others. "I appreciate the concern . . . but I really think I can handle this one."

"Ariane Austin of Humanity, you have had time to consider," the little sphere said, in Sethrik's voice. "I ask that you either select the nature of our Challenge, or concede and prepare to pay the price of that concession. How do you answer this Challenge, Captain Austin?"

She felt her grin broaden, and saw Steve's eyes suddenly go wide with understanding, as she answered. "I will accept your Challenge, Sethrik. And the nature of that Challenge will be . . . "

DuQuesne, never slow on the uptake, let out an abrupt chortle of comprehension, as she finished,

" . . . single-seat space obstacle racing."

Chapter 47

A glittering double-headed arrow, with a curved cabin section in the center, slid to a halt in the polished landing/launch bay. Barely had the movement ceased when DuQuesne saw the top hatch pop open and Ariane vaulted from the pilot's cabin. Carl was already in motion, running forward from his support and maintenance station.

"*Yee-ha!*" Ariane whooped, a sound so joyful that DuQuesne couldn't help but grin; he and Simon started forward, as Carl caught Ariane up in a hug that spun her around.

"I like the enthusiasm," Simon said, "but it seems a bit overmuch, given that we haven't even gotten to the race yet."

"But now I *know* I can win this race, Simon," Ariane answered. "This is a sweet, sweet ship, Carl!"

"You looked awfully wobbly at first, Captain," DuQuesne said slowly, a bit reluctant to throw a damper on things. "In fact, I'd wager money that you just about lost control on that second go-round."

"Oh, you are so totally right, Marc." The deep blue hair cascaded out of her helmet as she yanked it off. "But you are also totally wrong."

Carl nodded, smiling. "You get a brand new ship—especially one like this, for use in a type of race you've never been in—you do your best to *make* it screw up, if you think you can risk it, so that you know what the worst possible failure modes are."

"And this certainly is a type of race I've never been in," Ariane concurred.

"And that," DuQuesne said bluntly, "is what's got me dancing on pins and needles. We should've forced the game to go our way."

"We already *did*, Marc." DuQuesne felt a small part of him want to glare in disbelief, because he simply wasn't *used* to hearing people talk to him in that tone of voice, that said that he was a worrywart who just didn't know what he was talking about.

Sethrik and Ariane, with Orphan and Nyanthus and, sometimes, the Arena itself acting as intermediaries, had spent two days hammering out the details of the Challenge, partly through each making a refining proposal and sometimes outright argument. "Space racing" had at least two, sometimes three, definitions in the Arena, and Sethrik had insisted on it taking place *in* Arena conditions (i.e., not vacuum)—especially since her careful and deliberate specification of "single-seat" meant that he would be flying alone. Ariane had noticed that the Blessed never seemed to go anywhere alone, and Orphan had confirmed that there was a constant low-level link between Blessed that helped take some of the burden of being separated from the Minds. Her condition was going to negate that, place additional stress on him, and so Sethrik insisted on this as compensation. Ariane, for her part, had been equally adamant that it had to take place at least partially in null-gravity, and after considerable debate, both sides had agreed to make a course which would offer challenges familiar to both sides, but whose aggregate was unfamiliar to either side.

As Ariane had no Human vessels at all appropriate to an Arena-focused race, Nyanthus had proposed—with Orphan supporting—that both contestants use essentially identical vessels (with controls modified to fit their expectations) from some other race's base designs, so that neither would be any more or less familiar with the equipment. This was one point that Sethrik had balked at, but been overruled on; clearly he'd hoped to use a Blessed-designed racing vehicle and gain that advantage over Ariane. The race, therefore, would be performed in modified Vengeance scout-combat units called *thysta*, roughly translating to some kind of venomous fast-striking creature—cobra, viper, something of that nature.

The course as plotted would be at some location in the Arena (for which the Arena would provide passage to and from) which featured both gravity and non-gravity portions, with multiple obstacles of various types to maneuver around and through. The exact details of the course were being withheld until the time of the race.

"You're a *space* obstacle race expert, Ariane." Simon clearly shared DuQuesne's concern. "This race is . . . not space racing, as we know it."

"Exactly my point," said DuQuesne. "This is atmospheric racing all the way, although the lack of gravity in some portions will sure throw some weird curveballs at you. These clowns have been flying in the Arena for, what, thousands of years?"

"Marc, Simon, thank you for your worry, but please, stop it." Ariane's voice was as confident as he'd ever heard it, a calm contralto that was only somewhat like the worried, duty-ridden Captain Austin that was her usual face to the world. "You don't even *get* to space obstacle racing until you've shown you can beat the hell out of almost anyone in atmosphere racing. I won my first air obstacle race—the Texas Aero Unlimited—when I was fifteen, Simon, and I was racing against some guys more than ten years older than me who'd won that same race before. Sure, I've lost races, and I could lose this one—"

"—but don't you bet on that side, guys," Carl Edlund interrupted smoothly, "because you are looking at the lady who was almost unbeaten for two years in a row in the Solar Unlimited League, and whose overall record looks to beat out Hawke's—the only guy who beat her those two years—by the time she's thirty. It's been my privilege to work with her for almost five years now, and let me tell you, she's just the best there is."

Ariane blushed. "There's no way I'm beating Hawke."

"Well, maybe not now that we're missing the best part of the season. Then again, he isn't racing in *this* league."

Seeing her smile in answer to Carl's point, and the way she stood casually leaning against the sharp-edged surface of her ship sent a strange pang through DuQuesne. *I've never seen her like this. She doesn't need anyone's help here. She knows what she has to do, and she's going to do it, and she's as sure as anything that she can do it. This is her element.*

God, she looks good like that. Confident, ready to take on the world, and ready to go right through anyone who gets in her way.

As soon as he thought it, he realized how terribly dangerous that thought was. He could also see that Simon felt the same way. *That's a direction you do not want to go, Marc. Absolutely not. There's no chance of anything that would be able to last. Too dangerous for her. And nothing that doesn't last is going to work for me.* The elegant Dr. Sandrisson was at least a reasonably worthy match for her, and not a dangerous one.

But even forcing his thoughts down that path was difficult, leaving a bitter mental taste in his mouth. *I manage to avoid this kind of thing for almost fifty years, push K right out of my life, and now that I'm myself, I can't even make myself remember the reason I do avoid it? Idiot! She deserves a hell of a lot more than you could give her. Or maybe a lot less than you'd give her.*

"So you're sure you can handle the transitions, Ariane?" Simon was saying.

The tall, slender pilot smiled again. "Tested it out there. There's four gravity varying sections in the test course, plus the adjustable obstacles I was flying around. This little baby," she patted the ship, "has jets and control surfaces in all the right places; I can do a roll, a somersault, banking turns, whatever, choose which surfaces repond, use air brakes grabbing the wind or even full thrust reversers, choose which controls respond for which maneuver easily . . . it's one of the smoothest handling ships I've ever flown, even if she is awfully strange in some ways.

"Transition from freefall to gravity is a bit of a jolt at first, especially since it happens over a pretty short range in the Arena. We can hit multiple Mach speeds in these ships, which may be puny by our spaceflight standards but is pretty damn fast in the Arena, since you have to worry about maintaining speed in atmosphere, friction, all those kinds of things. But once you've done the transition a few times, you know what it feels like."

"What about dirty tricks?" DuQuesne asked, having gotten himself under control. Time to focus on the practicalities. "There's a lot at stake in this race, both objectively and from the point of view of face. We're the newbies—if we lose to a massively powerful Faction like the Blessed, okay, it's going to hurt, but it won't really damage our rep much, especially if we make a decent showing. But if the Blessed lose, it could *really* hurt. So they've got a pretty strong reason to try to get away with anything they can in this Challenge."

Ariane nodded. "I talked about that with Orphan. People try things even in our races, you know; hell, Simon was *there* when Hawke and I tried to get each other killed in a keyhole. Orphan says that there are some minor stunts that Sethrik might try, but any truly *major* cheating will be caught and he forfeits the race. Still, I'm going over the tricks he might try, and it *is* a fairly open-rules race. He's certainly not forbidden to try to cause me to crack up if he can." She grinned suddenly, a smile with a razor-sharp edge. "Of course, neither am I."

I love a woman who can swim with the sharks . . . and that's a bad, bad thought, he said to himself as that smile blazed out. *Mr. Superman, can't you keep your eyes off her?* He flicked his gaze to the side, only to meet Simon's level green glance; even that momentary meeting showed that the physicist was—as he had always been —completely aware of DuQuesne's focus on Ariane. *He knew even before I did. Well, before I allowed myself to recognize it, anyway.* "We're going to be able to watch, right?" he said quickly, realizing even as he did that he sounded . . . hurried, too elaborately casual, not quite himself.

It didn't seem to register with Ariane, fortunately. "From back at Nexus Arena, yes. At the actual race site, it will be just me, Sethrik, our support crew—one person each—and the two witnesses and intermediaries, Orphan and Nyanthus. Orphan's our advocate, Nyanthus is Sethrik's. Not because the Faith necessarily like the Blessed, but because each intermediary or advocate has to come from another Faction than your own in cases like this. So just six people . . . and the Arena, whatever *it* is."

He nodded and looked over the little modified fighter craft. It *was* very pretty, a sleek sharp central body with wings hearkening back to the classic jet fighters, with a second wing above and behind, angled back instead of forward, both with active-memory material control surfaces and control jets that could swivel in nearly every direction on each wingtip; the whole thing was polished a gold-touched silver except for the emerald-green of the cockpit; a huge jet intake began near the front and ran to the rear—though front and rear were more conveniences; the design of the thing would allow it to fly backward almost as easily as forward. "Well, you did handle her well through most of that practice, and allow me to say that the ship matches the pilot." *Watch it!*

"Well, as Gabrielle might put it, how sweet o' you to notice!"

"Got a name for her, Ariane?" Carl asked. "Gotta give me time to blaze it on her front, and it'd be bad luck to go out without a name."

"I sure do. A special name for me and for my second-in-command, even if no one else gets it. She's the *Skylark*."

As the name and her smile pierced straight to his heart, Marc C. DuQuesne suddenly truly appreciated how *very* much trouble he was in.

Chapter 48

Almost time, Ariane thought to herself as she ran her hand over *Skylark*'s forward contours once more, staring at the display of the race course. "Carl . . . " she started.

"Yeah, I know, time for your pre-race focus. Getting out now, you won't see me until launch time. You got . . . ten minutes." Carl gave her a quick friendly peck on the cheek and strode out, leaving her to her pre-race ritual.

She smiled and then began to concentrate. The basic details of the course were spectacular, yet simple. From their launch point within the gravity well of the selected Sphere (which, as far as she could tell, belonged to none of the races currently active), they would have to pass what Orphan and Sethrik called a Skyfall, something like an avalanche in space. There was then a carefully laid out, slowly shifting set of asteroid-sized bodies which

427

they had to weave between, not outside of; a huge cloudbank which included potential debris, living creatures native to the Arena, and so on; another gravity source (temporary—at Mach speeds they certainly weren't getting to another Sphere anytime soon!) around which they were to loop and return, going through the same very large cloud, a different set of asteroids, a small flock of *zikkis* (a rather stupid type of aerial predator which, while incapable of actually *damaging* the flyers, could deflect them or slow them down for a while), past the Skyfall again, and so around. Three loops, each probably taking a couple hours, for a six hour race. She was in her space and crash suit, which had adequate sanitary prep, and quite sufficient water and concentrated nourishment.

The inclusion of the *zikkis* had rather bothered her at first. It was one thing to put rocks in the way, but living creatures? However, Orphan had found her concern somewhat . . . amusing. "You will find that it is not a matter of using them as . . . how might I say it . . . disposable speed bumps, Captain Austin," he'd said, with his little buzzing chuckle. "The *zikki* is a terribly formidable creature in many ways, a pack-predator which hunts flying creatures capable of very similar speeds—if not armored nearly so well as your flyers —and which can also dig out other creatures that lair within solid rock and ice. You may injure one or two, I admit, but they will recover." She still didn't *like* it, but the Arena had selected that obstacle and refused to change it, so she had to live with it.

Recharging the ships in flight was done by matching alignment with a sort of "pit stop" through which the flyer would drag a superconducting charging loop connected to the main batteries. Part of their crew's duties was to make sure that the "pit stop" matched straight-flight vector with the ship (since they did have to divert from the main course to use them, and the longer it took to perform the more time they would lose) and that a full charge would be delivered. Carl had been practicing with that for the past couple of days. The energy demands of the course were such that at least one such refuelling would be necessary.

She began to go over the course in her mind, scaling the threats according to time. The first—

"Pardon me, Captain Austin."

The voice had come from behind her, space that should have been completely empty, and accompanying the voice was a buzzing undertone that sent shivers up her spine. She whirled.

Standing no more than ten meters from her was a shape in the black robes of a Shadeweaver. But unlike the vaguely humanoid Shadeweaver she had encountered before, even the loose-fitting robes here could not conceal the crab-like body and upright torso beneath, the seven leg-ridges and bulges in the upper area leaving no doubt that the thing in front of her was a Molothos. "What the hell are you doing here? I thought—"

"—that the Arena excluded all others besides the racers, their support, and Advocates from this area. Yes. But the powers of the Shadeweavers are not so easily set aside, not even for the Arena." The creature made no move towards her, but she shuddered again at the underlying sound and the semi-arachnoid outline she could make out under the curiously weightless cloak. "We can . . . perhaps not *trick* the Arena, but bargain with it, convince it to avert its gaze or to allow a door to remain open, a connection to remain accessible." Something in her posture must have finally become recognizable to it, for as it began to step forward it suddenly stopped and then stepped back.

"My apologies for upsetting you. It was not my intent to do so; indeed, I came to wish you good fortune."

What the hell are you up to? she wondered. "Well . . . that's very nice, but why here and now? For that matter, why at all?"

"Here and now, because the Shadeweavers do not, of course, publicly take sides in most conflicts, either Challenges or other. Therefore, only in privacy may I express these sentiments."

The fighting-claws emerged from under the cloak through unseen slits, made a strange crossing gesture that rocked back and forth. "Also, because I wish to both . . . apologize and warn you."

"As far as I know," she said warily, "I haven't encountered you at all before. And I have to say that I thought the Molothos were . . . a lot less polite overall than you."

A buzz translated as a chuckle. "It is even so, that my people do not speak kindly or well to others. Indeed, I am by their standards utterly mad, lacking the attachment to our people that most possess; from their point of view, I am a sociopath. Odd, is it not, that empathy and concern for other species is, to my people, what a lack of empathy and concern is to most others? Yet this is the price I have paid for the power of a Shadeweaver. In my mind, when I took the Oaths, their mutterings of leaving others behind were just that, mutterings of a deluded and inferior kind who simply had access to a power I did not; and with that power in my claws, I would then bring it to my people.

"Others with similar plans usually fail in their deception, or cannot complete the training; some simply die upon attempting their first . . . manifestation of power. Why I did not is unclear, even to many meditations of vision. But survive I did, though not as I was; instead the universe opened before me, and I saw my people through other eyes, and my own eye was shamed for the sights it had seen, and nearly I tore it from my head; but instead I opened it wide to see all that had never been seen by my people."

The Molothos Shadeweaver crabstepped sidewise. "But I waste your time in this. True, you have not met me; but others of my Guild you have, and they have an . . . interest in your people. I do not know all that they intend, for while there are basic rules that guide our actions, we are not a Faction in the same sense as many. We can act independently for many reasons, and even within the Guild may be webs within webs. Amas-Garao and his clique have some plan involving your people, perhaps even more focused upon one or two of you."

"That's the name of the one who spoke with me?"

"Yes. So I offer an apology, for those who have already attempted to channel you through a canyon of their own, and a warning that such will continue. I know little of what they intend, but I do know that we have long sensed turmoil approaching; portents have been clouded and difficult to read, and even charts of probability have been confused. The direction of the Survivor was one of the few clear indicia, yet its results . . . were unknown until the very event."

Ariane blinked. "The direction of the Survivor . . . you mean that Orphan was *sent* to us?"

"Did you not know . . . but I see, of course you did not. Yes, it is clear. Now I understand. Good luck again, Ariane Austin. You shall be in need of it."

"Wait a minute!" she said, stepping forward despite her inherent squeamishness. But even as the creature stepped backward, the shadows seemed to simply grow heavier, obscuring, blending with the black robes . . . and then the light strengthened, and there was nothing but shadow under *Skylark's* rearmost wing.

Dammit but I hate that! And right before the race? And what the hell is going on with Orphan?

A quick thought showed she had only two minutes left. *And with all this crap, I'm going to have a hard time getting in the groove. I wonder if that was the real point, and all the rest was just smoke and mirrors?*

"Fine," she said to the empty room. "I'm *still* going to win this race!"

Chapter 49

Skylark lunged forward at ten *Gs*, the most that Ariane wanted to risk for the initial run. With her racing and (relatively) new combat mods, she could take at least twice that, but she wanted to make sure she was really *on* before pushing both her envelope and that of *Skylark*.

In a way, it was almost comforting that Sethrik had also named his ship—a sense of commonality existed there. The fact that the ship was named *Dellak* after one of the six original Minds, however, was not comforting, and she felt almost sorry for Sethrik. She had nothing against AIs—she still missed Mentor, her own AISage—but the Minds were a different matter.

The Skyfall loomed before her, and seeing it for the first time in reality sent a chill of awe down her spine. A vast gray-brown cloud was trailing through the Arena's endless sky, a cloud composed of dust and pebbles and billions of chunks of shattered rock ranging up to several hundred meters across, the remnants perhaps of some pseudo-world that had formed, and been destroyed, somewhere in the inter-Sphere space.

But where that cloud crossed the almost knife-thin border—less than a kilometer across—where weight-lessness became fully 0.96-G—it became a roaring waterfall of destruction, a sheeting fall of screaming stones plummeting through a gravity field almost forty thousand kilometers high. Given the relative motions of cloud and Sphere, the edges of the Skyfall were not completely precise; some stones shot far forward, perhaps even moving fast enough to reach and impact on the habitable upper surface, and others formed a scattered spume-like spray at the edges of the mighty atmospheric cataract, carrying the brown tinge of the gas and dust with them and glowing in the light of the artificial sun, or "Luminaire," that was passing almost directly overhead.

Sethrik had chosen to accelerate somewhat faster, and for the moment she let him take the lead. He was more familiar with the environment, and—dirty tricks or no—he would take a course that he felt was reasonably safe. The Blessed pilot gave the Skyfall a wide berth, leveling into a flight that would stick with the flat plane of the general course outline.

The light of the Luminaire flickered some as her course took it behind the Skyfall, but there was still plenty of light. One good thing about the rather limited speed was that they wouldn't get all that far from the contest Sphere or its Luminaire, which was good; according to many accounts, there were parts of inter-Sphere space that were blacker than night and more dangerous than easily described; some of the rumors she'd heard sounded almost like ancient mariner's tales of monsters, haunted ships, and accursed seas.

Looming up through the mists she could see the vague dark outlines of the asteroids, massive chunks of rock drifting slowly in a contained ballet. She tried *not* to think about how much power was implied in this racecourse, in something so obviously assembled by the Arena specifically for this contest. The thought terrified her more than the Arena itself, mainly because *this* was something she could grasp.

Skylark's radar returns showed a line of at least twenty asteroids, between two and ten kilometers across, some less than a hundred meters apart, moving in a complex ballet. The *Dellak* adjusted course, dipping down slightly, then coming back on line; she realized Sethrik was trying to align himself for the straightest shot possible through the grouping. She thought he was slightly off, though the irregular nature of the damn things made it hard to tell; there were hundred-meter spiky mountains jutting from some of them, and they were not just drifting, but rotating like very lazy grinding wheels.

Time to start racing. Both of them had long since backed off on acceleration—since it wasn't possible to maintain such acceleration in atmosphere for long anyway, even if you had the power to do it; you'd burn up, no matter what you were made of (*Well*, Ariane thought, *unless the Arena gave us ships made of that CQC stuff.*). Now Ariane pushed that envelope, watching the energy and heating sensors, cutting a line just inside of Sethrik's. Slowly, she pulled up on the Blessed vessel.

Suddenly a jagged monolith loomed into view, black-edged stone so close that she thought she could see crystal formations in the rock. "Holy crap, Ariane, watch it!"

Carl's voice sounded in her ears. "Cut it too close and we'll have to send someone out there to bring you back in a butterfly net!"

Her heart was hammering from the close call, but it was exhilarating at the same time. She was *past* Sethrik now, and she had the line. She'd clear the entire line of . . . thirty, looked like, asteroids, in a full three seconds less time than Sethrik, who seemed to have been slightly taken aback by her daredevil passing move. "Don't you worry about me, Carl, you just have my pit stop ready when I come around the back turn of the second run-through. Unless Sethrik wants to just concede now?"

Carl chortled. A moment later, he said "Sethrik says to enjoy the view ahead, because soon the only thing you'll see ahead of you is him."

"Tell him and his crew to stop dreaming, because that's happening *only* in their dreams." She felt it now. The Molothos Shadeweaver had creeped her out, and she had plenty of questions, but she *felt* it. She and *Skylark* were one single unit, and unless Sethrik was the same way with his ship, they didn't even have a chance.

At Mach 3.5 they blasted out of the asteroid field, Sethrik behind her by a full ten kilometers (or, at their current speed, about eight point five seconds, more or less). But up ahead, both sight and radar were fading, as the massive barrier cloud, apparently including metallic and water particles that foiled long-range detection, roiled before them. *Skylark* and *Dellak* sped to its edge, both pushing high-speed competition until the limits of sensors required a sudden deceleration by airbrakes and reversers.

Green-blue flickered around her, the world was awash in mist of seafoam and glacier ice. *Dammit! Ice is real!*

she suddenly realized as both radar and visuals recognized something ahead that didn't shift like cloud, kicked in jets and airfoils in a shuddering turn that mashed her to the control couch, clearing the spinning block of ice, or maybe crystal, by meters, fighting to get back on course. Inertials told her the right general direction, but now she realized how tricky this part of the course was. You couldn't rely on long-range radar or imaging, and if you got off course in here you could exit *very* badly out of line, maybe end up on the wrong side of the far-post gravity well and have to circle back to pass it the right way around.

"Carl, can you give me a transmission vector? Make sure I'm staying on course? I can't see crap in this, it's like swimming in a stagnant pond."

"Trying . . . you're about six degrees off in the azimuth. Come down six point three." Carl said. "Sethrik's on the nose. Think he anticipated it, his pit crew's probably got him locked on a beacon."

"He's ahead of me now, isn't he?"

"By the time I get you back on line and coach you down, about ten kliks."

Damn; he's gained twenty on me in one stupid move. "Okay, well, we can't let me screw up like that again. You keep backing my vector for me, right?"

"Got your back. No worries."

She'd slowed to less than five hundred kilometers per hour, and even then visual range was terrible. She couldn't even see Sethrik at all. A flurry of rocks streamed by, and then, just visible to her left, a huge, sluggishly wavering, semi-spherical *something*, seeming gelatinous and alien; then her eyes and mind adjusted, and she realized she was looking at a massive floating lake, an aquatic environment in a weightless space. Tiny movement near the lake showed that something must live there.

Brown-blue clouds suddenly lightened, and *Skylark* cleared the cloudbank, her rear camera showing a trail of smoky gray following her. Ahead she could see *Dellak*, and shoved the throttle forward. Sethrik wasn't taking chances, though, and as they both flew the same craft, they reached their limits at the same speed. The Blessed retained his lead.

Ariane swung her ship completely around as they approached the red-marked gravity turn point and accelerated back towards the starting point, letting the gravity field suddenly whip her sideways and, with her properly-timed acceleration, send her shooting back the way she'd come, on a slightly different course. Sethrik had done the same thing, but she noticed (with some satisfaction) not *quite* as smoothly, so she'd made up a couple of kilometers.

But he was still *very* good, and she had to grudgingly admit it in the next couple of hours. He maintained his lead as they passed through the cloud again and the second field of contained asteroids. The *zikkis* came at them in clouds, somehow managing to match even these flyers in short, ragged bursts, adhering to the craft like armored five-tentacled squid and trying to pull them towards some presumably lethal destination. Turning and accelerating the ship sharply could dislodge them, shake them off, but it diverted you and slowed you down. Sethrik seemed to be able to anticipate their moves slightly, and mostly evaded them, while Ariane and *Skylark* had several incidents which drastically slowed them down. By the time they'd fought clear, Sethrik was more than fifty kilometers ahead.

*   *   *

"I think he may be better than I am."

Carl didn't immediately answer, which was a bad sign. Then, "I hate to admit it . . . but you might be right. Every time you start to catch up with him, he's managing to keep the lead."

"The only reason I'm this close is that you're a little better than his support crew," Ariane said. Sethrik's pit person had somehow slightly misaligned with Sethrik's speed and course, forcing the Blessed pilot to realign and costing him quite a few seconds, while Carl had practically flown the refuelling structure up *to* Ariane. She could see Sethrik, at least, but he was still over ten kilometers ahead and she just couldn't shrink that lead. They had passed around the far gravity turn for the last time, and were weaving through the rather tangled last set of asteroids.

As she emerged from that gauntlet, she could see that she *had* slightly cut the distance. *Okay, he's not better than me at that, but he's more than good enough that I'm not going to catch him unless he screws up or I figure out an angle.*

They were coming up on the *zikki* swarm again, and a small inspiration hit her. *If my inner ear and* Skylark *can take it, anyway.* She set her jaw. *I sure hope these creatures are as tough as Orphan says, because I'm going to feel* really *bad about this maneuver otherwise.*

As the swarm sighted her and jetted crazily at her from all directions, she slammed the throttle to full and, at the same time, inverted airfoils on opposite sides of *Skylark*.

The double-arrowhead racing ship leaped forward and began spinning like a drillhead along its main axis, whirling multiple times a second. It literally bored through the swarm, batting aside *zikki* like fish caught in a paddlewheel. Inside Ariane felt the world spinning crazily, the ship shuddering with impact after impact as it drove through the swarm by sheer power and centripetal acceleration, a straight-line brute-force approach completely different from—and considerably more dangerous than—Sethrik's ballet of evasion.

As the impacts subsided and the hard-driven *Skylark* began to accelerate beyond limits, she groggily took the controls and leveled the airfoils, throttling back. Carl came on the air, laughing hysterically. "My *God*, that's the funniest thing I've ever seen! Holy Jesus, though, are you all right, Ariane? That must've been *rough*!"

"It was," she said muzzily, still trying to clear her head and keep her high-nutrition, low-bulk lunch down. "*Skylark* held up pretty well, though. Where's . . . "

"Sethrik and *Dellak*?" Carl sighed. "You did great, you shaved about five kliks off his lead."

She cursed. "Which means he's still five ahead of me. And there's nothing really between us and the finish line."

"Just the Skyfall, and both of you've gone around that enough times so that I don't think there's much you can do there."

He's going to win. That son of a bitch is going to win, and we're going to have to pay him.

Far ahead, she could see the trailing cloud of the Skyfall. It wouldn't be long before they passed that, and then . . .

And suddenly she sat up, so suddenly that the delicate controls of *Skylark* caused her to wobble. "Carl, send me the course description again. The exact text!"

"Um . . . sure. Here. 'The first obstacle is the Skyfall. After passing the Skyfall, the second obstacle is a series of asteroids aligned in a cylinder; they move within this cylinder, of described radius thirty kilometers, and the contestants must remain within a concentric twenty kilometer cylinder; they may not avoid this obstacle merely by flying outside the asteroid region. The third—"

"*Got it!*"

Her gut had settled, and her grin was back. *Win or die, that's the way.*

She began to throttle back slightly. *But I'd rather win than die, so let's be a* little *tiny bit careful.*

Ahead, Sethrik and *Dellak* began the efficient turn, the minimum-deviation shift necessary to skirt the edge of the Skyfall.

Skylark did not.

"Um, Ariane . . . what the hell . . . "

"Quote: 'after passing the Skyfall'. *That's it*, Carl. *After passing.* Unlike all the others, there's no demand that you go around it. It's just *assumed* that you go around it.

"I'm going *through*."

"You're *nuts!*" Carl shouted, appalled. "*Look* at that, will you? It's a ten kilometer-thick wall of *falling rocks!*"

"Not as close together as they look. And what the hell, it's worth a try!"

"No, it's *not!*"

But it was far too late for Carl's argument to make any difference. *Skylark* was already destined for its encounter with the Skyfall, and the only question was whether it would come out the other side or not. Ariane slowed still more; the amount Sethrik had to divert to go around, she didn't need tremendous speed to still beat him.

She just needed to survive.

The gray-brown wall towered before her, blotting out everything else, and then began to resolve into specks, then dots, then hurtling boulders, asteroids, pebbles, falling freely in the gravity well that now seized her.

She made no effort to compensate for the gravity; here free-fall was more her friend than enemy, aligning her with the vertical vector of the rocks as they fell. But there were so *many* of them!

A black shadow from the side, pull up! Another ahead, dive—no, loop back, another behind it! A triad, huge black-toothed stones coming together, thread the needle, through it, *Oh crap!*

Skylark reeled as something smashed the tail of the little craft, sent it spinning. Ariane clung desperately to the controls, flying on instinct, surety of her bearing gone; for all she knew, she was now flying laterally down the center of the Skyfall, a thousand kilometers of plummeting death, and she couldn't spare even the fraction of her attention needed to check Carl's beacon. She had to hope she'd guessed right. Something else *banged* the hull as she careened around another miniature asteroid, and *Skylark* wobbled, feeling slightly less responsive, barely turning in time around the next set of falling stones . . .

But it was lighter ahead, lighter, gravel rattling on the cockpit, and they were clear—*clear!* She laughed, spinning the ship once for sheer joy at having survived, and—out of the corner of her eye—saw the *zikki* that must have been stuck in the Skyfall and hitched a ride out on *Skylark* go twirling away. She heard a confused gabble of voices in her ears, but that didn't matter, ahead was the station, the launch and landing area, and Sethrik was behind her, driving his ship for all it was worth, but it was too late!

She was approaching *waaaaay* too hot, still over Mach—maybe the Arena could use its Sufficiently

Advanced to stop her without injury, but she couldn't bet that it *would*—after all, dying in the landing might not qualify as winning! She went to full braking flaps, hit the main thrust reversers, added the nose thrusters. *Oh boy, that landing bay's coming up* awfully *fast* . . . and she was starting to slew, something thrown off by that little impact previously. Ariane fought desperately with the controls, cutting the thrust dangerously as she dragged *Skylark* back into line with the bay . . .

With a screech of misaligned metal, *Skylark* grounded in the Arena landing tunnel, was caught by restraining nets, rolled half over, and stopped, three scant meters from the rear wall.

"WINNER OF THIS CHALLENGE: ARIANE AUSTIN FOR THE FACTION OF HUMANITY," announced the calm voice of the Arena.

Chapter 50

"Why? *Why?*" Sethrik's translated voice echoed the clear shakiness of his posture. "Ariane Austin of Humanity, if ever I or any of the Blessed gave you reason to believe our price would be so high, so great and terrible, I apologize—in the name of the Six, I abjectly and completely apologize!" He dropped to the formal pushup-bow posture and remained there for a long moment.

Ariane was taken aback. She was sure that Sethrik's reaction was genuine, his regret as real as it was confusing. "But . . ."

The chosen of the Blessed leapt upright. "Only one thing would we have demanded, Captain Austin, only that you abandon your relationship with this . . . traitor." He gestured contemptuously at Orphan, whose posture somehow conveyed a mocking smile. "Nothing worth the death of the leader of a Faction!"

"Sethrik, please . . . " She was touched by the alien's concern. Though this reaction more than ever showed her the horror of the Blessed to Serve, for she had no doubt now that Sethrik really was just as much a person as any other in the Arena, yet he served the Minds, who had also beyond doubt efficiently, effectively, and deliberately enslaved his entire species. " . . . please, think no more of it. Really."

She suddenly realized that she had to be very careful what she said here. The advantage they had deduced . . . Sethrik's reaction confirmed it, in spades, and there was no reason to tell them about it. "I . . . I admit to being influenced by what I knew, and as Orphan has been our friend since our arrival . . . I did rather expect some terrible price."

Carl glanced at her oddly, but his face abruptly cleared in understanding. "You were *still* crazy to take it to that level, Ariane," he said, playing along.

"Then my apologies as well, Captain Austin," Orphan said quickly, in a somewhat shaken voice. "If my tales of the Blessed caused you to take risks to such extremes, truly I apologize for painting so terribly black a picture. Sethrik and I are enemies, yes, but he is no monster in truth."

Their reactions—with Nyanthus still almost frozen in sympathetic shock over the sequence of events—simply confirmed everything she'd suspected. They seriously—for some reason she didn't yet under-stand—did not *take* large risks unless forced into it. The times she'd been catching up to Sethrik or passing him were when she was making maneuvers which were, to her, acceptably risky, but were well outside of his com-fort zone. So from *their* point of view . . . if they had realized that she had simply taken the risk because she refused to *lose*, they'd think her a total lunatic, the sort of person who'd randomly tap dance through a field of landmines because someone dared them to. And *this* was the sort of person leading a Faction? She barely restrained a giggle, which would probably not have gone over well, but it was pretty funny, trying to see this from their point of view. "Apologies accepted, and accept mine as well, for frightening you so for what was clearly no adequate reason save that in my mind."

Orphan sighed, relaxing his posture. "Well, then, no matter what choices or reasons, it is clear that the Challenge was won, and won fairly, by Humanity. Are there any dissenting voices to be heard?"

Nyanthus' translated voice was somewhat faint at first, but soon returned to its strong baritone. "I . . . I cannot dissent, Orphan. Clearly she landed well in advance of Sethrik's vessel, and just as clearly she complied with all rules and all requirements of the course."

"So I can claim our prize now?" Ariane asked, tensely. *This could be it!*

"There is no doubt of it." Sethrik said reluctantly. "Though depending on your claim, it may require more or less time to grant, though never too long—such, as I believe you know, is enforced by the Arena."

She grinned. "Then, in that case, I know what I—what we all want. Ever since we arrived, in fact, we—"

Orphan was suddenly at her side, cutting her off. "I beg your indulgence for a moment; allow me to speak with the captain in private."

She stared at him through narrowed eyes, remembering the most recent revelation. "Can't you wait a couple *seconds*?"

"We need to talk immediately, Captain," he whispered. "I promise you, it is desperately important."

Interrupting me now? *Fine.* "Very well. Is the launch bay still available and private enough for my *Advocate*," she allowed a certain ironic emphasis to come through on the title, "to speak with me there?"

Sethrik looked mildly annoyed at the interruption, having evidently steeled himself to accept whatever —probably high—price Ariane had been about to demand, and now having to wait around for it. "I believe so. Be quick about it, if you may."

Nyanthus agreed that the launch bay should be sufficient, and so she allowed Orphan to lead her there.

As soon as the doors were fully shut, she whirled. "You lying son of a *bitch!*"

The Survivor was totally taken aback by her vehemence. "No, Ariane Austin, I assure you, I really do have something important—"

"I'm not talking about whatever bug you've got up your ass right now, Orphan! I'm talking about our first—our *very* first—encounter. That was a goddamn *setup* from the word *go*. You came to us deliberately—you were *sent* to us. *Weren't you?*"

She saw Orphan freeze, like a man emerging into a lethal crossfire. "H . . . how . . . ?" he finally managed.

"I had a visitor. A Shadeweaver. A *Molothos* Shadeweaver. And he said that you had been *directed*."

"Minds and Manipulation!" was the translation of the obvious curse Orphan gave. He was silent for a moment, then with a humanlike sigh he seemed to give up, slumped down on the deck. "It . . . is true. But not exactly as you envision it, Ariane Austin. I have never . . . precisely . . . lied to you."

"What you told us was true . . . 'from a certain point of view,' then?" she said, quoting the ancient line.

"Hm? Yes, I suppose that is an excellently sarcastic . . . yet I will admit, accurate . . . way to phrase it. From a certain point of view." Orphan's wings scissored halfheartedly. "Captain . . . Ariane . . . you must understand, please. I am indeed a formidable individual in my own way, as are many of you; perhaps more so than many. But I am alone. I have been alone for a very, very long time, and though I have—through a myriad of little tricks, subterfuges, carefully chosen alliances, and such—managed to stay a few steps ahead of the Blessed, no being can fight hundreds of billions alone forever.

"The Shadeweavers and I . . . have had dealings in the past. Generally good ones, for mutual benefit. But I owed them something from favors granted . . . well, some centuries back. A few of them came to me, some time ago, and offered me what seemed a marvelous deal; they would consider all my debts squared, and themselves even slightly in my debt, if I would permit them to perform a particular, shall we say, ritual upon me. They said that it would allow them a 'glimpse of the patterns of destiny,' by which I suspect they mean probable future events, and that doing it around my specific person was of especial value because I am, and have been, the only Faction of note to ever be composed of a single and singular individual."

"I don't believe in magic, Orphan."

"Oh, no more do I. Or I would prefer not to. Still, what they do, it has much of the air of magic about it." Orphan rose slowly, still without his usual jauntily assured air. "At the end of the ritual, they told me that my fortunes were nearing an end, and that the Blessed would soon catch me. But that there was one path that would possibly offer the Liberated salvation, if I had the courage to attempt it, and if I was strong enough to survive what it would demand of me. Part of that was to follow their direction at a specific time."

Ariane nodded. "Go on."

"There is, I am afraid, little more of substance to tell. They told me, at the appropriate time, that I was to flee to Transition when next the Blessed were close upon me with sufficient justification to capture, and to trust to the random fall of chance as I passed through the Gateway. Their advice seemed foolish, though perhaps no worse than desperation might suggest to me, but I had agreed to follow their direction, and follow it I did."

On a hunch, Ariane said, "But that wasn't the last of what they told you, was it?"

Orphan spread his hands and looked apologetic, somehow. "You have the measure of me, I see. There is . . . a small amount more. But I may not tell you, at this time."

"And you don't want me to tell anyone else, do you? Especially Marc."

"I think it would be most inconvenient for me, and perhaps others, yes."

She studied him for a long moment, and she could see that her silent, motionless gaze unnerved him almost as much as the equivalent did for her. "All right," she said finally. "But you *owe* me, Orphan, and one day—maybe real soon—I'm going to demand you pay up."

Orphan gave a bob-bow. "Understood, Captain Austin."

She sighed. *I hate this tap dancing. And I really wish I hadn't learned this about Orphan, because I was getting to trust him. Like him, actually.*

Of course, maybe that was the whole point of the Shadeweaver's visit. Not a slip of the tongue at all, but the entire purpose of his visit.

Damn, I'm starting to sound as paranoid as Marc. "Now . . . I almost forgot. Did you really have something to say to me about the payment?"

"Oh, very much so, Captain Austin. I believe you were about to make a mistake—one founded, I expect, in yet another failure of my own in communicating certain complexities to you."

As he explained, Ariane felt her face get tighter and grimmer. *Makes sense. And boy, is everyone* not *going to like this one.*

Chapter 51

The area before the Gate of Challenges was *crowded*. "Is it like this after *every* Challenge, Mandallon?" DuQuesne asked.

"Oh, certainly not after every Challenge, Dr. DuQuesne!" the young Initiate Guide assured him. "Now, give room, all of you!" He muttered something in what sounded like the supposed Voidbuilder language, and from nowhere a miniature whirlwind manifested, irresistably yet harmlessly shoving back the crowd, making a space around the gathered party of humans and the associated Blessed.

Unlike us, DuQuesne observed with a wry grin, *the Blessed to Serve don't look particularly eager. Given how they lost, that's not surprising.*

The Gate of Challenges was the entrance to most of the third level of Nexus Arena, and, in fact, so far

DuQuesne and the others hadn't seen much else of the third level. It was a huge, elaborately carved entryway which did have ceremonial gates—on actual hinges—but which was, according to Mandallon, never closed. Through the entryway was a truly stupendous, curved hall with dozens of corridors leading off from it, radiating out like the spokes of half a wheel; set back from these corridors, and about one for every three corridors, were Gateways similar to the Inner Gateways seen on the Spheres and in Transition, Nexus Arena's foyer area.

"Most challenges are actually held here, inside of Nexus Arena," Mandallon continued. "And there is often quite a bit of competition for seats to observe the Challenge live, when it involves any sort of exciting action. The next time such a Challenge occurs—which does not involve your people, of course—" He gave the flip-flop filter gesture that served his people for a smile. "—ask First Guide Nyanthus to assure you seats. It is very worth attending if you enjoy watching competitive contests."

"So in that case, we'd be seeing a lot of people trooping out of one or more of those corridors," Laila said, pointing, "And, possibly, if they were waiting to greet contestants or something of that nature, they would have done so in the sub-Arena where the contest took place. Yes?"

"That's right, Doctor C—"

"Mandallon, I've told you, please call me Laila."

"I'm sorry, Laila. It is a habit, to retain titles—believe me, if one is training to become an Initiate Guide, it is exceedingly poor form to address your own instructors in too familiar a manner!"

"Sounds rather like some professors I knew," Laila said. "Still, after you brought me back from what might as well have been the dead, you have the right to address me by my own name, and 'Doctor Canning' . . . just sounds too coldly formal."

DuQuesne was still not sure what to make of Laila Canning. She certainly wasn't the same as she'd been prior to their arrival in the Arena, but no one had really known her that well; it was certainly possible that some of the difference was due to change of circumstances. And, as she herself noted, going through the trauma she had could definitely rearrange your priorities and views. And in many ways she *was* the same; the same quick mind, the lack of concern with appearances (though always terribly neat and precise), the same fascination with scientific opportunities.

"But now," Simon said, returning to the original conversation, "as the contestants here left through one of those teleportation-style gateways, everyone has to wait for them to come back through here."

"And by tradition and practicality," Relgof put in from his place next to Simon, "the crowds are excluded from congregating in the hallway before the corridors; this prevents such traffic from too badly impeding the activities of other Challenges."

There was a pearlescent flash, and suddenly six figures stood before the central teleport-Gateway.

"*Ariane!*" Gabrielle and Simon shouted simultaneously. DuQuesne started forward, but the others were actually running; he saw Simon catch up Ariane and spin her around in a bearhug that almost caused them both to fall on the floor. "You did it, you crazy woman, you are utterly completely insane, do you know that, *baka!*" Simon laughed. Gabrielle hugged Ariane without waiting for Simon to detach, and snagged Carl into the scrum. DuQuesne felt a momentary pang of isolation, but ignored it. *Best that way*. Even Laila beat him to the group, although by then they were separating a bit.

"Well flown, Captain. Though I may have to agree with Simon's evaluation of your mental stability."

"Why, Marc, you say the sweetest things!" Ariane's smile was bright, but . . . there was something slightly off about it. He doubted anyone else could spot it . . . but in the following babble of people rehashing the race, of Ariane recounting events from her point of view, exclamations of surprise, and other such predictable interactions as they made their way back to the second level of Nexus Arena and the Embassy, he only became more certain. She was certainly proud of her victory, and she was enjoying the verbal celebration, but Ariane Austin was hiding something unpleasant . . . which really worried him. Following such a victory, there shouldn't *be* anything unpleasant, or at least nothing new, to put a damper on her spirits.

The mysterious appearance of a Shadeweaver—a *Molothos* Shadeweaver—certainly focused everyone's attention. But despite the detail of the encounter that Ariane recounted, DuQuesne became more and more certain that she was leaving something out. Subtle—she was damn good at that when she was prepared.

"So, when do we get to put the screws to old Sethrik?" Simon said, as they began to settle into comfortable chairs in one of the Embassy's meeting rooms.

This is it. DuQuesne could see the slight shift in her posture—and in Orphan's, now that he came to think of it. *Something's gone wrong here.*

"Already done." Ariane said after a moment.

"Already . . . You mean you were able to claim your prize right then and there?" Gabrielle asked in surprise. "So are we going home?"

Ariane took a deep breath. "No."

The single word turned the air in the room to gray lead. For a moment, no one spoke. Finally, Simon said, "Ah. So the people we had spoken to prior to the actual race—like Mandallon—were over-optimistic when they said that such a challenge would be sufficient to win us the power we need?"

"Not . . . exactly," Ariane said reluctantly. "I could have gotten that, but . . . "

"It is entirely my fault," Orphan broke in. "Yet another minor detail I neglected to mention until I realized it was crucial."

"What 'minor detail' was this?" DuQuesne asked carefully, trying to keep the annoyance from his voice. True, he didn't entirely trust Orphan, but the alien had been accurate when previously he'd mentioned how difficult it was to figure out all of the different details that would be crucial to the newcomers and intuitively obvious and not even considered to those native to the Arena.

"You know, of course, that you must leave at least one of your own in your Sphere whenever you travel to the Arena. But it appears that I did *not* make it entirely clear that you must *always* have at least one person present in your Sphere, even when you are not in the Arena proper and are returning to the normal universe. If you do not—if you empty your Sphere for more than the most fleeting of moments—your attainments here are mostly for naught."

"Wait, wait," Gabrielle said in a scandalized voice, "you're saying that if all of us go home, we'll be right back to being First Emergents again?"

"In essence, yes, I am afraid so, Gabrielle. And in some ways worse off, as for those who have been here, yet retreated, there is no tradition protecting them as with true First Emergents."

"So none of the 'First is forgiven' business the second time around," DuQuesne said grimly. "Important thing to know. No exceptions?"

"Very few," Orphan responded. "You have one standing before you; as I am, myself, the entirety of my Faction—including the home solar system I can claim within our Sphere—it is clear that I would be physically prevented from participating in the Arena at all if I had to follow this ruling to the letter. Another exception is if, for example, you leave one person behind and that person dies. No consequences would accrue at that point, and you would have a reasonable amount of time—following your being apprised of the situation—to obtain a substitute."

"So instead of asking for the power to go home," Ariane continued, "after discussing the situation and options with Orphan I decided to have the Blessed pay—however they can—the Faith to secure our Sphere. That way if we leave two or more people behind, we can still maintain a presence in the Arena—since we have absolutely no idea, once we go back to Earth, how long it will be before other people come back, and what they'll be looking to accomplish when they do—and we could also then safely have people like Dr. Relgof and Orphan and Nyanthus as guests."

"You *decided* this?" DuQuesne heard the question come out before he'd even realized he was going to say it, before he'd realized that there was considerable annoyance accompanying those words. "Without consulting us?"

"I'd already started to ask Sethrik for the prize, and Orphan stopped me just barely in time." Ariane looked annoyed by his tone. "Once it became clear to me that we had other issues to consider, I didn't see much point in forcing him to wait longer." She smiled faintly. "He was pretty shook up as it was."

"No offense, Ariane," Simon said slowly, "but Marc's surprise does have a bit of a point to it. This was a fairly important decision and, if I understand you correctly, you've made it already—that is, the wheels are already in motion and there would be no practical mechanism to reverse the decision, even if we were so inclined."

"That . . . is essentially the case, Dr. Sandrisson," Orphan answered, as Ariane was apparently trying to decide how to respond. "Mandallon, Dr. Relgof, perhaps we should leave our friends to discuss this matter."

The other aliens did not argue; with the translation facility of the Arena, the equivalent tones of expression had clearly made themselves heard. *No one else wants to be present at a family squabble.* The other humans were quiet until the three aliens had left.

"Carl, you're not saying anything," Gabrielle said.

The control engineer shrugged. "I was there, but . . . well, I never really thought about that angle. She made the decision, it was done, there it goes. But you're right she didn't spend much time consulting with me."

Ariane frowned at DuQuesne. "I think it's the right decision overall. And as you guys already said, it's no longer something we can change, so look on the positive side. We've been worried about that whole security issue ever since we arm-twisted Orphan into telling us what was going on when he tried to sneak in, so to speak. Now we don't need to worry so much."

"That isn't the issue here, Ariane. Leaving aside how well we can trust the security we get—and no, I'm not saying I think the Faith would screw us over, but it's still worth at least considering—the point is that you made a decision that affects us all without even giving us a chance to discuss it, put it to a vote." *Without even consulting me, which for some reason really rankles.* "We don't even know how a vote would've gone. Do *any* of us not want to go home?"

"Well," Laila said, "I wouldn't say never, but I have so much to learn here that I really wouldn't be particularly upset to be staying here a few years."

"Fine for you," Gabrielle said, "but frankly, I got myself plenty of reasons to want to get back. Doesn't mean I don't want to come back here right quick, but we've been gone and people that care about us must be worried sick, or even going through our funerals about now."

"Yeah." Carl scratched his head. "I hadn't really thought about that side for a while, but yeah, my family's probably real upset and so's Ashlyn, I'll bet." Ashlyn was Carl's on-again, off-again girlfriend; he'd mentioned her a couple of times but it was apparently a pretty relaxed relationship. "And you know, with Steve and Tom not even here, we should've waited until could go back and let them in on the talk."

"Well," Ariane said finally, with a tone that sounded like a person either picking their way through a field of landmines, or deciding whether to set one off, "I am sorry that you're all miffed over my making the decision, but that really is pretty much *your* fault, you know."

"What?" DuQuesne was caught off-guard by this statement.

"*You* stepped out of making the decisions about the whole party—all of you, remember? I've been *Captain*

Austin ever since we ended up in this insane place, and you've all been telling me what a great job I've been doing—which at least half of you have made clear means, in part, 'Boy, am I glad *I* don't have to do that stuff.' "

She glared at DuQuesne. "It was made pretty *damn* clear that I don't make engineering decisions, because I'm no engineer, and I don't do any of your science work because I'm not a scientist. You people—not just one, not just two, but *all* of you—decided to call me Captain and put me in this position.

"Well, fine, then, I've gone ahead and *been* the captain and until now you all seemed real happy with that. But if you didn't want me making the goddamn command decisions, you shouldn't have *made* me the goddamn Captain!"

DuQuesne wanted to immediately retort, but he stopped himself. He abruptly realized that part of the anger was simply selfish stupid pride; *he* should have been consulted, even if anyone else wasn't.

There was a tense silence following Ariane's outburst. Simon, characteristically, spoke first. "You . . . have a definite point, Ariane. If we aren't going to trust you to make such decisions, we shouldn't have let you think you should. And if that's the case, we shouldn't have a captain at all."

Gabrielle sighed. "And I don't think that would've worked out well before, so I'm not all that comfortable thinking we should do it that way now."

Ariane glanced around. "Maybe I should have asked you what choice to make. God knows I'm not saying I'm perfect. But the question is do I have the *right* and the *authority* to be the captain, the boss, the chief, or not? And if not, we cut this farce out right now, and I kick back and let all you brains run things unless you need a pilot, because I sure as *hell* am not going to get stuck with all the responsibility and the blame otherwise!"

"As far as I'm concerned," Carl said after a moment, "You're the captain, and you had every right to make that decision. Even if some of us might disagree with it. And I want to go on record as saying we need *someone* to be captain, and I don't know who else could do the job."

"I concur." Simon's nod was emphatic. "None of the rest of us—with the possible exception of Marc—are qualified for the position. So you were right, we were wrong to argue about it. Register our preferences, perhaps, but not argue after the fact."

"Like I said, I don't think we can afford to *not* have a captain. A committee's a good way to end up with a lot of talk and no action." Gabrielle smiled, and Ariane smiled back.

DuQuesne realized that now everyone was looking at him. Laila seemed to be exempting herself from the proceedings, mostly because she'd only been conscious a short time and probably didn't feel qualified to judge. He shifted slightly, then grunted. "We . . . do need someone who can make decisions. Not someone who's going to be second-guessed and blamed for anything that comes afterwards. You were right, I was wrong." *And I can't believe how hard it is to say that! The original DuQuesne had no trouble admitting his mistakes, and I thought I was better than him. I hoped I was better.*

But even as he thought that, he knew the truth. The "real" DuQuesne wasn't a human being, really, didn't have someone that he cared about so much that their opinion of him actually *mattered*. Someone that it *hurt* to admit that he'd wronged.

He stood up, hammering emotion back and feeling the sour taste of swallowed pride. "No offense, Captain. I . . . need to step out for a bit. But you are the Captain, and you had the right to make that decision, and I . . . I had no right to protest in the manner that I did."

He turned and walked out swiftly.

Chapter 52

DuQuesne found himself wandering the Grand Arcade. Like similar places in their home Solar System (at least since the Anonymity War), it was a place where the very volume of people could make you more alone and isolated than ever, just one in a sea of infinite faces, all different but all equally unknown to each other.

And that was exactly what he was looking for. Maybe Ariane . . . Captain Austin . . . wouldn't have quite figured it out, but Simon wouldn't have had any difficulty figuring out what was upsetting Marc, and he wouldn't be surprised if Gabrielle had more than an inkling, too.

Pretty ironic. They make a blasted superman but didn't bother to fix any of the little human problems. DuQuesne thought. *Of course, that was the thing that brought all Hyperion down in the end. Poor bastards.*

He always ended up going back to Hyperion, one way or the other. *Especially when I'm running from myself.* But he was one of the few who probably mourned any of the lost on Hyperion, especially the scientists themselves. Well, the dreamers, really. Only a few had been true scientists; the rest had been believers in a vision with some damn powerful AISages to help them. A fan club gone out of control. Their true sin, blindness in their own actions, and most of them had paid the final price, and caused the reorganization of a dozen branches of interplanetary law to ensure that nothing that monstrous could ever happen again.

And the few of us left—experiments or experimenters —shuffled off, swept under the rug, forgotten except as a Bad Example in the books. He thought of some of those embarrassing secrets . . . some living ordinary lives, one still running from the law (or sometimes making the law run from her), one disappeared almost as completely as though she'd died . . . a few lying in a special hospital ward in dreams that never ended, others in unique asylums that might have to care for them forever, and one old man hiding from his mistakes on a distant asteroid. He knew them all, knew where most of them were, and suspected that the only reason he didn't see the others is that they were afraid of contacting him.

But I'm just stalling. I want something to distract me, help me avoid this little issue involving my captain.

"Dr. DuQuesne, I believe?"

The voice had spoken from a dark area to one side, where he could have sworn no one was standing a moment before. Now a dark-cloaked figure, almost human in outline, regarded him calmly from that niche, green-yellow reflection of eyes visible in the dim lighting.

"Not a hard guess to make, I'm betting."

"Indeed." The Shadeweaver's voice was soft yet resonant, a deep thrumming behind the words like the purring of a great cat. DuQuesne wasn't sure if that was an actual sound from the creature, or one of the many subtle touches of the Arena's translation. "You are quite distinct from your comrades, Dr. DuQuesne. Unique, it would appear, in a number of ways. My fellows and I have, in fact, been watching you for some time."

"Odd. I would have thought it was the captain you were more interested in. You've sure focused on her a fair amount."

The Shadeweaver spread both arms slightly, circling the hands in a gesture which DuQuesne thought might convey agreement with a point. "This is a clear observation, but, as you state in implication, she is of interest because she is, in fact, the Captain, the leader. This despite the fact that it is not at all clear that she is the one most suited to the position, from an objective point of view."

What are you getting at? "I see. So what is it you want to say to me?"

"Say, rather, what is it that I wish to show to you, Dr. DuQuesne," the cloaked figure said, stepping forward slightly. Despite the additional light, DuQuesne could distinguish no more features within the cowl than the eyes. "You are clearly one of the most formidable of your people, and—for those with eyes to see—one who is perhaps not entirely one with your fellows."

He—or his people—are damn sharp to pick up on that. Figuring out that I'm somehow separated from the others means that they've managed to interpret cues that many humans would find pretty subtle. Either that, or their special powers give them a lot of free insight. They definitely play their Spooky Magic Man image to the hilt. "So get to the point."

"Ah, a being with little use for courtly evasion unless it serves his purpose. I appreciate that; so many here prefer it the other way." A flicker of something else in the cowl; bared teeth? A smile? Too quick and dim to tell. "The point, as you put it, is that I would like to show you something of our Faction—something you will not learn by clumsy inquiries in the Arcade, as some of your people have been attempting."

You know, I already think I see where he's going. Fine. I don't mind playing along and learning something. "I'm always interested in learning, especially if it's going to lead to something useful."

A laugh, with an eerie shrieking backtone. "Useful? Ah, Doctor, I believe you could indeed say that. Then in that case, follow me."

DuQuesne followed. As they moved along through the Arcade, he took careful note of the route he was following; no point in getting lost. But that also led to another observation: people didn't seem to notice him. Oh, they wouldn't bump into him, they evaded him in a crowd, but they simply never appeared to be looking directly at him or his dark-clad guide. Given the usual reaction to the Shadeweavers, that last bit was really odd. "So . . . hey, what do I call you? Mr. Shadeweaver would be kind of stupid-sounding, and there's a lot of Shadeweavers around."

"There are, yes. My name is Amas-Garao."

Thought as much. The one the other Shadeweaver mentioned to Ariane. "Noticed that we're not, so to speak."

A slight movement, perhaps a hesitation in a step, showed that he'd surprised Amas-Garao. "A perceptive observation indeed, Dr. DuQuesne. Yes, I have bound the forces to ensure that their interests lie elsewhere, that we are unnoted in the crowds."

And that no one knows I've gone anywhere with you. I wonder why? DuQuesne wasn't particularly concerned about a trap; first, if these Shadeweavers wanted to hurt someone, they probably could do it pretty directly without even being caught. Second, they'd already established that once you were a citizen of the Arena, the Arena acted like the universe's best comm net; just speak a message clearly directed at another person, and the Arena established the connection with one of those green lightballs.

And, of course, he wasn't exactly helpless.

The rather roundabout journey took them to a street within sight of the Five Great Faction Houses. Amas-Garao led him up the steps of a nondescript, blank-faced building, like several others on the same street, and gestured. The wall—not the door at the head of the stairs, but the wall next to it—opened like a curtain of mist. "Please, enter."

"After you," DuQuesne said, studying the opening with interest. There was nothing visible through this open archway, just blackness as complete as the inside of a cavern. Even his enhanced sensitivity to spectra that were normally closed to human sight didn't pick up anything.

The Shadeweaver passed through the dark, new doorway, and DuQuesne followed. As soon as he passed the threshold, he found himself in a long, trapezoidal corridor of dark, polished stone; glancing behind him, he saw a simple door, already closed. "Neat trick."

"Do you disapprove of theatricality? It is part of our mystique—and not entirely without practical justification, either."

"Not at all." *I've used dramatics enough times in my own life. My life was* built *on theatricality, in a sense.* "Just observing."

The corridor opened up into a seven-sided hall, walls intagliated with thousands upon thousands of symbols from what must have been hundreds or thousands of different written languages—mostly from different species. They were at the top of the hall, which DuQuesne could see—looking over a railing—descended a LOT of levels down. He wondered how that worked here in Nexus Arena; you couldn't very well just *dig*. Each level had a walkway and railing encircling it, and a single corridor leading out from each of the seven sides. "That's an awful lot of building for you guys. I got the impression you were a rare breed."

"Indeed we are, Dr. DuQuesne." There was another alien chuckle. "But please, do not play the innocent or innumerate with me. Even if we are rarer than genius itself, still there would be many thousands of us, would there not? And this, our Faction House, is meant to house us all in times of need or ritual."

Okay, I'm not going to easily lead this guy into thinking I'm stupider than I am. Have to be more subtle than that. These guys are all going to be Big Time Operators. "So why don't you have one of the big Faction Houses? You can't tell me you couldn't have one, if you wanted."

Amas-Garao nodded; the gesture was just emphatic enough to show that he'd picked it up by studying humanity. "Oh, indeed we could, Dr. DuQuesne. But why not tell *me* why?"

Marc snorted. "Fine. More dramatics, of course. You're the mysterious hidden force. Everyone knows you, no one knows where to find you—unless you want them to—and they know you're always there behind them. It's a sort of backhanded declaration of superiority. You don't take one of the big Faction Houses because it's simply not important enough to warrant the attention of the mighty Shadeweavers."

"True enough, so far as it goes."

"Plus, you're not exactly a Faction. Not the way people like the Faith, the Vengeance, and even the Analytic are." DuQuesne continued to follow Amas-Garao, who now led him down one of the corridors off the seven-sided hall.

"Indeed? And how do you know, or deduce, this?"

DuQuesne debated with himself about how much to reveal about what they knew. But if what he suspected was right, he needed something to start gaining, if not trust, at least an impression of mutual interests. So . . . "Because one of your people came to Captain Austin and basically said as much. Mentioned your name, in fact, and not entirely in a complimentary fashion, either."

The Shadeweaver paused at that, a faint hiss escaping the cowl. "Gona-Brashind, it must be." He moved on for a few moments in silence; DuQuesne took that time to confirm the observation that Ariane had reported; Amas-Garao did not seem to actually touch the ground, but floated above it by a few centimeters, drifting forward with an eerily smooth motion. "This is interesting news . . . and I am surprised you tell it to me."

DuQuesne shrugged. "I have no reason to trust this Gona-Brashind any more than the rest of you, and in my experience, someone who comes to you uninvited to tell you all the bad things about his comrades has got something of an agenda of his own."

"Perceptive again." Another Shadeweaver was heading towards them, as they were passing a huge set of double doors; Amas-Garao stopped and spread arms wide before the doors and held the pose as the other reached them. "Your pardon, Dr. DuQuesne; I must assist in this ritual momentarily."

The two exchanged a complex gesture and the newcomer turned and threw open the doors. He stood there a moment, which gave DuQuesne a somewhat-blocked view of the room within; it, like the hall they'd left, appeared to have seven sides (judging by angles), and it looked like there was a Shadeweaver standing in a doorway on each of the sides that he could get a look at, and seemed to be someone standing in the very center on a platform, with a lot of other black-robed figures circling it. A fragment of a chant or invocation was audible as the second Shadeweaver stepped through and the great doors swung shut: " . . . **dem orthar usat . . .** "

Amas-Garao stayed immobile for a moment, then made another gesture that somehow conveyed the impression of locking something to DuQuesne. "Any other observations, Dr. DuQuesne?"

"A couple possibles, but let me wait on those a bit. Anything else you want to show me?"

"Indeed. Quite a number of things, in fact, which I hope you will find interesting and instructive."

The first stop they made was several levels down; the door opened into what seemed, at first, to be blackness, but then as DuQuesne entered fully into the room, he saw an immense sphere glowing in the center, a sphere that seemed to be solid yet transparent, and within it a huge number of incredibly tiny swirls and dots and clouds. DuQuesne stared at it and felt a creeping sensation between his shoulderblades. "That . . . "

"Is the Arena, or our vision of it. Perhaps not perfect," Amas-Garao admitted, "yet you shall find none more detailed, even were you to search from the Halls of the Faith to the very farthest reaches of the Arena. The colored dots are the Spheres of the races, most of which we have seen. With this, we can guide ourselves—and others—through the Arena's endless clouded sea of sky." He gestured, and with dizzying speed the vision *zoomed* inward, showing finally Nexus Arena itself, then flashing back outwards to the universal view. "Intriguing, I am sure you will agree."

Not half enough words for it there. If that overgrown snow-globe's accurate, it's a map all the other factions would kill for.

The Shadeweaver led him to another room, gesturing him inside. DuQuesne, realizing that this was a tour with a purpose, walked in and looked around.

This room, a couple of hundred meters across, had a rough stone floor, with open archways of what appeared to be crudely-hewn rock standing every few dozen meters. But instead of seeing the same room and more distant archways through them, each archway showed something different; in this one, a sunlit field filled with blue-green waving fern-like vegetation and red fluttering, winged creatures; in that, a desolate rocky landscape, dark, with the twining-glowing cloudscape of the Arena above; in the next, a thunderstorm drove waves against a cliff of rock standing against the raging sea.

"The Hall of Portals," Amas-Garao said. "Step through any of these, and find yourself on another Sphere. And, if you are a Shadeweaver, conjure yourself another Portal and return, or continue onward. If you are not, hope instead that you have found a place where you can live, rather than die, for without our powers or aid you will never find your way back."

"And where do all these go?"

"A myriad different Spheres; perhaps one of them leads to your own." This time there was a definite hint of a smile within the cowl.

"But you were walking for some time before we met, and our journey here was also circuitous. Allow me to offer you some refreshment, if this is appropriate for your people?"

"If you mean, do we have anything against being offered something to eat, not at all."

"Then come, follow me again." As DuQuesne had more than half-suspected, this was not just a matter of his host remembering his manners; the fact that there was a simple-appearing dining-hall only a short distance away indicated that Amas-Garao had planned this stop as well. "Please, sit down, Doctor."

"Sure." DuQuesne complied; he didn't mind taking a load off his feet for a few minutes. "But I dunno if you've got anything I can eat."

"Of course we do not . . . at this precise moment. However . . . "

With a gesture, the Shadeweaver caused a platter to appear before him, with what appeared to be a grilled steak, thick-cut french fries, and a large mug of dark beer. *What the hell? We haven't given out any of our food templates, and if my nose isn't playing tricks on me, that beer's one that doesn't* HAVE *a template here.* He sniffed again, then cautiously sampled the steak. *Holy*

. . . That's genuine Kobe. Well, it tastes *like genuine Kobe. And that beer sure tastes like Forraker's Dark Secret.* He shook his head. "Okay, that's good. In more ways than one. And a little scary in some ways."

The Shadeweaver conjured a green-skinned oval something which he stuck a straw into while DuQuesne ate, which he did with gusto. *Again, doubt he brought me all the way here to poison me.*

Once he was done, he stood up, and Amas-Garao followed suit. "So, Dr. DuQuesne," the Shadeweaver said, as he led the way out of the hall, "What about those observations? Have you any more to add?"

Showtime. "Well, I'm guessing that your point in showing me all this was to impress me with what you can do—without showing me too much that was critical; letting me see and hear a little bit of some ritual, showing me the map, and so on. Which really leads to only one logical conclusion."

The Shadeweaver tilted its head. "And that is . . . ?"

"You want to recruit me."

"Very good, Doctor. Like our opposite numbers in the Faith, we also like to recognize the arrival of a new species of citizens in the Arena by a special ritual involving them. Unlike the Faith, however, we do not do this by asking you to perform some symbolic service and then 'assigning' you a member of our group who is, in actuality, serving our own needs, and who has no kinship to you at all save from this symbolic service. Instead we prefer to select an especially worthy member of the new species and teach them the ways of the Shadeweavers —awaken, if possible, the powers that lie within them, train them in their use, and welcome them into the Blood of the Skies."

"Blood of the Skies?"

"An expression of many meanings; so was my phrasing translated to you, but it could easily be something else. The Brotherhood of the Arena, in another sense. We are of no world, bound to each other by skill and knowledge, but also free to act as we see fit. You seem a man of great curiosity, of a desire to know and see all things, to travel as you will, to bring forth that which you envision. This is indeed what we seek as well, and what we can offer you."

Quite an offer. "But if I understand right, I'd also have to give up my own Faction."

"Say, rather, you would be expected to give your new brothers higher priority. But there is for Shadeweavers no absolute requirement that you refrain from contact with or assistance to your original people." Amas-Garao continued forward.

"I can't say it's not a big temptation. But my friends may need me."

Amas-Garao stopped. "With the powers of a Shadeweaver you could be of much more assistance."

That's certainly true. But from what he says . . . "I'm not sure; if your training takes significant time, I might be gone at a critical moment."

The Shadeweaver spread his hands. "All things are possible," he said softly, that powerful undertone to his voice again, "yet they have done well before, and is it not unlikely that the truly critical event must come when you are gone? Come. Join us, Marcus Cassius DuQuesne."

A grinding internal shock sent a flood of adrenaline through DuQuesne, as dizziness and confusion were opposed by the trigger of a cold iron-hard alertness he had never thought to feel again, that he hadn't thought was *possible* to feel outside of the lies of Hyperion. *Mind control! The son of a bitch is trying to control me!*

Alert now, he focused his will. *Damn you, designers, but you did some things right. Figured out a sort of mental checksum, a parallel automated process in my brain that makes sure it's following its own path unaffected by alien sources. Seemed such a totally useless addition, when we knew there was no such thing as psionics, when the Fenachrone were just a piece of a story . . .*

His head came up and he glared straight into the narrowing, startled eyes of the Shadeweaver. "That was a good try, but you don't . . . quite . . . ring the bell. And after that little trick, the answer is *no*."

The long-drawn hissing sound was a disbelieving curse. "How . . . this should not be possible!"

"Deal with it, you second-rate sideshow magician. It's not going to work. And I'm leaving."

"Fool!" Amas-Garao snarled. "Do you think I brought you here and showed you secrets so you could talk? You *will* be joining us—your unique resistance simply shows that you have something very much worth learning. And I assure you, it will not hold out forever against us!"

And he's probably right about that. Once they figure out how that defense works, whatever their mumbo-jumbo really is, it's bad medicine, and they can probably either rewrite me or overpower the resistance somehow. "Ariane!" he called, seeing a green shimmer appear in the air. "I'm in—"

The green ball vanished in a coil of black fury. "Oh, we won't be having *any* more of *that*, I assure you, Dr. DuQuesne. No one will be coming to help you—even if they could, which—I promise—they cannot."

DuQuesne turned and ran. *I may not be able to get away . . . but I sure as hell am* not *going to make it easy!*

The laughter from behind him . . . was already ahead of him.

Chapter 53

Ariane found DuQuesne's departure upsetting —something that surprised her, as he was clearly doing it just to cool off, and mainly because he'd been . . . well, speaking honestly, something of a jerk. Of all the people present, *he* should have known what he was doing when he made her captain.

Because, looking back on it, it really had been DuQuesne's doing. He could have taken that position any time, and he hadn't wanted it, and he'd made sure that his pick for the job got stuck into it. Without making it obvious that he was the real driving force.

Well, what do you expect? He's a superman. Best of breed, too, if the story is halfway accurate.

Which did make it all the more ridiculous that he'd screwed up so badly in this little argument. But enough of the musing—everyone was looking at each other with sort of deer-in-the-headlights stares. "Okay, Marc's gone to get some air, and we've settled that argument, right?" Ariane caught everyone's gaze. "Right? No more doubts about my being in charge?" *Well, none but my own, but that's my problem, not theirs.*

"None whatsoever, Ariane," Simon said, speaking for the others. "I'm quite sure that Steve and Tom will agree. Steve has, of course, worked for you for years, like Carl here, and Tom trusts your judgment."

"Well, in *that* case," she said, deliberately injecting more energy into her voice, "*I* think a celebration is in order!"

Carl leaped up with a grin. "Now *there* is an order I can get behind!"

"Well, before we get too far, might I have a word with you, Ariane?" Simon asked.

"As long as it's not another emergency. I don't want any of those for a while."

Simon laughed. "Oh, I would hope we've exhausted our quota for the week, at least. Actually, I was going to invite you to join me for dinner, unless you were dead-set on a party here. I've found a restaurant on the Arcade which is excellent at catering to biologies like ours, and as Steve generously donated a large chunk of his winnings to permit us to receive our pay here in actually useful form, I wanted to spend a bit of that doing something entertaining."

Ariane almost missed the real point of Simon's invitation; she was on the verge of asking the others if they wanted to come along when she remembered certain prior exchanges. *I think Simon's asking me out on a date.*

Why do some men have such terrible *timing? Right now I'm in the mood for a rowdy celebration, if I'm going*

*to do anything at all. After that race and this argument,
I'm sure not in a romantic mood . . . but I sure don't want
to just shoot him down.*

She was saved by the door rolling slightly open. "Captain Austin?" came the rough voice of Relgof. "We saw Dr. DuQuesne leave in what seemed something of a hurry, and wondered if there was a problem."

She held up a hand to Simon as if to say "hold on," and then turned to the door. "Come in, Doctor. And Orphan, and Mandallon, as I presume you all were waiting in the guest conference room to see what happened."

"She seems to know us well, my friends," Orphan said, striding in as the door finished opening.

"It is true, Orphan. I am afraid that I am revealed to be insufferably curious," Mandallon conceded. "But it is the way of a priest to be concerned with the doings of the world."

"Don't worry about it; we've all done the same kind of thing, I'm sure," Ariane said. "Excuse me a second, would you?"

She moved over to Simon. "Simon . . . I don't think the schedule's good for that right now. Given the circumstances. But that's not a no, okay?"

"Bad timing?"

"You are a master of it, Dr. Sandrisson. The first time you flirted with me, we ended up here. The second time, we were still in emergency mode. And whenever I win a race—or get in an argument—I want something rowdy with lots of people to blow off steam."

The elegant, long-fingered hand came up and brushed the snow-white hair from Simon's face, and he smiled. "Then I hereby resolve not to wait until the next emergency, but to wait for the very next quiet moment and ask again."

"Thanks. Now, if your restaurant can handle an actual *party* we might still benefit from your explorations!"

"I can certainly check. Mairakag Achan!" he called to the air. A green ball appeared, but surrounded by a sparkle of red that showed that the call was inconvenient at the moment—the equivalent of letting one's phone signal occasionally but not answering. As it was a restaurant, Simon simply waited. A few moments later the sparkle disappeared.

"The voice and cadence . . . if memory serves me correctly, this is Dr. Simon Sandrisson of Humanity! What can my kitchen do for you, Doctor?"

"Well, I won't be needing the special we discussed quite yet; however, we have a celebration for our recent Challenge win starting, and the question was asked whether your establishment would accommodate a perhaps noisy group of celebrants?"

The unseen alien's translated voice was rich and deep, as was his chuckle. "While I enjoy such celebrations myself as well, my own establishment is designed to focus on the experience of dining as only Nexus Arena can make possible. But I can recommend several excellent alternatives, Dr. Sandrisson."

"I believe I know a perfect choice," Relgof said.

"Dr. Relgof! Of course, you would indeed, as a patron of many of our establishments. Follow the Analytic's advice, Dr. Sandrisson, for they do indeed perform their research!" The green ball vanished.

Simon looked slightly disappointed, but cheered up visibly when Ariane leaned over to him. "Never mind, Simon; this way you can treat me to a place I won't have seen before."

"*So desu,*" he agreed with a smile.

The entire group headed *en masse* toward the doors. It struck Ariane suddenly how she was actually getting used to this—which immediately made her recognize how strange the picture before her was: Carl, Gabrielle, herself, Simon, and Laila, walking in a group with and talking to two tall, slender, six-fingered creatures with beard-like filters and an even taller, massive, insectoid creature with black beetleish wingcases, two curved crests at the sides of its head, and a disquietingly nearly-human face. *How quickly we adapt, if we're only willing to be open to the possibilities. Maybe we will make it here in the Arena.*

The place Relgof picked was closer to a nightclub than a simple restaurant . . . and the easy familiarity with which he walked them through and picked out a subdivision of the club which had tolerable ambience and food for all in the party indicated that, indeed, the alien scientist was familiar with the establishment. There were a fair variety of alien species present, including some of Relgof and Mandallon's people. It seemed that at least some other species enjoyed very similar entertainments to humanity, which was another reassuring part of this venture.

Carl caught her eye. "Hey, Cap'n. Let's enjoy ourselves, but not like we did at Hanover Station."

"What happened at Hanover Station?" asked Simon quickly.

"Carl—"

"Oh, the same thing that happened after the Mars Cup when we stopped off at Phobos Hab, and that happened at Kanzaki-Two after the Photon Limited, and—"

"*Carl!*" The tone in her voice brought him up short. *Dammit, I have to even watch out for people joking around. I sure hope he gets it* . . . She saw him wince and settle back.

"Don't be a spoilsport, Arrie. And what was it that happened, Carl? Stop with the suspense, don't taunt your medic."

"Um . . . never mind." Carl had clearly realized that talking about her . . . tradition of ending up in a post-race brawl would end up possibly giving away more about Humanity's risk-taking habits.

The others, especially the aliens, stared in curiosity for a moment, but then realized that, whatever they'd been talking about, it wasn't going to be discussed further. She saw Laila raise an eyebrow, then nod to herself, and Simon showed a similar expression. *I think they've got it, too.*

A waiter came by and managed to get orders from all of them—though it took the humans some time to figure out what was and was not safe. Ariane studied the crowd. If she had understood things right, this was the sort of establishment, back home, that *would* be pretty rowdy. And—for the aliens she'd met—it did seem somewhat rougher. But compared to the way a human bar would be, this was a genteel drawing room. *It's got to be that risk thing again. There's a chance of being really hurt in a brawl, and they just won't take that kind of chance if they aren't forced to.*

Simon was seated next to Mandallon, across from her and Relgof; this seemed to spark something in his mind, because he suddenly turned to the young Initiate Guide. "Mandallon, it just occurred to me that there is something we keep meaning to ask you."

Oh yes. "Thanks for remembering, Simon. It's been weeks now and I still kept forgetting it."

Mandallon gave a fluttering gesture. "So tell me of this thing you keep forgetting."

"When the First Guide Nyanthus greeted us upon our arrival," Simon began, "he was very courteous, as usual, but he did say one thing that was quite odd. He said . . ." there was a pause, as Simon obviously was consulting his headware to make sure he got the wording exactly right. " . . . 'In the seventh turning of yesterday's light that I saw this place, and knew you would come. Perhaps they are the ones?'

"So naturally, we have wondered exactly who 'the ones' are."

"Who . . . oh, but of course, you would not know, would you?" Mandallon laughed, then took a breath and brushed his fingers back and forth contemplatively across the filter-beard. "I suppose you still know little of the beliefs of the Faith, really."

Ariane smiled. "I have to presume your religion is at least as complex as one of ours, and it would take me a lot longer than a few weeks of casual contact to understand one of those. I know that you see the Arena itself as a manifestation of the Divine."

Mandallon chuckled, a sound in translation that was rather like his mentor Nyanthus's. "As Simon might say of my understanding of physics, that is . . . at best a vast oversimplification. But true enough.

"As with many other religions I have studied, from a hundred different worlds, we have our own . . . prophecies? Foretellings? Beliefs, in any case, in things that are to come. One of the most important—perhaps *the* most important—is that one day we shall pass the tests of faith and skill and will that the Arena presents us, and come to the *Canajara*."

Ariane blinked. "That word didn't translate."

"No more did my name," Relgof pointed out, "save perhaps only to become pronounceable. Word concepts that are specific yet have no direct equivalent are translated only as names are. The names of foods or creatures, for instance."

"And a few which have many equivalent meanings, such as 'Sandrisson Drive,' " Mandallon continued, with the multiplicity of subliminal words underneath the last phrase emphasizing his point, "are translated as many-in-one. The Canajara is . . . the Meeting of the Ultimate, the Choice of Path, the End and Beginning that may be. It is the time we strive for, and also what we fear most."

Simon raised an eyebrow. "Ah, I think I begin to see. When you reach the end of Faith, you believe that there is a great moment of choice, a potential for the greatest glory or complete defeat, as in my ancestors' Ragnarok."

"An end of the world? Mm . . . or the attainment of all worlds. Yes. But the Faith will not reach the Canajara alone. It is said that there will one day be newcomers, First Emergents, who will lead the Arena's people to the Canajara, with the Faith but not always of it. They will have followed the path of the Creators even before they knew the Arena; they will be set amongst the factions, though none will have Challenged them. The Blessing of the Arena will be upon them, and nothing to which they turn their hands—for good or evil—shall they fail at for long. And for good or evil none shall say, for the Sevenfold Path they tread in both directions, and they shall be exalted in light and terror." Mandallon's voice held a note of recitation, of speaking ancient words whose true meanings still were unknown.

"That doesn't sound all that fun. I hope it will be a long time before these people show up," Ariane said. "I suppose you might be able to shoehorn us into part of those prophecies, but other parts don't really fit, or are so vague that they'd fit anyone."

Mandallon's filter-beard flip-flopped apologetically. "Alas, Captain Austin, is it not the way of prophecies to be difficult to understand? They are hints and warnings, not roadmaps of the future. Yet there is much, much more in the teachings, far more than the, hm, simple summary that I gave you, which is part of what all the followers know. As an Initiate, and now Initiate Guide, I studied the visions far more deeply as I progressed along the Sevenfold Path."

"What *is* the Sevenfold Path, by the way? Another little thing I never asked."

"At least *that* is something I can answer more clearly, Captain Austin!" Mandallon seemed pleased. "I have spoken at some length with Laila, of course, and found that your people have some related concepts—especially a listing of—what was it . . . ah, yes, the Seven Deadly Sins. We believe that there are seven basic facets of a true soul which exalt us—the Seven Keys of Creation—and seven opposing facets which debase us, make us less than we were, the Seven Keys of Destruction.

"So the Sevenfold Way, then, is the Faith's . . . ritual schooling, path of learning, to emphasize the Seven Keys of Creation within us, and to reduce or eliminate from us those of destruction. The Seven Keys of Creation, what you might call virtues I suppose, are Compassion, Wisdom, Courage, Trust, Dedication, Generosity, and Wonder. Their opposites, respectively, are Hatred, Prejudice, Fear, Betrayal, Apathy, Arrogance, and Cynicism."

"Wisdom the opposite of Prejudice?" Ariane took a sip of her new drink—noting with pleasure that it managed to burn its way down her throat while also echoing the scent and sweetness of exotic flowers—and thought about that. "I wouldn't have thought of that. But . . . yes, I suppose I can see it. Wisdom in the sense of looking for true understanding, versus prejudice in the sense of assuming you already know and can judge everything."

"Precisely so, Captain! And well worded, I will say, for one who had not thought of the Key-Pairing before." Mandallon seemed to beam at her.

"Be careful, Captain Austin," Relgof said warningly, but with a flutter and glance that implied a wide grin. "Show too much insight of that level, and you may find yourself an Initiate as well!"

The others laughed, and this seemed to her a good time to move to a more pressing subject, while everyone was in a good mood. She turned to Dr. Relgof. "Doctor, there is something quite important I want to ask you. While I've had answers from other people, I think I'd like one more opinion from what may be the most unbiased source in the Arena."

The filter-beard flip-flopped as a rough chuckle resounded from behind it. "Ah, Captain, a scientist does attempt to avoid bias, and yet I could not say there are none, either within my own mind nor those of the Analytic. Yet it may well be true that we are the least interested directly in the petty politics of the Arena. What is your question?"

"As you know—from our little discussion earlier, before you, Orphan, and Mandallon absented yourselves —I have requested that the Blessed pay the fee— whatever it may be—to have the Faith secure our

Sphere. Meaning no offense to our good friend Mandallon . . . can we trust that this ritual, or whatever it is, will truly be secure?"

Mandallon did look somehow slightly hurt, but said nothing, as Relgof responded, "Indeed a wise question to ask, here in the Arena. How to answer it in a way that conveys the correct meaning, yet is precise . . . well, allow me to answer merely in the fashion of a true scientist. There is, as far as I am aware, no way to *know*, beyond any shadow of a doubt that there are no, how might it be put . . . "

" . . . Back doors?" suggested Simon.

"Back doors! An excellent word! Yes, no way to be absolutely certain that there are no back doors within the rituals. Yet, this *can* be said for certain: that never have I heard, or read, or even heard rumor of, the security of a Sphere being violated once secured by Shadeweaver *or* Faith. I have heard, yes, of people who had specified incorrect conditions of security, which had ways that they could be exploited by others, but never of an actual failure of security," Relgof said, picking up one of his appetizers, a misty greenish liquid in a peculiar container that seemed like a cross between a soup bowl and a faceplate. As the Analytic scientist took a deep draft of the liquid, she understood the design; the soup or whatever it was—*ocean water?* she suddenly guessed—passed through the filter-beard and then poured back out, far clearer and lighter in color, to disappear downward through a tube attached to the container. Relgof's filter-beard then flip-flopped a few times, presumably allowing him to actually eat whatever had been strained from the liquid.

"So," the scientist continued, "I can offer to you only the fact that in many, many tens of thousands of years,

there is no clear evidence of any failure ever occurring
—even when such a failure might well have been to the
benefit of the securing faction."

*Well, that does relieve me some. It was clear we needed
some kind of security on the Sphere, and we will have to
have other people from the Arena travel to Earth, probably often, as time goes on. I'm sure we'll try to set up
our own security, but without Arena-level security there
is no telling what tricks or traps might be waiting for us.*

*I'll just have to talk to DuQuesne when he gets back
about just what conditions to arrange, so we don't have
any of those loopholes Relgof mentioned.*

As though summoned by her thought, a green ball
abruptly materialized before her. "Ariane!" came
DuQuesne's voice, filled with a grim urgency she had
never heard before, not even at the worst times, and at
the same time with a hard eagerness she'd also never
imagined. "Ariane, I'm in—"

The green ball vanished.

She was on her feet now, as was Carl. "Heard his voice
like that before," Carl said, answering her unspoken
question. "When we were cornered by the Molothos."

"Marc!" she called. "Marc, answer me!"

But no green flickered. "Arena, connect me with Dr.
Marc DuQuesne! Marc!" There was no response, no hint
of a connection.

*What's going on? This has worked everywhere in
Nexus Arena, and everyone I've talked to has said how
reliable it is. The Arena simply doesn't fail . . .*

*. . . Unless someone is messing with it. And that
means . . .*

"Orphan." She gestured and the last of the Liberated
stood—slowly, as though he suspected what she was

about to say. "Orphan, I'm collecting on that debt you owe me. In full."

The black eyes, touched behind with ruby-red, studied her a moment. "What do you ask of me?"

"Help me get DuQuesne. I know where he is . . . except I bet I can't find it. But you can. Because you know *exactly* where he is."

Orphan took a step backwards. "W . . . what do you mean?" His hands almost unconsciously flicked outward, again and again. *No. No. No.*

"Only two groups could possibly be shutting off the Arena's little network: the Faith, who have no reason to do this, and the Shadeweavers, who might very well." She dragged him to the side, keeping the others from following with a savage cutting gesture that needed no translation even for Relgof and Mandallon. "You *worked* for the Shadeweavers. You know where their Faction House is. *Don't you?*"

"You are truly, utterly mad. You intend to go to the Shadeweaver *Faction House* and think you can somehow . . . argue? *Compel?* them to yield up DuQuesne? It will not work! You have no conception of these beings! What they can do!"

"You're three thousand years old, Orphan. You have to have some trick, something to help bring the odds down, even if they still suck."

"Even if I do . . . Please, Captain Austin, do not do this! They will not kill your friend, I am sure! Just wait—"

"I am *not* waiting. He called me because he is in trouble, and as his Captain—as well as his friend—I'm going. The only question, Orphan, is whether you're going to back out on what you agreed you owed me, or not."

The green-black coloration was definitely paler, faded by the stress. Orphan looked genuinely panicked, like a man trapped between two raging fires. "Please! Captain Austin, I *cannot* do such a thing!"

"Then your word is worthless?"

Orphan's mouth closed. His wingcases snapped shut. He stood for a moment, staring into her eyes.

Then he slowly forced his body to unbend, to stand upright. "No, Captain Austin. If this is your requirement, then I shall fulfill my promise. You will accept that if I can offer you any assistance in this matter, then my debt is paid in full?"

"Agreed."

Orphan closed his eyes; she heard a *whoosh* as his breathing organs took in a huge breath. Then the eyes opened, and his posture shifted. It was still stiff . . . but it was much more the Orphan she knew. "Then let us be off; if Dr. DuQuesne was indeed in trouble, we cannot afford to wait."

"Carl, you're coming with us. So's Gabrielle—but you stay in the back, understand? Simon, you get yourself and Laila back to the Embassy right away. Relgof, Mandallon, I'm sorry—"

The two simply stared at her. "You cannot go against the Shadeweavers. They will destroy you—or more likely simply humiliate you, then demand a price for your continued survival."

"Maybe," Ariane said, heading for the door. "But they'll also learn that you don't attack one of us without having to deal with all of us."

Hold on, Marc! We're coming!

Chapter 54

This is very much Not Good. DuQuesne thought grimly, as the black-cloaked Amas-Garao stepped out in front of him yet again. *I've used just about every trick I've got, and he's somehow managing to end up ahead every time. Isn't there any blasted* limit *to how often he can pull off that stunt?*

"You are achieving nothing beyond wasting time, Doctor DuQuesne." The Shadeweaver's voice was calm, certain, with just a hint of mockery.

"My time to waste, isn't it?" He moved slowly towards the Shadeweaver.

"Mine as well," Amas-Garao said, seeming to simply observe his approach. "Yet I will not argue that since the situation is of my own devising that it is not for me to complain. I find this rather entertaining. It is also *most* instructive."

"Always glad to be educational." DuQuesne said, stopping about ten to twelve meters away; that seemed to be about the limit before the wizard-like being decided to do his teleport business, or otherwise throw some kind of barrier up. *So far, he's made what amounts to a damn sci-fi forcefield that stopped me like a brick wall, caused a hurricane-force wind to blow me back, and of course just done that spooky disappear-appear-disappear trick. And he's right to do it, too, because I'm pretty damn sure I could take him if I could just get one hand on him.* "So what are you learning?"

"That you are indeed a quite formidable being—far more so, I think, than your companions. This had been our suspicion for quite some time, but your reflexes, your endurance, and a number of other little facets of this chase have verified it. You will be a most impressive addition to our ranks."

Damn. He isn't giving up on that either. "And after you give me these superpowers, what makes you think I'm not going to use them to do unto *you* exactly and precisely as you've been doing unto *me*?" He began to focus his will, speeding up his perceptions to full combat mode.

A faint chuckle. "Firstly, Doctor, because I have many, many years of experience on you, and it would be *most* unwise for you to challenge me in that manner. More importantly, of course, because you would not *remember* these circumstances. While your resistance to control is quite unique and fascinating, I do not think even you would be foolish enough to contend that it cannot be broken eventually."

DuQuesne shook his head. "No. You're right there. With all the stuff you people have—and it's a lot, I'll grant you that—I'm sure you'd figure out a way. Which is why I can't let you do that."

He'd been trying to avoid escalating the conflict. That way lay a whole huge fifty-five-gallon sized can of worms he didn't want to open. But with the Shadeweaver basically telling him flat out that he intended to recruit DuQuesne, and *make* DuQuesne think it was his own idea, and with every effort he'd made so far giving him exactly zero in progress, Marc didn't think he had many options left.

While he hadn't carried his main sidearms, he never went anywhere without something—actually, several somethings—on him for insurance. Feeling his readiness reach its peak, he triggered the action.

With inhuman speed and accuracy, DuQuesne brought up his arm, the holdout pistol sliding smoothly into his hand, the trigger being pulled in the very moment his arm aligned directly with Amas-Garao.

There was a subdued *click*. DuQuesne stared at the pistol, a sinking feeling in his gut.

The Shadeweaver had been startled by the sudden move; he'd twitched, moved half a step backwards. But then he laughed. "So, you are indeed fast. I did not, in all honesty, see that movement even begin. Yet how naïve of you, to believe that such mundane weaponry could be used against me."

DuQuesne looked at the pistol and popped the chamber open. The old-fashioned chemical pistol had functioned properly; he could see the dent on the primer case. The weight of the cartridge was correct, as far as he could tell. The gun should have fired.

But it hadn't. One more instance of impossibility in this insane place, but this one had been made to order.

I am still not beaten, and I'm not giving up no matter how *hopeless it looks!* Without warning, he whipped his arm back outwards, but this time *throwing* the pistol in a flat, hard arc, straight for the Shadeweaver's head.

The prior reactions had shown that Amas-Garao did not have DuQuesne's speed. Whatever barrier he might have had prepared to stop a full-blown charge by the former Hyperion, it was not triggered by the small and vastly faster improvised missile; with a sharp *smack* the heavy metal pistol slammed solidly into the side of Amas-Garao's head.

In that instant DuQuesne *moved*, sprinting forward while the Shadeweaver was distracted by surprise and pain.

This time, nothing stopped him. He slammed a hard-driven fist into the robes, where he figured the thing's gut was, following immediately with an elbow to the head, driving Amas-Garao into the wall with the force of his charge. The robes seemed to stiffen on impact, blunting the effect of punches and wall, but for a moment he had his hands on one of the Shadeweaver's limbs, and that was enough to turn, roll, and hurl the black-cloaked creature another ten meters into the far wall, to strike with muted yet groundshaking force. DuQuesne immediately sprinted again, trying to catch Amas-Garao between his hammer and the wall's anvil, but in the fraction of a second between movement and strike, the Shadeweaver vanished in a roil of smoky darkness.

He'll be back any minute. Probably take him a few seconds to recover, and maybe I've put the fear of God into him, but more likely I've just royally ticked him off. Even his damn clothes were protecting him. Actively. I've got to get out of here, and do it now. He broke into an all-out run.

The corridors of the Shadeweaver Faction House were
. . . confusing. DuQuesne had become aware of that as
soon as he'd started running. There was something about
them—and not in the construction, either—that threw
off perceptions of direction. But as a Hyperion, he'd had
an *awful* lot of experience, especially towards the end,
of being able to ignore confused perceptions and focus
on the facts—the real direction he was going, the actual
number of steps he was taking—and he knew *exactly*
where he was. He suspected Amas-Garao thought he
was lost. But one thing he'd been trying to do was slowly
work his way towards the exit. *This is it. I'll never get a
better chance.*

Why the other Shadeweavers weren't helping Amas-
Garao, he didn't know, but he wasn't going to complain.
He came to the central hall, scrambled up the railing,
leaped upward, grabbing the floor of the next level,
heaved himself up and over in an acrobatic flip that
landed him atop the next level's railing, right in front of
the corridor that led to the exit. He kicked into a flat
sprint, running as he hadn't run in fifty years. There was
the door, ahead of him.

And then it was gone. A flat, featureless wall loomed
up, and he barely slowed in time to keep from smashing
himself into it.

There was laughter—angry, vengeful laughter
—behind him. "A most impressive effort, Dr.
DuQuesne. You have injured me—something I would
have believed impossible in the circumstances."

*Not injured you bad enough, though. Damn, if only
Wu were here. I think we could take this guy, even with
all his tricks. Wu might even do it by himself.* He turned
to face the black-cloaked Shadeweaver, feeling behind

him with his hand. *They've got a lot of power, but they also do a hell of a lot of misdirection. I'm betting the door's still here, somewhere. Whether I can get it open, though, that's another issue.*

To his dismay, the Shadeweaver seemed to be reading his mind . . . or maybe he was just very perceptive now that he was taking DuQuesne seriously. "Even if you could find the door, you would not be able to open it. At the moment, it will only open from outside, and even then only to one who knows exactly where it is and how it is to be opened. A Shadeweaver, or one of our very, very few allies."

"Aren't you a little worried I'm going to finish the job I started on you?" DuQuesne said, straightening. "So far, you've gotten the worst of it."

"Indeed I have," the Shadeweaver said softly. "So I think that ought to change." He gestured with one hand, muttering a single alien word that DuQuesne half-heard as *thunder*.

A crackling sphere of energy burst into existence and screamed into the astounded DuQuesne, who heard a bellow of startled pain driven from his own lungs as electricity seethed through his body. He staggered and fell against the wall, using it for temporary support. *Holy Mother . . . that hurt. Like about a dozen stun charges. Would've killed most other folks.* He forced himself to straighten, but it was an effort.

Amas-Garao chuckled, and this time there was no attempt to disguise the sinister edge. *He may not indulge it often, but this guy likes this kind of thing.* "I think we have begun to even that little score, do you not agree?" He gestured again.

DuQuesne tried to dodge, but the quick-moving dot of light seemed to track him, detonating into another screaming sphere of lightning. The world wobbled around him and he collapsed against the wall. *Got to . . . get up. Break down the door, maybe . . . though a lot of these buildings are really CQC shells, which means I couldn't break out even if I were Superman himself.*

"What's wrong? You seem a bit less steady on your feet, Doctor." Amas-Garao said coldly. "I admit, your resistance is startling. One thunderball is enough to bring down most creatures; two will drop even a trained Molothos or a Genasi warrior."

Slumped against the wall, Marc concentrated and abruptly whipped his left hand out, sending a ring-carbon edged throwing knife straight for the Shadeweaver's chest.

The blade stopped dead in the air a meter from Amas-Garao, and the laugh burst out again. "The same trick shall not work twice, o desperate one." A flare of light that almost blinded DuQuesne accompanied the words, and a few drops of melted metal, smoking with burned carbon, dropped to the floor. "Your weapons are useless against a Shadeweaver, newcomer. Your impressive natural gifts, likewise useless." He sent another blast into DuQuesne; everything seemed to be darkening around him, and he did not know *how* he managed to force himself back to his feet, leaning hard against the unmoving wall.

"You have rejected the greatest gift to be offered anywhere in the Arena, and yet I am a being of infinite generosity." The translation of the Arena conveyed the subtle irony of his words perfectly. "You shall have this gift, no matter how much you fight it, and you shall thank me for it. You have run an excellent race, Dr. DuQuesne . . . but you have run out of room, out of tricks, and most of all, out of time. There is no escape, the door is shut, and it is over."

The dizziness rose up in a wave, and DuQuesne felt like he was falling.

Then he realized he *was* falling; falling *backward*, through the door that had without warning popped open, and he could see the Shadeweaver, frozen in mid-gesture with disbelief writ large in the very pose of his body.

He tumbled backward, rolling down two steps before someone caught him. He looked up, seeing Ariane looking down at him with a gaze of such concern that it almost made him forget where he was.

But only almost. "Captain, we—"

"Must go, *now!*" Orphan's voice was near panic as he heaved DuQuesne to his feet and started down the steps. "From the stairs to the gate is still the Faction House! We must go!"

Ariane looked like she wanted to argue, but turned to follow.

The air suddenly grew heavy, darkness swirled around them, and a wall of bladed ice reared up from the ground at the base of the stairs, towering fifteen meters into the air, mist cascading from it in chilling ghostly sheets.

Amas-Garao stood at the top of the stairs, a lambent green glow around him, fist clenched, glints of poisonous yellow sparking beneath his cowl. "I *assure* you, my friends," he snarled venomously, "No one is going *anywhere.*"

Chapter 55

"What the *hell* do you think you're doing?" Ariane demanded. She still couldn't believe what she was seeing. That . . . *thing* seemed to be able to create something out of nothing, and poor Marc looked like he was just about done in. "You didn't issue any Challenge, we haven't done a damn thing to you, and—"

"He wanted me to join his little club." DuQuesne said, already looking a little steadier . . . or maybe he was just making it *look* that way, for their sake. "I declined, and he wouldn't take *no* for an answer."

"Well, he'll take it now. The answer is *no*, and we're leaving. Now take down this sideshow stunt!"

The Shadeweaver shook its head elaborately, deliberately. "My dear Captain Austin, you appear under a misapprehension that you are allowed any say in this matter." He studied the group, gaze lingering on Orphan. "I will admit that you humans have so far proved a fascinating group—difficult to predict, defying the usual readings of omen. You have surprised us several times; the fact that you have convinced the Survivor to assist you in finding this place and opening the door perhaps the most surprising of all."

The voice dropped back to the angered snarl. "*Survivor*! You have dared to act against us? After all that we have done for you in the past, with all that you know of us, you would *dare*?"

Ariane saw Orphan literally *cringe* from the Shadeweaver's angry diatribe, a movement so alien when compared to his usual casual, confident demeanor that she felt almost sick. *He's absolutely terrified of these people, and I forced him to come here and help us.*

"I called in a debt." Ariane said.

"Yes . . ." Orphan said, looking at her gratefully, "I . . . had little choice. I owed them considerably, and . . ."

" . . . and what of your debts to *us*?"

Orphan straightened slightly, trying to face Amas-Garao squarely. He did not quite succeed, his own gaze never quite rising to meet that of the furious Shadeweaver. "You . . . you all had agreed that I had fulfilled any debt with certain actions. That perhaps you might be slightly in *my* debt."

"Indeed . . ." the Shadeweaver said, in a more neutral tone. It was clear that he was trying to judge the most advantageous way to play out this scenario.

Behind her, Ariane heard a few subdued clicking noises and a muttered set of curses. "They've got something that shuts down guns," DuQuesne whispered to

Carl and Gabrielle. "Probably works on any explosive. We're not blowing the wall down that way."

"Still, you have not yet entirely fulfilled that commitment, have you?" Amas-Garao continued finally. "On the other hand, your assistance to them—while infernally well-timed—has been small; you have merely shown them the way and opened the door. We shall consider our small debt paid, and the Liberated and the Shadeweavers to be even, if you leave now."

Orphan glanced at Ariane. She nodded. "You don't have to do anything more, Orphan. I can see what this cost you. We'll take it from here."

The tall, green-black alien hesitated, turned back to Amas-Garao. "I . . . I had committed to assist them, my promise was that I would be of use in their quest. I do not feel I could say I had done so if I had led them to their deaths or servitude."

The Shadeweaver's hand started to rise, and she could see Orphan restraining himself from backing away. Then the hand dropped. "Were you not one to honor the word given, you would not be one any could deal with, Survivor, so I will not have you feel you have been forsworn. I shall not kill them, nor bind them permanently to my service, though a few commands may be laid on them for the preservation of some of our secrets. Now you have what you have asked, and I give you leave to go; you may pass through the wall, even though no others may."

Orphan turned and began a slow, reluctant walk. He stopped, and looked at Ariane again. "You . . . you cannot beat him, even the four of you. Do you not know that?"

"Probably . . . not," DuQuesne agreed reluctantly. "But I did manage to get a shot in on him. There's not much of a chance, but if I spent any time thinking on the odds, I'd never have lived long enough to get here in the first place."

Orphan froze. "You . . . do not think on the odds?"

Even in this situation, she saw DuQuesne understood the need for caution. *Not that keeping our odds-defying attitude secret really matters now.* "Well, sure, in most cases . . . but not when my back's against the wall."

Orphan nodded slowly. "Of course. A cornered creature fights because it must." He turned away, looking strangely shrunken, his stance no longer proud and confident, almost beaten and humiliated, as he reluctantly walked towards and through the glittering wall.

Ariane drew her sword. "You might have ways of shutting off guns, but I don't think you can make a sword misfire," she said to Amas-Garao. DuQuesne began to move to the right as she circled to the left, and Carl drew his blade and began slowly stalking up the middle.

The Shadeweaver laughed. "Cleverly stated, and true, so far as it goes. Yet . . . it does not go nearly far enough!"

A screaming wind howled down the stairs; she stood againt it for a moment, but it redoubled in intensity and sent her tumbling backward, to smack painfully into the wall. She forced herself upright, bent down, and began to push her way forward. Another gesture and a mutter of alien words, and the wind concentrated, taking advantage of imbalance and surprise; she felt her sword wrenched from her hand. Carl's was ripped away as well, to dance above them for a moment before being hurled away and sealed into the icy wall. In her peripheral vision, she saw Carl and DuQuesne also forcing themselves towards Amas-Garao; the Hyperion was making much faster progress. *Maybe that'll distract the Shadeweaver; if he has to deal with DuQuesne, he won't be able to work on us.*

Amas-Garao suddenly noticed that DuQuesne was closing on him, and hurled a crackling ball of energy that sent the huge man tumbling limply down the stairs; to Ariane's dismay, the windstorm didn't decrease in the slightest. *Damn. He can keep at least two or three balls in the air at once, so to speak.*

"Why the hell are you bothering with this theatrical crap?" demanded DuQuesne as he levered himself upright again. "Okay, you're having a hard time with me, but why not just use your mindtwisting on the others?"

"Because," the Shadeweaver responded, obviously amused by carrying on a conversation during combat, "that does require personal focus. If I were to use such a technique, I would be unable to focus on all of you at once—which would, indeed, be potentially unfortunate for me, or at least quite annoying." Amas-Garao's voice was quite calm now, and eerily audible despite the howling wind. "Naturally, once all of you are unconscious, we will ensure that you will tell whatever version of events we find most useful."

"What about Orphan?" Ariane shouted against the howling wind. "He knows what's really going on here!"

"He is not called the Survivor for no reason, Captain Austin." The Shadeweaver's tone was cynically amused. "He knows not to oppose forces that outmatch him in a direct manner; he does not assault the Embassy of the Blessed, he doesn't contest the sincerity of the Faith, and he does not match truths and falsehoods and power with the Shadeweavers. He will never tell what he knows." He raised his hand. "But while I am no longer injured, I am now a bit bored with this insane resistance of yours. It is time to end it."

The wind was suddenly filled with crackling bolts of lightning, ripping a scream from Ariane, a curse from DuQuesne, and gasps from Carl and Gabrielle.

"*Stop!*"

The voice was Orphan's.

Amas-Garao stared; the wind and lightning died down, but while Ariane thought she could move well enough, DuQuesne was in no shape to take advantage of it, and the others didn't look too good either. *Maybe . . . if Orphan keeps him distracted for a few minutes . . . but we need time.*

"I have been tolerant and generous, Orphan. Do *not* try my patience further."

"I . . . I have no wish to. Yet . . . Yet I must correct a slight . . . misapprehension, a mistaken impression, that you are giving of me." Orphan's voice shook, but the Survivor stood straighter, and he made a hesitant step forward. "I am also the Survivor because I have, indeed, survived, longer, and through more perils, than many others.

"Indeed . . . when I think upon my past, is it not so that the odds of my survival to this point were truly poor? Would any of us have taken that bet?" Orphan straightened to his full height, though he still stood stiffly, fear written in every line of his stance, in the way his tail sought to curl forward and around. "I have been found—by your people, once—drifting in the Void, lost in the endless storm and wind between the Spheres. I walk alone, when all others walk together. It was a matter of survival—of the fact that once I knew and thought the truth of my very self, of my own mind versus that of the Great Minds—that drove me to join those I was sent to destroy."

She saw DuQuesne slowly gathering himself, and could see Carl and Gabrielle starting to recover.

Orphan forced his gaze upwards, looked full at Amas-Garao. "In survival—when the blade is at our hearts, when the coils constrict the breathing—odds are no longer the point. For the sake of ourselves, or for the sake of the species, some of us must risk all, and many times we die. Sometimes we die trying to save others, who also die."

"And what is *your* point, Orphan? Your survival is not bound to theirs."

Orphan's voice shook. "But . . . is it not? I am the only one of my Faction. I *am* the Liberated. I am my species, my race, my ideal. I am all of them. I am the only hope for the Blessed, the hope that they cannot even desire while the Minds hold them prisoner.

"You would have me walk away, when I swore to aid them. When I know what you are doing." His arms wrapped tightly around himself for a moment, covered partly by his wings as they, too, contracted tighter. "My survival is not my body, Amas-Garao. My survival is my freedom. I do what I will, because *I* will it." There was a manic, terrified edge in his voice, but Orphan forced his arms to release, though the hands remained tightly clenched.

Ariane felt as though they should move now, but she didn't. She was held spellbound, watching Orphan fight an internal battle on a scale she could not imagine.

Amas-Garao drew himself up. "Have a great care for what you say next, Orphan of the Liberated," he said softly, his tone that of a blade wrapped in blood-red silk.

"I have voyaged in search of the truth behind the darkest tales of those who sail the darkest reaches of the

Arena; I have returned alone after gazing on things no other has ever seen, remembering sometimes only that I dare not remember." Orphan's voice grew stronger. "I have dealt with Shadeweaver, Faith, Molothos, and Vengeance. I have won a Sphere in fair challenge. I am the Survivor.

"And I will tell myself no lies at the behest and in fear of others, even you—for then I have conceded the control of my mind—of *myself*—to you. Perhaps I will be their enemy one day. But who and what I am, that I shall *choose* . . . and never think of the odds, when it is my very self at stake!"

"Then," Amas-Garao said with an almost human shrug, "you shall die defying the odds—for I promised their survival, but not yours!"

DuQuesne tried to lunge to his feet, but there was no chance for him to close the distance. The Shadeweaver's hand stabbed out, and a blaze of fiery light streaked towards Orphan.

But in the same moment, Orphan had moved, one hand dipping into a pouch at his side. As the destroying light came down, the hand came up, and the white-hot flame sprayed off of an invisible barrier like a firehose hitting bulletproof glass.

"*What?*"

There was a hint of hysterical laughter waiting at the back of Orphan's voice, but it was strong and clear. "Alas, I failed to remind you—I am also the Survivor because I do not *rely* on the odds!"

His hand contracted on the odd carven rod, a tiny thing that glittered with hints of lights and circuits and, at the same time, bone and gems, a wand constructed by an engineer, or a transmitter assembled by a shaman.

A nigh-invisible sphere of force burst outward, and Amas-Garao staggered.

"*Now!*"

The four humans rushed the Shadeweaver. He snarled and gestured, unleashing his wind and lightning again . . . but this time it was weaker, and though it *hurt* Ariane drove through it, landed a blow. DuQuesne managed to hammer one shot home as well, before Amas-Garao faded and rematerialized a short distance away.

"You've damped his power down?" she said to Orphan.

"Yes. He is very strong, and I do not know anything about how long this device can hold him."

Seeing himself weakened and heavily outnumbered clearly didn't appeal to Amas-Garao; he raised his hand again. "Brothers, to me!"

Oh, DAMN.

A shimmer, and another black-cloaked form materialized; this one was broad and many-legged under the cloak, with a clawed upright torso. "We have been discussing this situation, Brother Garao," said Gona-Brashind. "It is our feeling that you must resolve this on your own, as you forbade any others from interfering earlier. I shall, of course, observe."

Ariane wasn't sure whether the translated curse was anatomically possible even for a Molothos. But she took advantage of Amas-Garao's discomfiture and charged again. This time he caught her in an unseen vise, stopping her cold and tightening, crushing the breath from her, as she stood only a few feet from the Shadeweaver.

At the periphery of her vision, she saw DuQuesne catch Orphan's attention; no words were exchanged, but the two of them seemed to understand the single glance perfectly, timing their lunges precisely. The Shade-weaver tried to evade, but a green-black chitinous knee took him in the side as DuQuesne's iron-hard fist smashed across the face inside the cowl.

That hurt Amas-Garao; she knew, because she felt the spray of warm alien blood from the impact; the taste in her half-open mouth was sharp, acrid. *I hope it's not poisonous*, she thought as she fell to the ground, no longer held in the Shadeweaver's grip.

The Shadeweaver staggered, nearly went down, but somehow rolled to his feet, sending another storm of energy outward, backing them up. Orphan tried to maintain a grip but was torn free; as Amas-Garao raised his hand to send another attack at him, DuQuesne seized his arm; Amas-Garao disappeared, reappeared, but looked less steady, tired, though still dangerous. Orphan was already on him, and he and DuQuesne exchanged other glances, both of them looking backward for a moment. Their strike didn't seem as well-coordinated.

Wait a minute . . . She followed their gazes, watched their movements.

I think I see. And if so . . . She ran to Carl. "You and Gabrielle, follow me!"

Amas-Garao screamed in fury and frustration; every time he *almost* had one of the two attacking him, the other would throw his aim off. He'd shattered parts of the stairs and left a hole in the nearby wall already.

But they couldn't maintain the rhythm forever. The Shadeweaver's defenses may have been weakened by whatever the thing Orphan held was, but they were far from down, and anger was lending a focus to the Shade-weaver despite his injuries. At the peak of his rage, he shrugged off DuQuesne, and saw Orphan, just two steps below him, stagger, a perfect target; Amas-Garao's hand blazed blue-white and sent a lethal bolt straight for Orphan's chest.

At the last possible second, Orphan dove—a dive so perfectly timed, so accurately calculated, that it was suddenly clear that even the stagger had been a deliberate ruse. And it was far too late for Amas-Garao to recall the blast he had just unleashed.

Blazing starfire thundered into the white-glittering wall, shattering it like glass before a sledgehammer into a billion razor-shards; Ariane, Carl, and Gabrielle were mostly sheltered by their position, crouched right against the sides of the gateway, which the wall had filled. Through the settling icy dust the three humans lunged into the street; DuQuesne and Orphan followed a split-second later.

Amas-Garao started down the steps towards them, but pulled up short as an Adjudicator seemed to materialize out of nowhere. The armored figure said nothing, but it was clear that even the Shadeweaver did not care to push things any farther.

"Thus is this encounter concluded," Gona-Brashind buzzed calmly. "While we cannot enforce and will not enforce our will upon you, Captain Austin, I ask—purely as a favor—that you not speak of this incident to the general public. Within your circle of allies and your own people, of course, I would not expect you to be silent."

Help you save face? Okay. Maybe you will owe me one. "I will consider it."

Orphan suddenly dropped the little rod with an oath; it smoked. He gingerly picked it back up, juggled it, and with difficulty replaced it in the bag.

Amas-Garao stared at them a moment; then without another word or gesture, he strode away, fading out of existence. The other Shadeweaver also vanished.

"I don't think this is over, not by a long shot." DuQuesne muttered, leaning on Carl. Carl did not look entirely happy to be trying to support someone who outweighed him by at least a factor of two.

"No," agreed Ariane. "But it is for now." She turned to Orphan. "Thank you, Orphan."

The leader and sole member of the Liberated suddenly collapsed.

"Orphan!"

Chapter 56

"Will they be all right, Gabrielle?"

DuQuesne had collapsed just moments after the hastily-located shuttle-taxi had brought them to the Embassy, and Orphan had been looking steadily worse, his color going from black and pine green to something closer to spring leaves and dark gray. As the only doctor present, Gabrielle Wolfe had immediately taken charge as best she could.

"Should be," the diminuitive blonde replied as she emerged from the Embassy room she was using as an impromptu sickbay. Simon followed her out, still packing various instruments into his own kit, with Laila trailing behind, clearly going over mental notes and only half-seeing everyone around her. "Hard to be sure, of course, what with Orphan being not at *all* human."

"Yes," Simon said, "The problem was quite a multidisciplinary one. Not just for Orphan, either."

Ariane blinked. "What do you mean?"

"Hyperions don't get sick, and ones like DuQuesne are hard to hurt, and when they get hurt, they usually take care of the problem themselves," Laila said absently. "Taking care of one is a delicate business, because they're all unique—one-off creations of bioengineering with some unknown set of modifications, whose origin isn't known and stability is uncertain. I wouldn't say he's as alien as Orphan, but Marc isn't one of us, either."

She remembered Marc's insistence—and pain—on the fact that he wasn't human. It somehow hurt worse to hear someone else confirm it so matter-of-factly. "So what's wrong with them?"

Simon put a hand on her shoulder. "Don't worry, Captain—Ariane. Marc's sleeping now, but he's going to be fine. He took an incredible beating for something like twenty minutes there, and fought for most of it. He wasn't a mass of broken bone because his bones . . . aren't bone, entirely. One of his modifications causes his bone structure and a number of other structural members like tendons to create natural—if you can call it that—ring-carbon composite. There's at least some of it protecting all vital areas."

"It's amazing, and explains a great deal about some of the described capabilities of the Hyperions," Laila said, more enthusiastically. "And, of course, he was running at top gear all that time—had to be, from your description of the opposition. That's what really has him down for now."

Ariane glanced at Gabrielle for clarification. "What does she mean?"

"Honey, you know we can't keep up with Marc, not even you. Well, nothing like that comes for free—something has to pay for it. Basically Marc's metabolism skyrockets during that kind of sequence, everything runs faster, and he burns through his reserves like lightning. Near as I can tell, he must have lost three to six kilos of mass in that long fight. Now he's trying to recover, and everything else really got to him. Also, I don't think he's exactly got insulation all through him, so the lightning balls that son of a bitch was throwing couldn't have been helping." She looked at Ariane oddly. "You seemed to throw them off pretty quick, though."

The gaze made her uncomfortable, and she didn't want to follow that discussion—it wasn't relevant. "Maybe I was lucky and didn't get shocked as hard as everyone else. What about Orphan?"

"Oh, now *there* is a very interesting situation." Simon said. "The issue of calculation of odds was rather thrown into sharp relief here, and so when I was helping Gabrielle examine Orphan, I was alert for certain . . . possibilities.

"Artificial intelligences don't work here, but it is possible for nanotechnological enhancements within the body to exist and function, and to some extent these can be used to augment brain as well as bodily functions. It appears that there is a long-established set of nanotech-biotech structures in Orphan's brain which, as near as Laila and myself can determine, basically assist in the accurate evaluation of situations and probabilities, on a much more basic level than we can perform them. This means that Orphan—and, by extension, I suspect many, if not most, of the alien species we have encountered —have what amounts to an instinctive 'gut feel' for probabilities that we essentially lack. They react to probabilities against them in the same way we would react to proportionate threats."

That does start to make sense of this. "So to them, facing down a probability against them of a million-to-one is like, what, nerving yourself to open a door when there's a T-Rex behind it?"

"Something not very far from that. There are, of course, survival-oriented cutoffs—there's no percentage in having people who are fighting for their lives just give up. As near as I can tell," Simon went on, "Orphan managed to trip those by focusing on how his mental freedom was, to him, equivalent to his physical survival. But it had the emotional effect on him of . . . oh, deliberately placing your head between a spaceship and its docking port. And he was at the same time *also* confronting something which, in and of itself, he viewed as nearly impossible to defeat. Add to that the quite considerable battering he took, and he effectively went into shock."

"Without Laila's advice, we might have lost him, too," Gabrielle said soberly. "My medical training didn't tell me anything about giving first aid to some kind of human-bug crossbreed."

Laila looked uncomfortable at the praise, and scandalized by the description of Orphan. "I simply was able to deduce what kind of mechanisms could be used to produce artificial respiration, and how he needed to be stabilized. He is *hardly* any form of crossbreed, Dr. Wolfe! His people are a magnificent, and alien, lifeform whose similarities to any Terran lifeforms are purely coincidence—and perhaps suggestive of some parallel courses of evolution, or of something even greater. We should never make—"

Gabrielle raised her hands defensively. "Sorry, don't you get so riled up."

Ignoring the exchange, Ariane pressed ahead. "How long before they wake up?"

"I'm not sure for Marc," Simon said. "He opened one eye, seemed to recognize he was safe, and shut back down again, so I would presume it's a semi-autonomic function which prefers to run its course if in safe surroundings. Orphan, on the other hand, is already awake. He wants to speak to you, Captain. In private."

She looked at the three with an exasperated glance. "Why the hell didn't you *say* so before?" She didn't wait for an answer—after all, she *had* asked other questions, too—but strode past them into the sickbay.

Orphan was laid on a bed tailored to his form; at least they'd learned how to control that sort of thing by now. He was propped up by the bed and, while still far from his normal coloration, no longer looked as though he were a terribly faded photograph. "Captain . . . Austin."

"Orphan." She sat down in a nearby chair. "Orphan, you gave far more than I asked. I didn't realize . . . how very much it was going to cost you. I'm sorry."

"*Please*, Captain! I . . . I hold no grudge or blame against you here. Indeed . . . I must thank you." The wingcases tried to shift, the body move in a way that she knew would be a weak smile. "It seems that only under such terrible duress was I truly able to see myself clearly, and recognize how I was being led to the service of others, where I had sought to free myself. As I said to Amas-Garao, perhaps one day you and I shall be enemies, not allies, but that will be because it serves my purposes, not those of some other Faction which is not my own."

The words were a clear cautionary warning; Orphan wanted her to be aware that he had not risked his life out of some noble heroism. She smiled. "Orphan, it doesn't matter to me *why* you did it. What *does* matter to me is that if you hadn't, we'd be either dead, or more likely going happily about our business without even realizing we'd been totally screwed by that bastard. Who," and her voice hardened as she spoke, "had better not think that this is over for *me*."

Orphan shuddered. "I overcame my fears in that moment, Captain, but hearing you so . . . *eager* to come again to grips with so formidable an opponent is enough to make me ill."

"Sorry." Ariane thought a moment. "You surprised the hell out of all of us with that little gadget—including the Shadeweaver. Where the hell did you *get* it? The Faith?"

He managed a small laugh, with a ghost of his usual ironic, superior tone. "Oh, never from the Faith, nor the Shadeweavers. Perhaps there are others—or rather, I must assume there are other such devices—but never have I heard of one elsewhere." He looked off into the empty distance, a very human pose. "I will not tell you exactly where, or how . . . at least, not at this time. That is a secret of inestimable value, I am sure you will agree. But . . . in the interests of our alliance, I will say that I still prefer to not believe in magic . . . but the place and time at which I acquired that device did indeed severely test my preferences. Then again, the Shadeweavers do the same."

She studied Orphan, whose body language and tone showed an unusual intimacy or openness . . . one perhaps born of the danger they had shared. "So . . . much as I hate to open this can of worms, but do you have any real reason *not* to believe that the Shadeweavers are magicians and the Faith the priests of the gods?"

Orphan's laugh was somewhat stronger. "Ah, Captain Austin, an excellent question. I have no direct evidence in that direction, no. If there were, undoubtedly the Factions would fragment more violently over matters of belief and doctrine. But it is, to me, rather suggestive that the Shadeweavers themselves insist that the Faith are but charlatans, by implications Shadeweavers in disguise, while the Faith appear quite sincere—most, at least—and describe what do indeed sound like a contact with something nigh unto a god." His hands flicked out weakly. "I am not sure exactly why this makes me doubt that there is a supernatural force, but something about it bothers me. Perhaps it will come to me later."

The interval had allowed her to figure out an approach for the important question. "So, if we are even now, does that mean we are not allies?"

Orphan tilted his head, then mimed the bob-bow gesture. "In that we have no direct and immediate commitment, yes. Yet . . . as I said to you before, I was told that there was one chance to save my Faction, my true people, and I have yet to finish the path I was shown. I have not been the Survivor by neglecting my interests, Captain Austin; while certainly this means that there may come a time when I must relinquish our association, and even work against you, in this case, and at this time, it would seem to me the height of folly to abandon you. Your stock, so to speak, is on the rise. We shall not speak of this incident outside, yet it will be known that *something* happened, and that it likely involved the Shadeweavers, and that we all returned. There will be whispers and rumors and all manner of useful uncertainty to be exploited."

"Glad to see I judged you right," came a low murmur from the other bed. DuQuesne was looking at them. "You're an opportunistic bastard who might sell us as soon as shake our hand . . . but you'd rather be up-front about it when you can."

"*Marc!*" She found herself by his bedside without even thinking about it, taking his hand. "You crazy . . . don't you *dare* go do anything like that again, you hear me?"

DuQuesne chuckled, then winced. "Believe you me, I've learned my lesson. How are you, Ariane?"

"I'm fine. A little bruised, nothing much else; Gabrielle said whatever species the Shadeweaver is, the blood's mildly toxic, but I'd have to practically bathe in it to be in danger." She squeezed his hand. "I'm just glad we won that one."

"We didn't win that one, Captain, and I hope none of you are really fooling yourselves into thinking we did."

"It was at least a tie," Ariane argued.

DuQuesne shook his head. "We got damned lucky. Twice over, in that fight. First that Orphan decided his personal survival was bound up with us, at least for that moment, and second that he had something to give us an edge. An edge that looks like it probably couldn't have held out more than a few more minutes, and maybe won't work ever again." He glanced at Orphan.

The alien looked uncomfortable. "You . . . may be right. I had of course never used it before. It was a reserve I have hidden for a long time, in case I ever found myself in a dispute with the Shadeweavers."

"In any case, it's for damn sure it won't *surprise* them next time. They'll be ready for it."

Ariane's elation at Marc's recovery was fast fading. "So you think they'll be trying this again?"

"Not the same thing, no. But something."

Orphan nodded, deliberately imitating the human gesture. "Dr. DuQuesne is, I am afraid, all too correct. The

Shadeweavers will not permit us to believe that we can escape without suffering consequences; even those who refused to participate in Amas-Garao's plan will not oppose a campaign to instruct us in the error of our ways, as long as it is reasonably subtle and not overly violent."

"If they're not going to do it directly, then what?"

"My guess?" DuQuesne yawned, looking astounded and realizing his own body wanted him to shut back down. He fought it off for a moment. "My guess? Things are going to just get a lot more difficult for us from now on." His eyes began to close, but he managed to finish his thought. " 'Just business . . . nothing personal.' " he quoted.

Oh, damn.

Chapter 57

There are times, DuQuesne thought dryly, *that I wish I wasn't right.*

It hadn't taken long for his prediction to come true. The day after the race, Carl and Ariane had gone to visit Ghondas, the Powerbroker Orphan had introduced them to previously, and she had been much more approachable. In fact, it had seemed that she was willing to discuss the possibility of selling them enough power to go home, based on the significant track record they had already established, and allowing them to simply owe something of a debt to her. The two had come back extremely cheerful, and spent much of the later part of the day searching through their possessions and knowledge for material that would make a useful "good faith" down payment.

The next morning, just before they set out to meet the Powerbroker, Ghondas had called and broken off the meeting. There was no explanation given. Ariane insisted on going anyway; DuQuesne, now at least somewhat recovered, had decided to go with her.

It had taken considerable argument to even see Ghondas—the normally-open area before her station was closed—and when she did come out, the usually expansive and pleasant creature was curt, nervous. "I have simply reconsidered my risks and decided that it would be unwise at this time," she said. "Can you not accept this is my right as a Powerbroker?"

"Of course it's your right." Ariane said hastily. "I just don't understand *why*. Everything seemed fine yesterday."

Ghondas quivered; DuQuesne didn't know much about her species' body language, but it gave him the impression of fear. She said nothing for a moment, then sank down slightly before raising her tendriled head. "I assess the risk differently today. Please. Do not press me."

Ariane looked as though she was about to argue more, so DuQuesne touched her arm. "Captain. Let's go. No point in making her angry, if she's not willing to deal, it's her choice."

"You think it's the Shadeweavers already?" she asked, once they were some distance away. He could see the lines of worry on her forehead—lines that were starting to show signs that they could become permanent.

"I can't think of any other reason. Excuses aside, someone like Ghondas doesn't stay in business by jerking her customers around, and doesn't negotiate idly. If she broke it off that fast, she learned something that took us from a reasonable business risk to untouchable overnight."

And the fun just doesn't stop. Steve and Tom had gone out for a night in the Grand Arcade. They came back just an hour and a half after they left. There was a puzzled, rather hurt look on Steve's face, and Tom Cussler's expression was like a thundercloud.

"What happened, Steve?"

"I don't *know!*" he said plaintively. "I mean . . . we went to some of the shops I've been to before, and . . . it was like the best stock would be put away when I got there. If it was visible, I was told it was already sold. The people who *would* sell to me wanted me to buy and get the heck out of the shop right away.

"Even Olthalis—the Chiroflekir that sold you guys our first alien food—even he didn't want to talk to me. Finally said 'it wasn't safe,' and told me to get away from his stall."

He exchanged glances with Ariane. She sighed, nodded, and turned to the others. "I think we have to discuss the situation, everyone. I think—"

"—Anathema has been declared against the Faction of Humanity," the rough voice of Relgof Nov Ne'knarph said, as he and Simon entered the Embassy common room. "My own Faction does not generally acquiesce to such things entirely, but I was forced to remove my friend Simon from the library, and myself from our Faction House if I wished to continue any conversation with him." The crest of feathers atop Relgof's head was bristling with what DuQuesne guessed was anger.

"What's 'Anathema,' Doc?" Carl asked.

"It's rather what we expected after that little conflict with the Shadeweavers," Simon said, throwing down his case in disgust. "A declaration—spread very quietly—that essentially says that the Shadeweavers are very displeased with our Faction, and will be for some length of time. No direct threat, no clear statement of consequences, just the statement that *they* don't like us.

"Any Faction can make such a statement, of course," Relgof said. "However, the Shadeweavers, I must confess, tend to have a vastly greater effect when they declare Anathema."

"So we can expect this crap to go on until whenever the Shadeweavers feel we've had enough?" Ariane looked furious enough to head down to the Shadeweaver Faction House by herself.

"I'm afraid so." Dr. Relgof flip-flopped his filter beard apologetically. "I, personally, will do what I can—there is very little the Shadeweavers can do to me directly, and if my Faction makes it clear that they are not directly aiding you, they will not push the issue. But very few indeed will dare go against the Shadeweavers. Except, possibly—"

There was a chime, and one of the green spheres appeared before Ariane. "Nyanthus of the Faith requests admittance."

"Show him in, please," Ariane said.

" . . . Possibly, as I said," Relgof continued, with a faint smile in his tone, "the Faith."

Nyanthus glided in, his symbiotes flying outward to enfold them all symbolically before returning. Mandallon followed immediately behind. "It was revealed to me that by now you must have learned of your predicament, Captain Ariane Austin. Know that the displeasure of the Shadeweavers holds no fear for the Faith. Mandallon has offered to be a go-between for you; while he cannot, of course, convince people to venture overmuch, the basic negotiations for the simple necessities can be much eased with his assistance—for few indeed are those who will deliberately insult the Faith."

Mandallon curtsy-bowed. "Indeed, it would be an honor to serve you in this manner. I know not how you have offended those . . . servants of darker powers, but it must be something truly wonderful for them to be so angered."

Ariane smiled; DuQuesne knew she liked the earnest young priest. "I would be glad to have your assistance, Mandallon—"

"—but," DuQuesne interrupted, "we'd really like to make sure it won't cost anything. Being honored is all well and good, but the Factions are still the Factions, aren't they?"

Mandallon started slightly, and Nyanthus's symbiotes jittered. After a pause, the rich "voice" of the First Guide spoke. "It is true that we cannot serve all people outside of the Faith without some form of return; this is Written in the way of the Creators, that for all services, eventually there is a payment. But we ask no immediate payment, only an alliance, a sense that you owe us gratitude—as surely you yourselves would acknowledge is fair, if this service we do for you?"

"It certainly seems fair to me," Laila Canning said. "Really, Dr. DuQuesne, that was quite rude—and I am not usually one to notice rudeness. The Faith have been completely open with us and incredibly helpful—and I owe them a debt I'm not sure I can ever repay." She looked with momentary softness at Mandallon.

"It's not rudeness," DuQuesne said bluntly. "Caution. We're still in a real precarious situation, and picking up debts that we don't know how to pay—and can't even count up in simple terms—isn't a good plan."

Simon studied them all narrowly. "I dislike anything that smacks of rudeness, but I find I must—reluctantly —concur with Marc. We have no way of knowing how long this Anathema will be in effect, and thus no idea of how large a tab we will have to run with your people, Nyanthus. Nor—as Marc says—a true way of making an accounting of that debt. When it involves money, it is a simple matter to determine if the debt is one can assume, but with services and obligations such as these, it is far murkier."

"Exactly." Ariane said, with some relief. "Nyanthus, Mandallon, it isn't that we don't appreciate the offer—even with the strings attached. I do, and I think we all do. But the last thing we want to do is end up with a debt which could by itself sour the relations between Humanity and the Faith. And any conflict on the exact extent and severity of that debt could do exactly that—and play right into the Shadeweavers' hands."

Nyanthus stood swaying a moment, and suddenly flowered open, laughing a deep laugh, joined by Mandallon. "Ah, Ariane Austin of Humanity, you have found an argument worthy of an Initiate Guide! Our very offer is now shown to be, perhaps, a snare set by the Dark Ones, based on our own motives and means. Now surely I must offer you at least some of Mandallon's assistance free of any burden."

"And I, as well," Orphan said, coming in from his own temporary room. The Survivor had very nearly fully recovered, and had been planning to return to his own Embassy the next day. "For surely the Shadeweavers may be displeased by me, but there is little, indeed, that they could do . . . and I like to believe that the Survivor himself is one that others would not wish to offend."

There's something . . . slightly different in the way he's standing and talking now. Wish I could put my finger on it. Maybe it's just the result of facing mental death, so to speak.

Ariane smiled broadly. "Well, we got this far with, basically, only you two as allies. As long as you'll stand with us in this, I'm sure we'll get through it somehow."

"With such confidence, and the blessing of the Creators, it shall be," Nyanthus said.

"Tomorrow I will help you lay in supplies of all essentials," Mandallon promised. "We should try to do this in carefully scheduled intervals, which will minimize the conflict with the Dark Ones."

"Thank you. That will help. If you'll stay here tonight, we'll go over everything we need and make a list."

Mandallon hefted an iridescent white, curved shoulder bag. "I had planned on it, Captain. Thank you for accepting this offer."

"Don't thank us until it's all over. We'll be thanking you, I'm sure."

DuQuesne looked around as everyone began to settle down, and more normal conversations started. *Seems that we have a solution to this problem.*

So . . . what am I missing? Because sure as God made little green apples, this isn't going to be that easy.

I can feel it.

Chapter 58

Simon stopped next to Ariane, and watched with interest as the nondescript floor blossomed out into chairs suited for their entire party. Around them, hundreds of other beings were taking seats in this . . . colosseum. He looked over to Mandallon, on his left, as they sat down. "Thank you so much for arranging this."

Mandallon gave a cheerful curtsy-bow before seating himself. "With all of the difficulties you have had, the First Guide agreed that this was the least we could do to give you . . . oh, an easement, a break I believe you have called it, from the tension. And for newcomers such as yourselves, Challenges are both entertainment and education."

"So who are the parties in this Challenge, what exactly is at stake, and what kind of Challenge is it?"

"Ah, Doctor Sandrisson," answered the mellifluous voice of Nyanthus, "this is a quite interesting Challenge, and one which I believe has a personal touch for you as well. In our discussions I recall that you mentioned the Powerbroker Ghondas as one who had clearly been intimidated by the Anathema."

DuQuesne looked over with interest. "So this is one of those required Powerbroker challenges? That they have to do every so often in order to retain their posts?"

"Precisely so, Dr. DuQuesne," confirmed Nyanthus. "In this case, Ghondas and her people, the Shiquan, have accepted a Challenge from the Vengeance. While, in theory, they could Challenge or accept Challenge from any Faction, including all of the lesser Factions, the Powerbrokers themselves have a sort of . . . traditional pride, in that as a group they consider it to show a lack of courage or dedication to maintain their posts by Challenging anyone other than the Five Great Factions—or, one would presume, the Shadeweavers, though I cannot recall any ever electing *that* route."

"Ouch," Ariane said. "Given that the major Factions have a lot of resources, that makes these pretty serious Challenges—not just a matter of formality."

"Oh, indeed they are serious, Ariane Austin," said Orphan, who had seated himself on the far right of their section—a section right up to the edge of the cleared arena-space below. "Yet the Powerbrokers have one great advantage over the standard participants in Challenge. Two, actually.

"First is that as they are not, technically speaking, a Faction, they follow slightly different rules. They do not have to select their participant in the Challenge until it actually begins, allowing them to, in fact, pick their champion to best offset the champion selected by their opposition. Between Factions, as you know, the representatives to meet in the Challenge must be determined well in advance of the actual contest."

That certainly is an advantage, Simon thought. *If you can wait that long, you can have a wide variety of candidates standing by, research your opponent's weaknesses, and select someone most likely to succeed in that specific Challenge against that specific participant.* "And the second advantage?"

Orphan gave a relaxed flutter of his wings that Simon associated with a smile; the accompanying buzz-chuckle confirmed it. "You recall, of course, the problem that one has in choosing, for example, myself to represent you in a Challenge?"

"Yes," DuQuesne answered, "The fact that you can grab the prize for yourself if you win."

"Exactly. Well, for the Powerbroker Challenge all that is necessary for them to retain their position is that the Challenge itself *be* a victory for their side. They make no direct demands upon the loser at all."

Simon felt his eyebrows raise. "Oh, my. So in essence they have an immense potential . . . prize, I suppose the term should be . . . to offer anyone who will agree to represent them. Their representative gets to demand a prize for themselves, not for the Powerbrokers, if they win, and is risking nothing if they lose."

DuQuesne grunted. "An edge for sure. They can get just about *anyone* to play the game for them with those kind of advantages. Doesn't guarantee victory, but sure does give them better odds."

"So what's the actual Challenge today?" Ariane asked.

At that moment, the space within the central arena area, which was roughly three hundred meters across, blurred, seemed to be filled with moving, shifting shadows; a murmur, a susurration of conversation, rose and fell with this, and as it cleared, Simon could see that the central area was now filled with walls making corridors, leading to various rooms and intersections; some were plain empty pathways open to the sky, some roofed over, others filled with what appeared to be trees and brush, some with figures that seemed to be standing at attention in the center. In the middle was a circular area with a beam of light emanating from the top of a tower, about thirty meters high, in the exact center of the circle, with four columns spaced evenly around it. From what Simon could make out, there were two openings into that central area, one on the left, one on the right.

"A Combat Challenge maze," Orphan said, both explaining what they saw and answering Ariane's last question. "This pits the contestants not against each other, but against various challenges—physical obstacles, traps, hostile creatures, intelligent opponents—in a maze intended to confuse and distract. The goal, of course, is to get through the maze and arrive in the center, interrupting the beam of light and thus ending the Challenge."

DuQuesne grinned. "Sounds like my kind of fun. And if I get the conditions right, it *could* still come down to the two participants duking it out."

"Oh, yes indeed it could," Orphan said with an answering chuckle. "If both make it to the center area at the same time, each will, of course, try to interrupt the light beam . . . and to stop the other from doing so. It is not unknown for both participants to manage to prevent each other from doing so immediately, and then having to fight each other until one or the other succeeds in reaching and interrupting the light."

There were small open spaces visible at each end of the arena area, clearly the places where each participant would start. Now a figure appeared on the lefthand side; tiny at this distance, but Simon still had an impression of something very large.

"There, the Vengeance's selected champion," Mandallon said, excitement plain in his voice. As he spoke, the air shimmered before them, and an enlarged, clear image of the far-distant contestant materialized in thin air. It *was* large, a semi-centauroid form with six armored legs supporting a snake-like body that tapered off into a tail that had bladed spikes at the end, and an upright forward torso with massive, human-like arms and a triangular head with two large glittering eyes and a broad, fanlike crest or shield protecting the neck. The entire creature seemed covered with both scales and hair, and the upright head could have looked Marc DuQuesne straight in the eye; Simon estimated its mass at close to a metric ton. "Sivvis Lissituras, a Daelmokhan."

"Looks nasty," DuQuesne said.

"Quite," confirmed Orphan. "Sivvis is a very well-known professional Challenge-warrior. As you might guess, there are a fair number of beings who make their livings by being very good at dealing with multiple types of Challenges and hiring their services out professionally. Despite his large size and—to many—brutish appearance, Sivvis is an extremely clever opponent; his last appearance in the arena ended in victory, and *there* the Challenge was to solve a mathematically-based light-puzzle in the shortest time. Here, of course, he gets to put his natural skills to the test. Now let us see what Ghondas and the rest of her family have chosen to try and compete with Sivvis Lissituras."

There was a distant sparkle at the other end of the colosseum, and a second image appeared in the air. Unlike the hulking Daelmokhan Challenge-warrior, the newcomer was . . . tiny. Simon guessed the height of the creature as no more than a meter and a half. Its body was covered with a smooth, shiny integument more like chitin than skin, mostly a polished white with some areas on the head and arms colored a rich royal purple, and had a body plan somewhat similar to Orphan's: a smooth, rounded head with wide, reddish-looking eyes, and streamlined inset ears, a small mouth, a well-muscled, almost human body, with strong, three-fingered hands tipped with black or deep purple clawlike nails, two legs ending in three-toed feet, and a long, sinuous tail. It wore a suit of some sort of armor, mostly white/silver plates on the chest inlaid with arcane symbols, layered bronze guards covering the shoulders and making a sort of four-section skirt around the waist and leg area.

"Oh, my, now *that* is interesting indeed." Orphan tapped his hands together in unconscious affirmation. "A Genasi warrior. If I read his armor-markings correctly, that's Tunuvun, one of their best."

"Amas-Garao mentioned that species once," DuQuesne said. "Implied they were pretty tough customers."

Nyanthus's trunk had leaned forward and his symbiotes orbited closely to the new image; it was clear that his interest, as well, had been captured. "There are some who believe the Genasi are the most formidable warriors in the Arena; unfortunately they are . . . impulsive and often given to acting before reasoning. They also are unusual in that they are one of the races native to the Arena itself, and have as yet no Sphere to call their own."

"So they're not actually citizens of the Arena?"

"Not in the sense that those of us here are, no," Nyanthus confirmed. "And they cannot Challenge directly without that legitimacy."

Simon frowned. "Rather unfair to them, given they evolved here."

DuQuesne shrugged. "Seems pretty clear to me the Arena isn't about 'fair' at all, except in pretty limited categories."

The voice of the Arena suddenly echoed around the colosseum. "**Are both participants ready?**"

A dual "Yes" came from the ends of the mazes—one rough and deep, the other a sharp, impatient tenor.

"**Will either of you yield now, before the contest begins?**"

Neither of the contestants even deigned to speak, apparently considering the question itself not worth responding to. After a pause, the Arena spoke again. "**The first to reach the center and, following that, interrupt—by any means—the beam of light from the central tower shall be the winner. Both of these conditions must be met for victory. By the ancient laws of the Arena . . . begin.**"

The two figures charged forward into the maze. Simon noticed that the mazes were the same size, but not identical. He wondered how the Arena decided what design was appropriate.

Sivvis halted suddenly, barely in time to keep from falling into a spike-lined pit that had appeared in front of him. The huge creature studied the pit for a moment, then backed up and made an amazing sprint and lunge that sent him literally running along the side of the wall like a gecko before coming to a skidding halt on the other side of the pit.

Meanwhile, Tunuvun of the Genasi was confronted by a grating blocking his passage—a grating that looked like it was made up of huge, razor-sharp sword blades, edges facing the contestant. With scarcely a pause, the tiny Genasi inserted his arms between two of the blades and levered outward. The glinting swordblades bent like twigs and the slick-skinned creature slid through the opening.

That was very impressive. Simon glanced over at Orphan. "His size is rather deceptive; I would hardly have expected such strength from so small a creature."

"Indeed, Dr. Sandrisson, it would be unwise to judge the Genasi by ordinary standards. Make no mistake, if by chance the two *do* reach the center at the same time, neither Sivvis nor Tunuvun will be in for an easy time of it."

Sivvis was speeding his way through a series of branching corridors. "Oh-oh, that's not good," DuQuesne said with a grin. "He's taken a wrong turn."

"He might make up the time, though. Look!" Simon could hear the excitement in Ariane's voice. *This element of the Arena . . . worries me. Though, thinking about it dispassionately, it is in many ways little different from the racing Ariane already participated in.*

Tunuvun was now in one of the small open areas, facing an armored figure of familiar outline: a Daalasan, the same species as Nyanthus's bodyguards. The compact form of the Genasi halted and stood waiting, not even assuming anything that Simon could recognize as a combat pose.

The Daalasan whirled a thick staff about his body in a theatrical gesture, demonstrating skill and speed, then sidled into action, the clawed, backward-bending legs shifting him sideways. Tunuvun did not bother to turn; he didn't even seem to be really bothering to watch. *That has to be a tactic in itself. Taunting your adversary with complete disdain.*

Without warning, the armored Daalasan gave a tremendous leap, the legs showing their strength, propelling the creature nearly nearly five meters into the air, coming down towards Tunuvun with the staff jabbing downwards..

There was a white and violet blur and the sound of a whipcrack combined with a head-on collision of two groundcars; the Daalasan tumbled limply away like a discarded doll and lay motionless on the ground as the crowd roared and the Genasi warrior moved with swift but unhurried strides towards the next tunnel. Simon blinked. "What the bloody hell just happened? I couldn't see a thing!"

"Not surprised," DuQuesne said, eyes narrowed. "Bastard's fast as a striking snake. He turned to face his opponent just as the Daalasan jumped, and then just before the staff could hit he did a flip, a sorta aerial somersault, and totalled the poor bastard with his tail. One shot, one takedown."

"Some of the maze is open," pointed out Ariane as they watched Sivvis desperately retracing his steps. "Why doesn't he just climb up, get a good view, and just run across the tops of a lot of these corridors? He could cut off a lot of time that way."

Nyanthus waved his branching tendrils in an amused manner. "So he could, were it possible to do so; yet not only would such an action be a gross violation of the expected protocol, but also the Arena relies not at all on others to adhere to its protocols. While one can jump and climb as desired during the contest, the participants here would see only black walls above, preventing an advance knowledge of the maze, and if they attempt to pass over, the barriers will prove to be quite solid."

The two contestants pressed forward; Sivvis literally ran over a creature that confronted him, Tunuvun was momentarily balked by a strange puzzle-lock that took him several precious minutes to resolve. A narrow passage barely wide enough for his body caused Sivvis to wiggle and drag himselv slowly forward, while his opponent leapt precariously from one trembling, unstable foothold to another over what appeared to be—*and, given the Arena's technology, could actually be*, Simon thought—a bottomless chasm.

The rustle and cheer and roar of the crowd rose to a crescendo as the two contestants each entered the final straightaway and charged into the central area as though shot from the same gun, catching sight of each other at the same moment, breaking into all-out sprints for the tower and the glittering beam of light at its apex.

Sivvis was ahead by perhaps the length of his massive torso, but as their two paths converged Tunuvun did not slacken his pace, but instead leapt onto the Daelmokhan's armored back.

Instantly the center of the arena became a whirlwind of furious motion. Sivvis whipped his head-crest backwards, an edged axe of evolution, as the Genasi warrior hammered downward. Tunuvun evaded the slash of sharp bone but was nearly crushed as the Daelmokhan rolled over; deep-purple claws dug in and he skittered around Sivvis's body like a squirrel running around a falling tree, jabbing and harrying. A massive arm caught at Tunuvun's tail, pulled, threw, but the tail curled around Sivvis's wrist, sent the Genasi slingshotting back directly for the glittering eyes, which were abruptly replaced from that angle by Sivvis's mouth, a great tearing beak like that of a monstrous eagle. Tunuvun's high-pitched curse was audible as the point of the beak scored a line across his body despite an amazing last-second release and twist by the Genasi. Now he landed, leapt over a swipe by Sivvis's bladed tail, and jumped back onto the vastly larger Daelmokhan's back.

"Holy *kami*," Simon heard himself whisper. He'd never imagined such a vicious duel of apparently-mismatched opponents.

Even DuQuesne looked impressed. "Damn, that's good. Almost a perfect matchup, both strong as hell, trained like nobody's business—Sivvis is a lot faster than he looks so Tunuvun never gets a good chance for a killing blow, but he sticks like glue and Sivvis never gets a really good shot at him either." Ariane was leaning forward cheering. Simon couldn't quite tell which one she was actually rooting for . . . or if she even knew.

The two combatants suddenly separated, glaring at each other across perhaps six or seven meters of space, breathing hard. Both were scored with at least four or five additional wounds garnered in the last few moments of vicious combat, and it was not at all clear which one was faring worse in this conflict. Sivvis edged sideways, and Tunuvun shifted as well, easing behind a cone-shaped pillar—one of four ringing the tower. The Genasi tried to scramble up the pillar, for a leaping vantage, but unlike the tower nearby, it was smooth as glass.

Sivvis took instant advantage of the momentary delay and lunged for the tower with that scrambling splayed-leg posture that had gotten him across the first pit. Claws and flat-padded feet grabbed hold and he began spiraling his way up the side of the tower.

Tunuvun bounced from the ground and sprinted in a whirl of long tail and short, sturdy limbs into a doorway of the tower, running and leaping up the interior stairway. Windows set at intervals around the tower showed him moving with incredible speed, gaining on the huge Sivvis. As the two drew even, Sivvis jabbed one arm through the window, missing Tunuvun by a hair's breadth; at the next window, the Genasi warrior leaped *through*, hammering both feet and his tail squarely against the climbing Daelmokhan, propelling himself off his opponent's body to the edge of the tower roof a meter or two above.

Adrenaline charging his system from this amazing combat, Simon felt his perceptions go into overdrive in that moment; time seemed to slow. He could see Sivvis, turning over in midair, starting a fall directly towards the point of one of the four sharp columns below. He saw Tunuvun's hands grip the top of the tower firmly, legs supporting him, the little Genasi throwing a last glance in the direction of his opponent. He saw the beam of light, now only two meters straight ahead of Tunuvun. One move, a flip of those arms and the Genasi would win.

But in that glance downward, Tunuvun undoubtedly saw what everyone else did: Sivvis plummeting directly for the sharp, smooth point, his massive weight driving him towards what was almost certainly unavoidable death.

The white tail lashed out, wrapped around Sivvis's own flailing tail, pulled taut; Sivvis was pulled inward, reached out, grabbed the side of the tower as the stone of the tower crumbled under Tunuvun's grip and the Genasi slid back to catch hold of a window on a level with Sivvis. For a moment, the two warriors looked into each other's eyes.

Then Sivvis's immense left arm snapped out, grabbed Tunuvun from the wall, and *threw* the smaller warrior with such speed and force that he streaked upward, completely over the edge of the tower, and tumbled directly through the beam of light.

A chime resounded through the Arena. "Challenge is concluded," the Arena's passionless voice stated evenly. "Sivvis Lissaturas for the Vengeance has interrupted the light beam using his opponent's body." As the roar of the crowd began to swell, the Arena continued, "At the same time, Tunuvun for the Powerbroker Ghondas has interrupted the light beam, using the strength of his opponent to do so."

A confused babble broke out. "As these are not merely simultaneous but in fact identical events, this constitutes a true tie."

"Amazing," Mandallon said. "I am not sure that one challenge in ten thousand has such an outcome. Truly are you fortunate to have witnessed this!"

"Does that mean they have to go through *another* Challenge to resolve the tie?" Ariane asked.

"Alas, I am afraid so. Poor Ghondas. The only way . . . but wait!"

Sivvis had raised his arms above his crested head and bellowed. "There is no tie!"

Oh my, thought Simon. *If that means what I think it does, Sivvis may be about to anger his patrons.*

The Arena responded immediately. "Clarify statement. Simultaneous accomplishment of goals clearly tie."

"Bah!" Sivvis's deep-voiced cough of dismissal was translated perfectly. "Tunuvun had won. He had taken me from the contest, was poised to break the light himself. He saved me from injury or death." His voice rose to a roar again. "There is *honor* in this Arena, is there not? Have I not always fought with that as my word and bond, in a thousand battles?

"When I threw him, it was with the full and direct intent to give him that victory which he had earned. Now declare the contest his!"

There was a pause. "Intent of actions can be considered when the situation warrants." Simon thought there might have been, perhaps, a touch of amusement in the normally passionless voice. "Physiological signs and past history confirm your statement.

"The Challenge is therefore concluded, victory for Tunuvun and the Shiquan Powerbrokers."

Tunuvun came forward from where he had landed, on the other side of the tower, crossing his arms across his chest and crouching low before Sivvis, clearly a gesture of great respect, and then straightened. "Then I have my prize—but the prize I ask can only truly be granted by the Arena itself." The tenor voice was precise, hard, and focused.

Orphan leaned forward. "Oh now. That sounds interesting, especially as I cannot offhand think of what the Arena could—or *would*—grant . . . "

"The Arena is not a participant and thus not normally subject to such requests. What prize is this that you require?"

"That which is controlled solely by the Arena: the right of Challenge," Tunuvun said, quietly. "Arena, we are born of you; we have never seen the dark skies of the other universe, never walked within our own Sphere. Give to me the chance to change that, the right to Challenge another Faction as though we were one of them, to Challenge them for a Sphere that we may call our own, that we shall *be* a Faction, not merely the pawns and soldiers of others."

A hush fell over the colosseum. For a moment, there wasn't a sound throughout the huge circular arena within the Arena.

"A prize whose value will depend entirely upon meeting another Challenge—a prize which may therefore be valueless, and costs nothing from any party at present. The Arena deems this reasonable. One Challenge you may give, and that Challenge must be accepted by those to whom you give it, and the stakes of that Challenge will be—for you—the chance to win your own Sphere. You may only issue challenge, therefore, to those who have a multiplicity of Spheres—ten or more.

"This contest is thus concluded. The Powerbrokers retain their position. Let this judgment be entered in the records as precedent." With that statement, the crowd began to slowly break up.

"Whew," whistled DuQuesne. "Quite a show. Thanks again for inviting us."

"You are truly welcome, Dr. DuQuesne," Nyanthus said. "And with such a marvelous spectacle, with such honor and strength displayed, I hope you have found your hearts somewhat lightened."

"Well, I don't know about anyone else," Simon said, glancing around, "but I certainly have."

He saw Ariane smiling agreement. *And with that said . . . I believe I have something else to attend to, before I make a mistake in timing again.* "Ariane," he began, as the others started to move off, rehashing the Challenge in conversation, "a moment, please . . ."

Chapter 59

"And a toast," Simon said, "to finally getting you alone at last."

Ariane laughed and tapped the flower-shaped glasses gently together and sipped. The *nallitiri*, as their host Mairakag Achan had called the drink, was mildly alcoholic, with a light fruity taste something like a grape crossed with a fresh cucumber, and a deep warm undertone similar to a touch of chipotle pepper. Ariane liked it and took another sip. "Mairakag, this is excellent!"

The tripedal Mairakag Achan touched all three of his four-fingered hands to the top of his head, a gesture of gracious thanks. "It is the purpose of the Kitchen to not merely satisfy hunger, but please the senses, of all who enter. I thank you for these words." He gave a graceful pirouette, elaborate dress robes of black, gold, and many-colored thread patterns flaring out from him momentarily. "I hope that you shall find all of the dishes presented by my chefs to be interesting, if not all to your taste. Have you selected your cuisine?"

"It's . . . almost impossible, sir," Ariane confessed. "You have sorted the offerings for things that aren't going to poison us and so on, but even then . . . I haven't even an idea of where to start. I don't know the traditions or tastes. But . . . " she glanced at Simon, "I'm not afraid to try new things. We've given you a few of our patterns, which should give you some idea of the range of our taste and smell senses. If Simon does not object, I would leave it entirely up to you. Let your experience be our guide."

Another three-handed touch and a pirouette. "You do my establishment much honor. I shall endeavor to show you the best that the Kitchen has to offer. I thank you for this opportunity."

"No, Mairakag," Simon said, "It is we who thank you, given that so few even dare speak with us these days; it is truly kind of you to accept us into your establishment, with the Anathema declared against us."

In a startlingly human movement, Mairakag Achan drew himself up, three eyes staring in all directions but still somehow focused upon them, the very image of the proud *artiste*. "Anathema? Preposterous! Do the Shade-weavers not eat? Do they not also come here when they seek the finest cuisine of the Arena? There are none in the Arena who would be foolish enough to task me over this, else I should declare Anathema against *them*, and let them try to find a restaurant worthy of the title that would serve them." He pirouetted again. "Please, think no more of it; enjoy your meal, and your time, for here there shall be no intrusions of your outside concerns." The elegantly-clad owner of The Kitchen swept away, a nobleman among his courtiers.

Ariane couldn't restrain a chuckle. "I see, a Faction of one like Orphan," she said quietly to Simon.

"Indeed. Not a Faction in the official sense, but he has apparently been running this restaurant for a very long time—long enough that Orphan calls him 'long-established'—and from what I've heard Mairakag has taught virtually all of the highly-respected multispecies chefs in Nexus Arena at one point or another, and hires the very best to be his kitchen staff. So if other species value their dining experiences—which the very existence of this place shows they do—yes, he can in a sense be a self-made Faction, or an artist above the petty concerns of politics." He took a sip of his own drink. "I'm just glad we were finally able to take this time. I was so busy trying to arrange this, though, I've lost track; what are the others up to right now?"

"DuQuesne is trying to talk with some of the second-ary Factions; he's also been talking off and on with Orphan about possibly arranging a crew for Orphan's ship, there are ways to make money trading and shipping stuff, but Orphan can't captain such a mission himself; he's apparently found it's cost him a great deal each time he's gone off on his own and left the Nexus unattended. Orphan himself has gone with Gabrielle to do some shopping, and Carl, Steve, and Tom are back at *Holy Grail* and our Sphere. Carl says the waterfall generator's about ready to come online, so we'll have at least our own internal power needs met for an indefinite period, and we can get materials we might lack here."

"What about Laila?"

Ariane couldn't restrain a frown. "With Nyanthus at the Faith's Faction House. Their high Temple, I guess. I'm a little worried about that, Simon. Everything I know about her from before was that she was a scientist—a complete analytical fanatic, as far as I could tell."

"Hm. Yes, true. But there are different types of scientists." Simon seemed to be considering his words. At that point, the first course was laid before them, a pair of plates holding long, curving, jointed things, steaming slightly.

Ariane studied them. They looked almost familiar . . . "Are these . . . ?"

" . . . *zikki*? Excellent eye, Captain Austin!" Mairakag said with a quick bow-gesture. "The feeding tendrils of the *zikki*, unlike the capture tentacles, are muscular but not tough, providing a firm, interestingly-textured meat which when steamed in a *klantel* broth should prove a worthy experience."

"The capture tentacles are tough, then?"

The gourmet chef laughed. "A too kind and gentle description. Native cultures of the Arena have been known to use their tentacle sinews as mooring ropes and motive cables. Enjoy."

Ariane picked up the provided utensils, clearly modified for human use, and cut the segmented shell open along the centerline. Red-purple meat wafted a sharp, tangy scent to her nostrils. The texture was, as indicated, interesting, a compressed set of individual slightly chewy fibers which popped something like orange pulp, releasing sparks of quick heat like wasabi that faded into a smoky flavor similar to roast duck with a touch of bacon. "My goodness. That's . . . fantastic."

Simon frowned. "I'm not sure I like the texture. The flavor is a bit . . . strong. But that's just an initial reaction." He took another bite. "About Laila . . . I didn't know her very well either—I'm a physicist and she was focused on the life sciences—but if you look at what we do know about her . . . There are people who explore science because they're curious. They want to *understand*. They want to poke into things and find out how and why they work. That is my principal motive.

"But there are other people who are scientists because they want something to *believe*. Because they like to have a support of substance under their lives. This is, of course, not at all unlike the reasons that people adopt a religion—saying nothing, mind you, about whether any of the religions are correct or not." He put down his spork-like scoop. "I've decided I'm impressed, but I don't particularly like it."

"I'd take your share, but I want space for whatever else he's bringing us," Ariane said. "I did look up Laila's simple bio that we have on board. That actually makes sense; she was raised almost in isolation from anything nonhuman until she was almost an adult, and when she visited Earth for the first time was completely fascinated by all the lifeforms she saw. Like . . . a religious revelation, maybe."

Simon nodded. "Her integration with multiple AISages could not have helped. I don't know exactly what Mandallon did to bring her back; was all of her there, or did the . . . well, power he used have to patch what was left back together? And what did it use for patching? Perhaps fragments of the only other persona available at the time—Mandallon. And not necessarily with Mandallon being aware of all this, mind you."

Ariane frowned. "That . . . would mean that she's not exactly the person we brought on board."

"True," Simon said, finishing his *nallitiri*, "but we all change with time and events, Ariane. I am quite sure *you* are not the person who first came on board *Holy Grail*."

She had to admit he had a point. And patched or not, Laila was definitely a person, not a vegetable, and Gabrielle had said in private that she wouldn't have given any significant chance that she could be restored at all back home. "Too much depending on those AISages and such, and all that's gone," she'd said. "If she'd made regular backups and we'd had the chance to apply them right away . . . but by now too much time's gone by."

"*Touché*," Ariane responded to Simon. "And at least she's functional." This wasn't the kind of discussion she had wanted to have on this night out, though. Time to start in the right direction. "So what have *you* been up to these days, Simon? We generally haven't seen much of you, you've been busy with the Analytic and Dr. Relgof."

"I suppose that's true. I've been trying to figure out how the universe works, I guess you could say."

"What do you mean?"

"Well." Simon leaned back in his chair as the next course—something looking like blue gooseberries in wine sauce—was set before them. He leaned back in. "I was intrigued by things Selpa'A At said before, about how nanoprobe replicators do not work in our own space. Obviously they work within our solar system."

"Yes," Ariane said, remembering the lecture by the leader of the Vengeance. "You said something about the 'Fermi Paradox' then." She tried some of the new dish, but this time she didn't like it; the texture was gluey, the flavor too subtle and heavy. It did, however, make an interesting dip for the *zikki*. And Simon was eating it up.

"Exactly," he said between bites. "And DuQuesne once spoke with me and Mio . . . " he paused as he was reminded of his own now-silent AISage, " . . . about unmanned probes to other systems seeming to fail, which fits very well with what Selpa told us. Now, the Vengeance see this whole phenomenon as a hostile one. It occurred to me—as I am sure I has to others—that you could interpret it very differently, specifically as a very positive action. The Voidbuilders wanted to make sure that no single species would dominate all reality, and thus prevent other species from ever evolving. In other words, without the Voidbuilders' interference, we would never have evolved at all. And, in all likelihood, neither would any of the species currently extant in the Arena, since given the apparent lifespan of intelligent species, none of those here are part of even the second or third generation of the Arena. We're not even really sure how old the Arena is—a hundred million years old? A billion?"

"Can you explain that? Not the age, I mean, but why we wouldn't have evolved?"

Simon nodded. "The basic idea is that once any species evolves that has an interest in exploration outside of its own solar system—and for a number of reasons, it seems very likely if not inevitable that most species would—they quickly realize that they can (A) explore much more efficiently with unmanned probes; (B) terraform worlds as they go with appropriately-designed probes; (C) even carry the basis of their biology with them in the probes, building up the initial population *ex nihilo*, as it were; and (D) with sufficiently advanced technology, take normally useless matter systems, such as blue giant stars and so on, and disassemble them for use later, effectively extending the habitable lifetime of the universe."

While she hadn't been familiar with the concept before, she grasped the outcome now. "Basically you're saying they'd have come here and either put our solar system into storage, disassembled it for use in a Dyson sphere, or made sure it was properly settled by *them* already."

"Exactly. The reason it's a paradox, of course, is that by everything *else* we know, it's not all that hard for life, and even intelligent life, to come into existence . . . so why aren't they here?"

"Ah. I see I have had one success with each of you. For diners with whom I have yet to gain familiarity, this is acceptable," Mairakag Achan said as he swept by the table. "I shall have to get your full evaluation later, if you would indulge me."

"Oh, certainly!" Ariane answered.

She turned back to find Simon's leaf-green gaze meeting hers. "You know, Ariane, I didn't really come here intending to bore you to death with lectures."

Oh, well, now we're getting to the fun part! "It's been . . . a long time since I had a chance for a date at all. Out of practice." *He is pretty darn gorgeous, though; that pure-white hair and those silly glasses work well together. And I love a good accent.*

"Obviously the same with me, or I might have found a more subtle opening line." He smiled disarmingly.

"Subtlety usually flies over my head." She mimed something zipping just above her hair.

He smiled again. "Then I'll try to be courteous, but not subtle. I realized I found you devastatingly attractive shortly after we met, about the time of my first similarly devastating *faux pas*. And you seemed not uninterested at the time. There is a certain chemistry between us, yes?" He reached out and gently took her hand.

Whew! Nice little tingles up my arm there. "I think so. Yes. But . . . " *But? This isn't a time to be saying but, girl, what's wrong with you?*

The elegant head tilted. "Perhaps I'd better not ask what would have followed that last word. Yet . . . Might it simply be that despite undeniable attraction, there's a certain other person you're more interested in?"

"Um . . . " *Hey, there, that's a great start. "Um." Speechwriters down the centuries will be quoting you.* "Who do you mean?"

"I would think it is obvious . . . or perhaps not, to you." Simon's smile was a tiny bit less bright.

"Well . . . look, part of the problem is the whole commanding officer thing, okay?"

Simon pushed back his glasses slightly. "Hm. Yes, there is that. But we are operating in a very different setting from the traditional vessel. And we have no way of knowing how long, or short, our wait to return home will be."

You're tap dancing and you know it, girl. "Oh, hell. You mean DuQuesne."

Simon nodded, white hair moving slightly over his face and then back.

"Argh. I wish I could answer that clearly, Simon. I really wish I could. There's times I think he's the most incredibly attractive guy I've ever met, then he's just plain scary, or so remote that I don't know how to *reach* him. You, you're . . . cool and collected, and I can see something not so cool underneath. And I like that. A lot."

There was a touch of pink on the aristocratic cheekbones. "Thank you. And you're direct, and fiery, and you have a fierce joy in everything you do that, to be honest, leaves me breathless. Not to mention that you're beautiful. I must say your choice of dark blue hair was inspired."

She blushed at the compliment. "Choice isn't the word; that just happened."

Simon gave a puzzled stare. "Gene or biomodification isn't something that 'just happens,' my dear; anyone around you as long as I've been can tell that your hair is naturally blue, so to speak."

"Unnaturally naturally blue, yes," Ariane agreed with a laugh. "But that's the truth. I only have one actual biomod, I was *born* with blue hair. The docs said it's not entirely unheard of; it usually means someone back in your family tree a generation or two had some kind of tweak done, and it pops up as hair color, sometimes a skin tone shift, and so on. Mine wasn't too bad, no reason to fix it."

"Well, that's something new to *me*. I've never heard of such a thing. Do you know who it was? Your father or mother?"

"Not for sure. Neither mom or dad had direct gene mods, but Dad's mom took off shortly after he was born, and Mom's parents . . . might have been any of a couple of pairs of people."

"Communal marriage?"

"Poly community, actually. Compared to them, Mom and Dad were practically throwbacks to a past era like Grandaddy."

"So you *do* have one biomod, you say?" Simon seemed to have decided to let things just go as they would, which was something of a relief. She didn't want to get pushed one way or another yet, especially since she did like Simon Sandrisson. A lot. But this question . . .

"Did I . . . yes, I did say that." She rolled her eyes. "It's a pretty stupid mod, and the kind of thing that only someone in my kind of profession—or maybe a thrillgang or something like that—would get. It just was so tough to get done that I hate to go through the trouble of getting rid of it. I—"

Green light suddenly appeared before her. "Ariane?"

Timing! Everything's about timing here, and the timing always sucks! "What is it, Gabrielle?"

There was a slight nervous backtone to the normally warm and calm Southern accent. "Somehow I've gotten separated from Orphan. I was in a shop browsing, and I turned around, and *poof*, no sign of him anywhere. I don't have to tell you he's not exactly easy to lose sight of, that man."

That's bad. What could have happened? "Where are you?"

"Grand Arcade. About halfway between Celenvia Fabrics and the casino what kicked Steve out."

Which means she's got quite a walk to get anywhere the robocabs can reach her. And with the Anathema on, I don't like the idea of her alone—of any of us alone. "Orphan!" she called. Another green ball . . . but this one sparkled red. Either Orphan was deliberately refusing contact, or he was far too busy to answer. And given the circumstances, "busy" would be a very bad thing.

She looked almost helplessly at Simon. "I'm sorry, Simon—"

"No need to apologize, let us go immediately!" Simon was already standing. "Mairakag Achan, a thousand apologies, but an emergency calls us away."

"I hope you shall be able to return soon, then." The alien gourmet had, of course, seen many similar events in his years there, she was sure. "Your account shall pay for what has already been created, but for no more."

"Thank you, sir. It was wonderful so far." She turned back to the other green sphere. "We're coming, Gabrielle. Find the least conspicuous point you can; we'll be there very soon."

Let's hope it's soon enough.

Chapter 60

The Grand Arcade was crowded, and many of the people there recognized the humans—perhaps not as individuals, but as a faction. Most of these moved aside, out of their way, almost afraid to touch. There were a few, however, who would subtly, or not-so-subtly, arrange to block their passage, impede their progress. Ariane knew better than to try to just shove her way past or bull through, but it was so damned *hard* to be patient and cautious when she was worried about Gabrielle. Not that Gabrielle was helpless, no, but with everything that had happened . . .

. . . and finally she came around the corner. "Oh, *crap*."

"*Shimatta*," concurred Simon next to her. "Of all the worst possible luck . . ."

Gabrielle Wolfe was in the midst of the arcade main promenade, and circling her were six of the Blessed to

Serve; Sethrik's darker mottled coloring and slightly taller figure was clearly recognizable, as was Vantak, slightly to his right. Scattered about the feet of the Blessed were broken jars, powders, torn strapping. All the massed aliens had given some way to the Blessed, but were watching with all the avidity of a human crowd, talking and whispering and buzzing in their own languages in a half-translated babble.

"Let me *through!*" Ariane hissed, and started shoving her way past the rubberneckers.

It seemed to her that Sethrik's head turned, very slightly, and that if he had been looking extremely carefully he might have caught sight of Ariane. But in that moment, the black-green arm lashed out and sent Gabrielle spinning, crashing into one of the other Blessed, who didn't budge. The small blonde shook her head, then leaped up into a combat pose.

No, no! Ariane opened her mouth to tell Gabrielle to drop; she'd seen Sethrik in action, knew that while DuQuesne could fold the Blessed leader up like a cheap cardboard box, and that she herself could probably hold her own against him, Gabrielle didn't stand a chance.

But things were happening way too fast, and as soon as it was clear that the human in front of him was ready to fight, Sethrik lashed out again. To Ariane's surprise, Gabrielle did not just go down, but blocked, parried, struck back. *That's right . . . Mentor said she'd had military-grade enhancements, and Carl said she implied she'd take* him *on if he wanted.* But Sethrik wasn't playing a game; one of the other Blessed struck at her from behind, and even though Gabrielle managed to block that, she couldn't stop Sethrik's next strike. This time his circle parted to let the *Holy Grail's* doctor go tumbling away unimpeded. Ariane could see, as she finally broke through the encircling onlookers, that there was blood running down Gabrielle's face, and the blue eyes were dazed and shaken. She caught Simon, whose face was furious as a samurai in battle, and pushed him in Gabrielle's direction, and then bellowed "What the *hell* do you think you're doing, Sethrik?"

The leader of the Blessed jumped slightly at her shout and spun to face her. She was even more furious as he did so; not only could she see a smear of red on his hand, the way he stood was familiarly arrogant, the usual posture of the Blessed. "Your crewperson deliberately impeded us, causing us to lose much of our valuable purchases, and then had the arrogance to accuse *us* of having run into *her*."

"And for that you're beating the hell out of her?" Ariane demanded incredulously. "You know, I'd half-decided you weren't all that bad, Sethrik, but now I know you're a complete asshole, a bastard, *and* a coward!"

The crowd around them grew suddenly silent. This barely registered with Ariane.

Sethrik took a careful, measured step forward. "What did you say?" he hissed. The stinger-tipped tail began to rise.

"What, are you *deaf*, too, as well as a bully?" she snarled. A glance back showed that Gabrielle was still not standing, sitting up while Simon checked her eyes. "I happen to know that Gabrielle was trying to stay out of *everyone*'s way the last few minutes, so you're *also* a liar."

"She was quite ready to fight me a moment ago, *Captain* Austin, and I simply instructed her. Or are you going to argue with the evidence of your eyes."

Her eyes were just about ready to see nothing but red haze. She'd never *felt* this angry before, but she knew she had to stay in control. "Sure, I saw her . . . after you knocked her down. Really impressive, taking on a *doctor* who weighs about a third your mass. Why not try taking on someone who can fight back, you son of a bitch?"

The eyes that met hers were strangely unreadable. Over his shoulder, she saw Orphan shoving his way through the crowd, trying to reach them. Something else was happening behind her, some kind of commotion, but she was focused on Sethrik, who finally sneered back, "If someone were to dare issue a Challenge on that score, I might even indulge them. *If* they dared."

"The last Challenge you were in, you lost." She smiled, a humorless grin, as she drove that home.

"There are fewer tricks in other challenges to allow simple fortune to rule your day, Human," Sethrik said.

"Fine," she said, not dropping her gaze. Vaguely she heard someone behind her, shouting something. "You want a Challenge? You've got one. I Challenge you, Sethrik."

As the words left her mouth, she felt some of the fury starting to ebb, and saw the Blessed's shoulders and wings droop slightly, the tail sag back to the ground, as he said, "And by the laws of the Arena I hear your Challenge, and accept your Challenge."

DuQuesne was at her side. "Captain, you haven't . . . "

A cold chill worked its way down her spine, as Sethrik turned to the side, still speaking.

"And by those laws I give to you my designated representative, whom you shall meet in the Challenge."

I should have realized. I should have felt it. Should have seen by the very fact that Gabrielle was hurt and nothing intervened. Stupid, stupid, stupid!

Coalescing from the thousand thousand shadows beneath the crowd, flowing in and forming darkness into solidity, Amas-Garao materialized before her.

Chapter 61

DuQuesne stared grimly at the dark figure confronting Ariane. Simon had called him as he and Ariane had been looking for Gabrielle, and DuQuesne had come immediately, a sinking feeling in his gut that something was badly wrong.

And it couldn't be worse. The Captain hadn't heard him telling her to stop as he came through the crowd, and he'd gotten there just in time to hear her issue the Challenge. *Bastard did it again. Worked her emotions somehow. Couldn't do it to me, so he had to target someone else, especially the Captain, so there'd be no doubt about our Faction being committed to the Challenge.*

He could see that Ariane had already reached the same conclusion—she probably had first-hand evidence in her own thought processes. The tall, blue-haired Captain of *Holy Grail* turned slowly on the Shadeweaver, hands balling into fists. "You incredible son of a *bitch*. You *made* me walk straight into that!"

Amas-Garao's deep voice echoed with amusement. "I forced you to do nothing, Captain Austin. Can you tell me truly that it is impossible that you would be angry enough to accept such a Challenge?"

No, she can't. It's blasted unlikely that she'd lose her head that badly, but it's not totally impossible. And she's too blasted honest to try to lie about it.

The cold, black glare Ariane focused on Amas-Garao would have worried just about anyone else; DuQuesne didn't see that it affected the Shadeweaver at all. "Fine, then. I suppose you already have the basic terms of the Challenge worked out?"

"But of course, Captain Austin. We of the Shadeweavers' Guild are a traditional people, following the ancient ways. Thus do I say to you that we shall resolve this Challenge—as you implied to my good friend Sethrik— in the most ancient manner of personal combat."

DuQuesne noticed Sethrik didn't look particularly pleased by the outcome. *The Blessed have been in a kind of tight spot lately; used all their credit with the Faith in securing our own Sphere, and the Faith never liked them much. The Shadeweavers must've made them an offer they couldn't refuse.* He noticed Orphan at the edge of the crowd, immobile, wings half-covering his arms, head down. *And there's the last piece of the puzzle. But first things first.*

"Personal combat," repeated Ariane. "And I suppose you have an idea what you want from us, if you win?"

"It is even so, Captain Austin," Amas-Garao replied calmly. "We want Dr. Marc C. DuQuesne."

"Don't you people ever give up?" DuQuesne said. "I am *not joining you*. That's the end of statement."

A hint of a sharp smile flickered inside the darkness. "I do not believe you quite understand, Doctor. Such a price is well within the stakes for a Challenge. It, of course, implies a far greater price if we were to lose," his tone became ironic, "but I do not fear that turn of events."

"Will you accept nothing else?"

The Shadeweaver seemed to consider. "Let it never be said that the Shadeweavers are unwilling to bargain. There is one other price we would accept, although Dr. DuQuesne is our preference." He gestured. "You, Captain, would be an acceptable substitute."

In any other circumstance, the dumbfounded astonishment on Ariane's face might have been comical. "*Me?*"

"You, Captain. Our auguries and visions, our research and questions, have shown that you have done much to bind your little Faction together; you have confronted and won a Challenge yourself. While the one named DuQuesne is in his way even more unique, there is much valuable in you and . . . your soul, if you will."

She glanced over at DuQuesne. "I'm . . . sorry, Marc. Sorry to all of you. I've screwed this one up bad."

DuQuesne shook his head. "Worry about it later. Can't we just drop the Challenge?"

"Alas," Orphan said quietly, finally having made his way to them. "It is not so easy."

"You've got a hell of a lot of nerve showing your face anywhere *near* me right now, Orphan," Ariane said evenly. "After that stunt—"

"I was honest with you, Captain Austin." Despite his words, Orphan looked neither proud nor particularly defensive. He just looked . . . tired, a little sad. "I had not quite finished my final obligation to the Shadeweavers. One service remained, which at the time I could not tell you."

DuQuesne glanced at Sethrik. "I get you."

"Yes . . . Yes, I suspected you would, Dr. DuQuesne," Orphan said. "The requirement was simple; that at some time I would have to cooperate, on a single task, with the Blessed, and the Shadeweavers would tell me that time."

"So you left and tipped them off as to where Gabrielle was." Ariane was not asking a question, but making a statement.

"Yes."

"And you are completely free of any obligation to the Shadeweavers now?"

Orphan gave a bob-bow. "Completely, Captain Austin."

"Fine." DuQuesne could see that she was now totally under control; anger might still be inside, but the exterior was calm, cold, rational. "Obligations and so on are the foundation of the Arena. You did what you have to, I guess. I won't cut off my nose to spite my face."

Orphan blinked. "That last . . . metaphor came through in a particularly disgusting fashion, and I am not quite clear on the meaning."

Ariane managed a tiny smile, barely visible to DuQuesne. "It means I'm not going to just lose a potentially huge resource because I'm pissed off at you, Orphan. I'm not *happy* with you but I'll get over it. So tell me why I can't just drop the Challenge."

Look at him straighten up. That's part of what the Shadeweaver sees, I'll bet. Here Orphan is, three thousand years old, sole survivor of his Faction, and he was standing there worried about what this Johnny-come-lately Captain thought of him. She's got it, in ton-lots, what my namesake's creator called 'look of eagles.'

"Because," Orphan was saying, "unfortunately while a person Challenged can choose to decline, the Challenger has implicitly agreed. He or she cannot just back out because they realize they have made a terrible mistake. In short, a Challenger backing out is as costly as a Challenger losing the Challenge."

Ariane's jaw dropped. "You mean that if we choose *not* to fight this son of a bitch—"

"That he gets either you or Dr. DuQuesne, yes."

"And what if," Ariane said dangerously, "I refuse to do *either*?"

Orphan shrugged. "These are the Laws of the Arena, Captain Austin. Do you believe that it cannot enforce them?"

Ariane winced at that. *No,* thought DuQuesne, *I'm quite sure the Arena can, and will, enforce those laws.*

Ariane wasn't giving up yet."What about the fact this . . . person messed with my head?"

"Supposition," Amas-Garao said, his tone amused and patient. "No proof of that exists."

"What if there *was* proof?"

Orphan sighed, his wings curving forward again, and DuQuesne shook his head. "Unfortunately," Orphan said, "such a protest only carries weight if one can seriously contend that the sequence of events that led to the Challenge would be impossible without the interference. And the Shadeweavers, as you know, enjoy . . . somewhat greater latitude than the rest of us."

"I noticed," Gabrielle Wolfe put in. She was still looking a little unsteady, supported by Simon, but her eyes were clear, and she seemed not too badly hurt. "Sethrik hit me, but none of those Adjudicators showed up. Would've spoiled the setup, I guess."

"It would have been inconvenient, yes," agreed Amas-Garao.

"So the only real choice we have is either meet you in the Arena—someone versus you in personal combat—or we just hand over either me or Dr. DuQuesne without a fight."

"That is indeed the essence of the matter," Amas-Garao said cheerfully.

"I see."

Ariane stood staring into nothingness for so long that finally DuQuesne touched her arm. "Captain . . . ?"

She turned and gestured for him, and the others, to follow. The crowd backed away, while the Shadeweaver stayed, unmoving and alone, even the Blessed having now moved far away.

Once they were a distance from Amas-Garao, Ariane turned back to them. "All right, people. I've stepped in it big—not without help, but it's still my problem. Any comments?"

"There is no point in fighting," Orphan said bluntly. "You have *seen* him in combat, Captain, and he was not—for most of that—even trying particularly hard."

"You sure of that?" DuQuesne asked. "He seemed pretty serious before."

Orphan flicked his hands out emphatically. "Understand me well, my friends. I have seen the Shadeweavers, watched them for many years indeed, and Amas-Garao is one of their best, old and subtle, and even what appears as anger, temper, ill-judgment, is almost certainly the result of deep policy and contemplation. He studies. He observes. He tests. He does nothing without thought, and of his true capabilities reveals little."

Ariane set her jaw, muscles so taut that DuQuesne could see every detail beneath her skin. "So you're saying I just hand over myself or one of my crew?"

Orphan looked torn. *Poor bastard doesn't understand our attitude at all.* "Captain, I'll take this guy. Maybe we can set up some of the duel terms to favor us. He's not indestructible."

Ariane shook her head. "I don't like the whole situation, but putting you in that ring I like even less."

Orphan looked up. "I am sorry for the part I have played in this, Captain Austin, but I want to be clear that under no circumstances will I take that place in the Arena against a Shadeweaver. I have withstood them once, I will not do so again."

"I don't expect you to." Ariane raised her voice. "Amas-Garao, you demand a great deal, especially if you would take our people and their knowledge and turn them against us. In a way, one might say you threaten our entire Faction."

Amas-Garao bowed. "I hear your concern. Let me ease this worry, then. The one who comes with us shall not be turned against his former comrades, nor controlled by us to do our bidding. If he—or she—has the strength, they will be one of us. While they may not be of your people, we shall make of them no enemy of yours; indeed, we shall be generous, and account you a small ally of the Shadeweavers, forgiving the prior Anathema, and instead offering you our assistance in many things. Of such an offer, many might say we are not demanding a price, but giving you a bargain of much worth."

"I see," Ariane said. DuQuesne saw that distant look come into her eyes again, and for minutes she stood motionless, while the silent crowd watched.

Suddenly her eyes focused and she turned to him. "Dr. DuQuesne!"

This is it. "Captain."

"I have a direct order for you, and the rest of you as witnesses."

"Ariane, I don't think . . . " began Simon.

"Dr. Sandrisson, I am the captain. You all agreed to that, and I am now acting in that capacity. Do all of you understand this?"

And she's about ninety Brinell numbers harder than a diamond drill right now. "Yes, sir."

"This is my order: under no circumstances whatsoever, Dr. DuQuesne, are you to allow the Shadeweavers access to your person again. You will not be risked, you will not risk yourself. You are far too valuable to humanity for us to take that risk, as you possess certain capabilities and talents that exist nowhere else in human space."

Dammit! And I gave my word! Can't even argue with her right now, given the conditions. "Understood, Captain."

It was the hardest two words he'd ever spoken.

Ariane turned back to Amas-Garao. "Fighting you would be incredibly stupid. I've seen what you can do. You've got abilities that I can't even understand, and you're as tough as anything I've seen. Maybe some of that comes from your Shadeweaver power, I don't know. Whatever the source, you were able to take us all on and not even work very much at it. I'd be an idiot to try to do it by myself."

Amas-Garao took a step forward. "Then I welcome y—"

"*I was not finished!*"

Ariane's shout cracked across the huge Arcade like a gunshot, halting even the Shadeweaver in his tracks. "Wh . . . what?"

"I said it would be incredibly *stupid*. But to just sell one of my crew for protection from this Challenge would be *cowardly*. It would be morally *wrong*, the action of one who would, in the words of one of our greatest men, 'give up essential Liberty to purchase a little temporary Safety.' It would be irresponsible of me to simply hand myself over to you; I am the captain, I am the leader, I am responsible for my Faction."

She had that *grin* again, that grin that was half-joyous, half-shark, and DuQuesne felt a warm chill down his spine as he saw it. "You want one of us that badly, to teach us a lesson, to learn what we really are? Well, I'll *teach* you what we really are! I'll meet you in personal combat, Amas-Garao—and come ready to lose, because by *God* you'd better remember this: *two* of us kicked an entire scouting expedition of Molothos off our Sphere; I won a challenge against the leader of the Blessed by going up against odds not *one* of you would dare even contemplate, and the last time we met we smacked you down on the doorsteps of your own Faction House, something not even our best allies thought was possible, so I will damned well *take* that chance instead of give it up!"

She took Gabrielle's other arm. "We'll finish working out the details after I get her back and all of my people assembled."

For the first time Amas-Garao's voice held something other than amusement and certainty; it was confused, slightly angry, a man balked by an unreasonable child. "There *is* no chance, you foolish creature!"

"More than you think," DuQuesne said, with his own hard grin. "You see, there's one point she's obviously thought of that you haven't."

"What is that, I ask?"

DuQuesne's grin widened. *It's still a piss-poor chance, but I know what she's thinking.* "Since I'm not the prize—having been specifically forbidden to be—*she* is. And that means you'll have to be awful careful not to break the prize you're fighting for, doesn't it?"

And for that, Amas-Garao had no answer, as they left through the parting crowd.

Chapter 62

"But of course she may bring weapons," Amas-Garao said. A hint of a smile—Ariane wondered if that was a real expression, or one put on for her benefit—showed within the cowl. "Any weapon that is powered solely by the combatant, that is."

"How very convenient for you, Shadeweaver," Nyanthus said. The Faith had volunteered to be the Advocates for Humanity in this Challenge. "As all of your powers are of the essence of your self, this strikes us as rather one-sided."

A tossing motion of the head from Amas-Garao. "It is of little concern to *us* that Captain Austin has chosen a Challenge she cannot win. I will not acquiesce to the use of powered weaponry; while it is true that a Shadeweaver may often triumph even against the most powerful weapons devised by any race, that is hardly the way of a true duel of warriors. She may bring any weapons that carry no force of their own, and that is all." Sethrik, still looking somehow unhappy and ashamed, bob-bowed his agreement.

No one else had stepped forward to act as the Shade-weaver Advocate, but this did not seem to concern Amas-Garao; he was conducting the negotiations himself, with his less-than-enthusiastic Advocate as pure formality, and Ariane found that particularly galling. Sethrik served a regime that was perhaps the most horrifying she'd heard of, but as an individual she'd come to respect him, and he didn't deserve this kind of abuse.

Her annoyance was useful to keep her focused on the problem at hand: namely, arranging things to her best advantage. "Fine, I won't argue that one any more. Our own traditions would generally agree with you. But one thing *I* will not back down on is that *you* have to have certain limitations on what you can do."

"What sort of limitations, Captain Austin? For I will accept very few such; as I said, it is no concern of mine that you have chosen to place yourself in the way of an infalling asteroid."

"Oh, I'm not going to try to say you can't use your special powers—much as I'd like to, that'd be like saying I have to fight with one foot in a bucket of sealing compound and both hands tied behind my back. But this is a fight, a duel, and it's *not* going to be decided by you messing with my head. I insist that you be forbidden to use your powers to touch on my mind, autonomic systems, and so on in any way, shape, or form."

Amas-Garao straightened. "This is a purely arbitrary restriction—"

"—yet one that has precedent," Sethrik said, also straightening, his wingcases sliding fully back to their normal position. Ariane could see the Shadeweaver twitch at the tone of the Blessed's voice, the tone of a man who had found a way to serve his own honor despite being in the service of another. "In the duels fought with species such as the Rodeskri—that of the honored Nyanthus—it is specifically forbidden that they utilize the species-specific capability of releasing a wide-area hallucinogenic/soporific gas, unless their opposition is known to be immune or is permitted sufficient protective gear."

Amas-Garao tilted his head dangerously. "An Advocate—"

"Is supposed to serve the interests of his represented patron, but not at the expense of justice," Nyanthus interrupted. Ariane's grin answered the cheerful undertone present in that of the First Guide of the Faith. "And he is quite correct; the specific reasoning behind that ruling was that the Dreamsleep directly interfered with the participation of the opponent in the duel, by removing their own self-direction, initiative, and will. In a broader sense, this is applied to all psychoactive, generally distributed materials in a personal confrontation."

The Shadeweaver stood immobile and silent for a moment, and Ariane felt tension growing in the room. Then Amas-Garao gave a deep chuckle and a careless gesture. "Well enough played, then. I confess that in the ways of my original people, the feelings on these matters would be much the same. It would be no combat at all if I could either convince you to surrender, or drive your emotions to remove your reason and thus render you ineffective and powerless. So be it. I shall use no powers that touch upon your mind or any other part of you without doing so in a direct physical manner. This does not mean that such methods will be ones that you can defend against, of course, but they will be ones that even Captain Austin—as a clearly honest and honorable opponent—will not consider any more unfair than the existence of my powers themselves."

"Are there other conditions to be placed on the contest?" the neutral voice of the Arena inquired.

"Ah, yes, there is one," Amas-Garao said, with an elaborate casualness. "Self-powered or not, my opponent will bring no device with her that is intended to suppress, shield against, or specifically counter my powers in a general sense, unless said device is one that her faction could and has created."

You don't want a repeat of that little beating that Orphan and DuQuesne gave you after Orphan unlimbered his secret weapon. Can't say I blame you.

Nyanthus's symbiotes weaved a complex thinking pattern around the central trunk. "But she is free to devise specific defenses against your abilities, so long as they are powered purely by Ariane herself, or from the nature of the materials she constructs them from?"

"I would have it no other way. I am simply excluding something that would seem, to me, to be the equivalent of your prohibition of my mind-control or psychoactive agents. Depriving a Shadeweaver of his powers is very much the same, would you not agree?"

Ariane saw by the uneasy movements of Nyanthus's openwork tendril-top that he was trying to figure out a way to argue that. "Never mind, Nyanthus. I agree with him, actually." *And I don't think Orphan has such a gadget that I could power, anyway, and if he did, he's not giving it to me. Amas-Garao's just covering all his bases like I'm covering mine.* "Agreed."

"This is the final condition?" the Arena inquired.

Can't think of any more that I could sneak by. "I'm done."

"We are finished," Amas-Garao said.

"Then the conditions are set, as follows: the two participants in the Challenge will be Challenger Ariane Austin, for the Faction of Humanity, and Challenged Amas-Garao for the Faction of the Shadeweavers. The basic form of the Challenge will be personal combat. Both participants may use weapons powered by their own natural inherent abilities, with the exception of influences on the mind or methods to negate the inherent abilities of the participants.

"The combat will take place within the Core Ring of Nexus Arena. The two combatants will enter simultaneously, from opposite sides of the Core Ring. The Arena will signal the beginning of the Challenge.

"Once the Challenge combat has begun, neither combatant will be able to leave the Core Ring, no matter what the circumstances. The Arena will maintain a protective seal around the entire Core Ring, thus permitting spectators to observe safely.

"Victory conditions are as follows: if the opponent is dead, if the opponent is unable to continue fighting for more than eight seconds, if the opponent yields the contest, if the opponent attempts to cheat any of the competitive conditions. In the event of a tie—both contestants meeting loss/victory conditions to within a tenth of a second—the Challenge will be re-negotiated; it will be possible at that point for either party to withdraw from the Challenge without prejudice." The Arena paused. "Do all of you understand and accept these conditions?"

Ariane took a deep breath. "I understand and accept these conditions."

"I, Amas-Garao, also understand and accept these conditions."

"**Then the Challenge shall be undertaken in precisely three days, seven hours, twenty-one minutes from this moment.**" That would, Ariane knew, put it at a time which would be the equivalent of mid-evening for the Arena—primetime, as Steve would say.

Thinking of Steve reminded her of one last issue. "Arena, one more inquiry, please."

"**State inquiry.**"

"As all know, we must keep a constant presence in our Sphere, or forfeit our current status. Yet all of our people have a great interest in the outcome of this Challenge. Is there a way for them to observe?"

A pause. Then, "**Precedent exists for this request. A display will be generated within your Sphere.**"

"Thank you, Arena."

"**Accepted.**" A subliminal tension—perhaps barely-perceptible white noise, perhaps something a lot more esoteric—seemed to vanish, and Ariane knew that the Arena, having made all arrangements, was now no longer focused on them at all.

Amas-Garao bowed, a nearly-human gesture that gave her hints of a very supple, not-quite-human structure beneath the robes. "Then we shall meet again . . . soon. I will not wish you luck, but I hope to see you perform well. Until then . . . farewell." The Shadeweaver sank downward, shadows running away in all directions as though Amas-Garao were melting into nothingness, and he was gone.

"Creepy bastard," she muttered. "Sethrik, thank you."

The leader of the Blessed to Serve bob-bowed. "I am . . . pleased to balance the debt owed you. Rare is the time that we would permit ourselves to be used in such a fashion, and it is an offense to the Minds that we be so demeaned. I fear that we shall be enemies often, Captain Ariane Austin, but I would have it that we respect and honor each other."

So would I. She dropped to the floor and gave a full pushup-bow. "Take this as token of my agreement, Sethrik."

Sethrik returned the gesture enthusiastically, and gripped hands with her in the human manner. "Though I acted as his Advocate, I will not be hoping for luck to be with the Shadeweaver. I will hope that you shall be glorious in your defeat."

You can't even imagine my victory, huh? Well, to be honest, knowing what I do about Amas-Garao . . . neither can I.

Chapter 63

"Good *Lord*, Marc, where did you guys come *up* with all this stuff?"

DuQuesne laughed, feeling a knot in his gut loosen slightly at Ariane's genuine surprise. "From all over, but you can credit some of it to Hyperion. See, a lot of the selected, um, template characters would have pretty damn strange worlds, their own signature weapons, that kind of thing, and they had at least ten AISages and four different human researchers working on ways to make something that worked close to the original's specs. Sure, in some cases it was pretty much impossible, but they came damn close in others."

Ariane poked her way around the mass of assorted weaponry and armor. "And I thought I was going to have a problem *before* figuring out what to take. What's this?"

He looked at the armored bodysuit she was indicating, with an internal tracery of lighter lines worked into a pattern all over the suit. "That was actually Simon's idea. Simon?"

The Japanese-Nordic scientist bowed and turned to Ariane. "As I read them, the fighting conditions are that you cannot use any weapons not powered by the participants. I did not, however, see any rules there that prevent you from letting Amas-Garao power *your* weapons. That armor—which is of course mostly ring-carbon composite with flexible mesh and thixotropic impact response—incorporates a superconductor mesh which should absorb at least some of the electrical energy that he seems to favor as a primary attack. The charge runs through here, where it is channeled into distributed superconductor loop batteries; you can link into it with your headware transceiver to trigger discharges at any of these four points."

DuQuesne saw a delighted look on her face. "Why, that's brilliant, Simon!"

"Which, of course, led the rest of us to make sure that there's some nice conductive channels built into all your other weapons," DuQuesne said. "Hit, discharge, and keep hitting until he says 'uncle!'—or until he can't say anything."

A pained expression crossed her features. "Marc, I don't want to kill him."

"Arrie, don't worry about that—worry about whether he's going to kill you!" Gabrielle said firmly. "I may be a doctor, but I'm not stupid, and it'd be really stupid of us to worry about anything but what you have to do."

"He won't kill me," Ariane said, certainty in her voice. DuQuesne could tell she was tense, but getting more into the kind of tension she'd had before the race, rather than the kind of tension someone who might be doomed to die might have. "That's one of my major advantages. He isn't getting DuQuesne, and if he tries to use any real big guns on me, he might lose by winning. And with him not able to meddle with my thinking, I can at least keep it on a physical level I might be able to exploit . . . especially with tricks like this."

"I still think it's damn unfair that they let the Challenge go through at all," Steve grumbled.

"Like I said before, I don't think the Arena is entirely concerned with 'fair,' " DuQuesne said. "And as we had Mandallon verify, Amas-Garao was *very* careful to not meddle with any of her choices *after* making the Challenge." *Which was damn disappointing, because not only might it have made it possible for us to argue our way out of this mess, it would* also *have let me argue them into letting me take the captain's place.*

Because good as she is, Ariane's going to get her ass handed to her in this fight, no matter what tricks I try to give her.

"There's no *way* I can carry all of this stuff," Ariane said finally.

"Pick and choose, then," Tom Cussler said. "I let 'em go wild on the construction—I can always feed the stuff you don't use back into the AIWish."

"A shame about that ruling on the drugs and toxins," Laila said. "I had been thinking of some concealable and effective drug dispersal methods to help even the odds."

"I appreciate the thought, Laila," Ariane said with one of the sharp smiles DuQuesne liked so much. "But I want to win this one straight-up." She picked up a complicated-looking wrist-mounted device. "This . . . Carl, you didn't!"

The controls expert grinned. "Took it right out of your character file. Astrella's Wrath of God."

First weapon he made, actually, DuQuesne recalled. *Odd . . . he did that even before the rest of us started in, but now that I look at the design, it already has conductive channels. Maybe he was ahead of us on that. The weapon could be easily used, if I understand the design right, to ground out a lot of Amas-Garao's thunderball trick.*

"Well, then how could I turn that down?" DuQuesne watched as she picked up the multifaceted, thick, complex device and locked it onto her wrist, a flat-levered panel extending from it across her palm; she finished the locking with a fluttering gesture that DuQuesne suspected was associated with the virtual game character that used the odd weapon. "You know, I feel like a kid in a lethal candy store. I'm taking the armor, no doubt, and my sword. What else?"

"A helmet," Gabrielle suggested. "We've got several—"

Ariane shook her head. "I hate helmets. Even the best restrict my field of view and muffle the sound. Yes, I know the arguments, but I won't wear one." Gabrielle sighed and shook her head, but clearly recognized an argument she wouldn't win.

"Take this." He handed her a small, thick rod, saw her raise her eyebrows at the density of the device. "That's a version of a weapon I know you know how to use, and that's got a lot of potential tricks in it." *And has a lot of sentimental symbolism for me. I don't pray, don't believe in it . . . but if the spirit of the guy who should be wielding it exists, maybe he'll help her.* "The original belonged to . . . one of my friends on Hyperion. It's a staff.

Extendable and retractable through memory-composites to lengths between, well, what you see there, up to slightly over ten meters. It'll harvest the energy to trigger the state changes during movement and combat, once we activate it, or you could channel some through the suit. Speed of shift depends on the power available to some extent."

"Oh, that *is* nice. Yes, I'll take this one." She examined the armor, found a latchpoint that would hold the retracted staff. "One of the Hyperions . . . Hanuman?"

"Close. Wu Kung." *Strange how much it still hurts to say his name. I wonder if they're still taking care of him? They must think I'm dead by now. I left instructions . . . but there's so much that could go wrong.*

We've got to get home soon. Too many people depending on us.

"The Monkey King . . . Well, I'll just hope I can borrow his skill, then, along with this replica staff." She started sorting through the other equipment.

I'll hope so too; but that'd be about the level of miracle we're going to need . . . and I don't believe in miracles. He could see his grim thought reflected on the other faces. Ariane was focused, not allowing thoughts of uncertainty or failure, and that was as it ought to be—it was the way she approached such problems, according to Carl, and it was pretty much the only way to go into this kind of fight. But the rest of them didn't have the necessity of combat—or, in most cases, the training—to push all worries and concerns aside like that.

And even training isn't enough for me. Amas-Garao made me feel helpless. *I haven't really felt that way since I was a child, a long, long time ago. That monster's completely out of my league. And Ariane . . . she isn't the type to give up. Ever. We saw that in her race against Sethrik.*

"Marc, I also need everything your headware learned about the Shadeweavers. I know there isn't much chance of it, but maybe something else you saw or heard or felt will give me a clue, a tactical advantage."

"Of course, Captain." He concentrated, linked, dumped the entire sequence of experiences from the time he met Amas-Garao up until the end of the battle into her open head-port. Well, there were some thoughts of his own he edited out, but those weren't relevant.

"Thank you, Marc."

"My pleasure, Captain." He could see her eyes temporarily unfocus, as she ran through the sequence of events. But he couldn't make himself feel much hope.

Even though he won't want to hurt her . . . there's also no way that I can see Amas-Garao quitting. If she dies, he still gets a human body, and maybe he can read a lot from even a dead mind, given the chance.

He closed his eyes and swallowed, feeling a lump that wouldn't go away in his throat, or maybe his chest. His eyes met Simon's, and he saw the same bleak fear in the emerald green eyes that he knew must be in his own coal-black ones.

Ariane wouldn't give up. And the Shadeweaver wouldn't stop.

In two more days, Ariane was going to die.

Chapter 64

This is it. At the sound of the chime, Ariane stepped forward, through the swirling portal in front of her.

The blaze of light and sound that met her was staggering. The roar of a human crowd in a stadium might, possibly, be as loud, but the sounds of the Arena spectators covered a vastly larger range, thunderous hoots and nearly supersonic shrieks and drumming of dozens of different types and sizes of limbs on floor, railing, chairs, or each other. She stared around with her jaw half-dropped for a long moment.

The 'Core Ring' stadium of Nexus Arena was an immense hexagonal space surrounded by level upon level of seating (adjustable for the wide range of species). Every space available was filled by something, many of them of species she hadn't even gotten a chance to meet, ranging from slender multi-tendriled rods that "sat" in slotted cylinders to amorphous blobs that had no seat, just a lot of floor space. As near as she could tell, there had to be at least one member of every known species in the Arena present for this Challenge. If she'd been vulnerable to stage fright, she was pretty sure she'd have surrendered to Amas-Garao right then and there; as it was, the sight was nearly overwhelming.

And they're all here to see me lose, she thought wryly. There wasn't a single bookie, gambler, or other odds-maker anywhere in Nexus Arena that would give odds for her on this contest. In fact, there basically weren't any bets going on because no one would take the other side of the bet. *Mandallon said the reason they'll all be watching is they can't believe I'll actually go through with it. They expect me to surrender just before things get ugly.*

Well, you just go on expecting that.

She spotted the human and allies contingent on the nearby wall. They had seats up against the invisible barrier—she might as well call it a "force field" because that's what it seemed to be: a transparent, nonmaterial, yet very real barrier between the Core Ring and the spectators—as close to the action as possible. All her crew was there, Steve and Tom as projected avatars (that apparently she could see, but others couldn't, so as to keep secret the exact numbers of their faction), along with Nyanthus, Mandallon, Orphan, Dr. Relgof, and a few others.

Odd. DuQuesne's not there! There's an empty chair . . .

She was surprised at the depth of her disappointment.

Across from her, Amas-Garao stood immobile, perhaps surveying the crowd, perhaps only studying her. Then he raised his arms, and the crowd roared louder.

There's DuQuesne! She spotted the huge Hyperion, striding through the crowd, pushing his way past other spectators to get to his seat. *Wonder where he was? He's not the type to forget to hit the bathroom before the main event . . .*

The Arena spoke, driving all other thoughts from her mind. "Are the contestants ready?"

Ariane felt adrenaline already starting to flow, the tightness of the stomach and cool tingle of fear/anticipation putting her to the edge of combat. She gripped the Wrath of God and spun it once, as Astrella would. *I'll need all the tricks of all my games and then some.* "I'm ready."

"I am ready." The deep voice of Amas-Garao echoed throughout the Stadium; she suspected it would have done so even if the Arena were not amplifying their voices.

"Does either of you wish to yield at this time, prior to any injury?"

The Shadeweaver spoke no reply; the clearly audible mocking chuckle was enough.

"Not a chance in hell," Ariane said. "And you're going to regret that laugh, Shadeweaver." *Nothing like a little bravado to start the day.*

"Then . . . by the ancient laws of the Arena . . . Begin."

Ariane exploded from her position like a sprinter hearing the gun. *He'll be expecting me to take the defensive, not the offensive, to look for an opening. Well, I'm not playing that game.*

Sure enough, she saw the still-distant, but rapidly-nearing, figure of Amas-Garao jerk, a jump of surprise, as she streaked towards him, hand reaching across to her katana. *If he'll just stay surprised for a couple more seconds . . .*

But the Shadeweaver was a veteran of many combats; before she was even within twenty meters of Amas-Garao, he faded into darkness, reappearing almost eighty meters away behind her and speaking in a soft yet penetrating voice the alien word that she heard as "Thunder."

The crackling ball of energy streaked toward her, tracking her as she tumbled aside; but unlike the prior battle this time she had enough range in which to act—she took a small globe from her pocket and threw it straight into the approaching ball of lightning.

The globe exploded on contact, the electricity coursing through it more than enough to trigger the state change, shattering the sphere and casting strands of conductive water solution everywhere, grounding the ball into the ground; a few ineffective sparks drifted forward a few meters more, but Ariane was already past them, running towards the Shadeweaver who reflexively hurled another lightning ball. The crowd was roaring and cheering, and now that she'd proven the tactic, Ariane continued straight forward, the second globe of liquid preceding her, neutralizing the seething mass of lightning, allowing Ariane to dive straight through, the widening eyes of Amas-Garao focusing on her as her *iai* draw tore its way through the narrowing distance.

She felt contact, even as the black-clad Shadeweaver vanished, and something fluttered to the ground. She tumble-rolled and grabbed it up, holding it into the air, grinning a killer's grin at Amas-Garao, who coalesced from shadow halfway across the hundred-meter arena. "First cut goes to Humanity, Shadeweaver! Want to concede?"

"An impressive beginning, Ariane Austin of Humanity." Was it just wishful thinking that made her hear a slight tremor in the very first syllables, a sound of someone more startled than they wished to let on? "There are those in our audience who would never have believed even so symbolic a strike against me; well done, indeed. Yet you hold nothing but cloth, child, no blood, no flesh, no substance. Am I a puppet, a thing of stuffing and stitches, to be threatened by the loss of a few threads? Try this, then, and see if you remain so confident!"

Twin thunderballs arced outward, crackling across the hard-packed dirt (*Genuine replicated traditional dirt*, she thought wryly) of the Core Ring, a trail of disturbed dust kicked up by their passage. She ran forward, trying to hurl one of her fast-shrinking supply of the globes toward the encroaching thunderballs, but they were too far apart; one vanished in ozone and sparks, but the other—

Ariane convulsed as the full power of the thunderball struck. *Even with the insulation and the channeling armor, some of it's getting through, and it* hurts. *And I have to make it look convincing, because any chance I've got against him depends on a sucker punch.*

And he's not going to be easy to sucker.

Amas-Garao hit her again, lightning coursing through her, sending her pitching face-forward to the ground.

The floor of the Arena's ring definitely *tasted* like dirt. Considerably more slowly than she actually had to, Ariane pushed herself up, began to stand, then desperately dodged as another thunderball streaked in.

This time, though, she was a lot closer to Amas-Garao, and as she dove, she chose her course carefully. Seeing what she was up to, the Shadeweaver dismissed the lightning-ball before her maneuver brought it close enough to potentially threaten its caster. Unfortunately, he also faded away at the same moment. *Damn! That would've been the perfect shot. I'm sure I've got some juice now.*

The Shadeweaver was getting her measure, unfortunately. He knew how fast she reacted, and he was no longer surprised that she was attempting to bring the fight to him as fast as possible. He materialized a bit more than fifteen meters off this time, but instantly a hurricane howled outwards from him. *I can fight my way forward through that, but I'll be doing it like wading through molasses . . . which gives him a perfect chance to aim and fire.*

But there's another way.

She knew from DuQuesne's experiences that the Shadeweaver had to think about it to throw up certain types of shields. Right now he had the hurricane up. *Which means . . .*

Kicking in the combat mods, driving her strength to full, she lunged forward, jabbing her arms forward as hard as she could . . . and triggering the Monkey King's staff to full extension.

Ring-carbon reinforced active-memory composite, powered by some of the Shadeweaver's own energy, jabbed outward like a ten-meter punch, hammering into Amas-Garao with an impact so brutal that the transmitted vibration sent splinters of bee-sting agony through Ariane's hands, making her drop the staff.

The air *whooped* from the Shadeweaver's lungs in an incredulous shrieking gasp, and Amas-Garao folded up like a greeting card, tumbling backwards limply. Ignoring the fading pain in her hands, Ariane sprinted forward, the hurricane winds now gone, drawing her sword, and diving towards the prone form of the Shadeweaver.

Amas-Garao rolled aside as she came, and *this* time there was no mistaking the desperation in his move, the shaking and wheezing sound of a creature barely able to force air back into its stunned body, no time to focus on arcane powers. Ariane's booted foot smashed into the robes, force blunted by the stiffening cloth but still hitting with considerable strength on what felt like a shin. The Shadeweaver grunted, and she thought she could hear a triumphant shout from DuQuesne, not far away. *If I can just keep this up, get one good contact cut . . .*

But the Shadeweaver contracted into a ball for a moment, and her kicks, punches, and cuts were blunted by the flexible yet tremendously tough robe. Knowing she was running out of time, she aimed a last cut at the head area, readying the electrical discharge. *One good bolt back . . .*

"Away from me!"

The voice was like the thunder of a vengeful god, and it was accompanied by a blue-white blast that crackled through her limbs like vengeance. *Oh, damn. I had him on the ropes, but he's just tougher than I thought. Or just has more defenses.*

Amas-Garao rose, darkness gathering about him. "A painful and well-considered attack, little Human, but not enough, not *nearly* enough. And what exactly gave such speed and power to that weapon, hm . . . ?" He circled her, fading in and out like a nightmare, keeping her turning in place to try and find him, never coming closer than twenty or thirty meters. He seemed to be considering. "Ah, yes, of course. A clever ploy indeed, Captain Austin, but do you think you are the *only* one to think of such things?"

Abruptly the temperature surged around her. She felt like she was in a sauna. "What, you're going to make me sweat to death?"

A dark chuckle. "Something very like that, yes. A network of superconductive layers, I think? Something to lead me into a false sense of security, while all the time giving you the power for quite a number of little tricks." The heat increased again. "But superconductors, alas, are such very touchy things, even in their advanced forms. Does the term 'transition temperature' bring anything to mind, Captain Austin?"

Oh, no. She was no engineer, but those words meant something to just about *anyone* who dealt with superconductor storage units—which meant pretty much everyone in the Solar System who used high-power equipment. A superconductor that got above its transition temperature would suddenly stop being a superconductor—and if it was storing energy at the time, that energy would be released. Immediately.

The transition temperature in question was 71 degrees C. And by the feel, it wouldn't be long before Amas-Garao reached that level.

The batteries are integral with the armor!

She tore at the fastenings, forcing them open, sweating now from fear as much as from the furnace-like heat. One arm out. Another. *Get that last fastener open!* She pulled the flexi-armor free and hurled it from her just as the temperature gave another surge.

The storage coils transitioned just as the armor left her hands. At a distance of about a meter and a half, all the energy she'd stolen from Amas-Garao detonated.

She'd had the presence of mind to duck and cover; even so, the blast felt like a wrecking ball, smashing her aside with irresistable force. She tumbled over and over, finally coming limply to rest against the side of the Core Ring.

That's funny . . . I thought the lights were bright . . . but everything's getting so very dim . . .

Chapter 65

DuQuesne gripped the railing so tightly he felt the metal give slightly. He hated this. He hated having to *sit* here and do nothing, while she gave everything . . . and all of it to make sure that *he* wasn't in the Shadeweaver's hands. He hated seeing her hurt.

He glared at Amas-Garao, the Shadeweaver gliding untouchably as Ariane tried everything at her command. And she was *good*. Oh, as a fighter she wasn't anything compared to him or Orphan (or, god forbid, Wu), but she had the *head* of a fighter, the guts and strategy and cold-blooded calculation. The Shadeweaver had the power, but even as he unleashed his lightnings, DuQuesne could tell there were more eyes on the hopelessly outclassed Ariane Austin. She dominated that battlefield through sheer chutzpah.

He heard a rhythmic muttering, a singsong chanting, and saw, out of the corner of his eye, Mandallon, holding a seven-sided crystalline object, turning it regularly after every muttered stanza; praying, praying for the impossible to happen.

Then Ariane took her shot, and DuQuesne was on his feet, shouting encouragement like a madman, along with everyone on his side, even Orphan, as the blue-haired Captain of the *Holy Grail* tore into Amas-Garao. *She's nailed him, she's got him right where she needs him, by God she's going to . . .*

But then he saw the Shadeweaver get up, heard his words, and realized that all the planning still hadn't been enough.

"Bloody hell, she almost *had* him, Marc," Simon muttered furiously.

"Bastard's tough, smart, and mean. I sucker-punched him once myself, and still lost." DuQuesne squinted down as he heard Ariane's comment about sweating, and suddenly went pale. "*Holy*—get the damn armor off!"

And then she did—and was caught in the explosion. Ariane tumbled across the floor like a broken doll.

"*Ariane!*"

The shout came from two men, both lunging forward, both smashing themselves ineffectually against the transparent, impenetrable barrier around the Core Ring. Gabrielle caught at Simon and pulled him back; DuQuesne felt an iron, alien grip on his shoulder, found that Orphan's grim face brought him back to a semblance of sanity. *It's worse than I thought. Haven't reacted like that since the last time I saw K.*

Amas-Garao drifted somewhat towards Ariane, then chuckled. "A good run. I look forward to seeing you later, when you have recovered." He drifted towards the exit . . . and rebounded. "What? Why can I not pass?"

"Because . . . " came a weak but iron-hard contralto, "the Arena knows that I'm not finished with you yet!"

The rising roar of disbelief echoed the rising of his own heart as he turned to see Ariane standing, leaning heavily against the wall of the arena within the Arena, a hell-bent grin on her face that either stopped his heart, or sent it leaping from his chest—he wasn't sure which.

Amas-Garao turned slowly, incredulously. "What is the *point*, human? I have taken all you can do, all the tricks and ruses you have devised—I have given you every chance! Yet you can barely stand! Do you *want* me to kill you?"

"*Want* has nothing to do with it." Ariane pushed away from the wall, moving painfully but straightening, tearing away gloves shredded by her tumble, drawing her sword again. "If you choose to kill me, I can't stop you. But I warned you more than once, Shadeweaver, that I *will not give up*. If you want me, you will have to *beat* me. I don't *care* what the odds are. Maybe you'll understand it better in *these* words: give me liberty, or give me death!"

And she was *sprinting* again, from what depth of focus and depth of reserves he couldn't tell, straight for the Shadeweaver, sword drawn back for a samurai cut that would cleave the creature from one side to the other. *You're gorgeous, but that's not going to work, Ariane.*

Amas-Garao did not even bother to disappear or step aside. He gestured, and the sword was torn from Ariane's grasp; he reached out, and his hand was around Ariane's throat, lifting her effortlessly from the ground; DuQuesne could see now that its hand was black-furred, taloned, like a humanoid panther. "I shall give you *neither*, arrogant little creature." The deep, pitiless voice of the Shadeweaver echoed throughout the stadium, slow, measured, certain. "I have no intention of killing you, as you shall be of vastly greater value to us alive; nor shall you win, and thus shall you have no liberty. Your choice—your *only* choice, Ariane Austin—is to either spare yourself further pain, and yield the Challenge, or to continue this futile contest until I choose to end it in pain. And pain it shall be, I assure you."

The Arena supplied them with many angles, many views of the contest, available at a simple glance. Now they could see Ariane, held in the unbreakable grip of the Shadeweaver.

And she was *smiling*.

"Pain?" she managed to choke out. "*I'll* give you *pain!*"

Her right hand lashed out and clamped on the exposed forearm of Amas-Garao.

The Shadeweaver shrieked and convulsed; a faint sound of buzzing and hissing reached their ears. Ariane dropped to the ground, still gripping Amas-Garao's arm, and with all the leverage of her body and fall *threw* the Shadeweaver, smashing him to the ground with stunning force.

"What the *hell*?" DuQuesne muttered disbelievingly.

"Way to *go*, Ariane!" Carl shouted, a grin a mile wide on his face. "You guys wondered about her biomod? *that* was her biomod. A built-in shock-stunner, electric-eel derived old-fashioned taser."

"So *that* was why you'd already put conductive channels in her weapons." DuQuesne liked things to make sense.

Ariane slammed a knee into Amas-Garao's back, then grabbed his head and tried to smash it into the ground. But the Shadeweaver rolled over; the cowl pulled away in the process, exposing a snarling, monstrous head, yellow eyes and fanged mouth and black fur and flattened ears, something like an unholy cross between a mandrill and a humanoid lizard. The great jaws snapped at her, backing her up, and a bolt of fire hammered her backwards. Amas-Garao rose, slowly, painfully, but still more swiftly than Ariane, and the snarl on the Shadeweaver's face was savage.

"And yet another trick, a much more surprising one, little human." The deep, measured voice was angry, but the anger faded swiftly. "Almost, almost you managed to force me to act from anger instead of policy. You nearly did succeed in achieving the goal of death instead of liberty." He faded, reappeared, as Ariane launched another exhausted strike that touched nothing. "You have done well. None will see you as weak or impotent; you have given much honor to your Faction.

"But now it ends."

With a simple gesture, Amas-Garao tore Ariane from the ground, sending her skyward, dropping her to the hard packed dirt. "You shall not touch me again."

Ariane struggled to rise, but another gesture hurled her across the ring, to impact against the wall. "You shall not even approach me."

"You son of a . . . " she muttered, and tried again to charge him, but her feet left the ground and she was pinned against the impenetrable barrier around the Core Ring.

Amas-Garao did not answer her, or even appear to heed her curses. As the crowd roared, and as DuQuesne found himself once more pounding futilely against the barrier, the Shadeweaver systematically, dispassionately, and implacably battered Ariane repeatedly against the walls, barrier, ground, again and again, impact after impact echoing through the stadium; the crowd grew quieter, realizing they were no longer watching a battle but a humiliation, a beating of a spirit as well as a body.

Finally there was nothing but silence and the sound of a body hitting the ground. A pause, and the young woman—barely more than a girl to DuQuesne— twitched. *No, please, Ariane. Let it go. Don't give him the excuse.*

But Ariane's wobbling posture, as she managed to get to her hands and knees, showed that even if he'd shouted, she probably wouldn't have been able to understand. She stayed there, unmoving, hair falling over most of her face, blood dripping into the dirt.

"Surrender," Amas-Garao said, and even his voice now seemed tinged with sympathy, or at least with less amusement, as though the enjoyment of this mismatch was finally beginning to pall.

The only part of her face that was unshaded by Ariane's hair was her mouth, bloodied, lips working, clearly trying to gather strength for yet another futile assault.

And then it stopped. DuQuesne could see that even her breathing had stopped, as though some thought had struck her so suddenly, so strongly, that even the need to breathe had been momentarily overriden.

And her mouth was curved in a smile.

Chapter 66

Ariane stared down at the dirt, trying to focus. Even the ground seemed to be moving, and not in a helpful way. She could barely hear anything, even the Shade-weaver's taunts. If he was still taunting.

Lost. I've lost.

She replayed all the facts she'd learned, but they were meaningless. All she saw were faces—DuQuesne's, as she'd seen it a moment before while she fell, white, furious, tears streaming down the usually impassive cheeks; Simon's, grim as a thundercloud; Carl's, teeth bared in a helpless snarl, Gabrielle's with tears running down her face . . . Steve's, half-covered by his left hand, Tom's with eyes closed, unwilling to watch any more.

And Orphan's, as she'd first seen it, alien and ironically confident . . . *Oh, not good, I'm starting to lose it.* She needed to focus on what was, here and now, not start drifting . . . drifting into the past . . . Mandallon's face as he became an Initiate Guide . . . Laila, two faces, the focused scientist, and the cold, alien smile seen only perhaps in her mind . . . Nyanthus' non-face, gesturing in the midst of ritual . . . Her own vision cleared momentarily, dark spots on the dirt . . . her blood. And the glitter of Wrath of God, impotent on her wrist.

"When your enemy surpasses you, you must defeat him beyond the battle."

Oh, wonderful. My brain's throwing cryptic quotes from a game sensei . . . think that was Astrella's master, that's why, saw the weapon . . .

"Beyond the battle", oh, thanks, that's *so* useful. Means that you have to beat him with something other than skill and strength, you have to change the rules. But this place changes *all the rules anyway.*

Entering the Arena, the end of nuclear power . . . all the AIs shutting down . . .

How can I change the rules, when the rules don't work any more?

Fragments of chants, the Faith, prayers of Mandallon, a few words through a Shadeweaver door.

A few words . . .

" . . . **dem orthar usat** . . . "

" . . . beyond the battle . . . "

Blood . . . a sharp, acrid taste . . .

And suddenly it was all there before her, as clear as though she had known it all along. It was an insane gamble, and probably wouldn't work, it had probably been tried many times before, but . . . what was there to lose?

Maybe my soul, she admitted to herself. *That's the problem; I might win, and lose everything at the same time.*

But if it works, it saves my friends; that's a good enough exchange no matter what the price.

She felt herself smiling. And then the laugh began, a faint chuckle that built up and threatened to dissolve into coughs in her pain-wracked chest.

"Why do you *laugh?*" demanded Amas-Garao.

"Because . . . I'm about . . . to beat you . . . "

Now the Shadeweaver laughed. "I think you are suffering from far too many injuries. Delirium does sometimes bring false senses of triumph."

Not "dem orthar usat" . . . or it doesn't have to be that. If I'm right . . .

The Shadeweaver said something else, but now she had to focus. Remember . . . get the pronunciation right . . . She opened her mouth, and began to speak. **"Recardisea tinduk wesni . . . "**

Chapter 67

Amas-Garao halted in mid-sentence, and burst into fresh laughter. "Fool! You believe it is so simple?"

Simon stared, listening hard. *It can't be that simple, no.*

Nyanthus' openwork tendrils shuddered dismally. "A brave last throw . . . but not possible."

But Ariane was continuing. " . . . **cotarey wademor tharus zatra** . . . "

Suddenly he understood. The words DuQuesne had repeated, overheard in another ritual, were very nearly the same. "**Dem orthar usat**" was just a slight change in emphasis and timing from " . . . **demor tharus zat**." The same, or similar, rituals, perhaps distorted through separation and time.

But just the words could not *possibly* be enough, else there would be no controlling the spread of the powers.

607

Amas-Garao smiled, a terrifying sight, and raised his hand for a final strike.

" . . : **setsdensu kama threy!**"

For a single split second, the Arena was silent, motionless, as though the Universe held its breath.

And there was a detonation of power like an exploding star.

"Impossible!"

The word was torn from Amas-Garao, even as his hands came down to block the wash of blazing energy that drove outward to the very limits of the barrier about the Core Ring. His feet dug in, but the force of the unleashed, uncontrolled energy was not to be denied; slowly, inexorably, he was being pushed backward, leaving a trail of earth in his wake, a trail being erased by the increasing vibration of the combat ring.

"A miracle!" Simon heard Mandallon say, a hushed and joyous whisper. "The Creators have heard, and they answer!" But Simon noticed that Nyanthus was still, unmoving, even the symbiotes flattened to the ground.

"Not . . . impossible." Ariane's voice was strained, the sound of a woman either in agony, or at the edge of ecstasy—perhaps both. "And . . . I've won."

"Won? *Won?*" there was strain in the Shadeweaver's voice now, strain and desperation and disbelief.

"Won." Her voice was stronger, but Simon couldn't even see her clearly any more, as energy blazed from her form, making her indistinct, dissolving in pure light. He became aware that the ground under his feet—*Nexus Arena?!*—was vibrating, shaking, as the uncontrolled power clawed at the barrier. The audience were suddenly on their feet, panic beginning to emerge as the impossible played itself out before them.

"You . . . can't control . . . this Awakening by yourself," Ariane said. Her voice echoed, contralto thunder, shaking the foundations of Nexus Arena itself, even though the tone was still that of a woman near the end of her strength. "I may survive it by myself—others have—but you, confined here, within a barrier you cannot escape . . . you are only one. Are you seven times greater than Nyanthus of the Faith? Are you?"

Amas-Garao's face was a rictus of fury and fear, teeth bared in a humorless, terrified grin as he fought against a power that was redoubled in that instant; the ground heaved under him, sending him staggering back. He realized at that moment that he was nearly to the barrier . . . an immovable object, with an irresistable force pressing in on him. DuQuesne could see disbelief warring with the need for self-preservation, but the Arena-born instincts won out. "I . . . I yield. *I yield!*"

But with that shout, the barrier came down, the contest ended. Blue-white energy lanced outward, shattered seats, scattered the now-fleeing watchers; DuQuesne stood frozen, staring at the featureless globe of light expanding from the center of the circle.

Higher-pitched in desperation, Amas-Garao shouted *"Now, my brothers! Now, O Faith! Initiate Guide and Shadeweaver, to me!"*

Six more shapes materialized around the great Core Ring; Shadeweaver and the Initiate Guides, Gona-Brashind across from Nyanthus, others of both sides entering, focusing the power of Faith and Shadeweaver to contain the energies unleashed.

A figure began to take shape, forged from flame and sunshine, taking on solidity, yet floating meters above the solid floor below. Eyes opened, eyes that themselves blazed with pure luminance for a moment before that faded. A figure with hair of blue, dressed in robes of midnight azure touched with gold, with a symbol—a cup crossed with a ship—of purest silver.

Ariane Austin's gaze met his own, a gaze filled with wonder and awe.

And still the Shadeweavers and Faith fought to contain the power, as the Arena shook to the thunder of her triumph.

Chapter 68

DuQuesne vaulted down, dropping the seven meters to the Core Ring floor as though it were a single step on a staircase. The incredible energy had finally dissipated, and all in the center of the Ring—Shadeweaver, Faith, and Ariane—knelt or sat or lay, recovering from near disaster. As he ran, DuQuesne heard a humming whirr behind him; a glance showed a ramp had extended down, allowing the others of *Holy Grail*'s crew to follow. The remaining crowd that had not fled during the devastating finale of Ariane's Challenge were starting to cautiously make their way down as well.

As he got closer, he saw Ariane slowly standing upright again; he noticed that her new outfit was not—exactly—a set of robes, but more formal than that; a *gi*, it seemed, was the base garment, but a *gi* with structured and clean

611

lines woven into the fabric, a martial-arts outfit crossed with a suit or uniform; rank bars on her shoulders, with the ship-and-cup symbol over the left breast, like an insignia. *It suits her,* he thought.

He slowed and stopped, putting out an arm and stopping Simon's headlong rush as though the tall scientist were an overeager child. "DuQuesne, what—"

He held up his hand, and all the others stopped. His gaze met Ariane's, and he could see her eyes widen. "Captain?" he asked cautiously.

The question in his voice caused her to nod. "I . . . think so."

Simon glanced from one to the other, looking puzzled.

"I see." Laila's voice was suddenly analytically cold. "And that must be one of the questions you have about me as well."

"I can't deny it," DuQuesne acknowledged, keeping his gaze on Ariane. "So, Captain, are you sure?"

She sighed. "How *can* I be, Marc? Would I know? If I did know, would I tell you, or would I play the part of myself well enough to fool you? All I can say is . . . I don't feel any less Ariane Austin. I feel . . . well, *more* myself, if that makes any sense." She glanced over to where Amas-Garao was also rising. "And we can deal with this later; it won't be settled in the next few minutes anyway, and I have to go shake down a Shadeweaver."

"Hold on, Captain! Before you do that, you need to know something. You don't need to bargain for power. I've got it covered now."

The delight that lit up her face—immediately followed by narrow-eyed suspicion—gave him hope that this really was the Ariane Austin who'd gone into the Ring. "That's wonderful, Marc . . . but I have a feeling we need to have a talk about exactly how you managed that."

"Later, I think."

"Don't think for a second I'll forget."

No, you won't. No matter who you really are, you're not going to forget that.

The Captain of *Holy Grail* had turned away and in three strides stood face to face with Amas-Garao. The Shadeweaver had pulled the cowl back over his head, and his posture was still wary. "You have achieved unexpected victory, Captain Austin," the deep voice said. "I congratulate you . . . for now."

"Thank you, I think," Ariane said, an edge of sarcasm in her tone. "I am claiming my prize."

"So quickly?" Nyanthus's voice was tired, and there was a strange catch in his voice, a sound of caution and unease. "You have won an unprecedented victory, and given the demands that the Shadeweavers were making, your price could be high indeed."

"Meaning no offense, Arrie, but he's right," Gabrielle said. "If Marc's taken care of our first need, why be in a hurry?"

"Because," Ariane said, voice hard as steel, "I know exactly what I want from these people, and waiting could be dangerous as hell."

DuQuesne had a suspicion, just based on the leashed anger in her voice, that he knew what she was going to demand, and couldn't quite restrain a slight grin. "Then far be it from us to question you on this one, Captain—especially after our prior second-guessing."

That earned him a quick flash of a smile, disappearing instantly into the glare that she leveled on Amas-Garao. "Amas-Garao, your price would have affected my entire Faction, and not in a good way. I am sure you agree with that."

"I . . . I cannot disagree. No." The reluctance in the deep tones was clear.

"Then my price will affect all of the Shadeweaver faction. From this point on, no Shadeweaver will *ever* read, sense, influence, brainwash, mentally assault, or in any other way outside of the mundane methods available to all other Arena species have any effect upon the minds of the Faction of Humanity or our direct and close allies." She grinned savagely, one of the expressions that DuQuesne couldn't help but find too dangerously attractive. "The *only* exception will be if you are individually, and specifically, requested to do so by an authorized individual of the Faction, and even in those cases you will never step one *millimeter* beyond the specific services requested."

Even Gona-Brashind seemed taken aback, and Amas-Garao sounded insulted. "Never? *Never?* This is a completely disproportionate penalty, compared with—"

A chime echoed through the Core Ring, and the dispassionate voice of the Arena spoke. "The requested prize is entirely appropriate and fair. The Shadeweaver Amas-Garao will accept this, and his acceptance is binding on his Faction."

Silence. Then Amas-Garao gave a surprisingly rueful chuckle. "I have been well outmaneuvered by you, Captain, and it would seem also by other members of your crew. A most disconcerting, yet exceedingly entertaining and instructive, sequence of events. I accept your demands; your prize for winning the Challenge is freedom from that sort of interference by the Shadeweavers, as you have specified and the Arena has adjudged fair." He bowed, and he—along with the other Shadeweavers present—evaporated into nothingness.

At that point Mandallon leapt forward and grabbed Ariane's hands, breaking into a strange sort of capering dance that was so joyous as to be infectious. "You *won*, Captain, you *won!* I prayed and prayed for a miracle, and was granted one! Did you not see? Was it not glorious?" He gave a hooting sound that translated as a laugh on the edge of tears of joy.

DuQuesne noticed Nyanthus make an abortive move in Mandallon's direction; the strange creature's symbiotes were almost all sitting internal to the candle flame-like upper portion, the tendrils of the top were tightly interwoven, like a man wrapping his arms around himself against cold . . . or fear. But his voice seemed normal, or close to it, as he said, "Indeed we congratulate you, and Humanity, on such a stunning victory. But I think you shall be needing rest, not excitement, for the next few hours."

Yeah . . . Ariane's coming down from the combat high, and even though—somehow—it looks like all her injuries were wiped away in that "Awakening," she's got a shell-shocked look around her. "He's right, Captain. I think we'd better get you back to the Embassy."

Ariane looked about to protest, and then stumbled slightly in her attempt to follow Mandallon's celebratory dance. "Whoa . . . You might be right, Marc." She let go of Mandallon, who suddenly stopped, crest feathers fanning out in a covering motion which DuQuesne guessed was something like a blush of embarrassment.

"I . . . I was overcome by the moment, Captain, I apologize . . . "

Ariane laughed, a touch of exhaustion now audible in her speech. "It's all right—I don't mind people getting excited about that win, I'm pretty excited myself. But

Nyanthus and DuQuesne are right, I'm starting to feel the aftereffects." She smiled around the group. "But you'll all be invited to the celebration later, I promise."

"Then we bid you farewell, and look forward to our next meeting." Nyanthus spread his openwork tendrils, enfolded Mandallon, and—apparently unwilling to be upstaged this time by a Shadeweaver—slid backward and vanished through a door of golden light.

"Now, Captain," DuQuesne said, as he and Simon put an arm out to help support an Ariane clearly reaching the end of adrenaline-fueled endurance, "let's get you home."

Chapter 69

DuQuesne entered Ariane's room and waited for the door to close before speaking. "You sent for me, Captain?"

Ariane was sitting on the edge of her bed, dressed in her regular clothes. A glance around the room didn't show the odd outfit she'd materialized in, back at the Core Ring, but she could have put it any number of places. She looked up. "Sit down, please, Marc."

He gave the gesture he'd selected to indicate to their Embassy "I need a chair"; the specially-designed over-size chair grew out of the floor near Ariane. He sat down and gazed at her for a moment. "Time for a private after-action talk, I suppose?"

"Before I go talk to everyone else, yes. Because we need to settle things between us first."

I'm not sure I like the sound of that. "Beg pardon, Captain?"

Ariane gave a snort of laughter. "I'm sorry, I didn't mean to sound *quite* that grim. I mean that you're the other rock this group relies on, and we need to make sure there're no questions between us. Right?"

"I check you there to about nine decimals," he said, relief allowing the old habits of speech to resurface momentarily. "You're rested up, I hope."

"Slept like the legendary log." Ariane shook her head, ran her hand through the deep blue hair with a laugh. "Which surprises the hell out of me; I'd have expected nightmares, freaky dreams, something. But yes, I'm all better now. I was hurt bad in that fight—you saw it—but the actual injuries just . . . disappeared when I triggered that Awakening."

"Which brings us to the first subject. What happened there, Ariane? How the hell did that work? It *can't* be the words, it's just not possible; if it was that simple, *everyone* would be a Shadeweaver or Initiate Guide."

"Oh, it's *not* that simple. Remember the conversation I had with Nyanthus? There's a very limited number of Initiate Guides, and a similarly limited number of Shadeweavers. And, according to Nyanthus, whenever a new species emerges into the Arena, they are 'blessed' with the opportunity to elevate one or two new people to Initiate Guide status. It's pretty clear, reading between the lines, that the same applies to the Shadeweavers."

DuQuesne nodded, thinking. "And since the Shadeweavers think the Initiate Guides are just using the same power, either that's true, or—as the Guides believe—there's two sources of power, theirs and their enemies', but either way they're getting just a couple representatives each every time a new inhabited Sphere comes online."

"Right. Which both explains why they're very picky about who they elevate, but also why they're very pushed for time. If these special slots are distributed between them, then they're competing for the slots, but don't dare waste them on the wrong person. And probably have evolved traditions that prevent them from coming to blows over it. That's why they initiate one person at a time; if there's a semi-random number of slots, say two to six, then if you do one at a time, everyone gets a fair shot at their share."

"Okay," DuQuesne said. "I'll buy that. And since you were present at the one ritual, you were able to connect the words I overheard with the ones you heard at Mandallon's Elevation. But you can't be the first person to ever find that out. And even if not, you can't be the first person to try just saying the words of the ritual."

Ariane grinned. "Sure, you're probably right. But you're missing two other points. First, with the limited number of slots, someone would have to see the ritual, make a guess that it's really those last few lines that trigger the Awakening, and then go out and try it . . . and do this all within a relatively few days or weeks of the arrival of the species in question. Otherwise, the slots would all be taken up—there'd be a full complement of Shadeweavers and Initiate Guides, and no room for a new Awakening.

"Second, the Shadeweavers call themselves the Brotherhood of the Arena, or the Blood of the Skies . . . and the ritual of the Faith involves blood from other Initiate Guides—"

DuQuesne could not restrain the laughter as comprehension burst in on him. "Dammit, that's brilliant! You figured blood was the final key—maybe there's some kind of nanotech or whatever transferred that way—"

"—and it has to be present in you for those key phrases to trigger the Awakening. And Amas-Garao had, without probably even realizing it, donated his own blood to the cause. Yes."

He shook his head in appreciation. "A hell of a gamble, but based on reasonable deduction. The combination *would* make it almost impossible for someone to stumble on it, too, especially given the time limits, and the fact that it would require the same person to have direct knowledge about both factions. Otherwise all the other training, meditation, and ritual involved would totally obfuscate the issue." He leaned back. "So . . . can you say who's right, or if they're both wrong?"

As she frowned, he knew the answer wouldn't be one he'd like. "I really wish I could, Marc. My *guess*, when I started this, was that it was just some mechanical access to power, like programming the biggest AIWish ever imagined, and these people had just ritualized it to the point that they didn't see it for what it was. Especially since everyone else who got this power would have gone through probably years and years of . . . training, or if I'm being less diplomatic, indoctrination bordering on brainwashing, to give them the 'proper' point of view.

"But when I finished . . . " He could almost hear the last words of the ritual again, echoing in both their memories. "When I finished, it was . . . transcendant. Mandallon tried to tell me what it was like, and I'm going to try to tell you, but now I know what he went through, *knowing* that nothing he said could possibly get across what he'd experienced. Not if I lived to be a thousand and spent every waking moment trying to talk about it.

"It was like . . . " she trailed off, searching for words, then starting again. " . . . like . . . you know the moment when you suddenly understand something? That instant where it's all totally clear, where all the things that confused you are for just that second perfectly in perspective? It was like that. But like having that feeling for the entire universe. I *saw* it all, Marc, I saw hundreds of billions of Spheres, and all the people living on them. I saw the expressions of every inhabitant of the Arena. And I saw how all of it went together, how every part of it works; I know I saw all of this, and more—I felt what my friends were feeling, and what Sethrik was going through, and I looked *out*, and I saw the Solar System and . . . " her eyes were glazing over. "I . . . I . . . " she shook her head, blinked, fell back on the bed, staring upward. "I can't . . . it's all there, but I don't have the words. I'm not a writer, Marc, I'm not a poet, I'm not a scientist, and I'd have to be all three of those and more to even make a stab at it."

I don't think even that would help, not if you really saw all that. "What about these 'Creators'?"

"There was . . . something. That's the problem, Marc. It wasn't just mechanical. I could *feel* something— somethings—watching me. Some of them I think were in the Arena, but some were . . . were . . . " she shuddered suddenly. " . . . *elsewhere*. I don't have a word for it. It wasn't here, in the Arena, and it wasn't back home, our own space. And some of them I thought I might almost be able to understand, and others . . . others were just beyond me. There was a sense of danger and malevolence . . . and at the same time, I saw a Light, something singing to me and protecting me, like what Laila described." She sighed. "So . . . I don't know. But

I wouldn't feel comfortable saying that there *weren't* things like Gods out there. Because there might well be. Or it might just be the old Sufficiently Advanced Technology schtick, and I'm a caveman with stone knives trying to make sense of it all."

For a moment the two were silent. Then Ariane looked up. "So am I me?"

"Why," DuQuesne asked after a pause, "do you ask *me*?"

"Because I saw *you*, too, Marc." She held his gaze, but there was color in her cheeks that hadn't been there before.

That's unfair. Reading a man's mind as a side effect of touching the numinous. "That hardly qualifies me to judge. Some would say it *dis*qualifies me."

"Not if they knew you. You were sure the Arena was real when Steve got us all convinced it was a fake, and then you argued him down. You're Marc C. DuQuesne, the Hyperion. If *anyone* can tell if I'm myself, it's you, Marc."

He studied her for a long time. "Ariane . . . I'm a superman with a very, very small 's.' On a human scale, and maybe a few of these aliens' scales, I might be something special. But I'd be a fool to believe that an artificial—or natural—intelligence capable of building the Arena, or overseeing it, couldn't fool me easily if it wanted to. Maybe it couldn't, but that wouldn't be the way I'd want to bet.

"That said . . . you're right, I'm not an easy man to fool. I've had the world's biggest lies played out through my life, and I saw through them." He took her hand, hardly even conscious that he was doing so. "And I think the hardest thing to fake for any alien would be a personality that I knew well. You're Ariane Stephanie Austin,

Captain. That's my professional opinion. It might be a *wrong* professional opinion, but it's the one I have, and—to be honest—it's really very much the same question as whether all this is real, or an incredibly convincing VR setting. It's pointless for us to worry about you being someone other than who you seem, unless we have a real good reason to believe it. With Laila, I've had some real questions, and they still haven't gone away. But with you, I don't have any doubts at all."

In the silence that followed, he was suddenly acutely aware of her eyes gazing into his, the warmth of her hand gripping his tightly.

She let go suddenly and stood up, cheeks pink, and spoke a little too briskly. "Well, that's good, now that we've cleared that up."

"Capt . . . Ariane, I think—"

"I think we have another couple of issues to deal with, yes, but that one can wait, Marc. It has to wait, for now."

Blast it. She's thinking of the dynamics of command, and once more, she's right. "I don't like it. You and Simon—"

"—Simon is in a different position. You're my second-in-command, Marc. And I have to be able to trust myself not to let any personal feelings get in the way when I'm doing this job that I got stuck with. Also . . . I thought it might be years before we got home. Which isn't true any more, which puts me back in the hotseat.

"And," she continued, before he could get a word in edgewise, "which also reminds me that you have some explaining to do, *Dr.* DuQuesne. How, exactly, did you manage to arrange for enough power to get us out of here, when I hadn't even won my Challenge yet?"

Let it go. She's right. For now. "It was simple, Captain. I just laid down a bet."

She looked at him skeptically. "Mmhmm. A bet. When I had it on good authority that there wasn't a bookie anywhere taking bets on this Challenge."

"True enough. But this was a private bet, and since I was taking the incredibly short end of the stick, Ghondas wasn't going to turn it down."

"And exactly *what* did you offer her if you lost?"

Bite the bullet. "Myself, Captain."

She stared at him, aghast. "I didn't have a snowball's chance in hell of winning that thing, and you went against my *direct orders* with a bet like that?"

"Begging the Captain's pardon, while it is quite possible that she *meant* to have the same orders extend to any risks I took, your precise words were that under no circumstances were the *Shadeweavers* to have access to me again."

She glowered at him. "I *also* made a point of your particular value to Humanity, which *should* have given you the hint that you weren't to be lost at all."

He certainly had, but implications that went against the interpretation he needed had been of course discarded. "I evaluated you as being at least as valuable, Captain, and you were already at risk. The bet would net us the power to go home in any case; Ghondas was willing to take what she saw as the infinitesmal risk of losing the bet in exchange for one of the few prices that we already knew would pay for the power, and in the guise of the bet it would not have any implications under the Anathema for her to worry about."

"But under what right—"

"Captain, it was my strong belief that the Shadeweavers would not be satisfied with you. Once they had you, they could—and eventually would—arrange something which would threaten our people again, until I was forced to comply with them. We are a new faction, a small faction, and overall a weak one. Give us the chance to go home, to let our people start really participating, sending out new ships, and all that, then we get a far better position. Eventually we could find a way to win me back from Ghondas, while keeping the Shadeweavers from harrassing us."

Ariane stared at him, then laughed and threw up her hands in surrender. "Fine. *fine*! I should know better than to argue with you. So you expected to lose the bet and arranged for the long-term consequences to be overall better."

"Actually, Captain, I expected to win."

She blinked. "You're completely nuts. I expected to get my ass whipped out there."

"No, Captain, with all due respect, you didn't. Your *conscious* mind might have expected that, but your heart didn't. And neither did mine. I believed in you, Ariane. I was *afraid* for you, but a part of me was still sure that somehow you'd do the impossible.

"And you did."

Her gaze was softer. "Thank you," she said quietly. "For everything, Marc. I do want to say . . . I'm glad we came here. And I'm really, *really* glad you were with us."

He looked back at her, searching for the right words to say. At that moment, the door rolled open. "Sorry to interrupt," Carl said, "But Nyanthus and Gona-Brashind are both here and insist on speaking to you, Cap."

DuQuesne raised an eyebrow. "That's . . . interesting."

"For apocryphal Chinese values of 'interesting,' yes," Ariane agreed. "I'll meet them in the main briefing room, Carl."

As Carl Edlund left, she looked over at DuQuesne. "Back to work, I guess."

"So it would seem."

I have a bad feeling about this.

Chapter 70

"Gentlemen," Ariane said, "what can I do for you? The party's tonight, and even you," she nodded at Gona-Brashind, "were invited, so I'm a bit concerned as to what brings you here now."

She noticed that Mandallon trailed behind Nyanthus, looking unusually subdued, with nothing of the elated animation of the prior evening. Nyanthus's movements, however, seemed at least superficially more normal. Gona-Brashind, much less familiar, was harder to read, but he did not appear to be overly tense. Perhaps this wasn't as bad as appearances would make it.

"I would hope that there is no true reason for concern," Gona-Brashind began, low voice speaking with soft courtesy. "It is merely that there is a minor . . . loose end which should be resolved before the festivities; the longer it waits the more difficulties it may present, and while it remains unresolved there will be much unnecessary tension in certain quarters."

She could see DuQuesne's face from the corner of her eye, and his frown was not comforting. "What loose end?"

"Let us say, rather, an opportunity," Gona-Brashind said, dipping slightly on his seven legs. "Though you have not had the training or discipline, you have shown that you have the talent that so few possess, and we would like to welcome you to your proper place as one of the Shadeweavers. You will need much teaching and practice to learn the control of that which was unleashed yesterday. But in this case you have the great advantage of being welcomed in as a full member, with none of the unfortunate implications of coercion which would have accompanied your entrance had you failed against my brother Amas-Garao."

Oh, crap. I can already see the light at the end of this tunnel is an oncoming train. "Join you? I'm a member of the Faction of Humanity, and I don't see any reason to join the Shadeweavers and abandon my own people."

The Shadeweaver bobbed its fighting claws side to side, a movement that seemed to indicate negation or disagreement. "You cannot remain solely here, Captain. You need to learn control and direction of those powers. And you are one of us now, despite that you gained the power under . . . unusual circumstances."

"I am most certainly *not* one of you, and of all the Factions, the Shadeweavers are one of the very *last* I would want to join. You people have been a pain in my ass ever since I came here, and I want as little to do with you as possible!" *Like I really want to be a member of a club that includes Amas-Garao?*

Mandallon seemed to straighten up slightly at that, and Nyanthus moved forward. "Indeed, it was my hope that this would be your reaction, though I had many fears. Captain Austin, you have had a great blessing, a miracle according to Mandallon—and I would be most reluctant indeed to gainsay him. In one thing is the Dark One correct, that you need to learn of the powers with which you are blessed, but he has clearly misjudged the nature of your blessing. The Temple of the Faith waits to welcome its newest sister, and teach her the Sevenfold Way—which, I earnestly assure you, you will find much to your liking. I have learned much of your people in your short time here, and there is much of the Sevenfold Way that the wise of your people have already grasped."

"Nyanthus," she said, carefully trying to pick the right words, "I'm honored by this invitation, but I'm not one of your people."

"But you *saw!*" Mandallon burst out, stepping forward, a pleading tone in his voice. "You must have, Captain Austin! You did, I *know* you did! The Creators revealed themselves to you, didn't they, just as they did reveal creation to me? Please, Captain, tell me they did!"

Crap. I hate to disappoint him. "Well . . . Mandallon, I saw many wonderful things in that moment. And maybe some of them were the Creators. But . . . I can't be sure what I saw, and I certainly don't believe I've seen any gods like you seem to think the Creators are."

With the drooping of the feathery material on his head, Mandallon was a literal picture of crestfallen.

Nyanthus was now more tense, his symbiotes flying tight, controlled arcs around his upper half. "So you deny the Creators, Ariane Austin?"

"I don't *deny* anything right now, Nyanthus. I'm just not sure what I believe about what I saw."

Nyanthus's openwork tendrils snapped out and back. "And you will not come to us and let us help you understand?"

"I'd gladly come," she began, and saw both Nyanthus and Mandallon start to relax, "but only to learn about what's happened to me. I'm not leaving my friends or my command."

"You cannot remain with them," Gona-Brashind said flatly. "The Shadeweavers cannot permit such an uncontrolled apprentice as yourself to wander, uncommitted and untrained; nor can we give us our secret teachings if you are not one of us."

"And equally we cannot allow the teachings of the Sevenfold Way to be given into uncommitted hands," Nyanthus said grimly, "as one who has not accepted the Creators may be empowered by something far darker."

"*What?*" she snapped in disbelief. "Are you saying you think I'm, what, a demon or something?" At her anger and tension, she felt something in her twinge, heard a soundless singing in the back of her head.

"I say it is possible and we can take no risks with our knowledge in these matters," Nyanthus said coldly. "Did you not call out the sacred words in desperation, Ariane Austin? Were you not furious and frightened? Did you not wish for power to destroy your enemy?"

Well, I can't entirely deny that. I was pretty pissed off at the time. And scared, yes. And half out of my head, I think. "Partly."

The great candle flame openwork shuddered. "These are the ways of darkness. Calling for powers in that spirit is all too likely to attract those that mask themselves as the Creators, the Deceivers. It is good," he said, with an air of one making a great concession, "that you do not immediately turn to the Shadeweavers for their knowledge, dark and corruptive as it is. It gives me hope that you may yet find your way to the Faith.

"But until that day, we can offer you no teachings. And in one thing we agree with the Dark Ones: you cannot be allowed to wander unchecked without such instruction."

"And just *what*," she said dangerously, feeling adrenaline surging up in her, "do you think you're going to do about that?"

A green-blue spark suddenly crackled around her, whipped out, shattered a dish on the table, and then dissipated. The floor vibrated. She stared, startled, at the wreckage, while the two emissaries seemed to nod in grim agreement.

"Last night we sealed your power away." Gona-Brashind said. "Temporarily, of course, as we had every expectation that you would go to one or the other of the great Factions and be trained. But now that seal must be made permanent. Until and unless you gain the knowledge to wield it, the Power shall be kept inside, inert, unreachable."

"A dual Sealing, by those of Faith and Shadeweaver, is necessary," Nyanthus continued, reluctantly. "A sealing away, with the support of your own Faction, shall resolve these issues for now."

DuQuesne stepped forward. "I don't think you guys get it. This isn't your call to make. She's her own boss. You don't want to teach her, that's fine. You guys learned on your own way back when, I guess she'll have to."

"You do not understand!" Nyanthus's voice was more urgent. "You have just seen a tiny fraction of her power, awakened when our intentions became known. The seal is temporary, it weakens, and as it becomes weaker she becomes less controlled and more dangerous!"

"Here we agree entirely with the Faith," Gona-Brashind said. "Imagine a power that may direct itself without conscious control, when you are angry, or tired, or even with more positive and focused emotions. A power whose limits you have no knowledge of, brought forth on the tide of passion, not reason."

Ariane tried to damp down the instinctive reaction of *but I'm not like that!*—but instead another blue-green crackle around her caused a chair to morph into a half-melted structure and shocked DuQuesne, causing him to give vent to an outdated curse. She bit her lip. "Damn. Marc, I think . . . I think they might be right."

"We *are* right, Ariane Austin." Nyanthus's voice carried slightly more emotion, a touch of sympathy. "We must seal it away now, where only knowledge and training, or another of power of Faith or Shade can reach it."

"You're sure, Captain?" DuQuesne asked. His body language showed he was quite willing to throw both priest and sorcerer-analog out into the street if she asked.

"You saw what happened in the Core Ring, Marc. If it's even a tenth that powerful, I could hurt a hell of a lot of people by accident." She looked to Nyanthus and Gona-Brashind. "Do it, then."

"As I said, Ariane Austin, it must also be with the support of your Faction," Nyanthus said. "You recall the ritual in which Mandallon became one of us?"

She nodded. "Oh. You mean you need five of us to round out the seven-pointed star."

"The idea is correct, but not quite correct," Gona-Brashind said. "We stand outside the figure, performing the ritual, as none of your people are of us. Seven of your people are needed, seven to surround you and bind you in the essence of your selves."

Seven? But . . . oh, dammit.

She could see DuQuesne wince. "This poses . . . a problem."

"What do you mean, Ariane Austin?" inquired Nyanthus.

Gona-Brashind gave a sigh of comprehension. "Of course. A total of eight of you have been seen throughout your presence here. It never occurred to us that you had rotated your entire population through. Your vessel, then, carried eight, and no more."

No point in denying it. "Correct. And you'd better not think that I'm going to sacrifice our citizenship here so that you can lock me down, which I'd have to do if I got Steve and Tom to abandon the Sphere. Why can't you just shift the design? A lot of our legendary rituals use a five-pointed star—"

Both Nyanthus and Gona-Brashind gave virtual identically translated snorts. "Impossible!" the Shadeweaver said, and Nyanthus, for once in complete accord with his adversary, continued, "All seven Keys are symbolized in the sealing ritual—they must be, that all aspects of your self are included and reinforced. And, while their ways are . . . very much different, the symmetry of seven is just as necessary for the D . . . Shadeweavers."

Somehow I sort of guessed that. "Then why my Faction? We could get a couple other people—Dr. Relgof and Orphan, for instance—to round out the seven."

Nyanthus and Gona-Brashind held a brief debate that used so many specialized terms that it might as well have gone untranslated. Finally the Shadeweaver turned back to her, attack claws bobbing in negation. "For the Shadeweavers, it is *possible* that such would work—though I would not wish to attempt it—and it clearly cannot work at all for the Faith. The unity of the Faction from the point of view of the Powers of the Arena is part of the strength of the sealing away. Seven Faction members for the Seven . . . Keys, as the Faith call them. No, it must be your people."

"Captain," DuQuesne said, in a reluctant tone, "we *could* move this whole party over to our Sphere, I suppose. Though I'm real reluctant to invite anyone else there right now."

Nyanthus quivered as though hesitating, but Gona-Brashind's claws gave a sharp, cutting gesture. "Not wise. Not wise at all. The seal is breaking down. We will have to work to keep it stable as you assemble, and this cannot be done while moving . . . and I have no idea what might happen to someone in her state attempting to transit through the Inner Gateway. The results could be . . . disastrous."

Mandallon looked almost ready to beg her on his knees. "Please, Captain Austin . . . can't you accept the Creators' gift?"

"I'd accept the *gift*, Mandallon . . . but I just can't be sure who's giving it to me." She looked at him sympathetically, then glanced back at the others.

Both Nyanthus and Gona-Brashind looked more agitated, especially as a faint glow momentarily traced its way around her and faded. "Ariane Austin, the problem shall only grow worse. You must sense this in your own heart. If you do not accept one side or the other, you shall be an increasing danger to all—especially your own people."

DuQuesne looked at her, clearly awaiting her decision. But she could see the worry, mostly for her, behind his calm black eyes.

Suddenly she remembered a prior conversation with Orphan. "Arena! Arena, do you hear me?"

"**The Arena hears.**"

"You are aware of the situation here?"

A momentary pause. "**The data have been reviewed.**"

"Then you are aware that I will need to empty our Sphere if I am to have this 'sealing' performed. You have previously made exceptions on occasion for particular situations which were beyond the control of the citizens, such as Orphan's ability to travel as he does. May I therefore summon all of my people here for this purpose without forfeiting our hard-won citizenship in the Arena?" She found herself almost holding her breath, and tiny sparks chased across her hand like skittering ants.

The pause was longer, as though the Arena was conferring with itself, or something else. But finally it spoke. "**This request is granted. You may empty your Sphere for this purpose. This exception ends as soon as one or more of your people leaves your Embassy following that ritual; at that point at least one of you must travel back to your Sphere within one hour.**"

She gave a sigh of relief and turned to DuQuesne. "Marc, go tell the others the situation. Then I want you and Carl to go get Tom and Steve and bring them here." She fixed a stern glare on the three aliens. "And you people will say *nothing* of this, understand? Or I don't go through with it, no matter what the cost."

Gona-Brashind crossed and rocked his fighting claws, Nyanthus gave that open-and-close gesture, and Mandallon bent in his people's curtsy-bow. "Understood, Captain Austin." Gona-Brashind said. "Until you have returned home and established a presence here with far more people, this is a vital fact that you have wisely concealed. We shall not speak of it."

She nodded and stood, calming herself to wait as DuQuesne left, almost at a run. A tension was building in her, and she realized that Nyanthus and Gona-Brashind were more right than they knew. *Hurry, Marc. I can feel . . . that I don't have much time.*

Chapter 71

Simon stared at Ariane, kneeling at the center of the seven-pointed star. *Oh, my, it's worse than I thought*.

The solid floor under their feet—a part of Nexus Arena itself—was vibrating erratically. Blue-green and blue-white sparks snapped outward at random intervals, and the smooth stone-like material was scored, blackened, and . . . changed at multiple points within that area. "Why is this happening? I had thought you sealed this power away just last night!"

"Indeed, we had." Nyanthus's normally smooth baritone was tense, worried. "Though it was a temporary seal, both of us would have expected it to last longer than this."

Gona-Brashind, inscribing a last sequence of glowing symbols—*Half mystical symbology, half circuit diagram,* thought Simon—around the perimeter, whirled on his seven legs as DuQuesne came barreling into the room, Steve and Tom at his heels. "Quickly! Into positions!"

"What the hell's going on? Ariane, are you all right?" Steve said, as he was shoved to stand at the sixth point of the star. He stared incredulously around at the others, each at one point of a complex glowing array with Ariane at its core.

DuQuesne stepped into position. Tom Cussler shook his head, then jumped as the entire room shuddered.

"Losing . . . control of the power, Steve . . . " Ariane answered; her voice was distant, in pain. "Seemed under control right after . . . the Awakening . . . "

"Yes, that can happen," Nyanthus said. "A temporary calm, perhaps from exhaustion after the power of the Awakening, who can say? But afterward, without the training and control that the Faith can give you . . . or," he admitted grudgingly, "that could be taught by the Shadeweavers, you are a time-bomb, a disaster waiting to happen."

Gona-Brashind nodded. "You must stay in your places and focus your concern upon Captain Austin. There may be much commotion—even danger, perhaps. Even in pain, *you must not move from your places*."

"We cannot emphasize this enough." Nyanthus glanced at Mandallon, whose prayers were apparently minimizing Ariane's reaction while preparations were finished. "This may seem a foolish ritual to you, unschooled in the ways of the Faith or Shadeweavers, but whether you believe or not, whether you see magic or miracle or simply unknown science, understand that the symmetry is as important here as in . . . as in a laser."

Simon nodded sharply in understanding. "Misalign even by the tiniest bit, and the entire device can destroy itself with its own power. I understand."

With Simon's concurrence and DuQuesne's grunt of agreement, the others seemed to accept the gravity of the situation. Ariane suddenly gave a small shriek that seemed to tear at Simon's heart, and he saw an echoing wince in DuQuesne's eyes. *"Hurry!"* she hissed, as a shockwave burst from her, an invisible sphere of force that hit them like a sudden gust of wind.

Nyanthus and Gona-Brashind began an invocation similar to the shielding/sealing one that had been used when Mandallon was initiated—Simon recognized "Vensecor secutai peheli ix" as the core chant—but added other words in low undertones she couldn't make out. Light and dark clouds of sparks began to orbit Ariane, closer, and closer, as Shadeweaver and Initiate Guide circled the septagon, one clockwise, one counterclockwise, their energies trailing them in counter-rotating circles. Simon felt as though a pressure was building up, not only on Ariane, but on him as well, as though they were being plunged deeper into the ocean's depths. A distant singing echoed through his mind, alien, yet almost familiar . . . *from Ariane?* Across from him, he could see Laila's eyes narrow, then widen, as though understanding had come to her.

The distant singing became abruptly louder, discordant. Blue-white energy erupted around Ariane, the ground shuddered so violently that Simon staggered, nearly leaving the tiny inscribed circle; so did the others, and red energy crackled around the entire star, burning into the seven other humans as they jostled the insubstantial edge of disaster.

"Stop . . . resisting!" Nyanthus said in a strained tone.

"I . . . I don't know *how!*" she said.

"Impressively . . . powerful," muttered Gona-Brashind.

Suddenly Simon *heard* Ariane, not speaking, but in his own head.

I've got to damp this down! But it's like trying to shove a cork into a hose!

The startled eyes around the points of the star showed that they had all heard it, almost—but not quite—as they would with a full comm link on board *Holy Grail.*

Focus, Captain. The deep mind-voice was unmistakably DuQuesne. *You're looking outside.*

Exactly. Laila's precise, measured tones picked up the thought. *This is focused on you. Not on us. You must ignore everything else.*

Simon concentrated as though linking in, and felt his own thoughts become words heard around the circle. *Is there a meditation? Some discipline in your training . . .* He suddenly smiled, despite a new wave of rose and sapphire agony. *Or that of your inspiring avatars that might . . .*

You're right . . . Have to calm myself, cut away from the world . . . A ripple of nervous laughter. *Astrella again, I think.* Simon saw her through a haze of blazing light, sliding down to a meditative pose. He caught sight of images from her . . . a mighty forest, silent, cool green of the spaces between . . . a symbol of five virtues, five elements . . .

Another shockwave blasted outward, unbalancing the seven and even causing both the First Guide and the Shadeweaver to pause. Simon felt himself ready to topple, reached out an arm desperately . . . as did all the others.

Arms cut through the circles around them but caught hold of each other, locked all seven into a unit that would not move. Energy moving inward now moved *through* all of them, circled and echoed through Simon, Laila, Steve, Tom, Gabrielle, DuQuesne, Carl. Simon saw/heard/felt an almost incomprehensible Babel of sight/sound/sensation; he felt rage and sorrow burning through him as he watched a vast space station receding behind him, speckled with sparks of explosions that meant the deaths of lies and men. He heard a voice calling Gabrielle's name, turned with her to see her mother standing in the doorway of a southern mansion. He stepped forth onto Earth for the first time, emerging from a sterile mechanical world into the brilliant lushness of a living world, and felt Laila's tears of wonder on his face; the flow of a thousand monitoring sensors' worth of data streamed through him like thoughts and he felt the power core of a colony beating like his heart, Tom Cussler's mind running it all; he remembered working at breakneck speed to assemble a makeshift control rig for DuQuesne, with Carl Edlund's hands doing the work; he felt the uplifting thrill of seeing the design of *Holy Grail* first emerging under Steve Franceschetti's direction.

Vaguely, he heard the strained desperation in the voices of Shadeweaver and Initiate Guide. "The symmetry is changed! Gona-Brashind—"

"Yes, I understand! No time for calculation! Do it! Now, priest, *now!*"

The two shouted out alien words simultaneously and energy detonated around them like a crushing sledgehammer. All seven fell to their knees, releasing at the same moment, catching themselves as they hit the ground. Simon was just barely aware of the fact that at that very moment, the circling nodes of power were just intersecting . . . on him.

White-black-green flame burned through him, screaming into Ariane along with his own scream, but he was not even truly hearing himself, because at that moment—for that one splintered instant in time— Simon *saw*.

For just that infinitesimal fraction of a second, Simon Sakuraba Sandrisson saw into Ariane, and through her, into the infinite maelstrom of energies and knowledge that intersected in her soul, connecting her to her crew, to Gona-Brashind and Nyanthus, and to . . . *everything*. He gazed into the heart of Nexus Arena, and heard words being spoken by the Blessed on a planet a universe and a million lightyears away, and read the archives of the Analytic in less than no time, stood on the surface of an exploding star and observed the symmetries of thermonuclear holocaust as though they were ripples on a pond, and outside all things, gazing at something else looking back, more than one something, a sense of vastness beyond comprehension, yet startlement, a sharp and uncomfortable sense of something unexpected and impossible.

And then there was silence, and isolation, and a return to awareness. The others, too, seemed to be just rising. *What . . . was that? I can barely remember some of it . . . it's fading. But some of it . . . I think some remains. Somewhere in me.*

What happened?

"It is done." Nyanthus said.

"Barely," Gona-Brashind buzzed, exhaustion clear in his sagging posture. "Yet disaster was averted, and it is finished."

"So . . . it's sealed away and can't come out?" Ariane asked, pushing herself to her feet.

"*Cannot* is a rather extreme word," Nyanthus said reluctantly. "It is possible in desperate circumstances that the seal could temporarily weaken. However, in general it will remain until you gain the skill and knowledge to actually wield the power you have—either through accepting the Creators, or through discovering what power has claimed your essence and thus using the techniques of the Shadeweavers."

Gona-Brashind gave a rattling which translated as a derisive snort. "I shall leave before your pompous self-delusions force me into more direct argument." He walked in slow, spidery fashion to the exit.

Nyanthus gave a flowering bow. "My apologies that this was necessary and my thanks to all of you for your giving us as much cooperation as you have." He glided out.

Mandallon lingered, then ran to Ariane. "Captain . . . Ariane . . . *I* will still believe in your miracle."

She smiled, her heart lightening some. "Then I'll try to think of it that way too. Thank you, Mandallon."

Simon looked at Mandallon. "What . . . what just happened there, at the end?" The young priest had been the only true witness, the only one who was not directly involved during the ritual.

Mandallon looked as confused as Simon—and to judge by the expressions, most of the others—felt. "I . . . I am not sure, to be honest. When unbalanced, you held each other up. That broke your immediate portion of the matrix, but by clasping arms you at least afforded a unified channel . . . but then you let go just as the final action was taken. I was afraid, for a moment, that you would be . . . "

Simon felt his head, gingerly; even the light pressure of his fingers seemed about to pop his skull. "I think I nearly was."

"But you are all right?"

"I think I shall be, yes. You had best move along, Nyanthus undoubtedly is waiting."

The young priest seemed a trifle less subdued as he exited.

"An interesting additional wrinkle. Not entirely unexpected," DuQuesne said.

"You expected this?"

"Well, something like it. Controlling the spread of those powers has to be uppermost in their rituals. You don't want five thousand separate little groups of people throwing that kind of stuff around, so you have to make sure your beliefs—on both sides—make it real hard to go independent. And with the power being hard to control, that's not too difficult to arrange."

"So I'll be seen as some kind of dangerous wild card . . . and I'm sealed up so I can't use the power. Unless I learn how, and the only people who *know* how won't teach me unless I'm committed to their cause." Ariane rolled her eyes. "Wonderful."

"Forget it." Carl said. "What we *really* need right now is a party, and then—we go home!"

Ariane looked gratefully at him, and Simon realized how, like Gabrielle, the cheerful engineer had been an understated but so very necessary support for their spirits at critical moments. "Thanks, Carl. You're right. I didn't even really WANT that power anyway; it was just a last-minute trick.

"So let's throw a party the Arena won't forget tonight!"

Chapter 72

"I must say, Captain," Orphan said, using his tubelike mouthparts to drink from a blue-green spherical something, "I was a bit hesitant about attending your 'party,' as your last attempt at celebration climaxed with an assault upon the Shadeweavers."

Despite the words, Ariane—by now becoming quite familiar with the body language Orphan used—thought she caught the tone of one poking a bit of fun at a friend. With a laugh, she answered, "I admit I do sometimes end up finding trouble after those kind of contests, to blow off the excess adrenaline, you know." She gave him a wink, which Orphan seemed to understand. "But I know other people have a bit less . . . exciting ideas of parties. So I let Steve, Gabrielle, and Carl plan this shindig, with a little advice and help from Mandallon and Mairakag Achan."

"Your celebration is greatly enhanced by his participation," Nyanthus said, drifting by; his central column was holding a wide bowl of sparkling liquid, into which the symbiotes would dip and fly back out like dragonflies taking drinks. "It is an immense honor that he would deign to personally participate in a private party; then again, your victory was utterly unprecedented and he, as well as others, recognizes the value of such publicity." He twirled slowly and flowered in front of Ariane. "I hope, Captain Austin, that you will bear me no great ill will for this afternoon?"

Orphan tilted his head, and backed up a step, signifying that he at least symbolically pretended not to hear (or so Ariane guessed). Ariane smiled. "Nyanthus, you're a true believer, as is Mandallon. But unlike Mandallon, you're responsible for your whole Faction—as I am—and so you can't take chances. I can't begrudge you the caution you have to take; whether or not *I* believe in the Creators, *you* do, and you have to act on that. Regardless of what happens with me and your people, I hope that—as Factions—the Faith and Humanity can remain close."

Nyanthus's branches relaxed slightly; the flowering bow he returned to her words was more fluid than his prior actions. "This is indeed one of my great hopes as well, and I thank you for your understanding." His two mostly-silent bodyguards gave their own squatting bows, echoing the First Initiate Guide's gratitude, and then followed the high priest of the Faith as he drifted back through the crowd.

Ariane saw Mandallon notice the movement from across the room; his crest rose and the filter-beard flip-flopped cheerfully. Looking much more relaxed, the gangly young Initiate Guide turned back to the motley group of people he was addressing, a group that included Carl, several aliens whose species she didn't know, a Chiro-flekir, a pair of Milluk, and three of his own species. Another significant knot of people, including the huge Challenge Warrior Sivvis, were watching with great interest as Simon and DuQuesne demonstrated human fencing; she'd been surprised to learn that Simon was extremely adept with a sword, though—unlike herself, Carl, and DuQuesne—he was not particularly skilled in hand-to-hand and other forms of combat.

"I suppose it is too much to hope that, having rejected the Faith and the Shadeweavers, you might join with us," a razor-precise voice said from behind her. Turning, she saw Selpa'A At. The Swordmaster First was carrying some kind of refreshment that looked like purplish beef jerky sticks in his underside manipulators. "Perhaps you saw something of the true intent of the Voidbuilders? Or was all as perfect and light-ridden as old Nyanthus would have it?"

You guys just make me uncomfortable. Fanatics in a nasty way, even if you can be courteous. On the other hand, there was no reason to antagonize them, and every reason to try to be reasonable. "I can't really say what I saw, to be honest. But no, it's definitely not all sweetness and light. Unfortunately, Swordmaster, it's also not all malevolence and torment, either. So I'm afraid I can't see my way clear to joining the Vengeance—even if I felt I could do that with a clear conscience, which I can't, as long as I'm the leader of this Faction."

The Milluk leader of the Vengeance dipped on his multiple legs. "Understood. But do I understand that you did, indeed, see or sense something malevolent, as well as something benevolent?"

"I can't deny it, no. What position all the things I sensed have, I don't know. But there are definitely forces out there that have anything *but* our best interests at heart, yes."

A rattling buzz, translated as a grunt of satisfaction. "Better than nothing, I assure you. Until now, we had only words of Shadeweaver or Faith; the one wave their manipulators and cast vapors of words to obscure the truth, and maintain that the power they wield is merely power, and nothing truly lies behind it; the Faith proclaim the perfection and wondrous glory they see, mentioning not the slightest flaw. You are the first to gaze upon this with unbiased mind, and you bring us a truth never spoken by others."

Ariane wasn't sure she liked helping to reinforce the paranoid beliefs of the Vengeance, but at this point it couldn't hurt to keep the Factions she could happy. "Glad I could be of help."

"You have, and I shall not forget this small yet very important service. A small favor I shall owe you, Captain Austin." Selpa dip-bowed to her and to Orphan. "Survivor." He then scuttled off through the crowd, apparently looking for someone else.

"I guess it's the time for everyone to check in with the winner," Ariane said wryly.

"Is it not also the case on your world that many contacts are made, deals arranged, negotiations begun, in such settings?" Orphan inquired, tossing the wrinkled husk of his fruit into a refuse container.

"I'm sure it does happen that way, Orphan. I'm just not used to any of this. I was just a racing pilot, for crissake, not a diplomat!"

"Is that so?" The precise voice was unmistakeable. Sethrik mimed the pushup-bow. "Then even more remarkable your people must be, for you have managed to make a very credible leader of a Faction . . . for a mere racing pilot."

"Sethrik! Glad you could make it."

The leader of the Blessed shook her hand. "Your victory was . . . pleasing to me. I was not proud of the part we were forced to play in that charade. No more were the Minds, I must note."

"Indeed," Orphan said dryly, "as the great Masters of Manipulation, they would find it most noisome to have some lesser beings forcing them into playing their game."

"Have a care, Mindkiller." Sethrik's tail twitched upward. "I have come here with civility and under truce."

"He's right, Orphan. Although, Sethrik, I would very strongly prefer that you not refer to him by that name within my hearing."

The two nearly-identical aliens locked gazes for a long moment, tails half-poised for striking. Somewhat to Ariane's surprise, it was Orphan who first stepped back and dropped his tail. "Our hostess is most correct, and I am at fault for attempting to provoke you. Habits of centuries are hard to break, Sethrik. Accept my apologies and my gratitude for the sympathy you have displayed to my ally Ariane Austin, instead."

Sethrik lowered his tail as well. "As all the stories have it, you can be well spoken. I accept both the apology and thanks, and out of respect for Captain Austin, I apologize for using that title which she finds offensive."

A twirling gesture of Orphan's stinging tail, giving the impression of an airy dismissing of concern. "Accepted." He glanced slightly to the side. "Is something amiss?"

DuQuesne was making his way purposefully through the crowd, the massive black-bearded, black-haired Hyperion having to do little other than glance at those in his path before they made way. Ariane glanced at the floating chronometer which showed time to each viewer in whatever manner they were accustomed. "Not amiss, no, but there's something we have to do."

"Captain," DuQuesne said as he came up. He nodded to Orphan and Sethrik, who returned the nod with minor bob-bows.

"Yes, I know. It's time to get moving." She turned to Orphan. "Would you be so kind as to help Simon keep an eye on things while I'm gone? Or," she said, as she located the scientist, "maybe Carl, as I see Simon's once again ended up in a corner with three of the Analytic and there's seventeen floating displays of equations around them. How they managed to get from fencing to physics, I have no idea." She spotted the other critical members of her crew, already heading in her direction, and waved.

"There is something you have to do *now*?" Orphan asked with some puzzlement. "In the middle of the celebration? What is it? Will it take long?"

"Shouldn't take too long," DuQuesne said with a slight sidewise grin.

"I'm about to turn into a pumpkin, and they have to get me back to my house before midnight," Steve said, coming up with Tom in tow. They'd volunteered to go back after they'd enjoyed the party for a little bit.

"Get a chance to hang out with the victorious group, meet-and-greet the aliens, that kind of thing," Steve had said. "But not take any chances. I don't think any of us are comfortable leaving our Sphere empty for very long." Everyone had agreed with that.

The expressions conveyed by the body language of both Sethrik and Orphan showed that Steve's vernacular had failed in translation. *Perhaps their society wouldn't have anything like the Cinderella myth, especially after the Minds got through with it,* Ariane mused. "Never mind, Orphan. We'll be back shortly."

She turned and headed for the exit. *With both me and DuQuesne escorting them, and no one knowing what we're really up to, this should be easy.*

So why am I nervous?

Chapter 73

"How much time have we got?" Steve asked nervously as the elevator closed to take them to the floor where Transition was.

"Relax, Steve." DuQuesne said absently, paying more attention to the actual dynamics of movement around him. He wanted to be fully alert to any potential problem. "We'll have you through the Inner Gateway with at least fifteen minutes to spare."

"Well, everything seems fine to me." Ariane said.

"So far."

The danger was obvious; with the Sphere of Humanity deserted but fully active, all a smart or malicious group had to do was prevent someone from returning there by the deadline, and suddenly there was a new Sphere for the taking—and the annoying new Faction eliminated, all in one fell swoop. Of course, no one *should* know that this was the case, except Gona-Brashind and Nyanthus, but you never knew.

"Seriously, Marc, what can anyone do? Violence is pretty much out, unless we assume the Shadeweavers are going to stop us, and I really don't think that's likely."

"I don't *know* what people might be able to do, Captain," he answered levely. "And that's the reason I'm worried. If I *know* what I'm up against, I'm willing to bet I can deal with it. It's the stuff you *don't* know that comes up behind you and bites you on the ass when you're not looking."

As the door opened, DuQuesne tensed, but there was nothing threatening; the usual mass of people (of all shapes, sizes, and descriptions) moving this way and that, but nothing that appeared organized. The only odd thing he'd seen so far was someone summoning one of those green comm-balls when they stepped out of their Embassy, and that wasn't really that odd; a lot of people ranging from the just curious to the Arena equivalent of journalists *did* spend a lot of time watching their Embassy and reporting on the activity they saw.

"Come on, let's move it." DuQuesne led the way, his size and presence carving a path for the others; Steve followed him, with Tom Cussler behind and Ariane bringing up the rear. As they approached Transition, DuQuesne had a sense of something wrong; the traffic wasn't flowing the way it usually did—in fact, there seemed to be far fewer people exiting the area of Transition than usual, yet it sounded like there was a lot of activity . . .

Then he was able to get a good look into the cavernous transfer and arrival area of the Arena. "For the love of—what in the seven flaming hells of space is *this*?"

Every single Gateway was a focus of activity—some with people and cargo emerging, hurrying across, to disappear through another Gateway. The movement was constant, fluid, clearly coordinated for the most part as a carefully orchestrated process. Only three Gateways seemed to be exempted from this, and there were deep, long lines extending from them.

A little fur-covered creature with four eyes and the nervous, twitching mannerisms of something used to having to be very cautious around larger, more threatening beings, hurried up. "Many apologies, honored citizens of the Arena, but the Masters are performing a major reconciliation adjustment, and thus only the three central Gateways are currently available."

With a creeping cold sensation that he already *knew* the answer without asking, DuQuesne demanded, "And just who are these 'Masters,' and how long is this going to take?"

A rattling, clicking noise translated to a nasty chuckle, as out of the crowd emerged exactly what he'd feared. "We are the Masters, as you will learn one day, Human DuQuesne." Dajzail, leader of the Molothos, said with a satisfied air. "As for when it will be done, not long at all; say fifteen to twenty minutes?"

The bastard knows. I have no idea how *he does, but he knows, or guesses, exactly how long we have, and he's timed his revenge to within a few minutes.*

"You can't *do* this!" Ariane snapped, striding to the front and glaring straight into the Molothos single yellow wraparound eye. DuQuesne noted that she had no hesitation in approaching Dajzail. *When she's mad enough, she forgets to be afraid of anything.*

"I assure you, we can, and we have." The savage mandibles with the grinder mouth behind clicked tauntingly.

"Resolving balance of trade and such through a quick exchange through the Gateways with all of our colonies, redistributing resources, troops, slaves, and so on, is something we do on occasion—as do a few other major Factions. As long as we do not take *all* of the Gateways, and do not take too long, neither the other inhabitants nor the Arena object." The Molothos preened one fighting claw with the more delicate mouth manipulators, like a casual, insulting gesture of polishing the fingernails while speaking. "I will admit that I have arranged for the precise timing of this event to be adjusted."

DuQuesne measured the timing by eye. The long lines in front of the few remaining open Gateways were not moving fast enough. He could see Ariane's quick estimation agreed with his; by the time Steve got to the front of the line, time would be up.

"We could butt in line," Steve said. "Just head up and—"

"Maybe. If someone lets you in." DuQuesne saw Ariane's fist clenching, hoped she didn't do anything stupid. "But if they're going through as fast as they reasonably can, you might find yourself going through a Gateway to somewhere else, because the Gate took the other guy's transport code. Unless they're smart enough to react directly upon contact?"

"Unfortunately," a familiar deep voice said from behind them, "while undoubtedly the Voidbuilders could have arranged such subtlety in the Gates, they are not so quick or foolproof." Amas-Garao regarded them from above, seeming to be seated on an invisible throne. "One stepping forward with intent to pass through activates the gate; others attempting to pass through at the same time may find themselves going to the first person's destination. Only if the platform is clear, or at least all those on the platform are not concentrating on passage, is it safe to attempt without risking visiting a destination one was not prepared for."

"You slimy son of a *bitch!*" Ariane whirled and glared up. "It's a good thing you're up *there*, or I'd be breaking your head! This was your idea, was it?"

"Your anger is understandable, but misplaced, Captain Austin." Amas-Garao's voice was amused. "I am, in fact, here only as an observer. This gambit is entirely the work of the Molothos, I assure you. I merely find the challenge an interesting one. How will you resolve this conundrum, I wonder."

Ariane's gaze seemed almost enough to bore its way through the Shadeweaver. "I'd really like to believe you, but if that's the case, how the hell did *he*," she jabbed her finger at Dajzail, "know what the score was?"

A rattling, buzzing laugh answered her. "So often the lesser races make the mistake of thinking they are so much more clever than the Masters. It was a matter of deduction, *Captain* Austin. Only eight had ever been seen, and never all eight at the same time. Now, suddenly, an observer reports that a pair of you leave abruptly, returning with the two absent individuals, and this immediately after both Shadeweaver and Faith arrive at your Embassy? Knowing the ending of the last Challenge?"

He's good, DuQuesne ceded grudgingly. But Dajzail was not finished.

"Obviously a bargain had been made to permit your Sphere to be temporarily unoccupied. Precedents such as dying individuals have previously been allowed, and in those cases the Arena requires that the Faction re-occupy the Sphere within a short interval following notification—not *quite* the minimum time for a notified individual to reach the Sphere, but not much more, either. Given the circumstances, we deduced that the next time any of you emerged, you would head for the Gateways—and thus to secure your Sphere. And so it was." The Molothos preened himself again.

DuQuesne stared hard at the three gates. *No way to get in edgewise. We might try to argue someone into letting us in . . . but hell, if I were Dajzail I'd make damn sure most, if not all, of the apparently innocent travellers in that line were ringers. These guys are just too used to these Gateways; there's barely a second's pause between one group disappearing and the next starting across the platform, already concentrating on their destination.*

Ariane glanced around, her gaze raking over the entire cavernous amphitheater of Transition; DuQuesne could tell she was reaching the same conclusion.

He became suddenly aware of Steve at his elbow. The curly-haired, short engineer was pressing fingers to his temples as though trying to *force* a thought out, or keep it in. "What is it, Steve?"

Steve Franceschetti looked up at Amas-Garao. "You're not interfering, and you're not going to interfere in any way?"

"You have my word. I am merely an observer."

"In that case . . . " Steve suddenly took off, running toward one of the lines. "DuQuesne, Ariane, come *on!*"

DuQuesne caught up with him almost instantly; Ariane was only a few steps behind. "What's on your mind, Steve?"

The narrow face gave a sharp grin. "How far do you think you can *throw* me, DuQuesne?"

"Pretty far," he admitted, as he jogged alongside the shorter man, noticing that Dajzail was not able to quite keep up. "But it won't do you any good for me to toss you through the gate the way things are going now."

"That's why the Captain has to get into trouble at the right time. Like when *I* got in trouble, and when the Blessed beat on Gabrielle . . . ?"

All of a sudden Steve's plan was clear—a plan so simple, so desperate, so last-minute-improvised, that there was no way anyone had ever anticipated it. He heard Ariane suddenly give a burst of breathless laughter. "You're just as crazy as I am, Steve!"

"What the hell are you all *talking* about?" Tom said, breathing hard in his effort to keep up.

"You'll have to time the offense just right, Ariane—and the distance I'll have to maintain is going to be iffy. I have no idea exactly how widespread the clampdown will be." DuQuesne ignored Tom's query. He'd understand once everything happened.

Dajzail started to screech out something that sounded like "Stop th . . . " but then halted, realizing that if his people *physically* intervened, the Adjudicators would intervene as well—and once they were present, there was no telling how things might go.

That, of course, is what we're counting on—and the whole point of Steve's question to Amas-Garao. The Shadeweavers could delay the arrival of Adjudicators, but the Molothos can't.

Ariane put on a burst of speed, heading for the central platform, and DuQuesne began, along with Steve, to separate from her, distancing himself in preparation for acting out his part in this last minute throw.

The captain of *Holy Grail* sprinted up towards the platform, the people in line beginning to murmur, point, and shout questions as she raced by. DuQuesne judged her progress, guessed at the timing and range, and adjusted his course. *A crazy idea from us crazy humans once again. But it's better than trying nothing.*

Ariane reached the top edge of the platform, with people progressing across it in orderly fashion. "Listen, all of you, one of us needs to get through!"

"Get to the back of the line!" snarled a semi-reptilian creature.

"How very rude!" said a Wagamia, one of the same species as Mandallon. "A wait will do you good! It is but a short time, and—"

There were shouts and screams of shock as Ariane's katana blazed from its sheath. "We don't *have* a few minutes, and by God you're all getting off this platform before I start cutting!"

"She's insane!" another alien shouted. "Adjudicator! *Adjudicator!*"

A massive figure in Adjudicator armor—something like a humanoid rhinoceros—materialized just above Ariane. Everyone in the area suddenly froze under the Adjudicator's field. "Threats of this nature and assaults on other citizens is a very serious offense. So," it said, glaring at another member of the now-frozen line, "is preparing to use additional ranged weapons in a crowd."

DuQuesne heard the rattling chuckle of Dajzail far behind. *Laugh it up, bugface, because I'm about to deliver the punchline.*

Turning, he caught up Steve, broke into a sprint that only a Hyperion could possibly have managed, and launched Steve straight for the ebony, blue spark-touched surface of the Gateway. Eyes closed, the smaller man bulleted forward, hopefully concentrating only on one thing: getting back to Humanity's sphere. All others on the platform—as Steve and Ariane had intended —were focused on Ariane and the Adjudicator. The Adjudicator glanced in startlement as the body flew past, clearing the heads of the crowd and plunging straight through the Gateway, a throw of over thirteen meters.

Dajzail let out an infuriated screech that echoed throughout Transition, and lunged forward, killing claws extended.

That got the Adjudicator's attention, and suddenly all of Transition was locked down, motionless. "These actions are connected." It was motionless, and no one else—except Amas-Garao—*could* move. The Shade-weaver gave a delighted-sounding laugh, and faded away into shadow.

After a few more moments, the Adjudicator straight-ened. "Captain Austin of the Faction of Humanity, did you intend injury to these people?"

"No, sir," Ariane answered immediately. "I was delib-erately trying to scare them, though, so that one of you people would show up, freeze the crowd, and keep them distracted."

A pause. "I can see from the stress patterns and other readings that you believe what you say, and the events and your personality are consistent with this." It turned slowly. "We do not need to ask whether *you* intended injury, Dajzail of the Molothos."

It seemed to consider for some more moments. "The Molothos' actions were legal, and an ingeniously non-violent approach to bringing about a defeat of their enemy. Nonetheless, they were also provocative of des-peration on the part of the Human Faction. There is no evidence of actual intent to injure on the part of Human-ity, and indeed the record shows multiple instances of

Humans having been deliberately provoked or harrassed by the Molothos or others.

"Ariane Austin of Humanity, you and Dr. DuQuesne will be confined to your Embassy for three days. Dajzail, you and your people will be similarly confined. Other potential penalties are waived in both cases."

With a blurring jolt, DuQuesne found himself standing in the doorway leading to the party, Ariane next to him. A number of partygoers gaped in astonishment.

Ariane gave a whoop that turned all remaining heads. "Hey, all of you! We've got another story to tell you, if you're not tired of hearing them!"

DuQuesne grinned and shook his head. *That vital secret isn't vital any more, I suppose. One more desperate crisis averted. Now let's hope we don't have any more until we get home.*

Chapter 74

"You are actually leaving, Captain Austin?"

"We are, right now, Nyanthus." Ariane smiled at the faceless Initiate Guide, whose expressive gestures had become for her nearly as good as a face. "Now that we *can*, we *have* to. The clock started ticking when we kicked the Molothos off our Sphere. They've already proven they're not going to let *that* drop. We need to get our whole species up to speed on what's going on here, and get a real force up there, before we find a whole fleet of Molothos upstairs."

"There is that, most certainly," Orphan agreed. "And all the other aspects of now having contact with the vaster universe. I would still go with you, if you like—"

Ariane shook her head. "Not quite yet, Orphan. With the Molothos carcass samples we're bringing back, and other things from our Sphere, we've got the actual proof of where we've been . . . and of course before I bring anyone else through our whole Sphere I need to talk with our people."

Orphan, she was relieved to see, took no offense at the implied lack of complete trust. Not that she'd expected him to. "We'll be back, of course—a lot more of us—and we're leaving half of us behind so things just don't go quiet while we're gone." She glanced around the Transition platform at the little farewell group.

"Indeed," Dr. Relgof said, shaking hands one last time with Simon, "it was my first fear that the Arena would become far more boring and tame when you had left!"

"We'll do our best to prevent that." DuQuesne shouldered a box of samples.

"Who is staying behind, Captain Austin?" Mandallon asked.

"Carl Edlund, Steve Franceschetti, Tom Cussler, and Laila Canning," Ariane answered.

She hadn't wanted to leave many people behind, but the practicalities of the situation pretty much demanded it. "No telling how long it will be before we get back," DuQuesne had pointed out. "And we *need* to know what's going on in the Arena. Our enemies here aren't going to sit still. Even if all we do is sit in our Embassy and thus avoid getting into Challenges, we need to be watching, listening, and learning. If the Blessed, the Shadeweavers, or, more likely, the Molothos start moving against us, we don't want to just drop into the middle of it without warning. So someone's got to stay in touch here—which means at least two people, because we need to leave someone on the Sphere, too. And since none of us like the idea of leaving one person alone in either place, I'd say that means we have to leave four of us behind."

Laila Canning had volunteered first. "I have a million things to study here, Captain, and I'm still catching up on everything you people learned while I was out. And after what happened . . . I'm not sure what would happen if I went back now. My AISages are still there, I think, dormant; no one removed them, as far as I know, and . . . " she looked rather lost for a moment, " . . . and I don't know if I could understand them, or they me, any more. If," she gave a twisted, sarcastic smile, "I am in fact me, something I know you are all unsure of."

In actuality, Simon had said he was sure that Laila Canning was in fact there, whether or not something *else* might also be there, based both on what he and Ariane had discussed before and on whatever he'd experienced during that sealing ritual. Ariane hoped he was right, but wasn't really concerned about it at this point; whoever "Laila Canning" really was, she'd been working with them ever since she awakened and showed no signs of being likely to be a problem.

Since Ariane *had* to go back—being the nominal Captain and the one who'd led most of the contact from the beginning, and DuQuesne insisted that he, too, had to go back, that pretty much left Carl by default as the one person they could leave behind who might be able to physically handle himself in a Challenge if something unforeseen happened. Steve and Tom would be continuing the development of the Upper Sphere installations, with Carl's assistance, but neither of them were really men of action.

She glanced over at Simon, who smiled back. "Are we ready?"

Gabrielle picked up her own case of data and samples. "I sure am. Got my family to see, and we both have to pass on hellos from Carl, Steve, and Tom." It said a great deal about Laila that she had no personal messages to convey, only professional communications.

"But you *are* coming back, Captain Austin?" Mandallon said, his crest lifting again.

"I wouldn't miss this place for the world." As she said it, she realized how much of her *was* going to miss the Arena. She'd loved being a racing pilot, still did . . . but here she had been something much, much more. Here she'd finally seen the cosmos waiting for her, and it was bigger, stranger, and more exciting than she'd ever imagined. "I'll be back, I promise. And not too long from now, either."

A few more waves and bows, and the four of them stepped through into the circular room of the Inner Gateway. Several corridors and turns later, they finally approached the door leading to the central area of the Sphere.

Passing through the obedient portal, they passed the automated security perimeter and into the now well-lit hexagon-tiled area in front of the door. Steve and Tom waved from the doorway of a fair-sized building they'd built nearby. Ariane could see the slightly unnatural stiffness of the cloth on Steve's right arm; the active fabric was still acting as a support splint, Steve having shattered his arm on landing during his flying re-entrance to their Sphere. With medical and internal support nanos it was almost healed now, but still needed a bit of additional bracing.

"Don't take too long!" Steve said. "Me and Tom want to get back sometime soon, too."

"Promise. Hell, they'll probably start sending more ships through before we get done, and you can come back on one of those as long as we leave someone else here."

DuQuesne winced. "It's going to be more complicated than that. We can't just dump a bunch of newcomers here and leave them without one of us old hands to watch 'em."

"Definitely not," Simon agreed. "According to all our acquaintances—Orphan, Dr. Relgof, even Sethrik —individual rapport is exceedingly important. Newcomers who don't understand what is going on could get us all in terrible trouble—and, of course, as far as the Arena is concerned, Ariane remains entered as the Leader of Humanity until some official change is made to that status."

Leader of Humanity. Boy, is that *going to make this an . . . interesting mess once it sinks into the SSC's collective heads.* "True. Well, guys, you'll just have to hang in there until we get back, okay?"

"No worries," Tom said. "We'll survive for a few months more without going home, now that we've got an established presence."

They continued on. "It's going to be more complicated still, Ariane," said Simon.

"Why?"

"If you recall, I did mention—oh, *way* back when we first had arrived—that the Sandrisson coils interfere with each other at range. Well, after going over the theory and design practice with Relgof and some of the others of the Analytic, I have hard figures for that, which show that—at most—you can have twenty starships in the Harbor at once before there is no safe place to activate a drive within the Harbor. If the ships are significantly larger than a two or three man vessel, the numbers become even lower. Ships will not be able to transition in, nor to transition our, until you either disassemble enough Sandrisson coils to stop the resonance, or you otherwise remove the excess vessels.

"Standard practice in the Arena, of course, is to get them out of the Harbor through the Straits, but we will have to design atmosphere- and gravity-worthy vessels before we can do that; *Holy Grail*, for instance, would almost certainly not survive the trip through the Straits."

Ariane nodded, then told the main door to open, letting them into the brightly-lit giant spacedock at which *Holy Grail* was docked. "That means we have to hammer these limitations home and *fast*, so that everyone and his grandmother doesn't go charging out to see what this 'Arena' is like, and end up blocking off access to the Arena for months while we sort it out." She sighed. "We're not even *home* and already I'm seeing the work piling up."

"You *could* just go back to being a racing pilot." DuQuesne said neutrally. She thought, however, she could see a slight upturn of the corners of the beard.

"And *you* could just go back to being a power engineer. I'm exactly as much the racing pilot that left as you are the engineer we started with."

"*Touché*. Then you're stuck with playing politics, Captain."

Carl Edlund was waiting for them at the airlock. "Welcome back, Captain. Your ship awaits."

Ariane gave him a huge hug, squeezing so hard that she heard him grunt. "Watch it, don't break my spine. I can't work nearly so well without it."

"You just keep an eye on everything until we get back, and don't accept any Challenges if you can help it . . . or put them off until we get back, at least."

Carl grinned. "Don't worry, Cap; by the time you come back, I'll have one of those big Faction Houses cleared out for you."

"I'm almost afraid you will." She watched DuQuesne and Simon shake hands with Carl, and Gabrielle gave him a quite emphatic kiss that left him blinking. Ariane managed to restrain what would have been a most undignified giggle at that.

She passed through the airlock and into the cramped, claustrophobic, yet somehow homey and welcoming confines of the *Holy Grail*. She made her way to the bridge, Simon following her and the others going to their original stations. She sat down and felt the straps and restraints lock in place, hearing Simon doing the same. "Is everyone settled in?"

"Power systems all secure. Sandrisson coil power supply fully charged and ready for activation. Reactor prepared for restart." DuQuesne's calm voice brought an echo from the past, from those last few moments before the universe changed. "Reaction mass reservoirs refilled. We're ready to go, Captain."

"Medical ready, and hoping to become totally useless in the next few."

"Don't rush it," Ariane said. "Remember, we first have to get down to the level of the model there, or we're going to be, what, two or three billion miles out above the plane of the solar system?"

"How long will that take?"

"Well, not *too* long. I'm going to use the chemical rockets, which Tom and DuQuesne were able to get recharged in the past few months, and that means I can kick us up to around, oh, five kps safely and still have plenty of time to stop if something goes wrong. Figure . . . a half hour from launch, a little less, actually, to transition. I'm aiming to come out about forty thousand kilometers from Kanzaki-Three."

"Ha!" DuQuesne laughed. "That'll give 'em a wake-up call, all right."

"Sandrisson Drive, ready." Simon said. "All coils check out, ghost-field test shows our configuration is within tolerances."

"Then *Holy Grail* detaching from dock." She felt the grapples and connectors disengage, and for the first time in months the first starship from Earth floated free. "Stand by for chemical rockets in five . . . four . . . three . . . two . . . one . . . firing!"

The roar of the chemical drive rumbled throughout *Holy Grail*, the force of acceleration pushed them back in their seats with a pressure of nearly two gravities. Ariane let out a whoop as she really realized that they were heading home.

The crossing of thousands of empty kilometers seemed somehow to be incredibly short, and as long as eternity. But at last, the coordinates showed a final approach to the target location. "Doctor Sandrisson?"

Simon took a deep breath, and activated the controls. "Sandrisson coils charging. Field building evenly. Countdown to transition begins. In ten seconds . . . Five . . . Two, one . . . "

There was a lurch, a wrench in the fundamental fabric of the universe; Ariane felt something inside her . . . click, almost like a ratchet moving a notch.

Full lights blazed on inside *Holy Grail*, and she felt/heard/sensed all systems coming back online.

"Reactor restarting. Power back to maximum in estimated forty-seven seconds." DuQuesne said calmly.

There was a confused babble from the various AIs as they tried to sort out their location, condition, time. A deeply resonant pseudo-voice echoed from a long-silent box at her hip.

Ariane Austin of Tellus, I confess that I find myself utterly inadequate. My Visualization seems to have failed me.

"Don't worry, Mentor. I'll fill you in. If you haven't managed it on your own." She was suddenly struck with wonder anew, as she saw on the forward screens the blazing cold blackness of space and stars, so different from the strange world of the Arena.

"Kanzaki-Three control is screaming at us, Captain," Simon said, with a bit of a laugh. "And the automatic controls are complaining about being cut off from the loop."

"They can just put up with it for the next few minutes. I'm bringing her in on manual." She activated the comm-net. "Kanzaki-Three, this is Experimental Vessel 2112-FTL, *Holy Grail*, reporting back." She grinned at the others, as she continued, "Control, you will not *believe* where we've been!"

THE FANTASY OF
ERIC FLINT

THE PHILOSOPHICAL STRANGLER

When the world's best assassin gets too philosophical, the
only thing to do is take up an even deadlier trade—heroing!

hc • 0-671-31986-8 • $24.00
pb • 0-7434-3541-9 • $7.99

FORWARD THE MAGE with Richard Roach

It's a dangerous, even foolhardy, thing to be in love with
the sister of the world's greatest assassin.

hc • 0-7434-3524-9 • $24.00
pb • 0-7434-7146-6 • $7.99

PYRAMID SCHEME with Dave Freer

A huge alien pyramid has plopped itself in the middle of
Chicago and is throwing people back into worlds of myth,
impervious to all the U.S. Army has to throw at it.
Unfortunately, the pyramid has captured mild-mannered
professor Jerry Lukacs—the one man who just might have
the will and know-how to be able to stop its schemes.

hc • 0-671-31839-X • $21.00
pb • 0-7434-3592-3 • $6.99

And don't miss **THE SHADOW OF THE LION** series
of alternate fantasies, written with Mercedes Lackey &
Dave Freer.

MORE ...
ERIC FLINT

Mother of Demons   0-671-87800-X ◆ $7.99

Rats, Bats & Vats   0-671-31828-4 ◆ $7.99
(with Dave Freer)
The Rats, the Bats & the Ugly   1-4165-2078-3 ◆ $7.99
(with Dave Freer)

Pyramid Scheme (with Dave Freer)   0-7434-3592-3 ◆ $6.99
Pyramid Power (with Dave Freer)   HC: 0-7434-2130-5 ◆ $24.00
                                            HC: 1-4165-5596-X ◆ $7.99
Slow Train to Arcturus)   1-4165-5585-4 ◆ $24.00
(with Dave Freer)

Time Spike (with Marilyn Kosmatka)   HC: 1-4165-5538-2 ◆ $24.00

Boundary (with Ryk E. Spoor)   1-4165-5525-0 ◆ $7.99

The Course of Empire   0-7434-9893-3 ◆ $7.99
(with K.D. Wentworth)

The Warmasters   0-7434-7185-7 ◆ $7.99
(with David Weber & David Drake)

Crown of Slaves   0-7434-9899-2 ◆ $7.99
(with David Weber)

THE JOE'S WORLD SERIES
The Philosophical Strangler   0-7434-3541-9 ◆ $7.99
Forward the Mage   0-7434-7146-6 ◆ $7.99
(with Richard Roach)

The Shadow of the Lion   0-7434-7147-4 ◆ $7.99
(with Mercedes Lackey & Dave Freer)
This Rough Magic   0-7434-9909-3 ◆ $7.99
(with Mercedes Lackey & Dave Freer)

Wizard of Karres   1-4165-0926-7 ◆ $7.99
(with Mercedes Lackey & Dave Freer)